HOT-SHOT DOC, CHRISTMAS BRIDE

BY
JOANNA NEIL

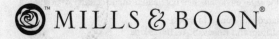
MILLS & BOON

First published in Great Britain 2009
Harlequin Mills & Boon Limited,
Eton House, 18-24 Paradise Road, Richmond, Surrey TW9 1SR

© Joanna Neil 2009

ISBN: 978 0 263 86884 5

Set in Times Roman 10½ on 13¼ pt
03-1209-48078

Harlequin Mills & Boon policy is to use papers that are natural, renewable and recyclable products and made from wood grown in sustainable forests. The logging and manufacturing process conform to the legal environmental regulations of the country of origin.

Printed and bound in Spain
by Litografia Rosés, S.A., Barcelona

HOT-SHOT DOC, CHRISTMAS BRIDE

BY
JOANNA NEIL

&

CHRISTMAS AT RIVERCUT MANOR

BY
GILL SANDERSON

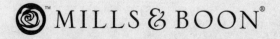 MILLS & BOON

A CHRISTMAS PROPOSAL—
the gift of a lifetime

Two gorgeous and talented doctors
are looking to swap their stethoscopes
for wedding rings this Christmas…

Dr Josh Bentley and Dr Mike Curtis aren't looking
for love…until they meet their irresistible
new colleagues and instantly lose their hearts!

They're going down on bended knee
and hoping to hear the words 'I do' in

HOT-SHOT DOC, CHRISTMAS BRIDE
by Joanna Neil

CHRISTMAS AT RIVERCUT MANOR
by Gill Sanderson

When **Joanna Neil** discovered Mills & Boon®, her lifelong addiction to reading crystallised into an exciting new career writing Medical™ Romance. Her characters are probably the outcome of her varied lifestyle, which includes working as a clerk, typist, nurse and infant teacher. She enjoys dressmaking and cooking at her Leicestershire home. Her family includes a husband, son and daughter, an exuberant yellow Labrador and two slightly crazed cockatiels. She currently works with a team of tutors at her local education centre, to provide creative writing workshops for people interested in exploring their own writing ambitions.

Recent titles by the same author:

THE REBEL AND THE BABY DOCTOR
THE SURGEON SHE'S BEEN WAITING FOR
CHILDREN'S DOCTOR, SOCIETY BRIDE

CHAPTER ONE

'THANKS for the lift, Tom. You're an absolute lifesaver.' Alison gave her neighbour a friendly wave and watched him drive away before hotfooting it into the hospital's A&E department.

What a way to start the day. She'd had nothing but trouble with the car for the last week, and then today, when she'd tried to start the engine, it had simply spluttered and died. It had been plain from that point that she was going to be late for her shift. Only by a few minutes, but of all the days to break her perfect record it had to be this one— when the new boss was due to put in an appearance.

No one seemed to know very much about him—except that he'd been brought in at the last minute after one of the consultants had been taken ill—and from what she had heard he was only going to be here for two days a week. What kind of job was that? And what did he do for the rest of the time? The only other thing she knew about him was that he was a friend of one of the managers.

The doors of the unit swished open and she hurried along the corridor, bypassing Reception and heading towards the doctors' restroom. If she could just slip off her jacket and sling her stethoscope around her neck before she made an appearance in the unit, perhaps he would be none the wiser.

'Whoa…steady on there. Where's the fire?'

She skidded to a halt and narrowly missed running headlong into the man who suddenly appeared in her path. As it was, her palms grappled with his chest as she sought to stop the collision, and at the same time a pair of large male hands reached out as though to steady her, circling her upper arms in a light but firm grip. The holdall that she carried over her shoulder swung forward with the momentum, and the man let out a soft 'oomph' as the weight of it slammed into his midriff.

'Oh, I'm so sorry,' she managed, sucking air into her lungs. Her fingers scrambled against fine-quality worsted material, and she realised that he was wearing a suit—dark grey and beautifully tailored. That was not a good sign, given that most of the male doctors of her acquaintance went around in rolled up shirtsleeves and trousers.

'I didn't see you,' she said, lifting her gaze. 'You seemed to come out of nowhere.' The faint note of accusation hung on the air as she tried to work out whether he had emerged from the side corridor or the supplies cupboard. What on earth would this man be doing in either place? Only staff had access to these areas.

Then she looked at him properly for the first time, and his features came into sharp focus—all clean, angular lines, and crisp black hair, with grey eyes that appeared to look deep down into her soul. The breath seemed to leave her all over again. He was altogether striking. The kind of man who, once seen, was never forgotten.

'Ah…' he murmured. 'That would be me in my ghostly

guise—stalking the corridors of the hospital in wait for the unwary. It seems I struck lucky this time.'

She laughed. 'Maybe. Though from the looks of you, you're anything but ethereal. Anyway, coming into contact with all that hard muscle and bone was a dead giveaway.' She studied him once again, her long, honey-blonde hair swirling about her shoulders with the upward tilt of her head. 'It's all right for you to let go of me now,' she hastily reassured him. 'I'm not running from a fire, but I *am* anxious to go on duty before anyone realises that I should have been here five minutes ago.' She frowned. 'I do hope you're not my new boss in A&E. I really wanted to show him my best side.'

He gave a wry smile, looking her over, his gaze taking in her softly curving figure outlined by the cashmere top and gently flowing skirt that she was wearing. 'I think you may have already done that,' he murmured, a soft gleam in his eyes causing warm colour to rush into her cheeks.

Her mouth dropped open a fraction. Had she heard that right? She decided to ignore the remark. Thinking about it would have made her far too hot and bothered.

'Oh, dear. That has to mean that you're the new man,' she ventured after a moment or two, her brow knotting. 'What are you doing out here in the corridor? Shouldn't you be in A&E, tending to the sick and injured?'

Slowly he released her, letting his hands fall to his sides. 'I dare say I could ask the same of you,' he countered. 'But in the interests of good working relationships I think we'll let that go for the moment. I'm sure you must have good reason for flying in here like a bullet from a gun.'

He looked her over, as though he was making sure she was still all in one piece.

'As for myself,' he added, 'yes, I'm the new locum. And as to what I'm doing here in the corridor…I thought it would be a good idea to acquaint myself with the lie of the land and get to know the people that I'll be working with. I must say I wasn't expecting it to happen quite this way, but here in A&E we have to be ready for any eventuality, don't we?'

'I suppose we do.' A wave of heat flowed along her cheeks. Had she really just asked her new boss what he was doing outside A&E? 'So, you'll be working here with us while Dr Meadows recovers from his heart attack?'

'That's right. I'm Josh Bentley. And you are…?'

'Alison Randall, senior house officer.' She winced, absorbing the fact that her worst fears had come to fruition. It seemed there was no end to what could go wrong today. How was she going to extract herself from this awkward situation? 'We were all shocked when Steven was taken ill,' she said. 'He's a lovely man…exceptional…irreplaceable…no one could possibly match up to him. He worked so hard, and he was so good with the patients.'

'I can see that I have a lot to live up to,' Josh said in a faintly whimsical tone. 'I promise you I'll do my best to fill his shoes.'

She groaned inwardly. Having her foot in her mouth was getting to be a habit. 'I didn't mean to imply that you wouldn't be able to do that.' She straightened her shoulders. 'And about my being late—you have to understand I'm not usually tardy. My car wouldn't start this morning. I had to beg a lift off my neighbour.'

He nodded, as though he had no problem with that, and then he turned his gaze to her holdall. 'What's all this, then? Are you planning on going away somewhere after work? Judging from the weight of it, you've packed for the long-term.'

She smiled as she shook her head. 'No, nothing like that. I brought in some goodies for the cheque presentation ceremony...just a few nibbles for people to snack on. I wasn't sure whether anybody would have thought to make an occasion of it, and it occurred to me that we should do something to make it special. I expect you'll be making a short speech, won't you?'

He frowned. 'I'm afraid you've lost me there. I've no idea what you're talking about.'

'Oh, dear.' She floundered for a moment. 'I was sure Management would have filled you in. They usually arrange for the press to be on hand—all in aid of good relations with the public and so on.' She ran a hand through her silky hair in a distracted fashion, conscious of time running away with her. 'I ought to drop off this holdall in the doctors' restroom and let it be known that I'm on duty.'

He nodded, and walked with her along the corridor. 'Perhaps you should tell me about this presentation? There's nothing in the diary, and my secretary doesn't come in until this afternoon. What's it all about?'

'Fund-raising. A group of people do their best to collect funds for the hospital—in particular the A&E unit. Of course most of the money they raise goes towards buying equipment for the hospital. Every year in December they drop by to present us with a cheque. Partly so that we can start arranging Christmas festivities for the patients. They bring presents for the children who will be staying in hospital over Christmas, either on the paediatric wards or in A&E, or on the observation ward next to A&E. Of course we don't give them out until Christmas Eve or Christmas Day.'

He was still frowning. 'Isn't it a bit early for this kind of thing?'

She looked at him askance. 'Hardly. It takes time to organise things around Christmas…decorations, presents, food. And sometimes we arrange a short entertainment or radio show. We can't throw it all together in a couple of days, you know, and if we have a pantomime group coming to do a brief production we need to pay them an advance.'

He shook his head. 'I don't see why everyone has to make such a fuss around the occasion. The world seems to go crazy at this time of year. It amazes me that the shops are full of Christmas stuff from as early as the end of September. Why we have to suffer three months or more of hype is beyond me.'

'Hype?' She sent him a doubtful look. Where was his sense of Christmas cheer? Was he one of those dour people who were averse to celebrations? 'Well, that's the way it is. Personally, I appreciate having plenty of time to make preparations—and I love the atmosphere in town at this time of year, with everyone crowding out the stores, looking for gifts for their loved ones.'

His expression was sceptical. 'You're a sentimentalist.'

'So what if I am?' She lifted a finely arched brow. 'I see nothing wrong with that, and I'm certainly not alone in feeling that way.' She straightened her shoulders and moved on towards the doctors' room. If he had a problem with the festive season that was his loss, and she wasn't going to argue the point.

'Christmas is my favourite time of year, when all the

family gets together.' She smiled, thinking about it. 'My grandparents live about fifty miles away from here, but they're coming over to the Pennines to spend the holiday with us, and my brother will be home from university.'

'Really? It sounds as though you have a good time to look forward to. I can't say I'm that enthusiastic about the season for myself.' He frowned. 'So, what's the plan for this cheque presentation?'

She studied him for a moment or two. How could anyone *not* enjoy this special time of year? Was there something more to his indifference than a simple aversion to hype?

'Well, Dr Meadows…Steve…always said a few words on these occasions. And since you're the one in charge here today, I imagine they'll expect you to be on hand if it's at all possible.' She added a warning note. 'We do try to show how much we appreciate all their hard work. They take on all sorts of fund-raising activities for us throughout the year, and they bring a lot of good feeling into the hospital.'

He pushed open the door of the doctors' lounge and sent her a thoughtful glance. 'I'm glad you told me about this. What time are they likely to arrive?'

'Around lunchtime, I would imagine…perhaps twelve-thirty. I expect one of the managers will deal with the actual proceedings.' She began to empty the contents of her holdall on to the table, and a variety of plastic containers filled with pastries spilled out. 'Perhaps I'd better ask one of the desk clerks if she can find time to put the food out in Reception.' She glanced at the clock on the wall. 'I hope no one in A&E is desperately in need of attention from me right now.'

'Only a youth with a badly gashed hand. One of the

nurses will tend to him in the first instance, but as soon as she's cleaned the wound it will need suturing. After that there are half a dozen walking wounded who could do with your help.'

'Oh, right.' She stacked the containers neatly on the table and then said, 'Again, I'm sorry about being late. My neighbour's going to have a look at the car for me to see if he can figure out what's gone wrong with it. He said it sounded as though there was a problem with the fuel pump.' She shrugged out of her jacket and hung it up on a hook at the side of the room, before going in search of her stethoscope. She found it in her locker, along with other bits and pieces that she pushed into the deep pocket of her skirt.

'Is your neighbour a mechanic, then?' Josh asked.

Alison shook her head, sending her hair into a flurry of activity. His gaze followed the ripple of silk before settling on her features once more.

'No,' she said, 'but he can turn his hand to most things. He fixed the plumbing when it went wrong, and then he looked at the washing machine when it refused to work. If we waited for the landlord to sort things out we'd still be waiting now.'

'We?'

'My flatmate and I…Katie. She's a senior house officer, too, working with me in A&E.'

'I see.' He nodded. 'I take it she made her own arrangements for coming in here today?'

'That's right. She had an early case conference to attend, so she was gone before I realised I had a problem.'

'Hmm.' He absorbed that. 'Wouldn't it have been better to have a garage mechanic look over your car? What if your neighbour can't fix it for you?'

She started towards the door. 'Well, then I suppose I'll have to do that.' She guessed he was trying to make sure that her lateness wasn't going to be a frequent occurrence. 'It would be unfortunate, though, because it will probably cost me an arm and a leg if I have to go to a garage, whereas this way I can give Tom a realistic amount of money for his time and trouble—that will give him a boost and help him to get back on his feet, and I'll benefit at the same time.'

'Does he need a boost?' They walked together towards A&E. 'Is your neighbour in trouble of some sort?' Josh's brows had come together in a dark line. Clearly he was having a problem coming to terms with her lifestyle.

'I'd say so. He's an engineer, but he found himself out of work when the company he worked for folded, and then he's had difficulty getting another job…which in turn means that he can't afford to pay the mortgage, and now the building society is beginning to make nasty rumbling noises about repossession. None of that bodes very well for a happy Christmas, does it?'

'It doesn't bode very well at any time of the year,' he commented.

They had only just set foot inside the A&E unit when his bleeper went off. He glanced briefly at the displayed message. 'That doesn't sound like good news,' he murmured. 'There's been an accident on the motorway. I guess things are going to become hectic around here very soon. Alison—I want you to stay with me.'

He moved away then, and went to organise the rest of the staff, directing who was to do what before striding towards the ambulance bay. Alison quickly followed him.

'Twenty-five-year-old male,' the paramedic reported,

wheeling a casualty towards the resuscitation room. 'Had to be extricated from his car. His blood pressure's low and he has a broken leg and arm. He also has chest and abdominal pain.'

'Thanks.' Josh took control as the patient's condition deteriorated even further. He began to insert a tube into the patient's throat, connecting it to the oxygen delivery system. 'Okay, let's get an intravenous line in and hook him up to the monitors.' He made a hasty but thorough examination of the patient, and then ordered a chest X-ray, skeletal survey and a CT scan of the head, thorax and abdomen.

'We've multiple injuries here,' he said, showing Alison the results a short time later. 'Apart from the chest injury he has fractures to his right arm and leg and a liver laceration. The broken bones have been splinted, so we'll concentrate on checking for abdominal injury.'

'His abdomen is slowly enlarging,' Alison pointed out. 'That means there must be some internal bleeding. We need to get him up to Theatre.'

He nodded. 'Make the arrangements. I'll do an emergency laparotomy to see what's going on in there.'

Just a few minutes later, after they had both scrubbed in, Josh began to operate on the patient. Alison assisted by retracting the edges of the incision he made into the patient's abdomen. 'He's bleeding from the hepatic vein,' she said urgently.

Josh was already tending to it. 'I'll do a resection of the liver, but I'm afraid I'll have to remove the gall bladder.' All the time he was speaking he was cauterising the tissues that were bleeding and checking for other damage. Alison was in awe of the way he worked. Every action was careful, precise, and no time was wasted. After a while, though, he let out a deep breath and said, 'That's it, I believe. We can close him up now. Would you do that for me, Alison?'

She nodded and prepared to suture the wound. This man had opened her eyes to what a skilled surgeon was capable of. 'What are we going to do about his chest injury?'

'Nothing for the moment. We'll keep an eye on things, but let's make sure his condition is stabilised before we do anything else.' He thanked the team who had assisted him and pulled off his surgical gloves, dropping them into a bin. 'I'll go and see how the other casualties are doing.'

It was some time later, after the mayhem finally subsided in A&E, that she was able to go along to the minor injuries treatment room to see the teenager who had hurt his hand.

He was a pale-looking youth, around sixteen years of age, she guessed, and even though he was lying on a bed, leaning back against the pillows, she could see that he was tall and lanky, with a shock of dark hair and strangely haunted, unhappy grey eyes. There was a bruise beginning to form around the lower edge of his jaw, as though he had been punched.

'Rees, I'm so sorry you've had to wait for such a long time,' she told him. 'We've been busy looking after some people who were injured in a road traffic accident.'

'That's all right,' the youngster said. 'The nurse let me know what was happening. I didn't mind waiting.'

'That's good.' She smiled at him. 'There aren't many people around here who say that.' She glanced around the empty room. 'Are your parents waiting for you somewhere?'

'No.' He looked anxious for a moment, and then started

to cough—a deep, chesty cough that racked his whole body for a second or two. 'Someone who was passing by brought me in. I said I'd be all right, but she insisted on bringing me here. She said she wanted to wait with me, but she had to go to work.'

'Would you like me to get in touch with your parents?'

'No…thanks. They don't need to know I'm here.' The words came out abruptly, in a staccato manner, causing Alison to wonder why he was so anxious at the mention of them. She sat down beside his bed and began to carefully inspect his hand. There was a ragged, deep gash across his palm. 'So how did this happen?'

'I stumbled over some rough ground. I was a bit dizzy and I wasn't really looking where I was going. I started to fall and put out a hand to protect myself, but there was broken glass on the verge and that's how I cut myself.'

She nodded, not quite sure whether or not she believed him. The edges of the wound were deep, as though his hand had been rammed by a broken bottle. According to his notes, the woman who had brought him in had said she'd found him wandering in the street, looking dazed. 'It looks nasty, doesn't it? Have you any idea what caused the dizziness?'

He shrugged. 'No, not really.' He coughed again.

'Everything all right in here?' Josh put his head around the door, and Alison wondered if he had come to check up on her. Perhaps he was looking in on all the A&E staff?

'We're fine,' she said.

Josh nodded, and looked as though he intended to hang around for a while. She would have preferred he didn't do that. How was Rees going to open up to her with Josh watching over them?

'Your trauma patient is still in recovery,' she told him. 'Last I heard, he wasn't doing too well.'

'I know. I'm going to do an aortogram. I suspect there's something wrong with the heart vessel.'

Perhaps he realised that she didn't want him around. His glance went from her to Rees, and then he nodded towards the boy and said, 'You're in good hands.'

Josh left, and Alison let out a slow, soft breath. She went back to checking Rees's neurological reflexes.

'Everything seems to be okay on that score,' she said quietly, 'although your blood pressure is a bit low. Did you have anything to eat before you went out this morning?'

He shook his head, and was overcome once more by a bout of chesty coughing that left him exhausted. No wonder he hadn't complained about being kept waiting. She guessed he was probably glad of the chance to sit and rest somewhere warm and comfortable for a few hours.

Something about him brought out all her tender instincts, and she wasn't exactly sure why. Perhaps it had something to do with the fact that he looked a lot like her brother had at that age. Anyway, she felt there was more to his story than met the eye.

'This is a pretty deep cut,' she said, examining the wound. 'I don't think I can follow the usual procedure and leave it open while we wait to see if there is any infection brewing. It will need several stitches—but I'll give you an injection of anaesthetic first, of course. We'd better make sure that you have an up-to-date tetanus jab as well.'

'Okay.'

'Did this happen on the way to school?' she asked conversationally as she set about preparing the anaesthetic.

'No. I left school in the summer.'

'On the way to work, then?' she murmured.

He shook his head. 'I don't have a job yet. I've been trying to find one.'

It was becoming clear that she wasn't going to make any headway on that score, so she contented herself with explaining the procedure to him. 'I'm going to inject anaesthetic into the wound,' she said softly. 'I'm afraid it will sting a little to begin with, but then gradually the area should become numb. When it's completely anaesthetised I'll start to put in the sutures.'

He didn't say anything, but kept up a stoic expression throughout the procedure, and she wondered what might have happened to him in his young life that made him appear so withdrawn and world-weary.

'There—that's the worst bit over with,' she said a short time later. 'We'll wait a moment longer for it to take effect.'

She studied his brooding features for a second or two. He had refused to give an address to the desk clerk, and that worried her. What was he trying to hide?

'That's a nasty bruise to your jaw,' she murmured.

'It's nothing,' he said, his voice gruff.

It was the kind of response she was beginning to expect. Coupled with the lack of information about his home or his parents, she couldn't help wondering if he was a runaway. Of course at sixteen he wasn't legally any concern of the authorities, but it worried her that he was here alone and injured, apparently with no relative for them to contact.

'I'll make a start on the stitches now,' she murmured. 'Can you feel anything when I press here—or there?'

'No, it's okay.'

She concentrated on her work for the next few minutes. 'I've noticed that you have a nasty cough,' she said after a while. 'When I've finished here, I think it would be a good idea if I run the stethoscope over your chest, to see what's going on in your lungs. I'll take your temperature as well— if that's all right with you?'

He frowned. 'What will you do if you find out there's something wrong?'

'It depends on what I find. If there's an infection you might need to take a course of antibiotics. I can give you a prescription for those, and our pharmacy will dispense them for you.'

He nodded. 'All right.'

She finished suturing his hand and began to clear away the equipment she had used. While she was doing that a commotion started up, somewhere outside the treatment room, and a hum of deep male voices reverberated through the department.

Rees was looking anxious again, and she told him, 'That'll be members of the bikers' club, come to present the hospital with a cheque from their fund-raising efforts. They've done that ever since we treated some of their friends here a few years back. As soon as I've examined your chest, I'd better go and make sure they're being looked after.'

There were a lot of crackles and signs of infection coming from his lungs, she discovered. 'It sounds as though you have bronchitis,' she murmured. 'I'll ask the nurse to take you along to X-ray as soon as she's put a dressing on your hand. That way we'll know for certain what's going on in your lungs.' She studied him closely. 'I'll be back to see you in a while, when I have the results. All you need to do is sit back and take it easy. Are you happy to go along with that?'

He seemed to relax. 'Yes, that's okay.'

She studied his pale, tired features. What had happened to this boy? Had he been living rough on the streets? It was cold outside at this time of year and he only had a thin jacket. He looked clean enough, though, and it was possible he had been staying with a friend. Perhaps she was letting her imagination run away with her?

Still, her instincts were urging her to do what she could to help him out. 'I brought some food in with me, to serve to the people who are here for the ceremony… Would you like something to eat after your X-ray? I'll see if we can rustle up a cup of tea for you, too, while we're about it.'

His face brightened for the first time since she had gone to see him. 'Yes, please…if that would be all right?'

'Of course it will. I'll find someone to bring a tray over to you.'

She hurried away. No doubt Josh was still tending to his patients, and she knew that the specialist registrar was busy in theatre, so unless someone from Management had put in an appearance at the presentation, the bikers were being left to their own devices—and that wouldn't do at all.

As things turned out, though, she needn't have worried. The chief administrator was there in Reception, and all due ceremony was being given to the burly bikers who had turned up *en masse*. A few bemused patients looked on from the waiting room, curious to know what was going on. And a man from the local newspaper was there, taking photos as the manager accepted a cheque from the leader of the bikers' group—a huge fellow, clad in leather biker's gear and sporting a tangle of wild black hair.

Alison asked one of the ward assistants if she would take a tray of food and a cup of tea to Rees in the treatment room, and then went to watch the proceedings.

Josh, against all the odds, put in an appearance a short time later, stepping up to the front of Reception in order to address the gathering of people. He began by thanking the bikers for their generous donation, and assured them that it would be put to good use.

The hospital managers, he said, would be exhilarated to know that a good portion of this money would be available for new diagnostic equipment, and when Christmas came around any children unfortunate enough to be in hospital at that time would surely find to their joy that Santa, after searching their homes in vain, had after all managed to discover their whereabouts. He brought chuckles from the crowd, and Alison couldn't help thinking that his impromptu speech was better than anything she had imagined it might be.

Bringing his speech to a close, he smiled, an action that lit up his features in a way that made Alison go unexpectedly weak at the knees. Standing next to her, Katie, her flatmate, said in a low voice, 'Oh, wow. That man is way too good-looking. How can any of us be expected to work at our best with him around? It's very difficult to concentrate when you're running a fever.'

Alison giggled softly. 'I'm with you on that one. Of course you could always plead that you need his personal attention…the touch of his cool hand on your brow.'

'Oh, don't…don't say that.' Katie's green eyes sparkled, and she wafted a hand by her face as though to fan cool air over her hot cheeks. 'A hand on my brow would hardly do it. Now you have me imagining all sorts of things—long, sensual sponge baths and the like. Oh, my…what am I going to do? I'll be fit for nothing for the rest of the day, and I have patients waiting to be seen.'

By now they were both chuckling, and Alison was doing her best to sober up when she became aware of Josh coming towards them.

'Something amusing, ladies?' he enquired. 'Anything that you would care to share with me?'

Katie made a strange gulping sound and covered her mouth with her hand, lowering her head so that the curtain of her chestnut-coloured hair hid her features. Alison aimed a discreet tap of her foot against Katie's leg to encourage her to restrain herself.

How on earth was she supposed to answer him? She felt as though she had been well and truly left in the lurch.

CHAPTER TWO

ALISON shook her head and made an effort to pull herself together. 'Take no notice of us,' she murmured, throwing a bland gaze in Josh's direction. 'It's just that having all these macho-looking bikers about the place has gone to our heads. Far too much testosterone for us to handle.'

'Really?' Josh's grey eyes held a quizzical glint. 'I noticed they seemed very taken with both of you. I overheard some mutterings about the possibility of coming over to ask for a date.'

Alison's mouth made a wry slant. 'Yes, well… Unfortunately for them Katie's already been down that route, and she decided that tearing along the road at high speed on the back of a bike doesn't do it for her—not to mention the mess it makes of her hair, being flattened under a crash helmet.'

Katie had recovered her composure by now, and chose that moment to dig her in the ribs. Alison clamped her lips shut in the vestige of a smile.

'Alison has had first-hand experience of that, too,' her friend interjected. 'She seemed to find it quite exciting for a time. For myself, I've decided that I'd far sooner feel the wind in my hair from the passenger seat of a convertible.' She sent him a look that would charm the birds out of the trees.

Josh grinned. 'Spoken like a true connoisseur. You look like a girl who was born to the high life.'

A flush of colour ran along Katie's cheekbones, adding to the shimmering intensity of her green gaze. Alison observed the interplay between her and Josh with a cautious eye. Were they taken with one another? Or was he simply the kind of man who charmed every woman in sight?

'I thought your speech was perfect,' Katie murmured. 'You said everything that needed to be said, and you kept it short, too. I'd almost go as far as to say that you must have done this sort of thing before. I certainly wouldn't have been able to come up with anything anywhere near as good as that on the spur of the moment.'

'Well, thanks.' He sent her a mock suspicious look. 'You aren't trying to haggle for a rise, are you? Because maybe I should tell you I'm not the one who gives them out.'

'Oh, shame. What a waste.' Katie frowned. 'And there I was, hoping that you'd be thoroughly mellow after all the food that Alison brought in… As if that wouldn't be guaranteed to melt the hardest heart.'

'Yes, I noticed the wonderful spread.' He cast a glance towards the far side of the room, where the impromptu buffet had been laid out on a couple of trolleys. 'It all looks very impressive—and most of it home-made, too, from the looks of things.'

Katie nodded. 'You should have seen our kitchen last night. There was flour everywhere, and lovely smells coming from the oven.' She paused, thinking about it. 'I can't imagine what came over her. In fact, with all that home baking going on I began to wonder if she was getting broody.'

'No way,' Alison put in, pretending to be affronted. 'Anyway, you know perfectly well that I'm off men—ever since Rob led me a merry dance.' She stopped, suddenly becoming aware that Josh was listening with interest. He didn't need to know about her unhappy foray into so-called love, did he? 'Well, anyway, never mind that… Let's just say it was an experience to take to heart, and one that's all in the past.'

She was on her guard now where men were concerned. Rob was history—a sad lesson that she shouldn't lose her heart to any man with a wandering eye. And maybe that should include steering clear of those like the one not too far away, who managed to ooze charisma as though it was a new aftershave.

She pulled in a quick breath and started again. 'As to the baking session—it was all because of the Christmas cake, you see,' she said, as though that explained everything. 'I felt I had to make a start on it.'

'In fact, she started the day before,' Katie put in. 'I saw her hugging the brandy bottle and wondered what on earth was going on. Of course she said she wasn't actually thinking of drinking it, but I didn't really believe her until I found her mixing currants, raisins and sultanas together with candied peel, and adding a generous slosh of brandy every now and again. Apparently you have to let the fruit soak overnight.'

There was a puzzled look on Josh's face, and Alison hurried to explain. 'My gran has this wonderful recipe that she gave to me. Since she's coming over to my parents' house for Christmas I thought I would bake her cake and surprise her with it.'

'And you have to start all that several weeks beforehand?' He was frowning.

She nodded. 'So I'm told. I popped the mix in the oven last night, and while I was about it I thought I'd bake a few treats for today. Then Katie started to help, and between us we seem to have been a little bit carried away.'

'I don't know about that—it's just as well we made stacks of stuff,' Katie said. 'It's a wonder there was anything left to bring after Taylor and Sam from the flat upstairs caught wind of what was going on. And then Tom's children from next door came in, wanting to sample everything, and pleading to be allowed to lick the bowl after she'd emptied the cake mix into the baking tin. They ate so much I was surprised they weren't sick.'

Alison grinned. 'It was lovely to see them happy, though, wasn't it? Things haven't been so cheerful in their house of late.'

'No, that's true enough.' Katie frowned. 'Imagine having the threat of being turned out of your own house hanging over you. Tom and Martha must be beside themselves with worry.' She glanced around. 'Anyway, I'd better get back to work. My lunch break is nearly over, and I still have a list of patients as long as my arm. I'll go and grab a bite to eat first, though.'

Alison nodded agreement. 'Me, too. And then I must go back to my own patients.' She sighed. 'There's no rest for the wicked, is there? Though it has been good to take time out.'

Josh went with them, glancing around the reception area. People had been busy putting up tinsel garlands over the last couple of days, and there were one or two sparkling bells adorned with red and silver ribbon. He didn't look impressed, thought Alison. In fact she couldn't be certain of his reaction… More resigned than anything else, probably.

He moved on, and soon started making his own inroads on the buffet, sampling a mince pie and adding a fruit turnover to his plate. 'I need sustenance,' he said. 'I have to operate in a while. It looks as though our motor crash victim is going to need a repair to his heart's main blood vessel.'

'Oh, I'm sorry.' Alison sent him a fleeting glance. 'That's bad news, isn't it? For the patient, I mean. Obviously you must have done the aortogram?'

He nodded. 'It showed a pseudoaneurysm. I believe there's a small tear in the vessel, so the nurses are preparing him for surgery now.'

'I hope it goes well.' It meant that the patient's heart would be linked to a bypass machine for a short time, while Josh inserted a repair graft in the leaking artery.

She lingered for a minute or two to chat, before heading back to Rees in the treatment room. Katie and Josh were deep in conversation when she left, and she doubted they would have noticed her departure.

The boy set aside his tray while she put up the X-ray film in the light box and carefully studied it. 'There's definitely an infection there,' she told him after a while, 'and you have a raised temperature. I think we'll start you off on antibiotics and keep you here for a few hours in our observation ward. Are you okay with that?'

He nodded. She guessed he was in no hurry to go back out into the cold, and perhaps he had nowhere to go. That was a worrying thought. Strictly speaking she had no real reason to keep him here under observation, or admit him to hospital overnight—which was what she would have preferred to do. That would give her more of a chance to talk to him, and hopefully encourage him to tell her more about the circumstances that brought him here. She wanted to help him in any way possible.

'All right, then,' she murmured. 'I'll arrange for a nurse to take you to the observation ward next door and get you settled.'

'Will it be all right if I take the food with me?'

She chuckled. 'Yes, of course. We'll make sure that goes along with you. I think, since your blood sugar was low, it's important to feed you. We also need to bring down your temperature and generally look after you.' She sent him a quick glance. 'I don't want to send you away from here while you're clearly unwell, and you haven't given us an address. I'm worried that there's no family around to take care of you.' She hesitated. 'Are you living at home?'

He didn't answer, but after a moment or two he shook his head.

'Have you been living out on the streets?'

He hunched his shoulders, and Alison wondered if she should take that as a yes.

'If you feel that you need to talk to someone about anything that's bothering you I'm here to listen, you know. Nothing you say will go any further unless you want it to.'

He returned her gaze, not quite meeting her eyes. He appeared to be deep in thought, and for a second or two she was hopeful that he might be about to confide in her.

But then he slumped back against his pillows without saying anything, and the moment was lost.

She left him in the care of a nurse, and went to tend to her other patients. With any luck Rees would pluck up the courage to open up to her later on. She just needed to win his trust.

For the next few hours she concentrated all her efforts on looking after the sick and injured. She hoped Josh's patient was doing well in the operating theatre. Still, she had seen Josh at work in the resuscitation room, and it was plain to see how effective he was in a crisis situation. No wonder he had been chosen to replace Dr Meadows. He was immensely skilled. There was no hesitation, no doubt, not a single moment when he wasn't in complete control.

That didn't change when he came back down to A&E some time later. He simply turned his attention to overseeing the work of his subordinates, and that was when Alison felt the first stirrings of unease. He began to leaf through all the patients' charts.

She went to check through the test results at the desk.

'Would you care to explain this to me?' he said, coming over to her a few minutes later. He was frowning as he held out a folder. 'I don't see any major problem with this patient, and yet young Rees is still here. By all accounts he could have been discharged some time ago. You've examined him and given him the appropriate treatment. Why haven't you sent him on his way?'

Alison's spirits plummeted. Was Josh Bentley one of the new breed of 'time is money; patch them up and move them out' doctors? How she hated that emphasis on efficiency at all costs. Somehow she had believed he would have better judgement than that.

Alison remained silent for a moment, glancing through the glass door of the observation ward. Rees was dozing peacefully, his face bleached of colour against the stark white of his pillows, and she couldn't help feeling that he was exhausted, worn out by a combination of factors. The boy's hair was an unruly tangle of black silky strands, crying out for the tender hand of a mother figure to smooth it into place. Surely Josh wasn't expecting her to wake him up and turf him out into the cold, soulless streets to fend for himself? What kind of man *was* he?

His dark brows rose in expectation.

'The boy's running a temperature,' she said, 'and he has a chest infection. Also, he's looking gaunt, and I don't think he's been eating properly. I prefer to wait for the results of tests, query pneumonia, before I decide what to do. It occurred to me that it might be wise to keep him in overnight.'

Josh gave her a long, thoughtful look. 'We both know he isn't that ill. I've seen the X-ray film. Besides, I heard he went walkabout for a while and a nurse had to go looking for him. What's going on here, Alison?'

'Walkabout?' She frowned. 'Where did he go?'

'The nurse wasn't sure. She found him in the corridor heading back to the ward. He must have slipped out through the security door when a visitor left.'

'Did he say where he'd been?'

'Only some vague comment about trying to find a washroom.' From his expression it was clear that he was unconvinced by that explanation. 'The nurse said he appeared to be on edge. She decided he must be feverish and led him back to bed.'

'Perhaps that's the truth of it.' Alison sighed. 'He's definitely unwell. I wanted to keep him here so I have a little more time to see if I can get him to open up to me. We don't know anything about his background, or what will happen to him once he leaves here. He won't say anything about his parents, and he's refused to give an address.'

'Hmm. I can see why you're concerned, but that isn't really our problem, is it? Besides, he might be on the run from the law. As to staying here, I already have Management on my back, emphasising the necessity to stick to targets and maximise throughput. Rees isn't seriously ill, and we're not obliged to notify the authorities about our worries since he insists he's sixteen. We haven't been asked to look out for anyone answering his description.'

'I know, but I'm pretty sure he's run away from home, and if he's living rough there's a strong possibility his condition will quickly nosedive. I don't want that on my conscience.' She frowned. 'There's a vulnerability about him that makes me want to do everything I can to help him—and surely we have to pay some heed to the welfare of the people who cross our path? You wouldn't send an elderly person out onto the streets if you feared for his well-being, would you?'

'Soft as putty, aren't you?' His smile was gently mocking. 'If you feel so strongly about him, why haven't you taken steps to contact the police or Social Services?'

'I don't want to betray his trust…and I want to give him the chance to confide in me.'

He shook his head. 'We're an accident and emergency

department,' he chided softly. 'Not a holding centre for waifs and strays.'

She glowered at him, her blue eyes sparking. Okay, ultimately he was in charge, but she wasn't going to allow her decisions to be overridden without a fight. She trusted her instincts and they had never let her down. 'We have spare beds and we're not overstretched right now. I don't see any reason for sending him away just yet.'

'Maybe not, but you know as well as I do that the situation could change at any moment if we have a sudden influx.'

'I prefer to base my judgements on the situation as it is at present. He's unwell, and I know of no responsible adult who will take over his care. It's my professional opinion that he should stay here.'

Josh was silent for a moment or two, his features taut, his mouth pursed in contemplation, and she began to wonder if perhaps she had gone too far. He was new here, and she didn't yet have the measure of the man. For all she knew he could take offence at her arguments and have her taken off his team.

'You may be right,' he said eventually. 'I'll give you the benefit of the doubt and go along with you on this one—if only because he complained of dizziness before his fall. That being the case, you'd better go ahead and admit him overnight on the grounds of suspected pneumonia and the possibility of wound infection. But if the situation changes, and we're overrun with trauma cases and the like, we'll have to do some creative thinking about where to place him.'

'That's great.' She stared at him, wide eyed, her face lighting up. 'I take it all back—every bad thing I was thinking about you. You've shot up ten times in my estimation. In fact, I could hug you.'

'Really? I thought you were finished with men?'

'Ah…well, yes, that's perfectly true. But then again, I wasn't planning on a relationship.' A ripple of warmth ran through her. What was the matter with her? Why couldn't she glue her lips together and stay out of trouble?

He studied her, a glint of humour flickering in his eyes. 'So you were thinking bad things about me, were you? That isn't good, is it? Given first impressions and all that.'

'Um, well, no,' she faltered. 'But then you did manage to redeem yourself after all, didn't you?' She studied him guardedly.

He chuckled. 'Think of it as a thank-you for warning me about the presentation…and for the fruit turnovers. Let's not forget them.' He rolled his eyes heavenward. 'They were out of this world.'

Her features softened in appreciation. 'I'm glad you think so. If Management complain about Rees being here, perhaps you should offer a few to them, too.'

He sucked in a quick breath. 'I'm afraid I can't do that.'

She blinked. 'You can't? Why…? Is it because it would reek of bribery and corruption?'

He shook his head. 'No, not that—though it's certainly a consideration. It's because they've all gone.' His mouth turned down at the corners. 'There's absolutely nothing left…only crumbs.'

She laughed. 'Oh, dear. Still, now I know I have the perfect bribe to use whenever I want something to go my way. I didn't realise how much influence I could bring to bear. Let's make the most of it. We're talking turnover power!'

He was smiling when Alison left him after a moment or two to go and get on with her work.

The rest of the day passed in a flash as she was kept busy dealing with new emergencies, but she managed to find time to look in on Rees in the observation ward before the end of her shift.

He still looked weary, and she noted that despite the antibiotics his temperature was a notch higher than normal.

'I think it would be for the best if we were to admit you overnight,' she told him. 'That way we can keep an eye on you while the antibiotics begin to do their stuff, and hopefully we'll be able to bring your temperature down. We can also keep an eye on the injury to your hand at the same time. How do you feel about that?'

'Yeah, that's all right.' He ran the back of his good hand over his forehead. 'The nurse said you might want to keep me in. She said she'd find some crossword books and a couple of videos for me to watch when I'm feeling a bit better.'

'That's good. You should try to get some rest.' She gave him a soft smile. 'I expect they'll be bringing your tea round before too long, and you'll need some energy to tackle that.'

His eyes brightened a fraction. 'That's great. I'm starving.'

She laughed. 'I don't know where you manage to put it all. Still, you could do with building up.' She smiled at him. 'I'm going off duty in a while, but the nurse will take care of you. If you have any problems at all, just let her know. She'll do whatever she can to sort things out. I'll drop by and see you in the morning.'

He nodded, and she left the bay, going in search of the nurse. She found her checking schedules on the computer, and spent a few minutes bringing her up to date on the situation.

'I'll do everything I can to encourage him to confide in

me,' Jenny said. 'So far he hasn't said anything that's of much help. He's a bit of an enigma, but I'm fairly sure that he's worried about something. Whatever it is, he's not letting on.'

'Thanks, Jenny. I'm sure he's in good hands in the meantime.' Alison left her and went to retrieve her jacket from the doctors' restroom.

As she walked back towards Reception a short time later, she saw that Josh was there, deep in thought as he pored over the contents of a folder.

'Ah, you're just the person I wanted to see,' he said, looking up, his tone brisk. 'I take it you're going off duty now?'

'That's right. Is there a problem?'

He shook his head. 'Not at all.' He waved a hand towards the corridor. 'You have some visitors…your neighbour and his children. I sent them to the relatives' waiting room.'

'Oh, that's good. Thanks for letting me know. Tom said he would come and pick me up. I just hope he managed to sort out whatever was wrong with my car.'

She would have gone to find them straight away, but she paused long enough to study Josh for a moment or two. There was something about his demeanour that put her on alert. 'Is everything all right? You look as though you have something on your mind. Has your first day here not gone as well as you might have expected? I know you've hardly had a minute to yourself all day. It's like that sometimes.'

She hesitated before adding, 'The work in itself can be challenging, can't it? We have to deal with things that you might come across only once in a blue moon, and there aren't always simple answers. But generally we're a sup- portive bunch of people, and we aim to rub along well together. Of course it's different when you're in charge, I suppose. You have a lot more to contend with, and you probably look at everything from a different perspective to the rest of us.'

'Well, that's certainly true. I wasn't expecting to see hordes of bikers about the place this lunchtime. Nor was I expecting to have to make a speech almost as soon as I arrived.' He frowned. 'As to this latest request...' He scowled at the folder he had been studying, tossing the file down on the desktop in a peremptory fashion. 'I can't imagine why I'm being asked to take part in a hospital radio show. Since I'm only going to be here for two days a week, I'm sure there are far more pressing demands on my time.'

Alison cast a quick glance over the file. 'Oh, I see. It's the outline for the Christmas radio programme. It goes out on air to all the patients, and they schedule it in advance. I don't imagine the radio committee meant to cause trouble for you. It's just that...'

'I know. You don't need to tell me...' He put up a hand to stop her. 'Steve Meadows always had a slot on the show. I've been hearing an awful lot about your former boss and his various good deeds. Apparently he was a member of the drama club and gave impromptu entertainment for the children on the wards, and he did charity runs and organised medical care for homeless people.' His lips compressed. 'He must rank among the saints, giving his time to every needy cause going. No wonder he suffered a heart attack. Was there anything that man *didn't* do?'

'Um...he did work tremendously hard, and he thought it was important to try to keep the patients happy—especially at Christmas time. It *is* the Christmas programme they're asking you to look at, isn't it?'

His jaw clenched. 'That's right… But they—the radio committee—had better think again. I'm a doctor, not a presenter, and at the moment I have more worthy matters to consider. Such as how to take care of the man I operated on this afternoon. If he manages to pull through after losing several pints of blood and having his heart put on bypass I shall count my blessings.'

He pushed the folder into the wastepaper basket with a broad sweep of his arm and then began to stride across the room. 'I shall be in the resuscitation room if anyone needs me.'

Alison nodded, watching him go. 'I'll be sure to let the desk clerk know.'

Clearly he was worried about his patient and not in the best of moods right now. Maybe it *was* bad timing for the radio committee to lay their request on him on his very first day in the job.

She scribbled a message for the clerk, who was temporarily away from the desk. As an afterthought, she pulled the folder out of the wastebin and laid it to one side in a wire tray. Some decisions would have to be made regarding the programme before too long—but they could surely wait for the moment? The new boss obviously needed more time to settle in.

She hurried along to the waiting room. 'Tom,' she greeted her neighbour, 'thanks for coming to fetch me. I'm sorry I've kept you waiting. I hope I've not put you out too much?'

'Not at all.' He was a tall man, with dark hair and features that were carved out of life's experiences—

crinkled lines about his blue eyes and a firm jawline that hinted at a rock-steady character. Alison had taken to him from the instant she met him.

He came towards her now, his arms enclosing her in a brief hug. 'I had to come into town anyway. I ordered a replacement petrol pump for your car, and the spare parts place promised me they would have it in stock by this evening. Of course Jason and Rachel wanted to come with me. They both needed new trousers, so my wife gave me instructions on what to look out for in the local store.' He frowned. 'I can't keep up with them. They're forever wearing them out at the knees or snagging them on something or other. Nobody ever told me about the downside of having a family. I've become a walking money tree, and I feel as though my roots are beginning to wither.'

She gave him a wry smile. 'It almost makes me glad I'm not a parent.' She glanced around the room. 'Where are they, by the way?'

'They went out to fetch cold drinks from the machine in the main waiting room. I thought I'd better wait here, in case you wondered where I was, but perhaps we'd better go and see what they're up to. They should have been back by now, and I daren't imagine what they might get up to left to their own devices for too long.'

'Good idea,' she agreed, nodding. The children were eight and nine years old, and full of the joys of life. 'Knowing Jason and his love of drawing, they could be trying out designs for a new mural by now.'

'Oh, heaven forbid! Don't say that, please. I can feel an ulcer starting already.'

She laughed, and they hurried away towards the main

waiting room in search of the children. Unfortunately they were nowhere to be seen.

Alison gazed around her in dismay. 'We'd have seen them if they were heading back to you in the waiting room, wouldn't we?'

Tom nodded, an anxious look spreading over his face.

'Can I help in any way?' Josh came out of the resuscitation room and strode briskly towards them, delivering the words in an equally vigorous, no-nonsense fashion. 'Are you looking for the children?'

Alison nodded, her heart sinking rapidly. He didn't look at all content with the way his day was going, and his questions didn't have the tiniest note of pleasant enquiry about them. Something was definitely wrong. 'They came in here to fetch cold drinks,' she said. 'Do you know where they are?'

'The last I saw of them they were playing in the courtyard outside the waiting room.' He looked directly at Tom. 'There's still a lot of snow around, and they were trying to slide down the grass verge. Unfortunately Jason slipped on the ice and cut his knee. He's okay, but I asked one of the nurses to clean it up and put a dressing on it before she brought the pair of them back to you. You'll find them in Treatment Room Two, over there.' He waved a hand in the direction of the room, and Tom thanked him and immediately rushed away.

Alison gave Josh a brief, apologetic look. 'I'm so sorry,' she said. 'It's probably my fault the children went exploring. I arranged to meet Tom at the end of my shift, but I was a little late.'

'So I gathered,' he said. 'Still, I dare say there's no harm done. If today's anything to go by, nothing in this place follows a normal pattern, does it?'

He walked away from her, heading over to the desk, where he began rifling through lab test results.

Alison sighed. He was right. This day *had* been singularly odd—and not just because of the biker invasion, or her car breaking down and Tom and the children coming into the hospital. She had come face to face with her new boss, and she still didn't have any idea of what kind of man he was. He was full of contradictions, a man of hidden depths. She had no real idea of how she was going to work with him on a day-to-day basis.

CHAPTER THREE

'YOU look like a sorry bunch of half-frozen characters,' Josh remarked, as Alison hurried into Reception next day. Katie and the men from the upstairs flat followed close on her heels. 'Perhaps you should grab a cup of coffee and warm yourselves up before you start work?'

Alison nodded, blowing on her hands as though to breathe life into them. Josh made an unexpected welcoming committee, though he was definitely a sight for sore eyes. He was every bit as immaculately dressed as he had been the day before, wearing a dark grey suit that drew attention to his broad shoulders and lean, tautly muscled frame.

He was on great form, poised and ready for work—while she, in contrast, was at a peculiarly low ebb, chilled to the bone from her journey to the hospital, and uncertain as to why Josh had chosen to make his presence felt at this hour. She wasn't used to having the boss watching over her. His predecessor had usually been found huddled in his office before the shift began, reading through a sheaf of papers.

'I think I'll do that,' she murmured. 'Sam gave us a lift into work this morning, but the heater wasn't working in his car so we've all forgotten what our hands feel like, they're so numb. Then we ran into a flurry of snow as we walked across the car park.'

'It sounds as though it won't be long before Tom has another mechanic's job on his hands,' Josh murmured. 'He's not doing too badly out of his neighbours so far, is he?'

'Much as I get along well with Tom, I won't be paying out for car repairs any time soon,' Sam retorted, shrugging out of his soft leather jacket. He was a sturdy, long-limbed young man, with mid-brown hair and blue eyes, and a matter-of-fact manner. 'Everyone will just have to toughen up. I need to save everything I have for Christmas. I'm planning on going away for the holidays…I have a skiing trip all lined up.'

'Ski slopes?' Josh's eyes lit up. 'That sounds like a good idea.'

Alison glanced at him briefly. Why would anyone want to go away at Christmas time and leave his family behind? Sam was a different case altogether. He had family overseas, and his skiing holiday was a celebration of their coming together.

'If this weather holds out you might not need to go away to ski,' Katie put in, heading across the room to the kitchen annexe, where a coffee pot steamed gently on a worktop by the sink. 'With the snow starting already, it looks as though we could be in for a white Christmas here at home. Wouldn't that be beautiful?' A dreamy expression settled on her face. 'I can just imagine it… A carpet of white over the Pennine Hills, with icicles hanging from the trees and masses of stars in a midnight sky. All the lights of the houses would give out a golden glow…'

'And we could sit inside, all cosy and warm,' Alison

added, rubbing her arms to bring about some heat. 'With a blazing fire in the hearth. And we'd drink spicy fruit punch and munch on hot mince pies covered with lashings of icing sugar. It would be wonderful, wouldn't it?'

'I'd sooner go on a pub crawl,' Taylor put in. 'Lots of singing and merry-making and people generally having a good time.'

'That's all a long way off yet,' Josh said in a laconic tone, pulling mugs down from a shelf. 'What *is* the obsession round here with the Christmas season? Snow means blocked roads and skids and lots of yucky snow melt on the verges when the thaw comes. Unless you like it so much you're planning a mass exodus to the North Pole some time soon? I hope you're not thinking of leaving me to manage A&E all by myself. I'd need a lot more than Santa and his little elves to help me get through the days.'

'You're a sad soul,' Katie said, sending him a pitying glance. 'What happened? Did you have your fun gland removed at some time?'

He nodded solemnly. 'Maybe I did—along with my nonsense nodule. Now, do you think we can push the subject of Christmas to one side and concentrate on limbering up ready for work? The rest of the staff are getting ready to hand over their patients to you. Apparently it's been a busy night. Several people came in with fractures and other injuries.'

'Well, that's brought us down to earth with a bump, hasn't it?' Alison poured coffee into the mugs and handed them around. She sipped her coffee and watched as Josh morphed smoothly from sympathetic colleague into leadership mode.

'We have three difficult cases to deal with on handover…
A patient with an aneurysm that needs careful management, a possible neck fracture, and a patient who suffered a collapsed lung. They're all under observation at the moment, but I'm assigning responsibility as per the whiteboard. You'll see there's a long list of people waiting for treatment, even at this early hour.'

He turned his attention to Alison, who put down her mug and prepared herself for action. He had that look about him that said he was up and running, and where she was concerned things were about to change…though not necessarily for the better.

'Your young patient from yesterday tried to go on a walkabout again early this morning,' he said briskly. 'For all we know he could be looking for drugs. Presumably you'll take a look at him some time this morning and find out exactly what's going on?'

'Oh. Right. Well, yes, I'll try to do that.' Alison blinked. Medical problems she could solve, given time and test results, but dealing with the intricacies of welfare troubles was not her strong point. Another walkabout? Something was obviously not right with Rees, and she definitely needed to find out what it was. First, though, she would make a quick check on her other patients. Right now they were her priority. 'As to the drugs, I've seen no evidence of any addiction.'

'Did you test for it?'

'No. I had no reason to.' He gave her an 'I told you so' look, and she was prompted to add, 'I was looking for a chest infection.'

'Of course you were. Have you come up with any

solution to the problem of what happens when you discharge him from the hospital?' Josh fell into step beside her as she set off towards the main area of A&E. She did her best to push aside the feeling of wanting to shrug him off. Didn't he have to go and see any patients of his own?

'Not yet. Other than seeing if I can persuade him to talk to a friend of mine from an agency that supports youngsters like Rees. I phoned Jack last night and asked what he thought I should do.'

'You're not about to give up on him, then?'

'Of course not.' She sent him a shocked glance. 'I'll do everything I can to make sure that he has someone to look after him when he leaves here.'

He gave a wry smile, but then his pager bleeped and he crossed over to the desk to answer the call. She went with him, checking the whiteboard for her patients' names and rummaging through the files for details of their conditions.

'I'll stop by the clinic later this afternoon when I've finished operating,' he said into the receiver. 'Make an appointment for him to see me around four-thirty and I'll decide what needs to be done.'

Alison frowned. What clinic was he talking about? Wasn't he going to be here in the hospital at four-thirty?

She glanced through the file she was holding, skimming through the notes outlining her first patient's symptoms. An aneurysm meant that the woman needed to be seen by a vascular specialist, and she must keep a check on her blood pressure.

Josh replaced the receiver on its cradle. 'Upper Regent Street,' he said, as though she had asked a question.

'The exclusive part of the city?' she murmured, a vaguely confused look crossing her face.

'That's where I have my private practice,' he responded, with a benign, obliging glance. 'You looked as though you were curious,' he explained. 'It's where I go when I'm not working here, and it accounts for two full days and two afternoons of my working week.'

She looked at him oddly. How was it he was so sure that he knew what she was thinking? It annoyed her even more to concede that he was right. 'You work in private practice?'

'I do—along with a couple of partners.' He studied her for a moment or two. 'You appear to be shocked by that information. Does it bother you? Do you have a problem with private medicine?'

'Um…not necessarily.' That wasn't exactly the truth. She had never been able to get over the unsavoury picture of people who were ill in bed being presented with bills for their treatment. 'I mean…I can see where it might benefit some people who can't get the treatment they want quickly enough, but I've always believed medicine should be freely available to all at the point of need.' Even the mention of it stirred feelings in her that she would rather stayed dormant. Hadn't her ex-boyfriend thrown away his integrity and gone for the option of wealth over ideals?

'Well, that doesn't always happen, does it?' He checked the wire tray on the desk for lab test reports. 'That's why people turn to me.'

'People who have money,' she said. 'Wealthy people.' She shook her head, feeling a little sick inside. 'Don't get me wrong…I don't blame them for turning to people like you for help. They can afford it. I just feel that everyone should have the same opportunity.'

'That will never happen, though, will it?' He grimaced. 'You're living in cloud cuckoo land if you think there will ever be a country rich enough to provide that level of care for all its citizens. You'll never have the idyllic situation where one system covers all.'

She snapped the folder shut. 'And that's where you come in, isn't it? Wielding your scalpel like a trusty sword. Only there's always a price to be paid, isn't there? Or should I say fee?'

He held up his hands as though to ward her off. 'Seems I hit a nerve,' he said. 'Have you always been this touchy, or is it something about me that brings it on?'

She frowned, studying his strong, determinedly masculine features with a cautious eye. 'I'd say probably a bit of both.' She started to walk away, heading towards one of the treatment rooms. 'Please excuse me. I have to go and treat a woman suffering from terrible headaches. Of course if she'd had the operation she needs to correct the anomaly in her blood vessels some time ago, she might not be in this situation now.'

He waved his hands in a gesture of exasperation. 'You know as well as I do that surgeons err on the side of caution in these situations. It isn't always a case of putting things off. Maybe it was a minor aneurysm, best left alone.'

She didn't answer him, but went instead to talk to her patient about medication to lower her blood pressure. Somehow or other they would keep her healthy until the surgeon deemed it was time to operate.

'I'm going to send you for another CT scan,' she told

the woman. 'If we find that the aneurysm has become slightly enlarged, I'll refer you back to the surgeon for his opinion. I believe he may want to bring the surgery date forward. In the meantime, we'll add another type of medication to your prescription to keep things under control.'

When she had reassured the woman about the situation, she left the room, and was about to go in search of her next patient when Jenny emerged from the observation ward.

'How's Rees doing?' Alison asked. 'I heard he was a bit restless again.'

'He's very jumpy and on edge,' the nurse told her, 'but I'm afraid he still hasn't told me what's wrong'

Alison nodded. 'Thanks for keeping an eye on him, Jenny. I'll go and talk to him later on and see if I can sort things out. How is he doing health-wise?'

'He's a lot better. His temperature is back to normal, and the chest infection seems to be responding to the antibiotics. He has more colour in his face, too, since we've been feeding him up. As to the hand, he's able to move his fingers well enough, and it appears to be healing nicely.'

'Good. Let's hope we can manage to find out what's behind his other problems.'

Some time later, when she'd finished dealing with all the urgent cases on her list, she headed back towards the central area of A&E, but stopped when she passed by one of the treatment rooms where monitors were bleeping warnings at high pitch.

Josh was at work in there. His patient was a young boy, around eight years of age, pale and gasping for breath, his lips tinged with blue. The child's mother looked on, her eyes wide and frightened as she watched Josh at work.

'He was out in the playground at school,' she said. 'I think the children were all running about at lunchtime, playing football, when he started to have problems. The teachers called me and said he'd collapsed. I don't understand what's happening.'

'I'm concerned that he might be suffering an asthma attack,' Josh murmured, listening to the boy's lungs through his stethoscope. 'He has a chest infection, and I imagine the cold weather must have added to the problem and brought on his breathing difficulties.'

He spoke gently to the boy, adjusting the breathing mask over his nose and mouth. Alison guessed he was breathing in a mixture of nebulised salbutamol and oxygen. 'I'm going to give you an injection of something that will help you to breathe more easily, Charlie,' he said. 'And we'll give you medicine to help clear up the problem in your lungs. Don't worry. You'll soon start to feel much better, I'm sure.'

The boy was clearly too ill to respond, and Alison went further into the room. Josh was working alone in here, so she guessed the nurse had been called away to tend to another emergency.

'Do you want any help?' she asked.

Josh nodded. 'Thanks. His oxygen saturation is very low, and I may have to intubate,' he said quietly.

'What does that mean?' the boy's mother asked, and Alison hurried over to the bedside to explain as Josh prepared to insert a cannula into the back of the boy's hand. With that in place, the child would be able to receive various medications that would act more quickly as a result of being passed directly into the bloodstream.

'He's not breathing very well on his own, so we might

need to put a tube down his throat and let a machine do the breathing for him,' she told the mother. 'The monitor bleeps every time his oxygen level falls below eighty-one percent. We need to bring it up as near to a hundred as we can manage.'

The woman sucked in a sharp breath. 'I'd no idea his chest was this bad,' she said softly. 'He was poorly yesterday, with a wheezy cough, but he wanted to go to school and be with his friends because there was a book fair on in the afternoon. I thought he would be all right. Of course I hadn't bargained on this bitter cold snap coming on.'

'It caught us all by surprise,' Josh murmured. He looked up at Alison. 'Will you start an infusion of aminophylline and add one hundred mg hydrocortisone to be given six-hourly? I'm going to add ipratropium to the nebuliser.' He turned to the mother and added, 'These drugs will help to widen his airways and should begin to ease his breathing. I'm also going to start him on a broad spectrum antibiotic to help combat the infection while we wait for the results of tests.'

All the time he was talking he was watching the monitors and assessing the boy's condition. Once the infusion was set up, and the drugs administered, he filled out the patient's chart and noted down what further action needed to be taken, so that the nurse would be able to continue with the treatment.

Charlie's breathing was shallow, his heart-rate rapid, and his little face was pinched and white. Alison wanted to comfort him and offer reassurance, but she knew that Josh was doing everything possible to pull the child back from the brink.

'I'll probably add intravenous magnesium sulphate to

the infusion when we have some of the results back,' Josh told Alison. 'It's been shown to be a safe treatment for acute asthma attacks, but we'll see how he improves in the meantime.' He turned to the boy's mother. 'Mrs Flanagan, it looks as though Charlie's oxygen level is beginning to rise slightly. That's a good sign. I doubt we'll need to intubate him after all, but we'll keep a close eye on him.'

Alison felt a modicum of relief. Josh had been calm and efficient throughout, and now he began to talk in a soothing tone to the child's mother, explaining the situation and letting her know what they were doing to combat the illness.

'We'll admit him to the children's ward,' he told her. 'If you would like to stay with him, the nurse will arrange for you to have a room close by.'

'Thank you.' Charlie's mother nodded. 'I'll stay, of course. I just need to ring my husband and let him know what's happening. He's out on a call somewhere, and his boss was trying to get in touch with him.'

Alison was touched by Josh's gentle manner with the boy and his mother. He managed somehow to instil confidence in the people around him, and she was glad he had come to work with them. He was someone they could trust to lead the team, she was sure.

The nurse, Jenny, came into the treatment room then, and Josh quickly outlined the situation and gave instructions as to how they would manage the boy's condition.

'I'll do that,' Jenny said. She gave Charlie a reassuring smile and then added, 'I thought you'd like to know, Josh, Taylor's hanging about outside the treatment room. He wants a word with you…something about advice on an orthopaedic matter…when you're not too busy.' Then she turned to Alison, saying, 'And you're in demand as well, Alison. Someone's been asking to see you. He's waiting for you by the reception desk.'

Alison frowned. Who might that be? She glanced towards Josh, and he nodded. 'You go. We've finished in here for the moment.'

He moved away from the bedside, and after a last check of the monitors they both took their leave of Charlie and his mother and left the room.

Sure enough, Taylor was waiting outside. 'What's wrong, Taylor? I heard you had a problem.' Josh studied him briefly.

'Uh, yes. I'm dealing with a particularly nasty shoulder injury,' Taylor said. 'I need to know what's the best way to treat it to preserve the patient's ability to use the joint in performance sports in the future.' He looked intently at Josh. 'That's your specialist field, isn't it—orthopaedic problems? I'd appreciate some advice when you have a free moment. I had to act quickly, but I'm not altogether sure I handled things the best way possible. You might be able to help me to put things right.'

Taylor was a lean young man, with soft brown hair that refused to be tamed. He was generally earnest, and eager to get on in his chosen career, and Alison could see that even now he was keen to do his very best for his patient. He wasn't going to miss any opportunity, and if Josh was the expert he was the man to ask.

Josh nodded. 'I saw you dealing with a complicated fracture early on. I think you probably did well to save the man's arm, let alone preserve any superior function, but certainly I'll come along and take another look. I was going to do that anyway. I know from the cases you've dealt with before this that you have the makings of a fine orthopaedic surgeon.'

Alison was astonished. Had he looked through *all* the case notes from the last week or so? This man was clearly making sure that he knew everything there was to know about the people he was working with and the state of play regarding their skills. He was awesome.

'I'll leave you both,' she said, scooting around the two men who stood in her path. 'I have to go and see someone.' She was still curious about her visitor in Reception.

She hurried over. There was only one man standing by the desk, and he had his back to her. Alison came to a sudden standstill. Whatever she might have been expecting, it certainly wasn't this.

'Fraser?'

Her brother turned around, his blue eyes widening in a sheepish smile. 'Hi, Allie.'

She went over to him and gave him a hug. 'What are you doing here? I thought you were supposed to be at university until a week before Christmas? Has something happened?'

He gave a nervous laugh. 'You could say that.'

She stared at him. 'I think I just did. Perhaps you should tell me what's going on, Fraser?'

'Yeah, well, I'm sort of having to get my head around it.'

'Fraser?' Her voice showed a hint of impatience. Mildly accepting that she was being given the runaround was not her thing. 'Out with it.'

'The thing is, Allie…I've been sent down.'

Her eyes widened in shock. 'You're joking? This is a joke, right?'

'Wrong. It's no joke, I'm afraid.' He pulled in a deep breath. 'What I came here for was to ask if I could beg a huge favour. I mean, I know you share a flat with Katie and all that, but do you think you could put me up for a while? The settee would do—or anything, really. It's just to get me out of a tight spot for a while.'

She gave him a perplexed look. 'Wouldn't it be better to go home to Mum and Dad?'

A pained expression crossed his face. 'They'd go spare,' he said weakly. 'Can't you imagine it? Dad's blood pressure would shoot sky-high, and Mum would be asking all the whys and wherefores, and then she'd sink to rock bottom and think the world had collapsed. You know how keen they are for me to get this degree. I am, too…my whole future career depends on it. I can't face them, Allie. Not just yet, anyway. Not until I've had time to think about what I'm going to say. Can you picture how this will go down at Christmas? It'll put a damper on everything. I'm in disgrace. I feel like the black sheep of the family.'

'Oh, Fraser… Come here. Give me a hug.'

She reached out for him and he put up an elbow to ward her off, squirming away. 'Give over, Allie. This is a public place.'

She made a wry face. 'You're right. I'll keep my hands to myself. It was a case of hug you or wring your neck, anyway. Best leave well alone.'

Just then Jenny's voice sounded in her ear. 'Alison, could I speak to you for a minute, please?' Jenny hurried over to her, a look of harassment on her face. 'It's about young Rees.'

Alison swung around to face her. 'Yes, of course, Jenny.

I'll be with you in just a second.' She turned back to her brother. 'Look, Fraser, why don't you go along to the hospital cafeteria and get yourself some lunch? I'll come and find you as soon as I'm free.'

Another wounded look crossed his face. 'I'm a student, Allie. Or at least I was. I don't have money for cafeteria lunches.'

'Sorry.' She winced. 'I forgot. Go along to the doctors' restroom and grab yourself some coffee and generally hang out for a bit. Try to amuse yourself. I've no idea how long I'll be.'

'Okay.' He started to do as she suggested, moving off in the direction she pointed out, and Alison turned back to Jenny once more. 'Sorry about that. What's the problem?'

'He's decided to discharge himself. I caught him getting ready to leave, and I thought you would want to speak to him first. He needs his medication organising for a start, and an appointment to have his stitches removed.'

Alison pulled in a sharp breath. 'I'll go and talk to him. Thanks, Jenny.'

By the time she reached the observation ward Rees was fully dressed, except for his shoes.

'I can't find my trainers,' he said, sending her a brief scowl as she walked into his bay. 'I think that nurse must have put them somewhere.'

'I'm sure we'll find them. Why don't you sit down for a moment?'

'You can't keep me here.'

She nodded. 'That's right, and I wouldn't dream of doing that.' She studied him. 'You look much better in yourself. That's good.'

'So where are my shoes?'

'I'll ask the nurse to look for them as soon as she comes back from treating her patient.'

Finally he sat down on the edge of the bed, and she couldn't help thinking he looked like a coiled spring, ready to shoot off at any moment.

'I'm worried that you won't have anywhere to go when you leave here, Rees. You haven't been in touch with your parents, have you?'

He didn't answer, and she went on softly, 'I'm not going to pry into what kind of troubles might have caused you to leave home—unless, of course, you want to talk to me about that—but I do want you to know that there are people who can help you.'

Still he remained silent, and she added in a careful tone, 'I have a friend who runs an agency that helps young people…runaways, mostly…who need help with finding somewhere to stay. The agency runs hostels that have accommodation where you would be able to stay alongside other boys of your age. Sometimes they can put in a word for you with training organisations or employers. I know Jack, my friend, has worked hard to enrol youngsters on work training courses.'

She gave him a searching look, wondering if any of what she was saying was having an effect on him, but his face was closed, as though he was shutting her out.

'I've met some of the boys who live in the hostels,' she told him. 'Some of them have been at a hostel for a couple of years and they've managed to turn their lives around. Others have stayed there for a month or so, and then left to go and stay with friends or be reunited with their families. They all found that it helped them to get back on their feet. Sometimes it just helps to be able to talk over your worries with someone.'

'Have you known this person—Jack—for a long time?' Rees was looking down at the bedcovers, plucking at the sheet with his fingers, but he gave her a brief, surreptitious glance. 'Why would he put himself out to help people?'

'He was in trouble himself at one time, several years ago.' Alison gave a faint smile. 'He knows what it's like to have problems at home, and when he came through it all he made up his mind that he would help others to sort their lives out.'

'How do you know he would want to help *me*?'

'Because I asked him.'

Rees's eyes widened. 'You've already set this up? Why would you do that?' He sounded angry and defensive all at the same time.

'No, I haven't,' she said hurriedly. 'I promise you I wouldn't do anything without your permission. I just told him that I know someone who seems to have a problem and asked him if he might be able to help in any way.'

Rees subsided. 'So I don't have to see him? He isn't waiting outside, or anything like that?'

'No, he isn't. He's at work, getting on with his job, but I asked him if he would come and talk to you if you agreed. He said he would. In fact, if you prefer, I could give him a call and you could talk to him on my phone. I'll leave you alone while you do that, if you like? Whatever you say to him will be in confidence. Just remember, you don't have to agree to anything.'

He didn't speak for a while, but stared into space,

mulling things over. Then he ventured in a quiet voice, 'Will you get into trouble for doing this?'

'Trouble?' Her brows shot up. 'No. Why do you ask? What makes you think that way?'

His shoulders hunched once more. 'Your boss said you were a real softie. He said you went out of your way to put things right that weren't really your problem…like seeing to it that those bikers were looked after, and making sure that I had somewhere to stay last night. He said your job was to help people to get well, and you were taking a risk by stepping over the mark.'

'Did he really? Well, that's an eye-opener, isn't it?' She frowned. 'I don't know why he said all that to you, but I promise you everything is fine. My boss was perfectly happy for you to stay here last night. I hope he didn't make you think otherwise? That isn't the reason you're so anxious to leave, is it?'

'No.' Rees shook his head. 'He said I should listen to what you said, because you were going out on a limb for me.'

'Oh, I see.' She frowned. 'Believe me, you don't have to worry on my account, Rees. I just want to do whatever I can for you, and make sure that you're safe when you leave here.' She studied him thoughtfully for a while. 'Would you like me to give Jack a ring?'

Slowly, he nodded. 'Okay.'

A few minutes later Alison left the room, closing the door behind her and leaving Rees to talk to Jack. She had no idea what might come of their conversation, but for now she had done all that she could.

She had a bone to pick with Josh, though. So she was out on a limb, was she? Overstepping the mark, he had said. He seemed to think he had her all worked out. Perhaps in the rarefied atmosphere of his ivory tower in the Upper Regent Street clinic he commanded all he surveyed, and everything was done to order in an expedient and profitable fashion.

She gave a brief, taut smile. That wasn't how things worked around here, and he surely had a major lesson coming his way. He'd find things were a lot more rough and ready in the lower echelons of Northern Mount Hospital's A&E department, wouldn't he? Here, people mattered for who they were, not what they could afford.

CHAPTER FOUR

'THINGS haven't been quite the same with Josh away from A&E for these last couple of days, have they?' Katie said, sinking back into her chair and taking a sip from a glass of white wine.

The sitting room was cosy, with golden flames flickering in the hearth and soft amber light pooling from delicately curved wall lamps and an illuminated display cabinet on the far side of the room.

'I was just getting used to having him around and then suddenly he wasn't there any more. I'm feeling quite let-down about it.'

'I wouldn't get all dreamy-eyed over him if I were you.' Sam leaned forward from the settee and picked out a handful of nuts from a dish on the coffee table. 'I heard he doesn't go in for serious long-term relationships.'

Alison was standing by the bureau, busy flicking through their selection of films on DVD just then, but Sam's words made her pause for thought. Was that true? Josh could be businesslike and efficient, but at the same time he exuded a casually friendly manner that appeared to encompass everyone. Except, of course, when he decided to take issue with *her* over various matters.

Like when she'd lent her phone to Rees. 'Are you mad?' he'd said. 'Didn't it occur to you that he might take off with it?' He had looked at her as though she'd taken leave of her senses.

'You are such a cynic,' she had told him, but his opinion had been reinforced when he'd learnt that her brother was going to stay with her for a few days. His brows had shot skywards.

'Won't that cause all manner of problems?' he'd remarked. 'After all, you did say you were living in a poky little flat. Surely he can find the courage to go home and explain things to your parents?'

'He's my brother, and he'll be staying with me no matter what problems that might cause,' she'd said.

Alison refocused as Katie responded to Sam's comment. Katie arched her brows. 'Does that matter? After all, I'm not asking for commitment—just a few weeks of sampling life in the fast lane. Have you seen that place where he works in private practice? It looks like a building straight out of Harley Street, all symmetrical Regency frontage and wrought-iron balustrades. The upper storeys have lovely Georgian-type doors that open out on to balconies and more wrought iron.' She sighed. 'I heard he has a penthouse apartment above the consulting rooms.'

Alison gave her a long, commiserating look. 'Poor Katie. You're well and truly hooked, aren't you?' She smiled. 'Anyway, perhaps it's not as perfect as you imagine. Maybe the inside of the building doesn't match up to the rest.' Her gaze clouded momentarily. And perhaps Josh was not all that he seemed.

'Oh, but it does.' Katie's eyes sparked with energy. 'My aunt Annie went to see one of the doctors there. She said the place was sumptuous inside.'

'Really?' Alison came out of her brief reverie. She couldn't help but think Katie was in danger of getting carried away. 'Well, remember what Sam said. It sounds as though you'll be asking for trouble if you let yourself fall for our new boss.'

Taylor nodded agreement. 'I went out with a girl who dated him some time ago. She said he didn't go in for anything more than casual arrangements.'

'It makes no difference. I don't care.' Katie tossed her head in defiance. 'As if *any* of you male creatures are looking for permanence and stability. Ask Alison. She knows all about fickle, dastardly men.' She glanced towards Fraser, who was hunched up on a corner of the sofa, listening to music through his headphones. 'I'm not including you,' she said. 'You're too young to be thinking that way.'

Fraser looked at her blankly, his mind far away with the latest chart sounds. He'd settled in well enough over the last day or so, but he'd retreated into a world of his own.

'Perhaps I expected too much,' Alison murmured. 'I was brought up to value firm bonds and everlasting love, but maybe my family was the exception. I've come to think that maybe what I'm looking for doesn't exist.'

'Oh, I don't know about that,' Taylor said on a musing note. 'I've always thought that maybe one day the right person will come along. I'm going to keep an open mind on that one.'

'That's because basically you're a steady kind of guy,'

Katie conceded, giving him a sisterly kind of smile. 'You're a one-off... But even that doesn't stop you from going after every reasonably attractive girl who crosses your path.' She drank the rest of her wine and smoothly unfurled herself from the deep armchair, sliding her empty glass on to the table. 'Anyway, I'm not going to change my mind— no matter what you say.' She went over to join Alison by the bureau and began to rummage through the selection of DVDs. 'He's gorgeous, and none of you are going to put me off. If he so much as looks my way with just a hint of interest, his future's sealed.'

Alison laughed. 'You're treading on thin ice there. Don't say you weren't warned... But I dare say we'll be here to pick up the pieces when it all falls apart. That's what friends are for, after all.'

The doorbell rang just then, but by now Taylor and Sam had come to join them in looking through the collection of films. Katie picked out a DVD, and Sam gave it a dismissive glance.

'We're not sitting through another soppy romance,' he complained. 'Anyway, you chose last time.'

'You needn't think I'm watching one of your spy films,' Katie retorted.

Alison left them squabbling like children and went to answer the door. She found her neighbour's children, Jason and Rachel, standing in the porch, their young faces earnest and anxious at the same time.

'Hello,' Alison greeted them. 'What's wrong? Do you want to come in? You look as though you need to offload on someone.'

Neither of the children moved. 'It's the puppy,' Jason

said, leaving Alison thoroughly bewildered. What puppy was he talking about?

'We found him yesterday,' he tacked on. 'He was wandering around in the cold down by the brook, and we're looking after him, but now he's poorly and we don't know what to do.'

'I'm sorry to hear that,' Alison murmured. 'I didn't realise you had a new pet. Has your mother called the vet?'

Rachel's face crumpled. 'She said we can't afford to pay a vet's bills,' she managed, blinking heavily to stop herself from crying. Tendrils of her fair hair trailed across her cheeks and she brushed them away. 'He's just a stray, and he doesn't belong to us, and we don't know where he's come from, but he looks really bad. He's trembling and his face is swelling up.'

'Oh, dear. That is a worry, isn't it?' Alison glanced down at her watch. 'And this time of the evening I expect the free vet's surgery is closed. I wonder if they have a number we could ring for advice?'

'Will you come and have a look at him for us, Allie?' Jason's expression was pleading, his blue-grey eyes showing desperation. 'You might know what to do.'

'All right.' She nodded. 'Of course I'll do that. But I'm not a vet, and I don't know very much about treating sick animals.'

Rachel looked relieved all the same, but just as they were about to head off towards the house next door, a long, sleek car drew up by the roadside. It was a gleaming graphite-coloured convertible, beautifully streamlined, and for a moment or two Alison simply stared. Who did they know who owned such a fabulous car?

Then the driver's door opened and Josh stepped out, locking the vehicle with a light thumb pressure on his key fob. He came towards them, greeting the children with a nod and a smile, and a quiet, 'Hello, there.' To Jason, he said, 'How's the knee?'

'It's okay,' Jason murmured.

Then Josh looked at Alison and said softly, 'Hi. I wasn't sure whether you would be at home. I just came to drop off these notes for Taylor. He wanted to know about special techniques in orthopaedics and I promised I'd hunt out some journal articles for him.'

Perhaps it was the deeply masculine timbre of his voice that made her pulse quicken, or maybe it was his strikingly male appearance. He was wearing a suit, all clean lines and understated elegance, as though he had come from work or a business meeting. Either way, Alison was not doing so well—and, whatever the reason, her heart suddenly seemed to slip into overdrive.

'Oh, I see,' she managed. 'You didn't need to make a special journey for that. I'm sure he would have been glad to receive them whenever you're back at work.'

She wasn't sure what to make of his sudden appearance in their neighbourhood, and she couldn't quite make out why he should have such a strange effect on her. Maybe it was something to do with seeing him away from work— or perhaps it was his sheer masculinity that took her breath away. He was long and lean, flat-stomached—perfect in every way. An odd fluttering started in her abdomen, something she'd never experienced before.

'I was passing by,' he murmured by way of explanation. 'I've just been to make a house call on a private patient, so it seemed logical to stop while I was in the area.' He studied her thoughtfully. 'If it's inconvenient I could leave.'

'No, please don't do that,' she said hurriedly. 'I didn't mean to be rude. I just didn't want you to be put out on our account.' She made an effort to pull herself together. So he made house calls, did he? 'Do you want to go and let yourself in? I left the door on the catch. Taylor's in the sitting room. For myself, I have to go with Jason and Rachel to help out with their new puppy. He's in a bad way, apparently.'

'Is he?' He frowned, his gaze moving briefly over the children. 'I'm sorry about that.' He looked back at Alison. 'Is there anything I can do to help?'

His offer took her by surprise, but she was more than happy to accept. 'If you want to come along, that would be really good.' She glanced at the children for confirmation, and they nodded. 'Thanks,' she told him. 'Perhaps between us we might be able to figure something out.'

'He was all right this morning,' Rachel said as they hurried along the path to her house. 'We found him wandering on the common yesterday, and he was cold and wet, but he started to wag his tail and came to us for some fuss. I think he was lonely. We stayed with him for a little while, and then he followed us home.'

'Mum said we should clean him up and get him nice and warm,' Jason put in. 'So we did, and he stayed at our house last night. He likes being with us. He's been playing out in our garden nearly all day.'

By now they had reached the back door of the house, and Rachel went inside, inviting them in. 'Mum's looking after him,' she said. 'We don't know what to do. My dad's not here. He went to see someone about starting a job at the factory down the road.'

Rachel's mother came to meet them in the kitchen, and Alison quickly introduced her to Josh. 'Hi, Martha,' she said. 'Josh and I work together at the hospital. He just called to see us at the house, but we thought perhaps between us we can work out what we might need to do.'

'Thank you so much for coming over.' Martha Selby grasped Alison's hands in a friendly gesture. She was clearly relieved to have someone there to help out. Her blue eyes were troubled. 'I've been trying to ring the vet, but according to the girl answering the phone he's on his way to a call. I don't know what to do. I can't afford to pay vet's bills, but the dog is in a really sorry state. I don't know whether it's something he's eaten that's caused all his problems. He's been pulling up plants in the garden and chewing on twigs and so on, and even in the house nothing is safe.'

She sighed, and ran a hand through her fair hair in frustration. 'I told the police I would look after him until someone claims him, but I'm beginning to think he must have been abandoned. No one could put up with that amount of chewing for long…and now I feel awful for thinking badly about him because he's so ill.'

She showed them into the living room where the puppy, a cross between a border collie and something indistinct, was standing in a corner, breathing with great difficulty, trembling and looking greatly distressed. He was much larger than Alison had expected. She could see that his face was swollen, especially around the eyelids, so that he could barely see out through the slits that were left.

'It looks like an allergic reaction of some sort,' Josh said, checking him over. 'He's a bit thin, so he may have been fending for himself for a while, and of course it's been very cold outside of late. I doubt he's been affected by that, though, if as the children said he was playing happily with them earlier today.'

He knelt down beside the dog, running a hand over his body, talking to him in a manner that was gently soothing. 'You're a poor young fellow, aren't you? What have you been up to, I wonder?' The dog's tail stayed in a drooped position, but he allowed Josh to touch him and gave no sign that he might become aggressive.

Josh tried to gently prise open the dog's mouth, and Alison guessed he was checking to see if there was any inflammation there. 'His mouth looks okay as far as I can tell,' Josh said. 'There's some swelling, but no burns, so whatever he ate was probably not caustic.'

'We can't give him an antihistamine, though, can we?' Alison said, going to join him. 'What if we're mistaken? And how do we know that our drugs can be used on dogs?'

Josh shook his head. 'We can't, but I've seen something like this before. One of my stepsisters had a dog that kept eating things it shouldn't, and he had a reaction like this.' He looked up at Martha. 'Do you have any Milk of Magnesia in the house?'

'Yes, in the medicine cupboard,' she answered, looking puzzled. 'Why do you ask? Will it help?'

'It may do. Give him a good tablespoon of it every hour while you wait to hear what the vet has to say. I don't see that it can do any harm, but it will help to speed whatever toxic substance he's eaten on its way through his intestines. It'll slow down the absorption of the toxin as well.'

Martha hurried away to find the medicine, and Alison tried to comfort the children who were standing by, looking anxious.

'Is he going to die?' Rachel asked, a quiver in her voice.

'We're doing what we can to prevent that,' Alison told her, putting an arm around the girl's shoulders. Jason sidled up to her and she embraced him, too. He had already formed a bond with this bedraggled young dog, and she felt his unhappiness as though it was her own.

Josh looked at them, a musing expression on his face. He stayed in a crouching position beside the dog. 'He's quite a big puppy, isn't he? I wonder how old he is?'

'Dad says he must be about six months old.' Rachel looked up at Alison. 'He says we should call him Dusty because he's like a dustbin. He takes everything in.'

'That's a horrible name,' Jason put in. 'We're not calling him that. We should call him Chaser, because he's always chasing us about.'

'That's not a bad idea,' Martha said, coming into the room and sliding a dog bowl on to the floor in front of the dog. 'He doesn't have a name on his collar, so we have no idea what he answers to. Anyway, someone might claim him, so I suppose it won't really matter.' She gently stroked the dog. 'Come on, lad, drink this.'

The dog was listless, but he briefly sniffed the contents of the bowl and moved away.

'Oh, dear. That didn't work, did it?' Martha frowned. 'Do you think I should add some milk to make it more palatable? But I heard that milk wasn't good for dogs.'

'That's because most dogs are lactose intolerant,' Alison said. 'They don't have the enzyme which allows the digestive system to break down the kind of sugar that is found in milk. I shouldn't imagine a small amount would do any harm, though.'

Josh nodded. 'That's true, and it will help to coat his stomach and intestines.'

Martha took the bowl away and returned a moment or two later. This time when she laid the bowl on the floor in front of the dog he tentatively obliged, slowly licking the bowl clean. Alison watched him, feeling a sense of relief, and Josh must have picked up on her thoughts because he glanced up at her and smiled. Then the dog moved away from the bowl and stood some distance away, facing the wall, continuing to tremble and struggle with his breathing. He looked thoroughly miserable, his tail resolutely down.

'I'll try the vet's number again,' Martha said. 'I can at least ask the girl to let him know what we're doing.'

Josh got to his feet, and both he and Alison continued to watch the dog, who stood unmoving, head down in dejection, as though he didn't know what to do with himself.

'C'mon, Chaser,' Jason coaxed, going over to him and rubbing his fingers lightly behind the dog's ears. 'You have to get better, 'cos we love you.'

Rachel added her pleas. 'We do, Chaser. We need you to get better.'

Martha placed the phone back on its hub. 'The woman who answered managed to get through to the vet and told him what's happening and what we're giving him. He says that sounds okay, but he'll ring us as soon as he finishes delivering a foal. Apparently it's a tricky birth.'

'At least the vet approves of what we're doing,' Alison said. 'That's something, at least.'

Martha nodded and looked over at her children. 'They've taken to the dog more than I would have ever thought possible,' she said softly. 'Before this they were begging us to let them have a puppy for Christmas, and I said we couldn't possibly afford to keep one. But now I don't know how they're going to cope if someone comes along and claims him.'

'From the sound of things, I wonder how you'll manage if you keep him,' Josh murmured with a faint smile. 'You said yourself that he chews everything in sight…and he looks as though he'll grow into a big dog.'

Martha rolled her eyes. 'I'm a fool taking him on, I know.' She glanced over to where the children were trying to coax the dog to lie down on an old blanket that they'd placed on the carpet by the radiator. 'Still, I could see he was in a sorry state, and I didn't want him to be locked up in a police kennel.' She looked back at Alison and Josh. 'I'll put the kettle on and make us some tea, shall I? We can have coffee and walnut cake with it, if you'd like? I'm going to have some. I feel as though I need cheering up, one way or another.'

Alison glanced at Josh to gauge his response, and he nodded. 'I'd like that,' he said. 'Thanks, Martha. Besides, I'd like to stay around for a while and see how Chaser gets on—if that's all right with you?'

Martha smiled. 'Of course. You're a good man. I can see that. Alison said you were a great man to have around in a crisis. She said you'd only been at the hospital for two days, and you'd proved your worth already. You had a man on heart bypass at one point, but he came through everything all right, she said.'

Alison withdrew into herself as her words were repeated. As to Josh, he began to look uncomfortable. 'Seems to me that Alison has had rather too much to say,' he murmured, throwing a sharp glance in Alison's direction.

She briefly hunched her shoulders in response. 'Sorry,' she mouthed.

He acknowledged her apology with a nod, and turned back to Martha. 'I just do what I feel is best at the time, and you know we still have to wait and hope that Chaser will come through this all right. He isn't out of the woods yet by any means.'

'Maybe, but I feel much more confident now that you're both here, and at least we're doing something.' Martha led the way into the kitchen. 'Sit yourselves down at the table,' she said. 'We'll be able to keep an eye on Chaser from here if I leave the door open.' She picked up the kettle and went over to the sink. 'I'll make a start on the tea. I expect Tom will be back soon, and he might be glad of a cup.'

Alison did as she suggested and sat down at the pine table. Josh took a moment to remove his jacket and lay it over the back of the chair, but then he came and sat down beside her. His glance skimmed over her, as though he was looking at her properly for the first time that evening, and she wondered what he made of her casual clothes— figure-hugging jeans teamed with a clinging cotton top. His mouth curved briefly, and she caught a glimmer of appreciation in his gaze.

He began to look around the room. 'It's very comfortable and homely in here, Martha,' he said, glancing in approval at the neat curtains and the bright touches of colour here and there, in the fruit bowl and the wooden stand laden with ceramic mugs. There were pine-fronted cupboards all around, and open shelving that held an assortment of cups, saucers and plates.

'Thank you,' Martha said. 'I've always loved this house.' There was a hint of sadness in her voice.

'Things haven't been so good for you lately, have they?' Alison ventured. 'But Rachel said that Tom was seeing someone about a job?' With any luck, her neighbour's fortunes were about to change.

'That's right. It's a long shot, and I'm not sure anything will come of it. I think they already have their full quota of workers.' Martha finished filling the kettle with water and set it down on the worktop, flicking the switch. She brought cake out from a cupboard and set it on a plate, pushing it towards them along with side plates and cutlery.

'Help yourselves.' As she spoke, the back door opened and Tom came in. Martha looked at him and an unspoken message ran between them. He shook his head. 'Nothing doing,' he said.

'I'm sorry.' Martha went over to him and gave him a quick hug. 'At least you tried.'

Tom nodded, then gently extricated himself from his wife's embrace. Alison could see that he was disappointed by his lack of progress with finding work, and guessed he was trying to be stoical about it. 'Is the dog still sick?' he asked. 'I didn't like having to leave you with him like that, but I had to keep the appointment.'

'He's still the same,' Martha replied. 'Alison and her friend Josh have been helping out. Josh said to give him Milk of Magnesia, and the vet agrees, so that's what we've done.'

Tom glanced their way. 'Thanks for that. It's difficult

to know what to do, isn't it?' He went over to the interior door and looked at the dog, satisfying himself that his condition hadn't worsened.

'He's lying down on the blanket,' he said. 'That's perhaps a sign that he's a bit more settled than he was.' Then he came back into the kitchen and gave Josh the once-over. 'So, you and Allie are seeing each other outside of work, are you? I thought she'd sworn off men.' He frowned. 'I hope you're going to treat her well. She deserves the best.'

'Tom…you're unbelievable,' Alison gasped, not knowing whether to laugh or be shocked. 'Josh and I simply work together. You sound just like my father, checking out everyone I'm with.'

'Well, if your father doesn't live around here he can't be expected to know what's going on, can he? And your brother has problems of his own right now. So you have to rely on your friends to look out for you.'

Alison shook her head, and then glanced at Josh to see if he was disturbed by Tom's comments. It appeared that he wasn't. He was calmly eating cake as though nothing untoward was going on. He paused only to wipe crumbs from his mouth with a serviette.

'Of course I'll treat her well,' he said, and Alison gave him an incredulous stare. Why wasn't he denying any involvement with her? 'Besides,' he tacked on, 'how could I do otherwise when she has you and the two young men from next door watching over her? I wouldn't put it past her brother to keep an eye on me, either. He gave me the once-over when we met back at the hospital. Believe me, I wouldn't dare put a foot wrong.'

Alison glared at him, but he simply laughed, and to

make matters worse Tom was beginning to look smug, as though all was well in hand.

'Take no notice of Tom,' Martha said, coming over to the table with a tray, laden with a teapot and cups and saucers. 'He always tramples in with his hobnail boots. Nothing I say ever makes any difference. In he goes—clomp, clomp, clomp.'

Jason and Rachel came in from the sitting room. 'Is it time for Chaser's medicine?' Rachel asked. 'He's still poorly. His tail's not wagging at all, no matter how we stroke him or talk to him.'

Martha glanced at the clock on the wall. 'I'll give him another spoonful and see how he gets on. Sit down and have some cake.'

Rachel went to hug her father first, and Jason followed, graciously submitting to his father ruffling his hair. Then they joined the group at the table and began to talk all at once about the fate that had befallen their new pet.

'He was eating stuff from the compost heap this morning,' Jason said. 'Yuk. That can't have done him any good, can it?'

'I think he was ill because he ate the shrub from out of the sink garden,' Rachel told her father. 'We found it in bits on the patio.'

Tom raised his eyes heavenward. 'I nurtured that plant,' he said. 'I fed it, watered it, and finally it sprouted a few green leaves. Now what's left of it after Chomper managed to get his teeth round it?'

'His name's Chaser, Dad.' Jason wasn't about to let his father win the battle of the names. 'Chaser. As soon as he's better he'll be running around after us, like before.'

'Chaser, Chomper—Destruction on Legs is what I call

him.' There was a half-smile on Tom's lips as he said it, but Jason prepared himself to launch a protest on behalf of the dog. Rachel sidled up to her mother, and Martha draped a comforting arm about her daughter.

Alison wondered what Josh was making of all this. He must live a vastly different life from the haphazard interplay that went on in this loving family. Did he prefer living a life of luxury in his fabulous penthouse apartment?

The look in his eyes caught her off guard, though. He was quietly watching the scene unfold in front of him, and there was a bleakness about his expression, a haunted look that she couldn't fathom.

It made her stop and think for a while. There was surely way more to her new boss than she could ever have imagined, and, strangely, she realised that she was curious to know more about him. Was he really alone and invincible in his elite world?

'I think I'll go and take another look at Chaser.' Josh pushed back his chair and stood up. 'It's all right,' he said, putting up a hand when Martha and Tom would have followed suit. 'You stay here and drink your tea. I'll keep an eye on him for a few minutes.'

Alison went with him. She sensed that the family needed to be alone for a while, to talk about Tom's efforts to find work at the factory and generally to unite after a difficult day. The children needed solace after the puppy's unfortunate illness, and their parents were the best ones to give it to them.

In the sitting room, Chaser was still a sorry sight. He lay on his blanket, stressed and uncomfortable, his face swollen and wretched. 'Poor lad,' Josh murmured, kneeling down and running a hand lightly over the dog's flanks. 'It'll take time for the effects of whatever you've eaten to wear off, but at least you're not any worse than you were before.'

'That's something to be thankful for, isn't it?' Alison knelt down beside Josh.

He glanced at her and nodded. 'He's lucky that he has so many people who care about him.'

'That's true. They're a solid family unit, aren't they? No matter what troubles they seem to have. There's something to be said for family ties, isn't there?'

'I suppose.' He turned his attention back to the dog, laying a hand over the area of his heart to check the rhythm.

'Do you have any family locally?' She studied him as he tended to the dog.

'Some. My parents don't live too far away, and I have a sister, Michelle, at the university in the next county. She's studying pharmacy there. She's a little older than her fellow students, because she worked for a while in research before deciding on a change of career.'

'That's a coincidence,' Alison said in astonishment. 'I imagine she must know Fraser. He's at the same university, studying the very same thing.' She broke off, frowning. 'Or at least he was…until they sent him home.'

He smiled briefly. 'It's a small world.'

'Yes, it is.' Her glance was curious. 'You mentioned stepsisters and stepbrothers? It sounds as though you have quite a number of relatives. It must make for happy family get-togethers around this time of year.'

He sat back on his heels and shook his head. 'I'm not so sure about that. I tend to avoid those sorts of occasions wherever possible.'

'You're not serious, are you?' She frowned. 'Why would

you want to do that? Is there a problem in your family?' Then she backed off, suddenly aware that she might have crossed a line. 'Maybe I'm treading where I shouldn't? I don't mean to be intrusive. I just can't imagine how it must be not to have the support of your family behind you.'

'That's because you live in a fantasy world where all is happiness and deep feeling. Don't get me wrong…I'm sure it *is* that way for a great many people, and my own parents are wonderful, caring individuals. They stand behind me and my sister in everything we do. It isn't that way for everyone, though. Take young Rees from the hospital, for example. Why do you think he ended up going to stay in a hostel? It wasn't because he was surrounded by the milk of human kindness, was it?'

She lifted her chin. 'You obviously have a warped view of life, and I feel sorry that you should see things that way. I love being with my family…even sharing my cramped living accommodation with my brother.' Her mouth flattened. 'I'm just sorry that Fraser has landed himself in trouble.'

'It's a pity he can't bring himself to tell your parents what's wrong, don't you think? What does *that* say about these happy families you're so keen on?'

'Fraser's going to talk to my parents soon.' She sent him an indignant glare. 'I'm sure they'll understand. He just wants to try to sort things out first, rather than upset them. He's hoping that he can persuade the university authorities that it's not a crime to set up a study group on the internet and exchange notes and information.'

He gave her a doubtful look. 'Maybe they thought he was cheating?'

'My brother doesn't cheat. He has no need to do that.

He thought he was setting up something on the lines of a tutorial or homework group. Of course now they're threatening him with expulsion, and that means he might not be able to complete his degree.'

She let her gaze run over him, taking in the hard line of his jaw and the stiff set of his shoulders. They were clearly opposites in both point of view and temperament.

'Rees's situation is entirely different. He was unfortunate,' she said. 'He's a troubled young man, and I'd dearly like to get to the bottom of what's hurting him. That's why I'm planning on keeping in touch with him.'

'Hah.' The word was a mild explosion of triumph. 'Well, there we have it, don't we? You're taking on far too much, getting involved with all and sundry, and in the end it will prove too much for you—mark my words. You need to keep a part of you separate from the job, or in the end it will overwhelm you. You can't take on the troubles of the world. No one can.'

Her mouth was set in a firm line. 'That's where you're wrong. I'll do my best, at least, to offer help where I'm able.' She studied him once more, watching the way his hand rested lightly on the dog's trembling body, as though to offer a modicum of comfort. 'Besides,' she murmured, her gaze softening, 'how can you imply that I'm being over-emotional and that I care too much when you stay behind to watch over a family pet that isn't even your own?'

He gave a wry grin. 'Ah, there you have me. I didn't say I was without feelings, did I? And they do say a dog is a man's best friend.'

She gave him a mock pitying look. 'As Katie put it the other day…you're a sad soul, Josh.'

'You're probably right.' He was smiling as he got to his feet. 'Talking of Katie, that reminds me that I ought to take those papers over to Taylor. Or maybe he'll be in the middle of something by now, and I'll risk disturbing him?'

'I'm sure it will be all right for you to go next door. Besides, Katie won't forgive me if I let you go without dropping in,' Alison said bluntly. 'She thinks you're chocolate and wine and exotic spices all rolled into one. But I'm warning you—tread carefully with her. She's my best friend, and if you break her heart I shan't forgive you.'

His expression was a pure treat. There was surprise there, humour, and a glint of something that Alison couldn't begin to read.

'I wouldn't dream of upsetting her in any way,' he said softly. 'After all, I really want, more than anything, to stay in your good books.'

She was still stinging from his remarks about happy families. 'You could have fooled me,' she said.

CHAPTER FIVE

'THIS poor man ran out of luck when he left home this morning, didn't he?' Katie said, frowning as she studied the ultrasound image on the screen. 'I'd imagine he stepped out into the road the same as he did every day, but today there was a car and now his pelvis is smashed to pieces.'

'It only takes a moment's lack of concentration.' Josh's expression was grim. His finger traced a line over the image. 'There's the iliac fracture…and we can see a tear in the liver, along with free fluid in the abdomen, so we know he's haemorrhaging. I don't believe the liver injury is sufficient to account for the persistent tachycardia, though. We need to look for something else that might be causing it.'

He turned towards Alison. 'Let's get him up to Angiography right away, and see if we can do something to change his fortunes.'

She nodded. 'I'll give them a call and tell them to prepare for the patient.'

'Good. Then both of you should scrub in. We need to do this fast.'

The next hour or so was an anxious time for all of them.

Josh's patient was losing a lot of blood, and when they started the angiography, looking closely at the state of his blood vessels, the picture was not good.

'His blood pressure's falling,' Alison said anxiously, checking the monitor.

Josh continued the painstaking process of progressing the catheter through the arteries, while Alison and Katie monitored the patient's condition.

'I believe I've found the source,' Josh said after a while. 'His pudendal artery is leaking, and the iliac artery is cut right across. I'll do a coil embolisation of the transected artery. Hopefully that will stop the bleeding.' He looked at Katie. 'You can help with that. Alison, will you prepare a gelfoam patch for the pudendal artery?'

They worked together to stabilise their patient. Time was running out for him, and Alison couldn't bear to think of this young man being cut down in his prime. He was barely in his mid-twenties.

Josh applied the patch to the torn blood vessel, carefully securing it in place and testing its viability, while Alison held her breath.

She checked the screen as he worked, and marvelled at his composure. His fingers moved with deft precision, guiding the instruments and sealing off all the leaks he found.

Soon the circulatory flow began to normalise. 'Blood pressure's rising,' Alison said. 'Heart-rate's still one-twenty.'

'That should stabilise soon. We'll finish up here now,' Josh said. 'We've done all we can for the moment.'

Some time later, when he had ensured all was in order, he finally moved away from the operating table. 'Katie, take him along to the recovery room, will you? And notify the intensive care unit that they need to prepare for him.'

'Will do.' Katie checked the patient's vital signs. 'So far, so good.' She sent Josh a look that was pure hero-worship. 'You did a great job. So smooth...so calm.'

'Thanks.' He gave her a brief smile and a mock bow, but he was already heading for the door, probably thinking about the next task ahead.

'You can see why they wanted him here, even if it is for just a small part of the week,' Alison said, watching him leave. She was full of admiration for the way Josh worked. Taylor had commented that he was an orthopaedic specialist, but as a vascular surgeon he was second to none.

Back down in A&E, the atmosphere was considerably lighter now that the most urgent cases had been dealt with and were under control. No one would dare say the words, *'At last it's quietened down in here,'* for fear of opening the floodgates to a torrent of emergencies, but someone had switched on the radio, and people were humming Christmas carols along with the programme being broadcast throughout the hospital.

The only event to disturb the general good humour came about when the Christmas work schedules were pinned to the noticeboard.

'Looks as though you're going to be working on Christmas morning, Alison,' Sam said, as he handed out warm doughnuts he'd brought in from the local bakery. 'I suppose you have the head of department to thank for that.'

Alison pulled a face. 'At least I should be finished by lunchtime, so there's a good chance I'll be able to sit down with the family for Christmas dinner. It won't be so bad.

They usually have Christmas music playing on the radio, and people generally try to keep things upbeat.'

Sam nodded. 'And you won't be on your own here. Josh is going to be working, too. I heard he'd volunteered for that one.'

Alison was surprised to hear that. The bosses were usually a rare sight in the hospital at that particular time of year. Looking at Josh, she raised her brows.

'That's right, I did,' Josh commented, coming to stand alongside them and helping himself to a doughnut. His shirtsleeves were rolled back to reveal lightly bronzed forearms. 'Sooner that than have some family man on duty, missing out on the great day. Most would prefer to stay home and see their children open their presents.'

'And he's even agreed to do a slot on the radio,' Sam added, 'sending out goodwill messages to all the children who don't get to go home. See—he does have a heart, after all.' Sam grinned. 'I knew it was in there somewhere.'

Alison brushed sugar crystals from her mouth and stared at Josh in astonishment. 'Is it true?'

'That I have a heart?' Josh felt around his chest in various places, as though to reassure himself of the fact, and then gave a nod of relief. 'I'm devastated that you should think otherwise.' He contrived to look wounded, but failed miserably when he took another bite from his doughnut.

'That you're doing the radio show.' Alison's voice held an edge of impatience. 'I thought you were dead set against it.'

'I wasn't really. I just had other things on my mind at the time. But when I gave it some thought I decided, why not? Hopefully it'll cheer people up, and I don't particularly have anything better to do.'

She slanted him a perplexed look as they moved towards the writing-up area in the annexe. Both she and Josh needed to commandeer a computer and add comments to the digital files.

Sam moved on, taking his box of doughnuts towards the reception area, where he paused to chat up the pretty desk clerk.

'I think that's so sad,' she murmured, accessing the patient's notes on the computer and giving Josh a fleeting, sideways glance. 'I mean, it's lovely that you've offered to help out, but to actually prefer to do that rather than be at home on such a special day seems like an awful shame.' She let her gaze run over him, taking in his clear, all-seeing grey eyes and lingering on the proud jut of his jawline. What must have happened to him to make him feel that way?

He shrugged. 'We can't all live in domestic bliss, can we? Life would be dull and boring if that were the case, wouldn't it?'

'Now you're being facetious.' She pinned him with a laser look. 'I've noticed you do that when you want to hide away your inner thoughts.'

His mouth softened a fraction. 'Maybe you're right.' He sighed, rubbing his hands lightly in a scissor motion to shake off the residue of sugar left there by the doughnut.

He started to key in his own notes on the second computer. 'Christmas was fine until I was about seven years old. It was around that time that I stopped believing in Santa Claus, and all the good things about the holiday season seemed to disintegrate.'

His gaze took on a faraway look, as though he was back in the past, living through that time all over again. 'My parents had been at one another's throats the whole year, and by Christmas Eve things came to a head. They had an almighty row—one to end all rows—and the next day you could have cut the tension in the air with a knife. Of course they tried to make the best of the day for my sister and me, but it didn't work. We played along, but we knew things were bad and that worse was to come.'

'I'm sorry.' She laid a hand on his arm, feeling the steady pulse of his blood through his veins and the warmth that emanated from his skin. 'I've been insensitive, prying like this. I should never have asked.'

He shook his head. 'It doesn't matter. Those days have long since gone by.' He smiled whimsically. 'My parents filed for divorce soon after that, and my father left home. It took us a while to get used to the change, and the next Christmas was difficult for all of us. We divided the time we spent with each parent, but we were always conscious of how the other was feeling. My father was living with my stepmother by then, but it was clear he missed us when he wasn't with us on Christmas morning.'

'Parents usually try to hide their unhappiness from their children don't they?' Alison said. But perhaps it wasn't so easy to do that when your heart was being wrenched out of you. She had no idea how she would cope if she ever found herself in that situation.

'I'm sure he tried. He phoned to see how we were doing, but there was a snag in his voice that made us realise he was finding it hard. He'd had seven years of seeing our excitement as we ran into our parents' bedroom on Christmas morning. It was a ritual, almost. We'd bounce on the bed to wake them up if they showed any signs of still being sleepy, and then when they sat up and took notice we'd hunt through our Christmas stockings to see what Santa had brought us. Later we tried to guess what was in the parcels round the tree, and we would all be laughing and happy and full of joy. All of that disappeared. Now he was miles away from us, and he was sharing his Christmas morning with his partner and her children instead.'

He stopped for a moment, as though he was glancing at the monitor, but his fingers hesitated over the keyboard and Alison knew that he was remembering those times with sadness. 'Then, when we went to stay with him on Boxing Day, we were naturally anxious about leaving our mother behind. We knew she was sad to see us go. She hugged us just that little bit too long before she handed us over. There were never any more cosy, united family celebrations after that.'

He gave up all attempts to key in any more notes. Instead, he leaned against the edge of the table, half sitting, half standing. 'Things stayed that way for a couple of years, and it didn't really get any easier. There was always that feeling of anxiety for the parent who was missing out, and it didn't change very much when each of them went on to marry other people. They were happier, of course, but the stable family unit had gone for ever.'

Alison went to perch on the table next to him. 'You said there were stepbrothers and sisters. Didn't that make things better for you?'

He gave a soft laugh. 'You'd think so, wouldn't you?' He shook his head. 'To be honest, there were a lot of wounded feelings going around. I think Michelle and I would have coped well enough, but our stepsiblings had

other thoughts on the matter. Like, Why have these intrud-
ers come to invade our space? Or, Why is my father paying
more attention to them? And, How come my mother's
being so sweet to her? Then, of course, there were new
siblings born into the various households, bringing new
jealousies and mixed feelings. Children can be cruel
without even meaning to be that way.'

'Do you still feel that way about one another?'

'Heavens, no.' He smiled. 'We've become the best of
friends. After all, we all had to compromise and try to
make the best of things. We grew up a little faster than we
might have done, and learned that the world can be a harsh
and unforgiving place if you don't begin to adapt.'

She studied him thoughtfully. 'Still, it's no wonder that
you have such a problem with everything that goes along
with the Christmas season.' Her expression was sad. 'I
don't suppose you'll be putting up any streamers in your
apartment, will you?'

He shook his head. 'I seriously doubt that.' His fingers
idly sifted through a sheaf of papers that had been left in
the wire rack by one of the computers. 'How about you?
Knowing the way you feel about it, I expect you've already
made a start on putting up Christmas decorations in your
flat, haven't you?'

She laughed. 'Well, we tried. Fraser helped Taylor to
bring down a box of bits from the attic, and we had an
initial look through to see what was there from last year.
We invited the children from next door to come round and
give us a hand, because they think it's a fun thing to do,
but unfortunately Chaser came with them. Somehow he
managed to get in on the act.'

She cast her mind back to the events of that evening. 'I remember thinking that his behaviour was a bit strange. At one point he stopped bounding about, getting under everybody's feet, and it was a relief for a while. But then it struck me that he was way too quiet, Chaser being the way he is, so I started to think that something might be wrong. He was walking about, though…very slowly, very carefully, but he appeared to be all right.'

She made a face. 'Then he disappeared for a while, and I suddenly began to think that he was up to something. Sure enough, we found him hiding under the table with a couple of garlands dangling from his mouth. He tried to stuff them in *en masse* when we found him, gobbling them up as fast as he could…hiding the evidence, so to speak. There really wasn't much left to hang up after he'd finished with them.'

Josh chuckled. 'I expect Tom's already regretting that moment of weakness when he said they would look after him. I wonder if the dog has been practising on *their* decorations?'

'They haven't made a start yet.' She frowned. 'I don't think they're ready to celebrate Christmas, not while things are looking so bleak. Tom had another letter from the building society, threatening that the house might be repossessed shortly after Christmas. He and Martha were really upset. They did their best to keep it from the children, but it looks as though their walls have ears… Jason and Rachel confessed to listening in. So now they're all worried. The children think they're going to be homeless, and it's as though their world is caving in around them. Even the fact that Chaser is back on form hasn't helped to make them feel better. That's why we asked them round last night to help with the decorations.'

She sighed. 'I think the building society would be prepared to hold off for three months if there was any sign that Tom was about to find employment, but that's not looking very likely. I feel so sorry for him. He's tried so hard to find work, even doing a few gardening jobs for people in the last few autumn months. Of course all that came to an end once winter was here.'

Josh's expression was grim. 'It must be a difficult time all round… But actually I've been giving it some thought. Perhaps I could help out. The hospital's building maintenance team is a man short since the new extension was built. Maybe I could put in a word for him? It sounds like the sort of job Tom would do very well.'

'Oh, would you really do that?' She stood up to face him and gave him a quick hug. 'That's a great idea,' she said, her mouth curving in a smile. 'I'll ask him about it.'

He moved towards her as though to return the hug, but just then her pager bleeped and he drew back.

Flustered, she glanced down at the message without really seeing it. What was she doing, hugging him like that? Was she losing control of her senses?

She focussed on the pager. 'I have to ring the flat,' she said with a frown. 'I hope Fraser's not in any trouble.'

'Do you want me to leave you alone for a while?' He straightened, as though he was getting ready to walk away from the annexe.

'No, it's okay. You go ahead and write up your notes. I'll move out of the way of the computer.'

Fraser was in an anxious frame of mind when he answered her call. She could tell straight away from his cautious, halting manner that he was in trouble of some sort.

'Fraser, what's wrong? Has there been more bad news from the university? Surely they can't have come up with a final decision this soon? I thought they weren't going to deal with it properly until the start of next term?'

'No, it's nothing like that. You're right, the Dean still has to meet with the university committee before deciding what to do about the situation.' His voice dropped, as though he didn't want to say what he had to say. 'Allie, it's about Gran. Apparently she slipped on the ice when she was walking to the shops. Someone called an ambulance and they've taken her to hospital.'

Alison sucked in a sharp breath. 'Did they say what might be wrong with her? How bad is it?' She reeled as all sorts of possibilities ran through her mind.

'Pretty bad, from what they're telling me. The paramedic said he thought she might have broken her hip. There was a lot of swelling and bruising, apparently. Mum and Dad are driving over there now. Mum says they'll stay over until they know what's happening. Of course Grandad's taken it badly. He says people can go downhill fast after a fall like that, especially when they're Gran's age. He's very worried. So am I. I love Gran to bits. They said she was in shock, and seemed to be confused about what had happened.'

'We're all worried, Fraser.' Alison was still trying to absorb the news. 'Once Mum and Dad arrive, though, I expect Grandad will cope a bit better. It must have come as an awful shock to him.' She hesitated, trying to think things through. 'Did Mum say which hospital they had taken Gran to?'

'No. I didn't ask, and she probably forgot to say. I think she was a bit taken aback when I answered the phone. She rang, expecting to leave a message for you, and then of course she wanted to know what I'm doing here. I think she's upset on both counts.'

Alison sighed. 'Well, it was only going to be a matter of time before she found out. At least that's one hurdle out of the way. Now all you have to do is think of a way to explain things to her.'

'Like she's going to understand.' Fraser was morose. 'And I daren't even *think* about Dad's reaction.'

'Just hang in there. They have other things on their minds right now.' She cut the call a moment or two later, and stood for a while, trying to take it all in.

'Is it your grandmother?' Josh tried to read the expression on her face, and she knew he was concerned for her.

She nodded. 'She's had a fall and they've taken her to hospital. It might be a broken hip.' Given that they'd just dealt with something similar in the angiography suite, it didn't fill her with confidence about her grandmother's condition. Their patient was likely to do well because of Josh's surgical skill. What if Gran wasn't so lucky?

She let out a slow, ragged breath. 'There are so many questions going through my mind… How bad is it…? Have they given her pain medication…? Are they making all the right checks…? When will they operate? I feel so helpless. I love my gran so much. I can't bear to think of her having to go through all that.'

She looked up at him, her troubled gaze clouding over. 'I feel as though I should be there with her, to make sure that she's all right, to see that the doctors are doing all they can for her. I know I should be able to trust them, but this is my gran and I need to know that she's safe.'

He reached for her, drawing her towards him, and then his arms closed gently around her. 'Of course you do. But she's being looked after. You should take comfort from that. Your parents will be with her, and your grandad. She'll be surrounded by people who care for her just as much as you. Between them, they'll make sure that she has the best care possible.'

'I know,' she said, her voice unsteady. She hadn't realised quite how vulnerable she had become in these last few minutes as the full import of what had happened began to sink in. She, who had always been strong, felt as though her legs were about to fail her at any moment.

'There isn't anything you could do for her right now. There are checks to be made and procedures to be carried out.' He wrapped her more securely in his arms, holding her against his strong body as though he knew exactly what she was going through.

'You're right,' she conceded. Somehow having him hold her this way lent her strength, gave her the courage to face up to whatever needed to be done. 'What would I be able to do if I went over there? I can't interfere with what the doctors are doing, can I? And I wouldn't really want to do that. I'm sure they're all far more experienced than I am. But I just feel I need to be with her.'

'Of course you do, and if that's what you really want there's nothing to stop you. If you want to go today, I could arrange for someone to cover for you…it isn't a problem. But it might be more sensible to wait until the weekend. That way you'll know a little more about what's happened and what they plan to do about it. And you'll be in a much calmer frame of mind. At the moment you don't know for certain whether she's actually suffered any major damage. Once you know the full extent of her injuries you'll be in a better position to influence the course of treatment if you're not happy with her progress.'

She nodded. 'Yes, of course. That's true. I suppose I'm jumping the gun a bit, aren't I? As to the weekend, I have to work on Sunday. Blame the head of the department for that. I can't change it…we're short-staffed as it is.' She was still feeling a little shaky, and her agitation was reflected in her voice.

'You're anxious and upset, and you want to do everything you can for her, but you know as well as I do that it's best to keep a cool head in these situations.' His hand moved lightly over the length of her spine, a sweeping, caressing motion that acted like a soothing balm. It made her feel warm and comforted, and she leaned against him, accepting the gentle solace he was offering.

'I have to think about my brother, too,' she said, her cheek resting against his chest. 'He's feeling quite shocked by what's happened. And the fact that Mum knows that he's not at university has just added to it.'

'But at least it's out in the open now. I suppose it means that he could go home to your parents' house, doesn't it? That might help to ease things at the flat.'

She shook her head. 'I don't think he'll want to do that. For a start the house will be locked up while my parents are away, and I think he needs to be with friends for the moment. He has an awful lot on his mind.'

He lifted a hand and ran his fingers tenderly through her hair, brushing the warm gold strands away from her face. 'I wonder if he appreciates having a sister who looks out

for him the way you do?' He smiled. 'He ought to, because
you're really very special.'

She gazed up at him. 'You would help your own family,
wouldn't you? Perhaps you and your sister have the
stronger bond, after what you've been through together?'

'There is that, I grant you.' He placed his fingers beneath
her chin, brushing his thumb lightly along the line of her
jaw. 'Don't let this get you down. I'm here for you, and I'll
help in any way I can.'

Then, before she realised his intention, his head bent
towards her, and he placed a gentle kiss on her mouth.

She was so startled that her lips parted a fraction and
her blue eyes widened. It felt for all the world as though
her lips had been touched by flame, but just as she was
getting used to the idea that it might be intensely satisfying to explore that kiss a little further he lifted his head and
slowly eased back from her.

'I have to go,' he said, stepping back and glancing down
at his pager. 'More problems on the work front. Go and
take a break for a while. Have a cup of coffee and think
things through. You'll feel better for it, I'm sure.'

CHAPTER SIX

'IT's just not going to be the same this year at Christmas, is it?' Fraser said, staring bleakly out over the snow-covered garden the next day. He was clearing the drifts from the patio so that Jason and Rachel could ride their bikes. The gate that divided the two properties was open, and they had the full sweep of combined terraces to explore. 'Everything's going wrong. Now Gran's in hospital, and we don't have any idea how things are going to turn out, do we?'

'That's because we're here and she's some fifty miles away.' Alison sighed. 'I'd sooner be there so that I can ask the questions I want answering. Mum and Dad are doing the best they can to keep us up to date, but neither of them are doctors and it's so frustrating. I want to know exactly how she's doing. I want to see for myself.'

'So why not drive over to see her?' Josh came to join them at the back of the house, with Chaser following hard on his heels. Alison's heart skipped a beat at his unexpected appearance, and she shifted her attention back to Chaser to cover it up. The border collie was obviously completely wowed by the untouched carpet of snow that was laid out over the lawn. Ears up, panting and ready for action, he bounded over it, racing around like a mad thing, leaving a trail of footprints in his wake. Every now and again he nudged the snowdrifts with his nose, and then jumped back in surprise before scooting off again.

'It will take a couple of hours to get there, but it's still early in the day. If you leave here before eleven you should be there before lunchtime, and if you start back some time in the evening you'll still have time to sleep and be back at work in the morning.'

'That's a fine theory, but the weather forecast predicts blizzards, and I'm not comfortable driving in snow and ice at the best of times,' Alison replied. 'It's one thing to make the short journey to work, but fifty miles or more is quite another.' She frowned. 'Then again, I really *do* want to go and see how Gran is doing.' She was silent for a moment, mulling over her options.

'I could drive you, if you like? It doesn't bother me.' Josh shrugged. 'I'm used to bad road conditions.'

Alison looked at him, her heart surging with relief. 'Would you? It's an awful lot to ask of you. Are you sure?'

He nodded. 'Besides, my car's probably a sight more comfortable than yours—and the heater actually works a hundred percent all the time… Plus there's a very effective anti-skid mechanism.' He grinned. 'Have I made a sale?'

She laughed, thrilled at the opportunity he was giving her to go and visit her gran. 'Oh, definitely.' She raised her eyes heavenward. 'As though *I* can afford a top-of-the-range model… Katie will be so jealous.'

'Not really. She begged a lift to town the other day. Katie's not backward in coming forward, you know.' He turned to Fraser. 'How about you, Fraser? Do you want to come along with us?'

'Yes…please. Definitely.' He raised his brows. 'I wasn't actually going to let you take Alison without inviting myself along.'

'That's settled, then.' Josh zipped up the front of his soft brown leather jacket. 'You get yourselves ready to leave, while I go and have a quick word with Tom about the interview I've lined up for him at the hospital. It's all set for tomorrow, so I hope he doesn't mind losing part of Sunday morning.'

Alison stared at him, open-mouthed. 'So soon? How did you manage that?'

'I spoke to the maintenance supervisor about it yesterday. He has to work tomorrow. There's a particular check that needs to be done, so he's going in early. He said he'd talk to Tom and find out if he has the right qualifications for the job. As an engineer, and from what you've told me, I'm sure he has.'

Alison circled her hands around his arm, tugging him towards her. 'It's so good of you to do this. What made you decide to help him?'

Josh made a wry face. 'He looks after you, doesn't he? He helped you out with your plumbing problems, and made sure that your car was back on the road… Not to mention he keeps an eye on you to make sure that you're okay. I think he deserves a bit of luck, don't you?'

'I certainly do.' She smiled up at him and he bent towards her, moving closer, as though he was about to kiss her. His arm brushed against the curve of her breast, and even though she was wearing a soft fleece jacket she felt the shockwaves reverberate throughout her body.

'If you two are going to get soppy, I'm going inside,' Fraser said, heading towards the kitchen door.

Alison recovered herself in a giddy instant. What was she doing? Hadn't she sworn off men? Allowing herself to be drawn in by his easy-going, friendly manner was a dangerous game. It could lead her down all sorts of heart-breaking pathways.

Her wayward thoughts were interrupted, though, as just then Chaser decided he'd had enough of running around. Panting with exhilaration from his exercise, and the sheer joy of living, he came and stood beside them, his coat covered in snowflakes. Clearly that didn't suit him, and the next minute he started shaking himself so vigorously that icy droplets showered in all directions.

Alison gave a yelp as she was sprayed liberally with ice water. 'No, no!' she said. 'Stop that right now, Chaser.'

Josh straightened, giving her a rueful smile. 'I'll go and see Tom,' he said. 'I expect he'll be back from the news-agent's shop by now.'

They were ready to set off on their journey within the half-hour. Alison had gathered up a few things that she thought Gran might like…magazines, a couple of paper-back books and a tin of sweets. Fraser had added his own choice—a bunch of flowers from the corner shop, wrapped in cellophane, with their stalks dipped in moist cotton wool fastened tightly within a polythene bag.

'Do you think they'll survive the journey?' he asked, frowning.

'I should imagine so,' Alison said. 'Aren't they beauti-ful? She loves carnations and chrysanthemums, especially in those soft colours.'

Fraser looked pleased. It was the first time he'd seemed happy all morning.

The roads were every bit as bad as she'd predicted, clogged with snow in parts, but clear where the snow ploughs had been busy. Josh was a careful driver, though, and his car covered the miles with ease. Alison sat back in the passenger seat, enjoying the luxurious feel of leather upholstery. It would be great to be reunited with her family.

When they arrived at the hospital, her parents hurried to meet them in the reception area. 'The nurse told us you were here,' Alison's mother said, coming to give them a hug. 'Your grandad's stayed in the waiting room to be near to your gran.' She looked at Josh and added, 'Thank you so much for bringing Alison and Fraser to us. We've been so worried about my mother, but I know she'll want to see her grandchildren. Having them here will help her to recover, I'm sure of it.'

Alison went to embrace her father. 'How is she?' she asked. 'Mum said they had taken her to the operating theatre. Is she still there?'

'No, they've taken her to the recovery room, but they're not allowing us to see her yet. They say her blood pressure is low, and they have to work with her for a while to bring her out of the anaesthetic.'

Alison frowned and looked briefly at Josh, anxiety sparking in her eyes. 'Sometimes that can happen,' she said.

'The nurse said it would be some time before we can see her. Maybe an hour or more.' Her mother looked worried.

Josh had been staying back, out of the way of the family circle, but now he came to stand beside Alison and laid an arm lightly about her shoulders. A fleeting moment of understanding passed between them. Having him here with her to lend support was comforting.

'Did they say what kind of operation she'd had?' he asked.

'They had to put pins in the bone to support the break,' Alison's father said. 'The doctor said that sometimes they have to replace the joint, but he was hoping that he might be able to preserve hers. They haven't really said much to us as yet. I think they're more worried about bringing her round.'

Alison pressed her lips together and tried not to let her family see her fear. All manner of things might have happened. She might have lost too much blood, or the whole episode might have placed too much of a strain on her heart. Josh's fingers curled around her shoulder, holding her by his side and silently letting her know that he understood what she was going through. Her grand-mother wasn't strong, and the shock of breaking her hip could have caused huge problems. Surgery would have added to that.

'Perhaps we should go and get a cup of coffee while we wait for news?' Josh suggested.

Alison's mother nodded. 'And then Fraser can tell us why he's been sent down from university. I can't believe that this has happened.' She gave her son a long look. 'And you a straight A student.' She shook her head. 'It's unbelievable.'

Fraser looked glum. 'I knew you wouldn't believe I was innocent,' he said.

'Of course we believe you, son,' his father said. 'We just need to know a few more details.'

Alison glanced at Josh once more, wincing. This was not good. The last thing Fraser wanted just now was an inquisition.

They headed towards the hospital cafeteria, and once in there Josh went to buy coffees for everyone. Alison picked out a tray of food, choosing items that everyone could share—sandwiches, flapjacks and fruit. She doubted anyone had eaten very much, judging by her parents' weary features. Food would sustain them.

'So you don't even know if you'll be able to go back to university next term?' Alison's father said a few minutes later, finishing off his cheese sandwich. He studied Fraser from across the table.

Fraser shook his head. He was picking at his food, clearly wondering about the wisdom of coming here.

'I would hope the Dean will think again about expelling Fraser,' Josh said. 'The idea for a study group was sound, and from what I gather it was only the actions of one or two people that caused things to go wrong.'

'They used other people's work,' Fraser explained, swallowing his coffee as though that would give him strength. 'That wasn't the idea. But I don't see why I should be blamed for their actions. There were plenty of other people who used the site in the way it was meant to be used. I've been singled out simply because I started it.'

'Perhaps you ought to have known some students would take the opportunity to cheat.' Her father frowned.

Alison could see that he was not entirely convinced, and somehow it seemed unfair that Fraser should be quizzed while she and Josh were listening in.

She glanced at Josh. 'I'd like to look around the local shops for a basket of fruit for Gran,' she said. 'There might even be somewhere within the hospital where I can find one. I know she probably won't feel like eating for a while, but it'll be there for her when she does.'

He nodded. 'I'll go with you. I saw a couple of general stores as we drove in here. We're right in the centre of town, so we don't have far to go.'

Alison stood up, laying a gentle hand on her brother's shoulder. 'We'll be back in two ticks,' she told her parents. 'I want to be here when Gran's up to seeing visitors.'

Her mother nodded. 'I'll phone you if anything happens.'

The air outside the hospital was crisp and clear, and Alison breathed in deeply, trying to rid herself of all the worry of the last couple of days. As she walked along the street with Josh towards the shops they passed by some children who were enjoying an impromptu snowball fight, and the sound of their laughter filled the air.

Further along the street a man with a covered barrow was selling hot chestnuts, and Josh said, 'Have you ever tasted these?'

She shook her head. 'Never. I've often wondered what they're like.'

Josh stopped and handed over a few coins, and the man scooped up a couple of dozen nuts from a rack above the hot coals, emptying them out into a paper bag.

Josh thanked him and they moved on. He crushed a chestnut inside the paper, and Alison heard a faint cracking sound as the darker surface of the nut broke away.

'You peel them—see,' he said, and then offered her a palely golden nut, holding it to her lips. 'Careful in case it's hot,' he warned. 'When you bite into them they're softer than you might imagine—a strange, creamy kind of texture.'

It was somehow an oddly intimate experience…his fingertips just a breath away from her lips, the chestnut hovering within reach. Alison bit into it and savoured the taste in her mouth. 'They're slightly sweet, too,' she murmured. 'I hadn't expected that.'

They shared the chestnuts as they walked along, and the heat from them warmed her inside, adding to the gentle flame that was already glowing softly inside her. It was good to have him near. She felt that she was safe. He would protect her from the ills of the world. Nothing could go wrong while he was around.

She stopped at a grocery store to buy a basket of fruit, filled with shiny red and green apples, bright oranges, bananas and succulent grapes. The wicker basket and its contents were packaged with cellophane and tied with ribbon. 'I think she'll like that, don't you?'

'I'm sure she will.' Josh draped an arm around her, reaching for the basket with his free hand to carry it for her. 'Your gran's lucky to have so many people around her who care about her deeply.'

'She's always been there for us. I remember her helping me learn to ride my bike, and she used to let us help her whenever she baked cookies or cakes. She and my grandad have played a huge part in our lives. I was sad when we had to move away from the area because of my Dad's job. It meant that we didn't see them so often. But they still made the effort to come and see us, and we would go and visit them.'

'It's strange how people can have such different lives, isn't it?' He sent her an oblique glance. 'You and I have had a totally different upbringing.'

'Perhaps that's why you're so independent?' She studied him briefly as they walked back towards the hospital. He lifted a quizzical brow and she explained, 'You work as part of a team, but at the same time you're definitely the boss. You're self-assured, you take on the responsibility for other people, and you don't seem to worry about what other people think. If you don't want to do something you have no qualms about saying so. That must come from a background where you've been left to decide things for yourself, surely?'

'Possibly. Though my stepfather tries to influence me wherever he can. He's a surgeon in private practice, and I suppose it's because of him that I became interested in taking up the profession.'

'And is that why you followed him into private medicine?'

'I suppose he showed me the way. He talked about the possibilities of my going to work in the States. I thought about it, but I'd done my training here, and I felt I needed to stay at least for a few years, give something back. After a while I began to realise that I could help people in some instances to gain access to treatment faster than they would if they waited for the health service to act. I don't see anything wrong in doing that.'

He looked at her as though she might disagree, and she hunched her shoulders and said, 'I'm not going to argue with you on that score. You've been good enough to help me out today, not to mention giving Tom the chance of a job, so I couldn't possibly do anything to upset you...no matter how much I disagree with your point of view.'

He laughed and squeezed her shoulder, tugging her into close proximity with his long body. 'So I can do practically anything I like, can I? Seeing as how my score sheet's way high?'

By now they had reached the environs of the hospital,

and they crossed the main thoroughfare, heading towards a covered walkway that led towards the rear entrance and the cafeteria.

'That depends what you have in mind,' she murmured cautiously.

He chuckled, drawing her into a deserted corner on the outside of the building, sheltered on all sides by three blank walls. He carefully placed the fruit basket down on the pavement and gently pulled her into his arms.

'Something like this,' he said, bending his head so that her lips were just a whisper away from his. 'I've been wanting to do this all day.'

His hands were moving over her as he spoke, slowly shaping the soft contours of her body, while his cheek lightly rubbed against hers. His mouth sought the ripe fullness of her lips as though he was giving her the chance to change her mind. She could have pulled away. She could have stopped things there and then. But she didn't.

She wanted him to kiss her. She wanted to feel the warm, firm touch of his mouth on hers and discover once and for all whether the fire he'd stirred in her the last time he had kissed her had been a fluke.

And then it was too late for any going back, because his lips were pressuring hers, brushing them apart, taking her on a slow, sweet journey of discovery. His body moved against her as he deepened the kiss, and every part of her turned to flame, responding to the tender invitation of his mouth and hands.

His hands caressed and stroked, urging her closer to him, so that their bodies melded together, her softness crushed against his hard, male torso.

Her hands lifted, curving around the back of his neck so that her fingers encountered the silk strands of his hair, and at the same time his arms folded around her, holding her even closer to him, if that were possible, so that her breasts were pressed against the wall of his chest and her thighs tangled with his.

'Do you have any idea what you're doing to me…how you make me feel?' Josh's voice was roughened, a husky, breathless sound from deep within his throat. He sounded surprised, almost, as though it had taken him unawares, and it was a heady feeling to know that she could have this effect on him.

It was a two-way exchange. There was no mistaking the ripple of excitement that raced through her veins. What had happened the first time he'd kissed her was definitely no happy chance of fate. She had never felt this way before with any man. Josh alone had the power to send her spirits soaring heavenwards, there was no doubt about that.

Was it possible that he could send her plummeting down to earth just as easily? She had travelled this way before, and found to her cost that emotions could be fickle.

The errant thought crept up on her even as Josh reluctantly eased back from her. 'Perhaps we should go inside,' he murmured. 'I can hear people coming.'

She nodded, unable to trust herself to speak just then, and as he glanced at her he must have realised something of what she was thinking.

'Are you all right?' he asked.

She nodded. She bent down to pick up the basket and tried to brace herself for what might lie ahead. Gran was ill, coming round from surgery, and she needed to focus all her attention on that.

'Did I step out of line?' he murmured, as they started to walk in the direction of the cafeteria. 'Perhaps I read the vibes all wrong?'

'I'm not really in a fit state to make up my mind on anything,' she told him, her voice quiet. 'I'm not sure that I know what I want. Except I vowed I'd never let any man hurt me ever again.'

'And I can understand that.' He stopped momentarily in the corridor, causing her to pause along with him. 'I don't mean to hurt you, Alison,' he said, running his fingers gently beneath her jaw. 'Can't we just live for the moment…enjoy what we have with no strings on either side? I'll be honest with you. I can tell you straight off I'm not looking for a long-term commitment. I've seen for myself that nothing lasts for ever. But I'm here for you now—right at this moment and for the foreseeable future. You can be certain of that.'

Alison didn't answer. Before Josh had dropped into her life she had told herself that it didn't pay to give your heart to any man. She had learned to be cautious, to be wary of letting her emotions get out of hand. In some ways it had dampened her natural exuberance, made her feel like half a person. And then Josh had come along and she had forgotten everything. He'd smiled at her and held her in his arms and every sensible thought had flown out of the window.

Fraser and her parents were back in the waiting room with her grandad when she and Josh caught up with them a few minutes later.

'They say we'll be able to see her in a while,' her mother said. 'They're trying to make her more comfortable. But we have to take it in turns to visit her. No more than three people at a time.'

'That's all right. Did they tell you any more about her condition?'

Her mother frowned. 'Only that it will take a while for her to fully recover. She had pins and a metal plate put into the leg. They'll make a start on getting her back on her feet as soon as possible, but she'll be in hospital for up to a fortnight.'

It was more or less what Alison had expected.

'That brings us almost up to Christmas, doesn't it?' Fraser was pacing the floor. 'Poor Gran.'

'She looked very frail when they brought her through,' her grandfather said. 'And the operation took so long. She was in there for hours.'

Alison nodded. 'It can take a long while,' she said. 'It's major surgery. It's the kind of thing Josh does in his private practice. He'll be able to tell you what's involved.' She knew she could trust Josh to explain in layman's terms, without going into detail about anything that might cause her grandfather to worry, and he didn't let her down.

After a while the waiting room door opened, and a nurse came into the room. 'Hello, there. She's all ready at last,' she said. 'Now, who's going in to see her first?'

It was some time later when Alison finally managed to go and see her grandmother. Fraser and Josh went with her, drawing up seats by the side of the bed.

'Who's this young man you've brought with you?' Gran was still drowsy from the anaesthetic, and Alison could see that she was in some pain despite the medication she had been given, but her blue eyes had homed in on Josh straight away.

'This is Josh,' Alison told her. 'We work together at the hospital. He knew how anxious we were to see you, so he drove Fraser and me up here. We were very worried when we heard you'd had a fall.'

'Well, I should be a whole lot stronger now,' Gran said. 'They've turned me into a bionic gran now, by all accounts. There was a very nice doctor who operated on me. Said he wanted my phone number—but your grandad saw him off.' She tried a smile, but her voice was already fading with tiredness.

They chatted for a while, with Fraser telling her about his pharmacy course, omitting any mention of being sent down for fear of upsetting her, and Josh telling her about his own role at the hospital.

'They want me to do a radio show and read out Christmas messages,' he said. 'I thought I might impersonate a few cartoon characters to cheer up the children.' He gave them a sample of a wacky duck and a world-weary dog delivering advice on how to cook the Christmas dinner, making them chuckle.

'Stop making me laugh,' Gran said. 'You're making my side hurt.'

'It sounds as though they're looking after you anyway, Gran,' Alison said a little later, stroking her grandmother's hand. 'You gave us all quite a scare. We were worried about you.'

'Ah, well, I gave myself a bit of a fright as well.' Her eyelids started to droop, prompting Alison to quietly stand up.

'We're going to let you rest now, Gran,' she said. 'I have to go back home, to get ready for work in the morning, but Mum will phone me and let me know how you are.'

Her grandmother's eyelids fluttered. 'You take care, sweetheart.'

Alison dropped a kiss on her cheek, and moved away so that Fraser could say goodbye. Fraser loved his grandmother as much as she did.

It was upsetting to see Gran pale and in pain, and she could only hope that she would be well looked after. A major operation such as she had been through was no simple matter. She would need a lot of physiotherapy, and not the least of her problems would be to gain her confidence again in walking.

As things stood it would be some time before she would be back to her old self. There was certainly no chance that she and Grandad would manage the journey to her parents' house for Christmas this year.

At the door she paused, letting Josh and Fraser pass her by on their way out into the corridor. She took a final look at her grandmother, lying in the bed.

'He seems like a good man, Alison,' her grandmother said, turning to give her a gentle smile. 'Just take care he doesn't break your heart like that other one.'

CHAPTER SEVEN

Snow had been falling steadily during the night, laying down a crisp carpet of white over everything. As she drove to work Alison looked out over the sprawling landscape of hills and dales and wondered at the beauty of it all. The branches of the trees were decked with a frosting of ice crystals illuminated by a watery sun, and in the distance the rooftops of a farmhouse and its outbuildings had received a thick blanket of snowflakes that glistened like diamonds.

'Isn't it lovely?' Alison murmured to Katie, sitting beside her in the passenger seat.

She turned the car on to the main road. She was so much more cheerful now that she had heard from her mother that Gran was up and about, using a walking frame to help her get about in the hospital. It had been more than a week since her operation, and with any luck the danger time was past.

'This is what you were dreaming about not so long ago, isn't it?' she said, looking out at the hedgerows and fences glistening with frost. 'A Christmas card picture? Except that this is daytime and you were thinking of night.'

'Perhaps I'd been sneaking a tipple from the sherry bottle

back then,' Katie responded in a less than cheerful manner. 'It doesn't seem nearly so romantic when you have to get up early to come in to work and the roads are slippery.'

'You're right. I'll grant you that.' Alison smiled. 'At least the car heater's working, after a fashion, which is more than I can say for the one in Sam's rattlebox.'

Katie laughed. 'He's a fanatic, that one. He actually had his skis out this morning, trying them on for size. That man's a hoot.'

'Oh, he is,' Alison agreed. 'There's no doubt about it. And when he told me about his exploits on the ski slopes I began to realise why he has such a yen for spy films. I'll bet as he zooms down the piste at high speed he imagines he's a secret agent on a mission.'

They both chuckled at that, and just a few minutes later Alison parked her car in the grounds of the hospital. She walked with Katie towards the main doors of the emergency department.

In the ambulance bay the paramedics were checking their equipment in preparation for their next call, and Alison stopped for a while to chat with them—until her fingers began to tingle with the cold.

'I have to go,' she said. 'See you later. Much later, I hope.' She grinned. 'Keep safe.'

She hurried to catch up with Katie.

'I'm glad to see you made it in to A&E,' Josh remarked, coming across the two of them as they walked towards the doctors' writing-up area. 'With this awful weather half the staff are struggling to get in, so it looks as though we'll have to take up the slack until they get here.'

'Then again, with any luck most non-hospital people will

stay home and stay safe,' Alison remarked, reaching for a folder from the desk. Her fingers were still numb with cold, but she persevered and flipped open the manila cover. She quickly scanned the patient's notes and then checked the entries against a sheaf of blood test results, before searching in her pocket for a pen. 'It looks as though our aneurysm patient came through her operation without suffering any adverse effects,' she murmured. 'That's good to know.'

She attempted to add a comment to a paper in the file, but gave up when her stiff, cold fingers refused to respond. 'Ah...no. Too cold, too cold,' she mumbled. 'You wouldn't think a walk across the car park would give you frostbite, would you?'

'That's because you stopped to talk to the ambulance crew,' Katie said. 'You would insist on talking to them about Mrs Flanagan's son.'

'Well, they were the ones who brought Charlie into A&E, after all. He could barely breathe when they picked him up, and they just wanted to make sure he was okay. It must be difficult for them, worrying about the patients and not knowing the outcome. At least I was able to tell them he was admitted and now he's almost back to normal. He'll be going home in a couple of days.' She tried again to write, and failed miserably.

'Here—let me,' Josh said, taking the pen and the folder from her.

'But you don't know what I was going to write,' she protested. 'How do you—?'

'That wasn't my plan,' he murmured, setting them down on the desk. 'Give me your hands.'

Without waiting for her to respond, he began to chafe her

hands between his, so that her fingers tingled and her palms heated. After that a response kicked in throughout her whole body. She felt warm all over, and she was sure her cheeks by now must be flooded with pink. There was something strangely compelling about the way he was holding her, his large hands engulfing hers, and somehow in that moment she felt completely secure and cherished, as though by that simple act he had staked a claim on her heart.

She quickly tried to shake off that wayward thought. Why was she even imagining such things? Perhaps the cold had affected her more than she'd realised.

She looked up then and saw that Katie was watching, with an odd expression on her face and a kind of startled awareness freezing her smile, and Alison felt an immediate surge of guilt run through her. Did Katie think that something was going on between them? It wasn't like that…of course it wasn't…was it?

She would not hurt her friend for the world, and yet already Katie was backing away, turning on her heel and heading for the observation ward.

'I'm fine now, thanks,' Alison mumbled, looking into Josh's eyes. 'Really, I'm thoroughly warm.'

'Hmm.' He studied her face for a minute or so, and she was mortified because she was sure her cheeks must be burning. 'I'd have thought you would have learned your lesson last time you had this problem,' he murmured. 'We have to do something about it. Winter's moving on, and we can't have you suffering from the numb fingers every morning, can we?'

'I'll sort it,' she said. 'I'll remember to bring along a pair of gloves, even though I'm travelling in the car.'

'Hmm. Make sure you do. And get yourself a hot drink before you attempt to start work next time.' He hesitated for a moment, before finally letting her go. 'Where did Katie disappear to?' he asked, frowning as he looked around. 'I need to talk to her. She wanted to follow up on one of her patients.'

'I think you'll find her in the observation ward,' Alison said. 'After that she'll be working in paediatric A&E for the rest of the morning.' She couldn't help wondering what Katie was thinking, and how she would react to him seeking her out.

'Of course—I remember now. And you're both off this afternoon, aren't you?'

She nodded, thankful to be on safer ground at last. 'We should be spending an afternoon in the lecture theatre, but the session was cancelled yesterday. I guess that means we both get the afternoon off.'

'Lucky you.'

He walked away, and after that she found she was much too busy to dwell on what went on inside people's heads. Her whole morning was taken up dealing with broken limbs and sprains brought about by falls on icy pavements, reminding her of how badly her gran had been injured. Whoever said winter was a wonderful season? Surely it couldn't have been her?

By lunchtime she was almost ready to hand over her patients to a colleague, when Katie stopped by the fracture clinic.

'Hi. Jenny said I'd find you in here,' she murmured. 'I just dropped by to say I won't be needing a lift back to the house this afternoon. I thought I'd do a spot of Christmas shopping while I have the opportunity, and Taylor's going to pick me up from town at the end of his shift. I know you said you would look after Jason and Rachel this afternoon, otherwise I'd have suggested you come with me.'

'Okay. Thanks for letting me know.' Katie's manner appeared to be as natural as ever, so it was possible she had decided to put the events of the morning to one side. That was something of a relief. 'Perhaps we could shop together some time next week? I've a stack of presents to buy.'

Katie gave a brief smile. 'Of course. Me too. Today will just see the tip of the iceberg.' She paused before she turned away. 'By the way, I thought you'd like to know…I was up on the second floor a short time ago, and I saw that young lad Rees going towards the women's surgical ward. I suppose he must be visiting someone up there.'

'That's interesting.' Alison frowned. 'He said he would keep in touch, but I haven't heard anything from him up to now. I think I might go and see if I can catch up with him. I'd really like to know how he's getting on at the hostel. I've been talking to Jack on the phone, but he says Rees is keeping his cards close to his chest.'

'You're way too soft for your own good,' Katie said, her mouth curving. Now, where had Alison heard that one before? Maybe she and Josh were two of a kind. 'Anyway,' Katie added, 'I'm off to shop till I drop. See you later.'

Alison gave her a light wave, and went back to checking her patient's X-ray film. 'That looks fine,' she said, glancing at the woman. 'The bones in your wrist are perfectly realigned now. You'll need to wear the plaster cast on your arm for a few weeks, though.'

'Do you think it will be off by Christmas?' The woman

was frowning. 'I just can't see it going with my little black dress, somehow.'

'Oh, I don't know. It might be quite a fetching accessory—especially if you get people to do a few drawings on it.' Alison smiled. 'Seriously, though, I think you'll have to get used to it until the New Year at least.'

'Ah, well, thanks anyway.'

Alison finished writing up her patient's prescription for pain medication and scooted off, intent on tracking down Rees.

Josh caught up with her as she was heading for the lift. 'Are you off now?' he asked.

She nodded. 'In a few minutes. I just heard that Rees might be visiting someone up on women's surgical. I was hoping to catch up with him and say hello. Did you want me for some reason?'

He nodded. 'I wanted to talk to you about your plans for this afternoon. Katie said you had arranged to babysit?'

She nodded, treating him to a brilliant smile. 'That's right. Thanks to you, Tom has a job at the hospital, and they can actually begin to think about doing some Christmas shopping. The building society has granted them a three-month stay on their mortgage, so things are looking up. I said I'd look after the children when they come out of school, so that they can take advantage of the late-night shopping in town.'

'That's more or less what Katie said.' He hesitated momentarily. 'It occurred to me that they've been a bit down lately, up until their father managed to get his new job, and they're due for some fun. I think I've come up with something to help you keep them amused…if you're agreeable, that is?'

'Um… Yes…I'd love to do something for them.' She frowned. Why was he doing this? Was it that he had formed some kind of bond with the children after looking after their dog? Or was it that he wanted to spend time with *her*? Either way, she felt a sudden quivering of excitement in her abdomen. 'What did you have in mind?'

'I'll tell you when you come back from seeing Rees,' he said in an enigmatic way. 'Meet me in the doctors' restroom in, say, half an hour?'

'All right.' She went on her way, intrigued. What had Josh come up with that was so mysterious?

She shook off the perplexing thought. He was a man— a totally different species. Who could know anything about the inner workings of their minds? She certainly couldn't claim to be an expert.

She hurried along to Women's Surgical, wondering whether she was already too late. Might she have missed Rees?

'I saw a young man go into the end bay a while back,' the nurse on duty told her, 'but I think he left a few minutes ago. In fact I'm sure of it. I remember seeing that the dressing on his hand was coming undone. I was going to suggest that I change it for him, but he left before I had the chance.'

'Oh, that's a shame.' Disappointment ran through her. 'I was hoping I might be able to talk to him for a while.'

The nurse was sympathetic. 'I expect he'll be back here tomorrow. He's been visiting Mrs Brackley on a fairly regular basis, but we can't allow anyone to stay with her for more than a short period. She was in a bad way when she first came in here, and she tires easily.'

'Mrs Brackley?'

'That's right. She seems like a pleasant woman, but she hasn't really been very talkative. We don't know an awful lot about her, and the boy has been her only visitor so far.'

'Well, never mind. Perhaps I'll be able to catch up with him tomorrow.' Alison gave the nurse a quick smile. 'Thanks for your help.'

'You're welcome.' The nurse glanced at Alison's name-tag. 'If I get the chance, I could give you a ring next time he turns up?'

'Would you? That would be brilliant.' She wrote her pager number down on a notepad that the nurse handed to her. 'Thanks—I really appreciate this.'

Alison left the ward and took the lift back down to the ground floor. It was a shame that she had missed Rees, but at least she had moved forward a little. She had discovered that there was someone in his life that he cared about, and that made her feel a bit more cheerful about his situation.

'Something's changed. There's definitely a spring in your step now,' Josh said, his dark brows lifting as she walked into the restroom. 'Did you manage to have a chat with the boy?'

She shook her head. 'I was too late… But I did learn that he's been visiting someone up there—I'm wondering if it could be his mother…a Mrs Brackley. The nurse didn't say much—because of confidentiality, I imagine—so I didn't press her, but apparently the woman is quite ill. Maybe I'll be able to persuade Rees to tell me more eventually…and then there's a chance we can begin to help him.'

He studied her thoughtfully. 'You don't mean to give up, do you?' His expression was wry.

'No. Never. Why would I?' She sent him an odd look.

'That's what we're here for, isn't it…? To help one another wherever we can?' She frowned. 'Anyway, what was it that you wanted to talk to me about? Something to do with keeping the children amused, you said?'

'That's right.' He poured coffee from the percolator and offered her a cup. 'It was the blizzard this morning that made me think of it. I remembered the first time I saw them, when they came with Tom to pick you up from the hospital, Jason said he wished it would snow some more. He wanted to get the toboggan out, he said, but Rachel pointed out that it was broken. It occurred to me then that I have one gathering dust in my attic. I was saving it for my various nieces and nephews, but they're all still a bit too young, and it seems to me that Jason and Rachel might as well have the benefit. It seems a shame to miss out on the snowfall.'

Alison put down her cup, and on the spur of the moment wrapped her arms around him in a quick embrace. 'You're such a star. You're not so much of a toughie after all, are you…?' she said, her cheek resting briefly against the material of his jacket. 'All that protesting about not being responsible for waifs and strays…and all this dismissal of the Christmas season. Have the ghosts of Christmas past, present and future paid you a visit? It might be snowing outside, but your heart is beginning to melt isn't it?' She looked up at him, smiling, her gaze meshing with his, her hand flattening against his shirtfront to encounter the warmth of his skin and register the heavy beat of his heart.

He had been so wonderful this last week or so, taking her to see Gran and her parents, helping Tom to find a job.

He didn't answer. He was very still, almost as though

he was holding his breath, and in that fleeting moment it
was as though something sparked between them. It was
unbidden, thrilling, and altogether unexpected—a total
awareness that held them both in thrall. Neither of them
stirred, but Josh's eyes held a stunned, dazed kind of look,
as though he had been knocked for six, and slowly she
began to realise what she had done.

He was watching her steadily, flame kindling in the grey
depths of his eyes, and now he moved closer to her, his
hands coming to rest lightly on the small of her back. 'I
don't recall saying that I don't care about people,' he
murmured. 'I just don't go along with all the sentimentality
that seems to affect everyone at this time of year.' His hands
stroked the length of her spine, pausing to linger on the soft
curve of her hips. 'Anyway,' he said softly, 'you more than
make up for any shortcomings I may have. I get the feeling
you'd take on the world and its problems if you could.'

Alison couldn't think straight. Having his arms enfold
her in that way was proving far too great a distraction. It
made her body fizz with excitement, and she was beginning to feel as though nothing in the world mattered except
to have him hold her like this. That would surely be a dangerous path to tread?

She had been hurt once before, and instinct warned her
to draw back. He was a man, and his reactions were totally
male, his whole body responding to the subtle invitation
of her warm embrace. She had to be more careful from
now on, or her impulsive actions would drive her headlong into trouble.

'Even I couldn't manage that,' she said with a shaky
laugh. 'I let my heart rule my head—I know I do. But I've

always been part of a loving, caring family, and I'd rather cherish that ideal than keep people at arm's length and not get involved in their troubles.'

'You don't apply that same philosophy to the men in your life, though, do you?' he said softly, his voice becoming rough around the edges. 'You haven't let anyone get close to you for quite some time.'

'That's different.' She stiffened. 'It's much more personal, and it doesn't bear any relation to what I'm talking about.'

'But I'm right, aren't I?' he persisted. 'You have all this feeling for the people around you who are suffering in various ways, and yet you keep your own heart walled up, out of reach of anyone who might make the slightest dent in your defences.' His hands moved to encircle her arms, as though he would shield her from harm, and yet *he* was the one who was provoking her unhappiness, stirring up things that she would sooner have let lie.

She drew in a ragged breath. 'I vowed I wouldn't let anyone hurt me ever again. I thought Rob was someone I could care for, that maybe we might have a future together, even. But he let me down, and I'm not going to go down that route again.'

'What happened?' His voice was coaxing, tender, as though he really cared, and Alison realised that this was something he wouldn't drop.

She sighed raggedly. Maybe it would be simpler to tell him what he wanted to know and get it out of the way once and for all.

'When I first met him,' she said, 'Rob was trying to establish his own medical supply business. But things were difficult for him. I could see how hard he was working, how determined he was to make a success of things, and I admired him for that. I thought it was great that he wanted to supply products that would be useful in diagnosing illness, and I really wanted him to do well. I was behind him every step of the way.'

Josh frowned. 'But something went wrong?'

She gave a broken laugh. 'Oh, no. It all went very well. I introduced him to my father, and he agreed with me that Rob had a good enterprise going. He helped him to find contacts, and even lent him money so that he could build up the business.'

'Was there a problem with that? Did he pay the money back?'

She nodded. 'He did. The problem for me was that he changed course and decided that it would be much more profitable to supply private hospitals and clinics with consumables like examination gloves and surgery packs. Somehow that didn't seem to me like such a praiseworthy venture.'

'But there was nothing untoward in itself in him doing that, was there?' Josh's brow indented with a crooked line.

'I suppose not. But he became very money-orientated, and he seemed to be overrun by the notion of private medicine and how lucrative it could be. Once he had established a position for himself I discovered that Rob actually cared more for his business venture than he did for me. He decided to move on. It was a case of thanks for everything, but I'm okay now. I don't need you any more.'

'I'm sorry. That must have been a bitter blow—both for

you and your father.' Josh held her close to him, as though he would soothe away her pain.

'My father managed to shrug it off. He said we had put our trust in him and we weren't to blame for thinking he was something other than he was. Rob could turn on the charm at the drop of a hat, and you wouldn't know you were being led down the garden path. He made me believe that he loved me, but it was all a sham. I fell for it. But I won't let that happen again—ever.'

'It would be a mistake to judge all men by his example, though, wouldn't it?' He ran a hand along her arm, but his gaze was questioning, as though her answer really mattered to him.

'I don't know about that.' Her voice wavered a little. 'I just don't think I'm ready to take any risks on that score.' She tried to ease herself away from him. 'Anyway, I don't know what all this has to do with my wanting to help other people. Just because I have a problem with getting romantically entangled with a man it doesn't mean I can't get involved in helping out where I see trouble brewing. I won't stand by and see young people like Rees being left to fend for themselves, or watch my neighbours' lives fall apart without doing something to ease their burden. Someone, somewhere has to care—otherwise it would be a poor world we're living in.'

Slowly, he let her go. 'That's an admirable viewpoint…honourable, decent, but sadly flawed. Some people prefer to be left to their own devices, you know, and I'd hate to see your dreams dashed.'

'I can live with that. Besides—nothing ventured, nothing gained.' She smiled. 'At least I feel I've scored a small victory with you. You've offered to help out with Jason and Rachel, and that must mean that you're beginning to think my way just a tiny bit. Between us we could do our best to cheer them up, couldn't we?'

'We certainly could,' he said, a perplexed look crossing his face. 'Only after what you've said I'm not so sure you'll be too pleased with what I was going to suggest.'

CHAPTER EIGHT

ALISON stared at Josh. 'Does this mean that you've changed your mind about the toboggan?' Her spirits plummeted. What had she said that would have caused him to think twice about it? What had seemed like a wonderful idea that would bring joy to the children was dissolving as rapidly as snow-melt in the glare of the sun.

'No, nothing like that.' He looked around and saw that her coffee was untouched. 'Aren't you going to drink that?' he asked.

'In a minute.' Her mouth flattened. 'You said I might not be too pleased about what you had in mind?' she prompted.

He shrugged. 'It's only that I need to stop by my clinic for a brief consultation with one of my patients when I leave here, and I was going to suggest that you might want to come along with me.' He winced. 'Except that since you've told me about Rob and his links with private medicine I have the feeling I might be tarred by association... You've made your views about private practice pretty clear, so now I have to do a quick rethink. I don't want to upset you unduly by bringing you face to face with my business premises.'

'You wanted me to go with you?'

'It doesn't matter.' He swallowed the rest of his own coffee, and she watched in absorbed fascination as the line of his throat moved. 'I live above the shop, so to speak, so I was thinking I could bring the sledge down from the attic and you could check it over to make sure it's suitable. I wouldn't want Jason and Rachel to get their hopes up and then be disappointed. It's not that important, though. It'll be just as easy for me to pick up the sledge and bring it over to your place.'

'I don't mind stopping by your clinic,' she said, picking up her cup and savouring the hot liquid. 'Perhaps I *have* been guilty of letting Rob colour my judgement, and I hope I can keep an open mind. I'm not obsessed with the idea of free medicine for all… It's just that I believe people should get their priorities right, and there should be a balance of some sort.'

Besides, she was suddenly curious to see where Josh lived and worked, and the idea of being with him for a few hours more held an intense appeal. 'Katie said your practice is on Upper Regent Street, so it's *en route* from here, isn't it?'

'That's right…just a couple of miles away. I could make you lunch, and you might want to relax in the apartment while I see my patient. It won't take long.'

'Nice work if you can get it,' she said with a wry smile. 'Are all your afternoons so light on patients?'

'You think I have it easy, don't you?' There was a glimmer of amusement in his eyes. 'It's not the case, unfortunately. I had to change my schedule to allow for redecoration of the surgery, and my afternoon appointment is one that was slipped in at the last minute before the painters get to work. As to the rest, it means I have the ideal opportunity to spend the afternoon with you and the children.'

A ripple of exhilaration ran through her. Did he really want to spend the afternoon with her? The thought gave her a welcome lift, but after a moment's reflection she batted it away. Weren't the children his prime concern?

'If you're ready, perhaps we should set off?' he suggested. 'I'm aiming to have you home by the time school ends for the day.'

'That's good,' she said. She rinsed her cup under the tap and then went to find her jacket.

Outside the hospital the ground was covered in snow that had drifted in parts to bank up against the line of fencing and edge the verges with borders of white. The car park had been gritted, though, making it easier for vehicles to negotiate the driveways.

She drove out of the hospital grounds, following his lead, and tailed him as he headed for the main road towards his prestigious consulting rooms. It was a short journey. Once there, they garaged the cars securely in the old stable block at the back of the building, and then he ushered her inside through the private entrance.

'Would you like a quick tour of the clinic before we go up to the apartment?' he asked. 'Or we could skip that, if you prefer?'

'No, I'd like to see around.' She gave a mischievous smile. 'I'm interested in seeing how the other half live.'

In fact she was already impressed by the sheer grandeur of the place, and as he led the way into the main foyer she could see why Katie's aunt had called it sumptuous.

'This is the reception area,' Josh said. 'Most patients will come in here first of all. We wanted to make it light and airy, so we chose pale, warm colours and made it welcoming, with the occasional picture on the walls, and we've added plants here and there.'

'I think you succeeded,' Alison said. 'It's perfect. I like the friendly touch, with the magazine table and the children's corner, and I imagine the tropical fish tank over there helps people to relax.'

'That was the general idea.' He seemed to be pleased by her comments. 'Come and see the rest,' he said, walking through a small vestibule.

As she toured the consulting rooms she could see that the same light but opulent touch remained throughout. All the desks were made of natural oak, as were the glass-fronted bookcases that housed collections of exquisitely bound gold-embossed medical books. Again, there were plants to add greenery, and the ambient lighting added an extra glow to the pale sunlight that spilled over all from the Georgian-style windows.

Examination couches were housed behind discreet carved wooden screens, and in each room there was a corner basin and storage for medical equipment.

'I don't see any need for decorating of any kind,' she murmured. 'Everything looks quite perfect.'

He smiled. 'That's because we decorate every year,' he said. 'Each room is done in rotation, so as not to cause too much inconvenience. This week it's my turn.' He laid a hand lightly around her waist, sending little shockwaves of pleasure to pool in her abdomen. 'Shall we go up to the apartment? I'll fix you a light lunch, and then you can

relax while I go up into the attic and retrieve the sledge.'
He smiled, his gaze warm as he looked into her eyes.

'That would be good.' She couldn't understand why he
made her feel so strangely off balance. It was as though she
had drunk deeply of a glass of wine and it had gone straight
to her head.

They took the lift up to his apartment, and once again
she found herself captivated by the luxurious feel of the
rooms. Natural light poured in through long, square-paned
glass doors that opened out on to a balcony overlooking a
nearby park.

'I sometimes eat breakfast or supper out here,' he said,
opening them up and pointing out the distant hills.

'I can see why.' She looked out over the horizon. 'The
view must take your breath away on bright, clear days.'

'That's true. It's also pleasantly warm when the sun
shines... Not quite so good when everything's covered in
snow and ice and your breath literally freezes on the air...
like today.'

She chuckled, and turned back into the room as he shut
the doors behind them. 'You've made this place totally
different from the rest of the clinic, haven't you?' she said,
looking around. 'I mean, there's still the lightness of touch
and the beautiful wood finish, but the sofas are warm,
coloured upholstery instead of leather, and there are more
subtle, artistic touches in the ceramics.' She gazed at the
softly curving lines of a vase and the marbled surface of a
shallow bowl, filled with palely gleaming pebbles of glass.
'It's lovely.'

'It's good to hear you say that.'

She laughed. 'It wouldn't last five minutes if you transported all this to the flat Katie and I share. What with Taylor and Sam tramping through at regular intervals, and the children from next door racing in to tell us what's going on in their lives, it wouldn't stand a chance. And that's without Chaser racketing about the place.'

He raised a questioning brow. 'Does he do that? I know he was racing about the garden on the day we went to the hospital, but I thought maybe that was a one-off.'

'Oh, yes, he does. According to Martha he's supposed to be confined to the house and garden, but he wants to be with the children, and where they go, he goes. He's like lightning, whipping through the doors and getting under everyone's feet.'

'I'll bet they wish he'd stayed a little bit under the weather—at least for long enough for them to get their breath.' He was smiling as he led the way into the kitchen. 'I'm not sure what you would like for lunch,' he said. 'I could whip up some pasta, or there's salad in the fridge… unless you fancy some soup, or maybe some crusty bread rolls and a selection of cheeses? Is there anything else that you might like to eat?'

'Salad with crusty bread and cheese sounds fine to me,' she told him. 'I could sort that out while you go and find the sledge, if you like?' She glanced at her watch. 'There can't be too much time before you have to see your patient.'

'True. Are you sure you don't mind?'

'I'm sure. It shouldn't be too difficult for me to find what I need, should it?'

'You're a trouper.' He filled the kettle at the sink and set it to heat, and then laid out a teapot, cups and saucers on the central table. He retrieved bread rolls from the wooden storage box and butter from the fridge. 'Cutlery's in the drawer,' he said. 'I'll be back in two ticks.'

She heard him crashing about in the attic while she added cheese and the salad bowl to the items on the table. There was a ham in the fridge, and she set that out as an afterthought. He looked as though he was a hungry man. He was always lean and lithe, and he had to get his energy from somewhere, didn't he?

The tea was steaming in the pot by the time he came back into the kitchen.

'It's a lot bigger than I remembered,' he said, placing the sledge down on the floor. 'But then again it's a two-seater.'

Alison stared at it, open-mouthed. It wasn't at all what she had expected, given the modern-day preoccupation with all things plastic. Instead this was a beautiful creation, carved from solid mahogany and beautifully varnished so that it gave off a faint sheen.

'What's wrong?' he asked, looking concerned. 'Is it too big?'

'No, nothing like that. I'm amazed, that's all. Surely that must be a work of art? It isn't something you'd buy from any old shop, is it? It must be hand-made.' She crouched down and ran a hand along the smooth slats that made up the seat, and then examined the runners, in the shape of skis, with curved ends that arched up to join with the seat. 'It's fantastic.'

'Actually, my grandfather made it. Well, we made it together. He was the one who showed my sister and me how to scoot down the slopes and how to pull on the rope to guide us where we wanted to go. The guide bit doesn't work all that well, but we had a lot of fun trying it out when we were small. He made it to last.'

'He certainly did.' She stood up, sending him an anxious look. 'Are you sure you want to lend this? I mean, if anything should happen to it I'd be devastated.'

'It's not doing any good in the attic, is it? Besides, Grandad would be pleased to know that children were still getting joy from it.'

He went over to the sink and washed his hands. 'Come and eat,' he said. 'You'll need some food inside you if we're going to face the cold and take Jason and Rachel to explore the slopes.'

She did as he suggested, helping herself to salad and cutting a wedge of cheddar. 'Is you grandfather no longer around?' she asked on a tentative note.

Josh shook his head. 'No, he passed away a long time ago, when I was about ten years old. My grandmother followed soon after. They were wonderful people…and in a way they were my salvation. They were there for my sister and me after our parents divorced.' He stopped then, hesitating as though he'd said too much, and Alison wondered whether she ought to ask him any more about them or whether it would be best to stay silent.

In the end he made up her mind for her. 'My grandmother was a great cook,' he said. 'I remember we would go out collecting blackberries and scrumping apples, and she would turn them into mouthwatering apple and blackberry pies.'

He started to butter a crusty roll as Alison poured the tea. 'She made delicious Christmas puddings, too,' he said, 'and there was always a coin hidden away somewhere inside. We always joked that Grandad would find it and break a tooth on it, but he never did. I think she secretly made sure that one of us children would find it. Then we'd rib one another because the other one had lost, and we'd make up for it later on by pulling the wishbone on the turkey. Of course if the winner had the coin as well a lot of squabbling went on.'

Alison smiled at that. 'When my brother was very young,' she said, 'he asked why it was called the wishbone, and Grandad said it was because the turkey wished it had run faster. So of course my gran told him off and said he was lowering the tone.'

Josh laughed. 'You're a very close family, aren't you?'

'We are.' Her expression became sad. 'I was really looking forward to my grandparents coming over for the Christmas break. Of course that won't happen now.' She sighed. 'You saw him when he was worried and on edge at the hospital, but my grandad's a dear old thing, and he always manages to make us laugh.'

Josh began to carve the ham. 'He was friendly towards me, and he listened to what I said even though he was pre-occupied… And your grandmother seemed like a pretty stoical woman, even though she was still semi-anaesthe-tised and in pain.'

They finished off their meal with fruit for dessert, with Alison telling him how her mother served whipped cream mixed with brandy with the Christmas pudding. 'I've been adding brandy to the Christmas cake I made,' she added. 'It's supposed to keep it moist. You have to add a little every so often, maybe once a week, and then just before the big day I'll ice it and top it with sugar fir trees and snowmen.'

Her smile faded. 'I'm not sure when we'll be eating it, though, now. I don't know what my parents are planning to do about Christmas, now that Gran can't travel. I hate the thought that we'll all be separated.'

'Maybe they'll work something out? Your mother seemed very anxious to stay with your gran and grandad to make sure they were both all right.'

She nodded. 'I suppose they might stay over there for the Christmas period. Fraser will be able to travel down there on the train, but I'll be working.' She glanced at him. 'The same as you… But I expect you'll be spending Christmas with your sister and maybe your mother or father, will you?'

'Possibly. They've asked me, but I haven't finalised anything yet.' He smiled wryly. 'You know how I feel about the holiday season. But, as to your celebrations, it sounds to me as though you would all be sozzled—what with brandy in the cake, and wine with dinner, and brandy cream on the Christmas pudding.'

She laughed. 'More than likely. Mind you, Grandad says he's going teetotal ever since he lost the plot last year and sang "Happy Birthday" when the Queen's Speech came on the television. I actually didn't know you could make the words fit to the tune of "God Save the Queen", but somehow he managed it.'

Josh chuckled. He finished off his tea and started to get to his feet. 'I have to go and see my patient,' he said. 'He'll be here at any moment. I gave him a total knee replacement a few weeks ago, and I need to check that everything's progressing as it should.' He hesitated. 'Feel free to relax—read the paper, watch television, whatever you want while I'm gone. I'll clear away as soon as I come back.'

'Thanks. I'll probably ring my mother and have a chat.'

'Okay.'

Alison ignored what he'd said about clearing up, and sorted it out herself. She stacked the crockery in the dishwasher before sitting down to ring her mother, and then started to wipe down the surfaces in the kitchen.

Josh came back to the apartment after around half an hour. He looked pleased with himself.

'His knee was looking good,' he said. 'He isn't on painkillers any more, and he's walking well. He'll soon be able to drive his car again.'

'Another satisfied customer, then?' Alison glanced at him as she placed a tea towel over the oven bar.

He nodded and glanced around. 'You didn't need to do all this,' he said. 'You've obviously been busy.'

She smiled. 'It means we can set off for my flat. I need to go and take over from Martha. They have some serious present-buying to do once Tom finishes work.'

'He's doing well from what I hear.' Josh picked up the toboggan and went with her to the door. 'The maintenance supervisor says he's a good worker—one of the best.'

Alison was glad about that. Things were looking up for the family next door, and she kept that cheerful thought in mind as they went in search of the children.

They were pleased that she was going to be looking after them, and happy that Josh was with her.

'Come and see what we have in the boot of Josh's car,' she suggested, after they had waved their parents goodbye.

They both stared at the magnificent sledge, their eyes growing large, while Chaser danced around them on the pavement, getting in everyone's way. 'Josh thought you might like to try it out on the slopes by Sawyer's Dell,' she said casually.

'Oh, *wow*... Wicked,' Jason exclaimed.

Rachel's eyes lit up. 'Do we really get to use this?' she asked, looking at Josh for confirmation.

He nodded. 'As long as you wear your bike helmets. Some of those slopes are pretty steep, and we want to make sure you're safe in case of a tumble.'

The little girl jumped around excitedly. 'Brilliant!' she exclaimed. 'My friends are going down to Sawyer's Dell, and I was feeling miserable because I couldn't go with them.'

'Well, that turned out all right, then, didn't it?' Josh grinned.

'Is Chaser coming with us?'

'No, not today,' Alison said. 'We thought he might get in the way of the sledge and be hurt, so I asked Fraser to take him for a walk instead.'

She made sure they were well wrapped up, with coats, hats, scarves and gloves, before she led the children back out to the car and saw to it that they were strapped securely into their seats.

Chaser watched them from the pavement, jumping about and howling in misery as he was prevented from going after them, restrained by the lead that Fraser was holding firmly in his hand. 'Not this time, lad,' Fraser said. 'You're with me. You'll like it, I promise. Maybe not a lot, but it won't be so bad.'

They set off. Just a few minutes later Josh parked his car on the roadside by the hilltop, and lifted the sledge out of the boot.

'We'll try a gentle slope first of all,' he said, position-

ing the toboggan and holding it steady while the children
seated themselves on the wooden slats. 'Jason, you hold
on to the guide rope, and Rachel, you put your arms around
your brother's waist. Hold on tight. Okay?'

They both nodded, and a moment later he gave them a
gentle push to start them on their way. The toboggan slid
effortlessly over the snow-covered hillside, and the
children shrieked with joy as they careered down into the
valley below.

'That was *mega*,' Jason said, breathless from helping to
haul the sledge back up the slope.

Rachel tugged on his coat. 'Let's do it again,' she said.

For the next half hour or so Alison watched as they
raced down the hill, competing with their friends for speed.
'They're having a great time,' she said, gazing up at Josh
and shivering a little from the cold. She stamped her booted
feet in an attempt to warm herself up.

Josh wrapped his arms around her. 'Here, let me give
you some of my heat,' he offered, and she laughed, going
into his firm embrace.

'That's just an excuse,' she said. 'You're as cold as I am.'

'W…w…what m…makes you th…think that?' he
asked, his brows lifting.

She chuckled, and snuggled closer to him. It was a
blissful experience being in his arms like this, and she
found herself wishing that it could go on for ever.

He lowered his head and rested his cheek against hers,
before stealing a brief but definitely determined and pas-
sionate kiss.

'Have I told you I think you're something very special?'
he asked, his breath warm against her cheek. 'You likened

me to Scrooge a while ago. Does that mean that you're my very own Christmas angel, come to save me from myself? I think I like that idea. Even if you *do* have a cold nose.'

She turned to face him fully then, laughing up into his eyes. 'You're pretty wonderful yourself,' she said, 'doing all this to cheer us up. Have I said thank you for that—a very special thank you for all that you've done?'

He nodded. 'I think you may have, but then again there's special and *very* special. What exactly did you have in mind?' He looked hopeful, his gaze heating, his head lowering towards her, his mouth seeking hers once more.

'I'm thirsty.' Jason's voice pierced the warm exclusion zone that surrounded the intimacy of their embrace. 'Can we go home now and have some hot chocolate? Mum always makes it with melted marshmallows on the top.'

Rachel added her voice to the plea. 'I need the toilet,' she said.

The bubble of contentment burst in a flash and Alison blinked, trying to gather her thoughts together. 'Yes, of course,' she said, as Josh's arms gradually released her.

'Can you hold on while Alison and I try out the sledge?' Josh asked, looking down at Rachel.

'Yeah, sure.' Rachel's eyes widened a fraction. 'This is something I want to see. Alison doesn't do sledging, or fairground rides, or anything like that. She says it makes her tummy go funny.'

'We can't let her get away with that, can we?' Josh looked from one to the other, and both children shook their heads.

'No!'

A moment later Alison found herself bundled on to the sledge behind Josh, with instructions to hold on tight. She did as she was told, putting her arms around his waist, closing her eyes and leaning her head against his solid back. She put her trust in him that he would get her there and back in once piece.

They were poised at the top of the longest, steepest slope, and she pulled in a deep breath as he pushed against his heels and started their glide down the hillside. She clung on to him for dear life, her stomach clenching against the swift descent, the cold air whistling past her cheeks, and somehow, in that mad, whirlwind of time, she realised that she had done what she had vowed never to do. She had fallen for him—big-time. Love had crept up on her without warning, without giving her the chance to push it away.

The ride ended in a flurry of snow as they crashed into a snowdrift, and she gasped and spluttered, shaking herself to throw off the impact of what seemed like a dozen or more snowballs. Love, she was discovering, was a chilly, ice-drenching experience.

Josh was grinning from ear to ear. 'You look just like Chaser,' he said, copying her actions and giving himself a good shake, splattering her with even more snow.

'Oh, do I?' She gave him a wicked smile. 'Perhaps you'd better watch what you say—unless you want to haul that sledge up there all by yourself.' She sent a long look over the steep gradient of the hillside. 'Looks quite a marathon from here, doesn't it?'

'Oops,' he said.

Back at the house, Alison made sure that Rachel and Jason changed into warm, dry clothes—while Josh searched Martha's cupboards for chocolate powder and marshmallows. Alison drew the curtains against the darkness, and then they sat in front of the hearth, gazing into a glowing fire. Chaser lay on the rug, blocking a good deal of the heat, his tail thumping with the satisfaction of having his favourite people back where they belonged.

Josh came to join them, handing out hot drinks and home-made cookies, and for a while all was peace and contentment.

Then Josh's phone rang, and he answered the call, listening carefully for a while before getting to his feet.

'I have to go,' he said, snapping the phone shut. 'I've been on call at the hospital since some twenty minutes ago, and they need me to check on a patient who's been brought in. He's a young man—a motorcyclist who came off his bike in a skid.'

'I'm sorry.' Alison followed him from the room as he prepared to leave for the hospital. 'I'm sorry for the motorcyclist and for you, having to set out. It's a shame the day has to end like this. We've all had a lovely time.'

He put his arms around her and kissed her soundly, as though he, too, regretted having to leave. Her lips tingled in the aftermath of that kiss, and she gazed up at him in wonder. It was a kiss of passionate intent—one that spoke volumes without a word being said.

'This wouldn't be happening if I'd listened to my stepfather, would it?' he said with a rueful grimace. 'He said I should have gone into private practice in the States, and I said I'd think about it. I was even offered a job just a couple of weeks ago. If I took that there wouldn't be any late-night calls to take me away.'

She watched him get into his car and drive off. The mist of happiness that had surrounded her all evening suddenly began to dissolve. Was he actually thinking about doing as his stepfather suggested? Was he going to accept the job he had been offered?

She felt nauseous all at once. She had done it again, hadn't she? She had fallen in love with a man who never meant to get involved in a serious long-term relationship—a man whose priorities lay elsewhere. They didn't even share the same principles, a belief in a health system that treated everyone equally.

Only this time it was far worse. This time she knew that her love was the real thing. She loved Josh, despite any faults he might have. She had come to believe that she might share her life with him, and now all that had gone in an explosion of broken dreams.

CHAPTER NINE

ALISON put the children to bed later, tucking each of them under their duvets and planting a kiss lightly on each cheek. 'Sleep tight,' she said, closing the doors to their bedrooms before she made her way quietly downstairs.

Katie knocked on the back door as Alison was rinsing dishes under the tap. She stepped into the room. 'Are Jason and Rachel settled for the night?' she asked, looking around.

Alison nodded. 'I don't suppose it will be long before they're asleep,' she said.

Katie had brought a shopping bag with her. 'I bought loads of things this afternoon. I spent far too much.' She started to empty the bag. 'I thought I'd show you these while Tom and Martha are still out. I bought a cosmetic set for Martha, and a marquetry set for Tom, since he likes making things with wood. And there's a doll for Rachel and a football for Jason. Do you think they'll like the gifts?'

'I'm sure they'll love them.' Alison smiled. 'It sounds as though you had a good shopping trip.'

Katie pulled out a chair and sat down. 'I did. It was lovely in the town centre. There were Salvation Army people singing carols, and stalls in the cobbled square selling hot food. And inside one of the big stores they had a display with Santa's sleigh and reindeer. It was so sweet. There were little elves who nodded their heads and moved their arms, and I saw one little boy talking to them as if they were real.'

'I expect he was telling them what he wanted for Christmas.' Alison smiled. 'I hope his parents were listening and taking notice.'

'That's what Fraser said. Great minds think alike.' Katie started to put her purchases back into the bag. 'I thought Tom and Martha would have been back by now? Didn't you say Martha wanted to tuck the children up in bed?'

Alison nodded. 'She did. But perhaps they needed a bit of extra time to search for gifts—or maybe they stopped to enjoy the atmosphere of the city centre for a bit longer?'

'Maybe.' Katie frowned. 'Where's Josh, by the way? I saw you both go out with the children, and he unloaded a sledge from the back of his car. Seeing how cosy you two have been getting of late, I would have expected him to stay around.'

Alison glanced at her. 'You don't mind the two of us seeing one another outside of work? I know how keen you were on him.'

'Nah. I was just keen on the illusion. Drop-dead gorgeous and at the top of his profession, too…who wouldn't be hooked? But it was just idle fantasy.'

Idle fantasy and illusion… Alison mused on that. Wasn't that exactly what she had been guilty of while she'd been letting her feelings run away with her?

'He had to go back to the hospital,' she said. 'A motor-cyclist came off his bike.'

'Oh, I heard about that. It was on the local radio. A

couple of cars skidded, trying to avoid him, and several people were taken to hospital. That's not good this side of Christmas, is it?'

'No, it isn't.'

Alison made coffee for both of them, and they sat by the kitchen table and chatted for a while, nibbling on cookies. The phone rang, and she brushed crumbs from her mouth, going to answer it.

'Alison?' Josh's voice came over the line, and her heart made a quick jump.

'It's good to hear your voice,' she said. 'How are things? How is the motorcyclist?'

'He'll survive. He has a head injury and a few broken bones, but we've managed to stabilise him, so that's a relief.'

'I'm glad. Does that mean you'll be able to go home now?'

'No...' He hesitated, and Alison was immediately on the alert.

'What's wrong?'

She glanced across the room and saw Katie mouthing a query—'Josh?' She nodded.

'There were a few more people who were injured when the motorcyclist came off his bike.' He paused once again, and then asked, 'Are the children asleep in bed?'

A frisson of alarm rippled through her. 'Yes, they are. I checked up on them a few minutes ago. Why? What's happened? Has something happened to Tom and Martha?'

He let out a slow, heavy breath. 'I'm afraid so. It's nothing too serious... I mean they'll have to stay in hospital for a couple of days, maybe a little longer for Tom, but they're worrying about the children. They don't have any relatives living close by. Do you think you could make arrangements so that Jason and Rachel will be looked after'?'

Alison reached for a chair and sat down. Katie, after seeing how shaken she looked, came to stand beside her, listening in.

'I'll sort something out. What happened? How bad is it?'

'They both have concussion and possible whiplash injuries, which is why we're keeping them under observation. Martha has a dislocated elbow, caused when the steering wheel jerked her arm, and Tom has injured his knee. We're not sure quite how much damage has been done, but he suffered a nasty twisting motion and it's swollen. So far we've done a physical examination and taken X-rays, but I suspect he has a meniscal tear, so he'll probably need surgery.'

'Oh, no. I can't believe this is happening. Just when things were starting to go well for them.'

'Yes, it's bad luck all round.' There was the sound of another voice in the background and he said, 'Anyway, I have to go and check on a patient. I'll see you in the morning.'

He cut the call, and Alison stared blankly ahead for a while. Katie shook her head in bewilderment.

'It doesn't seem fair, does it?' Katie said in shock. 'Just when things were beginning to go right for them. Did I hear him say it was a meniscal tear?'

'That's right. It's been one thing after another, hasn't it? Apart from the pain and discomfort they must both be suffering, it means Tom won't be able to work for several months. It's not the sort of thing that will heal up on its own, is it?'

Katie shook her head. 'He could have a repair operation once the swelling goes down, but the waiting list is probably six months long.' She closed her eyes briefly, thinking about it. 'That poor man. He doesn't deserve any of this.'

'No, he doesn't.' Alison pressed her lips together as she contemplated the enormity of what had happened. 'I have to think of a way to tell the children. That isn't going to be easy, is it? They've only just started to think that there's something to look forward to.'

She thought about it at various intervals through the night, while she tried to get some sleep on the couch in the sitting room. Would Fraser agree to look after them until their parents were able to come home?

Fraser came round to the house first thing in the morning. 'Katie told me what had happened,' he said. 'Have you told the children yet?' Chaser, still half asleep in his bed in the corner of the kitchen, lifted one eyelid.

She shook her head. 'They've only just started to wake up. I'm concentrating on making breakfast and getting them off to school on time. I still haven't worked out what to say to them.'

'You have to go to work, though, don't you? Do you want me to take over? I'll take them to school, and fetch them when it finishes. Between us we'll sort something out.'

She gave him a hug. 'You're a treasure,' she said. 'Thanks.'

'What are you two doing here?' Rachel said, coming into the kitchen, rubbing sleep from her eyes.

'Where's Mum?' Jason looked around. 'Has Dad gone to work? He's left his toolbox over there.' He absently reached down to pat Chaser on the head as the dog bounded around his feet.

Alison tried to appear cheerful, so as not to alarm them. 'Sit down and have some juice, and I'll explain what's happening,' she said. 'I've put your cereals out for you, so you can make a start while I see to the toast.'

'Did they finish all their shopping?' Jason asked. 'I wanted a fire truck for Christmas. I wonder if they bought me one?' His eyes widened. 'Or a ray gun? I *definitely* want a ray gun.'

'You're always thinking about yourself,' Rachel chided. 'I think something's the matter with them… Why else would Allie be making our breakfast?' She looked solemnly at Alison, waiting for her to answer.

'You're right,' Alison said. 'Your mum and dad had a bump in the car last night, when they were coming home, and they've been hurt a little bit. Your mum's banged her elbow, and your dad has hurt his knee.'

'Are they in the hospital?' Jason's eyes were round and unblinking.

'Yes. They have to stay there for a little while.'

'Who's going to look after us?' Ever practical, Jason was concerned about the fundamentals.

'I'll take you to school and bring you home,' Fraser told him. 'After that we'll work something out. You don't need to worry.'

Rachel was clearly thinking on a deeper level. She came over to Alison and rested her head against her. 'Will my mum and dad be all right?'

'I'm sure they will,' Alison said, putting a protective arm around her.

After breakfast she cleared away the dishes, and left the children in Fraser's care. She was anxious to get to work and look in on Tom and Martha, find out how they were bearing up.

Martha, she discovered, was sitting in a chair next to Tom's bed. Her arm was in a sling, and she was wearing a soft supportive collar around her neck.

'It was just a partial dislocation,' Martha told her. 'They gave me a sedative and painkillers, and Josh and a nurse manoeuvred the bones back into place. I have to wear the sling for about three weeks, and after that they say I'll need physiotherapy. It doesn't feel too bad.'

'That's something, at least.' Alison noticed that both she and Tom had saline drips attached to their arms. 'It doesn't look as though they'll be letting you go home for a day or so,' she said.

Martha made a face. 'No. We both had wounds that meant we lost quite a bit of blood. I think they want to make sure our test results are normal before they'll release us.' She pulled in a deep breath. 'Tom had an MRI scan, and Josh told us the shock absorber part of his knee is torn. He'll need an operation to put it right. We've no idea what's going to happen about his job.'

'It could have been worse,' Tom said, and Alison guessed he was trying to put a brave face on things since Martha was becoming anxious. 'We're still alive—and the presents we bought are still intact, so I'm told.' He looked anxiously at Alison. 'Are you sure the children are okay?'

'They're fine. They both want to make cards for you at school, and they're planning to surprise you with a snowman in the back garden. That's if they can persuade Chaser to leave it alone.'

Tom laughed. 'We heard from the police that we can officially keep him, since no one has staked a claim. I don't know whether to be pleased or to start taking anti-depressants. Did I tell you he tried to eat our Christmas tree? I brought it down from the loft, getting ready to put it up in the sitting room, but while I was working out what I'd done with the base he tore a chunk off the top. It's such a mess I haven't had the heart to put it up.'

'It's in the shed,' Martha said. 'Tom reckons that's where the dog should be. In disgrace.'

Alison chuckled. 'I'm glad to see that you're both managing to keep your spirits up, anyway.' She glanced at her watch. 'I have to go. I'm on duty now. But I'll drop by and see you again as soon as I get a free moment.'

Josh was not anywhere to be seen when she went back down to A&E, and she guessed he was taking a break after his unexpected spot of night duty. She missed him. She wanted the chance to talk to him properly, to find out whether her feelings for him were truly misplaced. Was he going to be staying around, and if so had he changed his mind about relationships not lasting?

It was easy to understand why he felt that way. Having witnessed his parents' acrimonious divorce, and suffered the aftermath, who could blame him for losing faith in the possibility of true love? It was just that she didn't think she could cope with a loose-ended relationship. She had realised that she was an all-or-nothing kind of woman.

For the next several hours she tended to the patients who were unfortunate enough to come into the emergency department. Most were straightforward accident victims, but one was a man who had just returned from a trip abroad and discovered an insect bite that had started to give him a good deal of trouble.

Alison suspected a parasitic infection, and referred him to the tropical medicine consultant.

She was typing up her notes when her pager bleeped, and she saw that she was being called to the women's surgical ward. She frowned, wondering what was afoot, and then remembered the nurse who had told her about Mrs Brackley.

Was Rees back in the hospital, visiting the woman? She finished dealing with the open file, and then hurried up to the ward to find out what was happening.

'Hi, Alison,' the nurse greeted her. 'I thought you'd like to know that the young man is back here today. He looks a lot happier than usual, and his hand seems to have healed up nicely. At least, he isn't wearing a dressing on it any longer.'

'Thanks for letting me know,' Alison said. She peeked along the ward, debating whether to take a chance and disturb him, or wait until he came out of the bay.

She waited, chatting to the nurse about this and that, until after a few minutes Rees emerged from the bay and started to walk towards her.

'Rees, it's good to see you,' she said, and he came to a sudden halt, as though he was surprised to be acknowledged.

The nurse moved away, going to check on her patients. 'Doctor?' Rees stared at her for a moment, and then his mouth curved in a smile. 'Hello. I wasn't expecting to see you up here.'

'No. Nor me you.' She gave him a fleeting scrutiny. 'You're looking good,' she said. 'How are you? Has your chest infection cleared up?'

'Yeah. I'm doing okay,' he answered with a shrug. 'Your friend Jack set me up in a hostel with some other lads. It's good there. You were right. He's okay.'

'I'm glad to hear it.' She looked at his hand. 'I see you've had your stitches taken out. How does the hand feel?'

'It's good.' He demonstrated how he could open and close his fist.

'I'm pleased about that.' She looked beyond him to the bay he had come from. 'I see you're visiting someone? Is everything all right?'

He nodded, and then his mouth flattened. 'I don't want it to get out that I'm here. You won't tell anyone, right? You won't tell Jack?'

'Of course not…unless you want me to. Is there a problem? I'm sure Jack would help you if he could.'

He looked doubtful. 'I can trust you, can't I? You won't say anything to anyone?'

'You can.'

He seemed to relax a fraction. 'It's my mum, see. She was beaten up, and we had to get away because my stepdad would have come after us. He punched her, and then he went for her with a bottle, but I managed to stop him.' He pulled in a ragged breath. 'I hit him over the head with a broom handle and he fell down. I pulled my mum outside the house and my mate helped me take her away from there, so he couldn't find us. Then I called the ambulance.'

'Is that how your hand came to be injured? You got in the way of him attacking your mother?'

He nodded, but he was looking scared—as though he had said too much.

'Why didn't you tell anyone?' Alison was baffled. 'The ambulancemen, for instance?'

'Because I'd hit him…my stepdad, I mean. I think he was only dazed, because he fell and he'd had too much to drink, but I didn't go back to find out. I thought the police would lock me up. I wouldn't be able to look after my mum then, would I?'

Alison laid a gentle hand on his arm. 'Rees, you were defending yourself and your mother. You were doing what you had to do. Your injury and your mother's injuries are proof of that.'

His expression was uncertain. 'What if I hurt him badly?'

'Your friend would be able to tell you if he's all right, wouldn't he? Haven't you seen him?'

He shook his head. 'I've not been back.'

'Then I think you should tell Jack what happened, just as you've told me. Let him deal with it for you. He's had experience of this kind of thing. He'll help you, I promise.'

They started to walk towards the door. 'You really think so?' he said.

'I do.'

She parted company with Rees by the lifts, and when he headed down the stairs to the rear exit of the hospital she took the lift down to A&E. She hoped he *would* confide in her friend Jack.

Josh was back in the department, looking at the MRI scans of Tom's knee.

'What's the verdict?' she asked, going to stand alongside him.

'His best chance of decent recovery is to have keyhole surgery to remove the damaged portion of the meniscus. That way, with physiotherapy, he could be back at work in around four weeks. A more complicated repair would mean several months before he could return to work, and it might not achieve a particularly good result.'

She winced. 'Either way, he has a long wait ahead of him. I checked the schedules for surgery, and most of the surgeons have waiting lists.'

'Hmm. There's another possibility, of course.'

'Is there?' She sent him a puzzled look. 'Apart from private surgery I don't see what option there is. And you know as well as I do that he can't afford that. He doesn't have medical insurance.'

Josh made a wry smile. 'Oh, ye of little faith. There are ways of sorting these things out.'

'There are?'

'Oh, yes. You perhaps aren't up to date with the details because you work solely in A&E, but the health service has been buying in services from the private sector for quite some time. Some people are fast-tracked for things like MRI scans or eye treatment. At the moment there's a drive to clear orthopaedic surgery cases, among others, and that's where I come in. I can arrange for Tom to be put on *my* operating list.'

She stared at him open-mouthed, prompting him to smile and bring up a curved fist to gently close her jaw. 'I'd do the operation without charge, but Tom's a proud man and I have a strong feeling his pride would get in the way of him accepting... Or he would put himself in the difficult position of making sure he paid the charge at a later date. This way seems the easier option.'

Alison managed to find her voice at last. 'If we weren't in a public place, I'd kiss you.'

Flame sparked in his eyes. 'And if I didn't have a ton of urgent work to get through I'd whisk you out of here and take you up on that offer.' His mouth curved as his gaze drifted over her. 'Only I'd probably want to do a whole lot more than simply kiss.'

A tide of heat flooded her cheeks. 'You're only saying that because Tom's incapacitated and can't watch over me,' she said with a teasing smile. 'You're forgetting that my brother's still around to make sure your intentions are honourable.'

'Oh, shoot.' He contrived to look crestfallen. 'You're right. He's looking after the children, isn't he? And those two youngsters have a way of cutting in on the act too.' He shook his head. 'Never mind, I'll figure something out.'

She didn't know whether that was a threat or a promise, but either way she couldn't help thinking it would be good to have Josh hold her and kiss her and tell her that everything was going to turn out just fine.

She had her doubts. Josh wanted her, that was for sure, but he had made no mention of love or commitment. Perhaps those words weren't in his vocabulary?

And as to the rest… Christmas was just a few days away, but it was nigh on cancelled in several households. Her grandparents, her parents, and now Tom and Martha were struggling to find a reason to celebrate. And what of Rees and his mother? And poor Fraser, who still didn't know whether he had a career in pharmacy ahead of him.

And the weather was closing in. A steady fall of snow had blocked the roads and led to police warnings for people to stay at home where possible. As if *she* could do that.

She finished the rest of her shift, trying to keep her mind occupied with positive thoughts. Her patients would recover from their injuries. She would see to that. She put them first and gave them the best care possible.

Josh followed her home. 'I wanted to make sure you and Katie were safe on these icy roads,' he said.

'You are so sweet,' Katie murmured, sliding out of the passenger seat as he held open the car door for her. 'But the truth is you wanted to be with Alison, isn't that right?' She gave him a long, thoughtful stare. 'She's been hurt before, you know. Play with her feelings and you have to answer to us.'

Alison nudged her in the ribs. 'I can take care of myself, Katie. Now, scoot into the house and tell Taylor and Sam to clear up the mess they made last night. I have to go and check on Fraser and the children.'

'How do you know they made a mess?'

'When don't they?'

'True.' Katie nodded and went into the house, leaving Alison to park the car in the garage and head next door.

'Come in and I'll make some soup,' Alison said, gesturing to Josh to follow. 'I doubt Fraser will have thought to make something hot for the children. He can run to sandwiches, or maybe even toast, but his culinary skills don't extend much further than that.'

Fraser was already in the kitchen, but he looked pale and anxious, and Chaser was whining—a pathetic, mournful sound that grated on the ears. In the corner of the kitchen a scattering of broken wood pieces surrounded the wicker bed that Martha had managed to obtain for him, and there were teeth marks all around the edges of the bed. Chaser had been busy.

Josh went over to the dog, stroking his head and tickling him behind the ears.

Alison knew something was wrong. Despite his problems, Fraser was usually outgoing and full of life.

'What's the matter?' she asked. A shiver of fear clutched her chest. 'Is it Gran? Has something happened to her? Has she had a relapse of some sort?'

Fraser shook his head, almost as though he couldn't bring himself to speak. 'No,' he managed finally. 'Nothing like that.'

'What is it then?' She gazed around the kitchen and peered into the sitting room. There was no noise—no sound of children's voices. 'Where are Jason and Rachel?' she asked. 'Did you pick them up from school?'

He nodded and tried to speak, but his voice was strained and no sound would come out. He tried again. 'I've lost them. I'm useless. I gave them milk and biscuits and said they should go and play in their bedrooms while I finished off some work I was doing. Then Dad rang, and I spoke to him for…what…? fifteen minutes…no more than that, I swear. When I went to check on them, they'd disappeared.'

'Have you looked outside?' Josh was already peering out into the darkness of the garden.

'Of course I have. There aren't even any footprints because the snow has covered everything.'

'You've shouted? Called their names?' Alison was concerned, her conscious mind telling her that nothing major could have happened to them, but her subconscious was working overtime.

'Yes…yes, I've done all that. I've looked all through the house. I've checked every nook and cranny in case they were playing hide and seek. I don't know where they are. I've even told Chaser to go through all the rooms, but they're not in the house.'

Josh was thoughtful. 'There's only one thing to be

done, then. We'll let Chaser loose outside and see if *he* can find them.'

'We'd better put him on the lead,' Alison said. 'I don't want to have to tell Tom and Martha we lost him, too.'

Despite the seriousness of the occasion, Josh gave her a look of wry amusement. 'I'm not so sure Tom wouldn't be inclined to thank you for that.'

Alison hooked the lead on Chaser's collar and opened the back door. The dog raced outside like an animal starved of all the good things in life and, nose down, followed a zigzag path all over the garden. Then, confused, he followed his tail for a while, before taking off once more and hurtling in the direction of the shed. There he stood, barking and whining and causing so much commotion that Katie, Taylor and Sam came out to see what was going on.

Fraser opened the shed door and peered into the darkness. 'It's pitch-black in here,' he said. 'I can't see a thing.'

Chaser dashed inside, sending brooms and spades and garden tools crashing to the floor. They heard a child's muted shriek, and then Rachel's voice said, 'Get off, Chaser. Stop slobbering over me.'

'Now you've given the game away,' Jason said crossly. 'And I bet it's your fault they found us. I told you to keep the torch switched off. Now they'll take us away and make us live in a children's home. It's all your fault, Rachel. Why couldn't you keep quiet? Ouch. Chaser—get off me.'

Alison let out a huge sigh of relief. She let go of the dog's lead and turned towards Josh, who obligingly held her tight and let her cry out her feelings all over his leather jacket.

They all trooped back towards the house. Reassured, now that the children had been found safe and well, Alison remembered that Fraser had said he'd spoken to their father on the phone.

'Did Dad call for a special reason?' she asked him as they went into the kitchen. 'Or was it just for a chat? You said Gran was all right?'

'She's fine—healing up nicely, he said.' Fraser relaxed for the first time since she'd arrived home. 'He called to tell me that he spoke to the Dean about me being sent down from university, and apparently between them they worked out a solution. The Dean's going to put it to the committee that I acted with the best of intentions, and they're going to look into the possibility of changing the rules on internet use. He seemed to accept that I hadn't been cheating in any way, and he says he's sure I'll be allowed back there next term.'

Alison laid a gentle hand on his arm. 'That's wonderful news. You must be really pleased.'

He nodded. 'It's been a worry. It didn't occur to me that Dad would talk to the Dean, but I'm glad he did.'

They concentrated on looking after the children after that, with Alison making hot soup while Josh and Fraser did what they could to warm the children and make sure they'd suffered no ill effects from their time in the shed.

Later, when they were seated around the kitchen table, enjoying soup and crusty rolls along with hot jacket potatoes, and the dog had been treated to extra rations for finding them, Alison explained to the children that there was no chance of them being taken to a children's home.

'But that's what the Year Six children said at school,' Rachel protested. 'They said if your parents aren't there for you you have to be taken away.'

'They said you don't get the chance to say you don't want to go. They just come and take you anyway.' Jason added his piece.

'That's not going to happen,' Alison said. 'We're going to look after you—Fraser and me—until your parents come home.'

'Really?'

'Really.'

There was a short silence. 'Will they be back for Christmas?' Jason asked. 'Will we still get our presents?'

Rachel glared at him. 'That's not important,' she said.

'Yes, it is. Why are you looking at me like that? I didn't do anything wrong.'

Fraser cut into the argument. 'Tell you what,' he said, 'if you two go upstairs and get ready for bed, I promise you that tomorrow we'll put up some Christmas decorations and make the place ready for when your mum and dad come home.'

'Yes!' Jason said, making a victory salute.

'Chaser ate the top of the tree,' Rachel said, looking doubtful.

'I know.' Fraser pulled a face. 'We'll sort something out.'

An hour later the children were fast asleep in bed, and Fraser went next door to listen to music through his headphones.

Alison sank down on the settee, exhausted by the day's events. Josh came and sat down beside her, sliding an arm around her.

'Everything's turned out for the best, hasn't it?' he said. 'The children are happy now, and I've arranged to operate on Tom's knee the day after tomorrow. Both he and Martha will be out of hospital in time for Christmas… But you still look sad. Do you want to tell me about it?'

She snuggled up against him. How could she tell him that she wanted him to stay with her for ever and a day? With him by her side she could face pretty much anything.

'I'm fine,' she said. 'I suppose I'm feeling a little strange because nothing has gone quite the way I planned. It'll be Christmas in a few days, and usually it follows a lovely, comfortable pattern. I'm unsettled, a bit worried about how things will turn out. But that can't compare with a fraction of what you go through every year.'

She gazed up at him. 'What are you going to do about Christmas?' she asked softly. 'Have you made up your mind? If you haven't, you could come with me and spend Christmas with my family. My parents are going to stay over at my grandparents' house, but I know they would all welcome you. I'd like you to be there…but of course I understand if you've already made arrangements to go home.'

More than anything she wanted him to spend the time with her, but she wasn't going to be selfish and ask him to upset his mother's plans, or his father's, or even his own.

'Thank you for that.' He dropped a kiss on her forehead. 'You know, I haven't given it much thought over these last few weeks. I've been trying to push it to the back of my mind for a long while now.' He flashed her a rueful smile. 'Like you, I'll be working on Christmas morning—my mother knows that, so she's keeping that in mind. She'll have a houseful, with Michelle and the rest of the brood.' He ran his fingers idly through her hair and seemed to be preoccupied. 'What's Fraser going to do about Christmas?'

'I think he's planning to go home on the train on Christmas Eve.'

'That's good.'

He changed the subject, starting to talk of Fraser's good news about university. Alison commented here and there, simply glad to have him near, but as she curled into his arms she gave an inward sigh.

Without Josh the holiday season would seem empty. But he hadn't taken up her invitation, had he? He wasn't offering to spend Christmas with her.

CHAPTER TEN

THE bells rang out at the first stroke of midnight. Alison stood very still and listened as Christmas Eve turned into Christmas Day, and the sound of carols being sung at Midnight Mass floated on the air throughout the emergency department.

Then the music was drowned out by the sudden bleeping of monitors, and Alison hurried into the treatment room where Josh was examining a patient. The man had complained of tightness in his chest, and difficulty in catching his breath.

She could see straight away that he was very ill, in a lot of pain, and his skin was clammy and pale. His ECG reading was erratic.

'I believe you're having a heart attack, Martyn,' Josh said quietly, adjusting the oxygen mask over the man's nose and mouth. 'The paramedic who brought you in here gave you aspirin to help thin your blood, but now we're going to give you medication through a tube in your arm. It will help to break up any clots that might be blocking your circulation.'

Alison was already preparing an infusion of thrombolytic drugs, along with painkilling diamorphine and something to prevent sickness.

'We'll add a beta-blocker to help widen the blood vessels,' Josh said, glancing at Alison, 'and then, once he's stabilised, we'll run some tests.'

They worked with the man for some time, monitoring him and making sure that his distress was eased. Alison was conscious that his wife and young children were anxiously waiting for news in another room, but he was too ill for them to be allowed to see him. It would have been far too upsetting for the children, a boy and girl.

Josh waited until it was clear that Martyn was feeling more comfortable, and appeared to be free from pain and breathing more easily, before he told the nurse she could bring his family in.

'I'll do a nuclear scan of the heart and blood vessels,' Josh said, as he walked with Alison away from the treatment room and into the central area of the department. 'The tracer will pick up any signs of abnormality, and we can decide what to do from there.'

'Poor man. He'll definitely be spending the next few days in hospital.' Alison made a face. 'It must be very hard for his children.' She thought about it for a moment or two, but then her expression lightened. 'It makes me feel so much better to know that Tom and his family are at home together…and all thanks to you.'

'It wasn't just down to me.' He began to walk towards the annexe. 'The team that helped me with the operation deserve some recognition, don't you think? But it was an operation well worth doing. If he sticks to his physiotherapy he'll be back at work within a matter of weeks. His boss will be pleased about that, at any rate. The supervisor thinks it was sheer bad luck, the way things happened.'

'But in the end everything's turned out well because of you.' She went over to the worktop where the percolator was steaming, and started to pour coffee into two mugs. 'I was wrong about private medicine. I take back everything I said.'

He raised his brows at that, and her mouth quirked into a crooked shape. 'Perhaps my opinion was soured by the way my ex-boyfriend behaved. What began as a feeling that the situation was a bit unfair turned into a distaste for practices in medicine that were money-orientated. Perhaps I was simply acting out my unhappiness and frustration for the way Rob treated me. I don't know what I ever saw in him.'

She offered him a cup of coffee, a smile hovering on her lips. 'I realise that you're not at all what I expected of doctors who work in the private sector.'

'So you don't think too badly of me after all?' he murmured, looking at her over the rim of his cup as he sipped the hot liquid. 'There's a chance for me to redeem myself? I'm no longer a lost cause?'

'You know what I think of you,' she said huskily. 'I was full of preconceived ideas, and you've turned all of them on their heads. You're a wonderful man—the best—and I just wish that I could help you to change the way you feel about family and relationships in general.'

He frowned. 'I love my family. And I told you once before, I do care about people. I just think relationships become skewed somewhere along the way.'

'Not all of them.' She smiled. 'I spent the evening with Tom and his family, and despite their injuries they are so happy together.'

She had hoped that Josh would come and join them for the evening, but he had disappeared after finishing his shift and hadn't answered his phone when she rang him.

Perhaps his feelings for her were as he had said in the beginning…light with no strings, just a fun arrangement.

She tried to shake off the thought. 'Jason and Rachel were tucked up in bed, dreaming of dolls and fire trucks and happy family gatherings, I imagine. The whole house was filled with the joy of the Christmas season, though I dare say a lot of that was down to Fraser's handiwork. He decorated it with beautiful Christmas bells, and mobiles that catch the light, and he even managed to rescue the tree. It's covered in baubles—in a bit of a haphazard fashion, because the children did most of it and one or two of the baubles had to be thrown away after Chaser tried to get in on the act—but Fraser stuck a huge star on the top, and it makes the whole thing look perfect, somehow.'

Josh smiled. 'I'm glad everything's worked out well for them. You're right. They're a lovely example of how things can be within a family, aren't they?' His expression changed, becoming darker. 'It's very much like that with the family who are here with us today. They seem to be a strong family unit. I just hope we can pull Martyn through and give him the chance to enjoy being part of it for a lot longer.'

Alison would have answered, but a nurse came to the annexe then, saying, 'You're needed in Resus, Josh. There's a woman suffering an asthma attack.' She turned to Alison. 'And someone in the treatment room needs stitches to his arm.'

And so it was for the next few hours. Alison hardly had time to think about the fact that it was actually Christmas

Day. If it hadn't been for one of the nurses setting up a nativity scene in Reception—a wooden stable, with a manger filled with straw and the baby Jesus in his mother's arms, Joseph looking on—she might even have missed the significance of the day.

That same nurse seemed to sprinkle a liberal helping of Christmas cheer around the department. 'There's someone to see you, Alison,' she said. 'He's in the waiting room.'

Who did she know from around here that would make a point of coming to see her? Her curiosity aroused, Alison went to see who it was, and when she opened the door and saw Rees standing there her heart gave a little flip. But he wasn't alone. Her friend Jack was with him, along with a woman Alison guessed must be Rees's mother.

'Rees—Jack. I'm so pleased to see you,' Alison said. She nodded a greeting towards the woman, who smiled back at her.

'I just came to say hello, Happy Christmas, and thanks for putting me in touch with Jack,' Rees said. 'Everything's changed since I talked to you, and Jack has helped me to sort things out.' He put an arm around the woman, holding her in a warm embrace. 'This is my mother,' he said. 'She was hurt, but now she's so much better, and we're going to make a fresh start—thanks to Jack.'

'I'm so glad for you,' Alison said. 'I knew things would work out if you told Jack what was going on.'

Jack came and gave her a hug. 'I've managed to find them a house to rent, and the police are dealing with Rees's stepdad. He won't be causing them any more trouble, and I'll be there to keep an eye on them, make sure they're all right.' He smiled. 'In fact we're all having Christmas dinner together at the house, so I'm hoping things are looking up all round.'

'That's great news.' Alison looked at Rees's mother. 'I'm pleased you have somewhere to stay. Jack's a good man. I knew he would help you.'

The woman nodded, her lips curving. 'Yes, he is.' She reached out and took Alison's hand in hers. 'I wanted to say thank you for looking after my son. We both appreciate it—very much.'

'You're welcome. Any time.'

Alison went back to A&E in a jaunty mood, and she was more than ready to assist Josh when he judged Martyn well enough to be taken to Radiology.

'I'm going to inject a small amount of a tracer substance into your vein,' he told Martyn. 'When the scanner is in operation it will show us images on the computer monitor, and if there are any blockages in your blood vessels we'll be able to see them. We'll also be able to tell if there are any problems with your heart.'

A few minutes later Josh and Alison retreated into the computer room beyond the scanner. The images that came up on screen were crystal-clear.

'There's a massive blockage in the coronary artery,' Alison said, watching the screen. 'I'd say he was a candidate for angiography, wouldn't you?'

Josh nodded. 'And I think we should do it this morning. Before the clot has a chance to cut off the blood supply any further and cause damage to the heart muscle. We can't afford to wait or he might not see next year. I don't want to even contemplate the possibility of those children losing

their father. I'll book the angiography suite for the procedure. We'll take a couple of hours, to enable us to talk to
him and his wife about what's involved and to prepare him.'

Alison was fully conscious of what was at stake here.
Josh was always calm and in control, and she knew how
skilled he was as a vascular surgeon, but would he be able
to save this man's life? She didn't dare think about what
might go wrong.

Despite their worries, the atmosphere in A&E was light
as the staff worked to bring about a feeling of seasonal
goodwill. And somewhere around mid morning Josh's
voice came out over the hospital radio, announcing the
imminent arrival of a very special visitor. Alison put down
the lab test results she was reading and listened. His alter-
egos, the wacky duck and the downtrodden dog, had a
comical, animated conversation about the event, hotly
debating the question of who the visitor might be, and
what it was that could be wrong with him. In the end, as
they apparently saw the man coming in through the door,
they decided the problem was that he'd been eating too
many pies and must have a huge tummy ache.

The maintenance supervisor walked into Reception just
then, heavily disguised and padded out as Santa Claus, and
began distributing presents to any children who were unfortunate enough to be spending the day there. With a
twinkle in his eyes he stooped down to talk to Martyn's
children, and then pressed large parcels into their hands.
They gazed up at him in open-mouthed wonder, their eyes
wide, and then hastily began to tug the wrapping paper
from their gifts.

'I've got a racing car,' the boy exclaimed. 'Look, Mum,

it goes all by itself.' The car zoomed along the floor of the waiting room, shooting out into the reception area.

'That's great,' his mother said, smiling in spite of her anxiety about her husband's condition. 'But bring it back in here, where it won't get under people's feet.'

The little girl carefully opened up her box and lifted out a baby doll in a cradle. 'She has her own feeding bottle,' she said, her voice tinged with excitement. 'Isn't she lovely? My very own baby.'

Alison watched them. Now all she and Josh had to do was make sure that Martyn would be around to stay with them through the coming years.

Josh came back into A&E after finishing the live part of his broadcast. His stride was vigorous and he exuded energy, so that Alison, watching him, felt her heart skip a beat.

'I think we're all set up to go ahead with the operation,' he said, walking with her to the observation ward where Martyn was resting. 'I'd like you to administer the sedative and keep an eye on his blood pressure. I'll prepare the stents, and the nurse will help to keep him calm and relaxed.'

Josh had to insert a catheter into a blood vessel in Martyn's leg. From there it passed into the artery of the heart, and Josh had to work using tiny instruments on the end of the catheter to remove the blood clot that was causing so much trouble. If the clot broke up and split into smaller pieces there was a risk that Martyn would suffer another heart attack.

She gave a sigh of relief when he sucked the clot back through the tube. 'Okay, let's get the stents in place,' he said. The stents were small wire mesh tubes that were inserted into the artery to hold open the blood vessel. They remained in place, allowing the blood to circulate freely around the heart.

'You did it,' Alison said, smiling up at him as he left the angiography suite a few minutes later. He'd changed out of his green scrubs and was wearing a crisp pale-coloured shirt and dark grey trousers. He looked immaculate. She wanted to hug him there and then. 'You saved his life.'

'That's why we do this job, isn't it?' he answered in a droll fashion. 'To save lives so that people can be with their loved ones.' They walked together along the corridor until they reached the lift bay. 'And that's exactly what I want to do. I want to spend Christmas with the person I love most in all my life.' He pressed the button for the lift and then gazed at her. 'I want to spend it with you...not just for now, but for all the Christmases to come.'

She was stunned by his words. 'You love me?' she said. 'Am I hearing this right or am I imagining things? Am I caught up in the middle of a dream? Tell me again what you just said.'

The lift doors opened and they both walked inside, waiting until the lift doors closed on them.

He reached for her, his mouth curving as he drew her into his embrace. 'I love you,' he said. 'I've wanted to tell you for such a long time, but I thought you were sworn off men after Rob. And I had this worry that love is something fickle that never lasts. I was afraid that I'd be forever living on the outside, looking in.'

His hand stroked her, gliding along the length of her spine, leaving a trail of fire in its wake. 'Then I realised that I've never loved anyone before this. I've never felt so completely out of my depth. But I know that with you my life will be complete. I've discovered that love *can* be for ever, and that people can grow old together and know the joy of being a contented, loving family. I saw that when I met your parents, your grandparents and your brother.' His hands lifted to stroke the golden strands of her hair. 'And, yes, I would love to go with you to your grandparents' house and stay with you over Christmas.'

She laid her head against his chest, sighing in content-ment. Then, on a sudden thought, she looked up at him and said, 'What about your mother? Won't she be expecting you to go and be with her?'

'I think she'll understand. I went to see her last night and we had a long talk. I told her how I feel about you, and she told me to forget about the problems that she and my father had and go with my instincts.'

'And that's what you've done?'

He nodded, but Alison was still uncertain. 'What about your notion of working in the States? Is that still on the cards?'

'It was never an option. I just said that I would think about it, but I already knew I preferred to work here. After I met you it was never going to be something I would consider. I know how much your family means to you.'

She lifted her hands and cupped his face, drawing him gently down towards her so that her lips made fiery, pas-sionate contact with his. 'I'm so happy to hear you say all that,' she whispered. 'I've known for a long while now that you're the only man for me. I love you so much.'

The lift doors opened and they both stared bemusedly out into the corridor. 'I don't remember pressing the button for the ground floor,' he said. 'But perhaps it's just as well that we're here now.'

'Is it? Why?' She looked at him in confusion as he led the way outside the hospital to a paved area in a secluded spot, bordered by trees and shrubs.

'Because otherwise I might have ended up proposing to you in a lift. That would never do, would it? Imagine telling our children that I proposed in a hospital lift. Even I have more romance in my bones than that.'

'Our children?' she murmured. 'Isn't that jumping the gun a bit? You haven't actually asked me anything yet.'

'Oh… Well, I can sort *that*,' he said. Then he smiled, and it was like the sun glittering on a wide blue sea. 'Will you marry me, Alison? Please? Will you be my wife and share my life and my family, share all your Christmases with me from now on?'

'I will,' she answered softly.

He wrapped his arms around her and kissed her—a thorough, sweet, perfect kiss that sent the blood straight to her head and made her toes curl. 'You've made my dreams come true,' he said softly. 'You're everything I've ever wanted.'

'Me, too. That's exactly how I feel about you.'

He kissed her again—a long, wonderful kiss that left her heady with delight. Then he looked down at her, his fingers tracing the contours of her face.

'I love you,' he said again, then seemed to hesitate. 'Alison…?' he murmured, breaking off his words.

'Yes?'

'Let's go inside, shall we? It's freezing out here.'

CHRISTMAS AT
RIVERCUT MANOR

BY
GILL SANDERSON

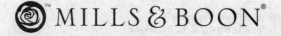

All the characters in this book have no existence outside the imagination of the author, and have no relation whatsoever to anyone bearing the same name or names. They are not even distantly inspired by any individual known or unknown to the author, and all the incidents are pure invention.

All Rights Reserved including the right of reproduction in whole or in part in any form. This edition is published by arrangement with Harlequin Enterprises II BV/S.à.r.l. The text of this publication or any part thereof may not be reproduced or transmitted in any form or by any means, electronic or mechanical, including photocopying, recording, storage in an information retrieval system, or otherwise, without the written permission of the publisher.

This book is sold subject to the condition that it shall not, by way of trade or otherwise, be lent, resold, hired out or otherwise circulated without the prior consent of the publisher in any form of binding or cover other than that in which it is published and without a similar condition including this condition being imposed on the subsequent purchaser.

® and TM are trademarks owned and used by the trademark owner and/or its licensee. Trademarks marked with ® are registered with the United Kingdom Patent Office and/or the Office for Harmonisation in the Internal Market and in other countries.

First published in Great Britain 2009
Harlequin Mills & Boon Limited,
Eton House, 18-24 Paradise Road, Richmond, Surrey TW9 1SR

© Gill Sanderson 2009

ISBN: 978 0 263 86884 5

Set in Times Roman 10½ on 13¼ pt
03-1209-53088

Harlequin Mills & Boon policy is to use papers that are natural, renewable and recyclable products and made from wood grown in sustainable forests. The logging and manufacturing process conform to the legal environmental regulations of the country of origin.

Printed and bound in Spain
by Litografia Rosés, S.A., Barcelona

Gill Sanderson, aka Roger Sanderson, started writing as a husband-and-wife team. At first Gill created the storyline, characters and background, asking Roger to help with the actual writing. But her job became more and more time-consuming, and he took over all of the work. He loves it!

Roger has written many Medical™ Romance books for Harlequin Mills & Boon®. Ideas come from three of his children—Helen is a midwife, Adam a health visitor, Mark a consultant oncologist. Weekdays are for work; weekends find Roger walking in the Lake District or Wales.

Recent titles by the same author:

THE COUNTRY DOCTOR'S DAUGHTER
THE MIDWIFE AND THE SINGLE DAD
A MOTHER FOR HIS SON
NURSE BRIDE, BAYSIDE WEDDING*

Brides of Penhally Bay

To Oliver and Joe, latest grandchildren.
Have a good life.

CHAPTER ONE

DISTRICT NURSE Grace Fellowes looked at the patient in front of her with mild exasperation. The trouble with these moors farmers—even ones like Albert who'd long since handed over the reins to his son—was that they thought if they slowed down for more than a few minutes they'd be dead. She put on a severe expression. 'You've been walking on this leg, haven't you?'

Albert shifted his ulcerated leg irritably on the foot-stool. 'Give over, young Grace. As if you haven't already found out from my boy that I just stepped down to the barn to run my eye over the flock and a sheep got in my way.'

'I'm not young Grace today, I'm your nurse and I know what I'm talking about. One in fifty people over the age of eighty get ulcers like yours and because of your blood-pressure problems there isn't enough new blood getting to the tissue to repair it very quickly.'

In truth, almost the only hope with venous ulcers was to dress the wound and then cover it with a compression bandage, but Grace didn't mention that. 'We've kept the germs out so far, but you must be more careful when you move about. Your son's right to be worried about you. How does your leg feel now?'

'Not too bad. Sometimes it itches, sometimes there's a sort of heavy feeling.' He watched as Grace dusted on the dressing, then covered the ulcer with an antiseptic pad and eased on the elasticated support stocking. 'Thanks, lass. That's tight, but I can feel it working. Still seems odd, you junketing all over the moors to see to us. Who'd have thought twenty years ago that young Grace Fellowes from Rivercut Manor would grow up to be our district nurse.'

Grace stood, went to wash her hands in the sink at the side of the farmhouse kitchen and then put on her fleece jacket. 'Be glad I am,' she said lightly. 'You might have a fearsome stranger telling you off instead. I'll be back in a week for another look. Any problem before that—give me a ring. And don't go banging into anything!'

'I suppose,' said Albert. He hesitated. 'Before you go— I'm sorry you've had to put the old place up for sale.'

Grace swallowed. 'Ah, well. That's life. I'm luckier than most. I've got a job I love, a cottage that needs hardly any housework and the nicest patients in the world.' She blinked to clear her eyes and walked quickly to the farmhouse porch, slipping her feet out of her comfortable flatties and into her Wellingtons. It might look a bit odd—a nurse in a smart blue uniform with rubber boots up to her knees—but in most farmyards it was necessary even when they weren't ankle-deep in snow like today. A couple of quick words with Albert's son and then she was back in her car.

As she drove through the high moor tops Grace grinned. 'Young Grace from the Manor' indeed! When was Rivercut valley going to emerge into the twenty-first century? It was

GILL SANDERSON 9

a bit isolated—but not that much. You could get to London from York in three hours. Then she chuckled. Provided you could get to York at all with the North Yorkshire moors snowed up as they were at the moment.

The back road she was on dropped down into a narrow valley. She slowed, seeing that the surface ahead was covered in water. This often happened in winter—the drain under the road was just not big enough to cope with the stream that ran through it. It was fortunate that Grace had grown up here and knew all about the local hazards. Her elderly Land Rover only skidded a little as she carefully drove through the flood.

Climbing the hill again, she caught her breath at how beautiful the countryside was with its blanket of white. Snow had come very early this year—this was only the beginning of December. And the forecast was that the snow was going to last. She knew a cold winter would cause trouble but they were used to it round here. Garages would be stocked with snow chains and antifreeze, dispensaries would have supplies of cough linctus and crutches.

Grace's next call was at a village called Nestoby. Not that anyone in the large Leeds nursing college where she had done her training would have called it a village. There was only a handful of houses, no pub or post office, just a corner shop that sold an incredible range of goods even though it was situated in the front room of a cottage.

Mr and Mrs Kipps ran the shop—and had done for the past forty years. They'd taken it over from Mrs Kipps's parents. Grace parked outside, opened the shop door and was greeted by an outburst of coughing. She looked at the wizened figure bent double behind the counter. 'Not doing very well, are we, Mr Kipps?' she asked sympathetically.

Mr Kipps was suffering from emphysema. He had smoked all his life until he'd had a bad attack of bronchitis which had laid him up for months. Even so, James Curtis—the GP Grace worked for—had had to put the fear of God into him before he had been persuaded to stop. Now Grace called in regularly to check up on Mr Kipps's condition and to arrange for physiotherapy visits to drain his lungs of fluid.

Mrs Kipps came through to look after the shop. She was a large, unsmiling woman and as a child Grace had found her rather frightening until she had realised her bark was worse than her bite, and most of that barking was directed at the lads who were intent on getting tuppence out of their penny-worth of sweets. 'I'm sorry about the manor,' Mrs Kipps said abruptly now.

Grace gave a rueful smile. 'Thanks, but it's the way of the world. I just hope I can sell it to a family who want to make a home rather than to some faceless company to use for corporate entertaining.' She followed Mr Kipps into the back room to take his blood pressure, listen to his heart and check up on his general well-being. His condition was as good as could be expected for a man who had smoked forty a day for more years than the twenty-eight Grace had been alive.

'How are you feeling?' she asked. 'Not too much pain from the coughing? I know these cold days must be hard on you.'

A voice came from the shop. 'He came home late last Wednesday with the smell of tobacco on him. Told me it was because he'd walked home with one of our neighbours who smokes. I told him that if I found him with a cigarette in his mouth, he'd be out on the moors all night with only his cigarettes to keep him warm.'

'I wasn't smoking!' Mr Kipps wailed.

Grace decided to say nothing. The situation appeared to be under control.

Outside it was snowing again, the hard small snow-flakes that landed and settled adding another layer to the smooth, soft outlines of the winter landscape. Grace loved the way snow turned the moors into a whole new land, more beautiful even than the myriad greens of the heather and scrub. She could forgive it making the drive to her last call of the day tricky. She noticed that the Christmas spirit seemed to be abroad. All the isolated farmhouses on the way to Fellowes Top had illuminated Christmas trees in the windows. Grace felt an excited wriggle inside her at the sight. She did love Christmas.

At Fellowes Top Farm she made short shrift of Young Jack Stanley (so called to distinguish him from Old Jack Stanley, his father), who seemed to think that the proper care of a pitchfork wound in his upper leg so deep that it had only just missed the femoral artery was to sweep up slurry in the pigsty. Leaving him chastened, she set off for home. It was a longish journey, Fellowes Top being the most outlying of the properties her family had once owned, but Grace quite liked a drive at the end of a good day. It gave her a chance to unwind from the busyness of health issues resolved and problems fixed.

It was dusk now and the snow was still falling. Grace's dashboard thermometer indicated that the temperature was well below freezing. She snuggled further inside her warm fleece as she drove, thankful that the Land Rover had four-wheel drive. She really must make room in next week's schedule for a service. Maybe Bert Machin wouldn't charge her too much, especially as he would also have heard about the manor going up for sale. Grace bit her lip. Everybody this afternoon had mentioned it, saying how sad it was and how brave Grace was being. And Grace had smiled cheerfully and uttered platitudes and hadn't admitted once that it was tearing her apart to have to sell her childhood home in order to pay off the twin burden of death duties and her mother's debts.

She blinked back tears and concentrated on the road— and realised with a spasm of alarm that she'd automatically chosen the shorter cross-country route home from the farm instead of the gritted main road. Oh, heck, she'd really need her wits about her now. Still, she'd driven along part of it earlier and it had been okay. She'd just have to be extra-careful.

She was miles from the nearest farm when the accident happened. She was taking a right-angle bend, not at all too fast, when the rear wheels broke away and slid sideways. She couldn't believe it! She did everything correctly, didn't over-steer, braked very gently and steered into the direction of the skid. All to no avail. She was coming off the road.

At quite a slow speed the Land Rover slid backwards. There was just a moment when Grace felt completely helpless, then a jerk as the back wheels dropped into a ditch and her head whiplashed forward. The engine cut out. The car was still. *Oh, no,* she thought.

For a minute she simply sat there stupidly, her head-lights pointing upwards at an odd angle. *Shock,* diagnosed a detached, professional part of her brain, and with that she clicked back into being Grace Fellowes, District Nurse, again. No part of her was injured, that was good. She was facing the right direction, also good. She had four-wheel drive. With any luck she'd simply be able to drive out.

She took a deep breath and started the engine again. The car lurched forward a couple of feet and then slowly slid backwards. She could hear the whirring of the wheels skidding in the slush of the ditch. *Grip,* she told them, *grip.* Then she remembered that at her last MOT the mechanic had told her the tyres were only just within the legal limit and had nothing like the traction that they should have. Buying new tyres had been a luxury she had been putting off.

She was not going to panic. She turned the lights off to save the battery, took out her mobile to call the garage, re-membered—irrationally—that she'd once seen an adder slither out of one of these ditches and cross in front of her and decided she'd get a much better signal on the road. So she clambered out of the car, *not* thinking about snakes, and took a large step up the side of the ditch.

Under the snow it was more slippery than she'd expected. She lost her footing, fell on her knees then pitched forward. Her phone flew out of her hand into the slush and the mud. No! Grace scrabbled frantically for it, but when she eventually closed her fingers around its solid, comforting form it was obvious that no way would it work.

It was as much as she could do to bite back a sob. She felt bewildered. All this had happened so quickly, so easily, that she was having difficulty in comprehending it. Not ten minutes ago she had been happily driving through the snow-covered landscape, looking forward to getting home. And now she was stranded on a lonely country road, she was covered in mud, the light was failing, she had no means of calling anyone and it was at least three miles to the nearest farmhouse. What had happened to her good day?

Another deep breath. This was simply shock. Think positive. She had a torch, she knew exactly where she was and there were worse things in life than an early-evening walk in the snow.

But before she could take a single step she saw lights in the dusk ahead. Oh, thank goodness. What a stroke of luck! A car was coming this way. She stood on the side of the road and shone her torch across it, preparing to wave the driver down.

The car was travelling quite slowly, its engine a muted mutter. She waved vigorously. The car's lights flashed, telling her she'd been seen. Then it drew up to her and stopped.

She recognised the make of car, a top-of-the-range Range Rover, just the kind of vehicle she would love for herself. Hard on that came a momentary touch of apprehension. She knew most of the people around there and none of them had a car like this. The car was driven by a stranger.

A man got out. 'Are you all right?' he called.

'Yes,' Grace called back, 'but I've slid the road.'

'Just a moment.' The man opened one of his rear doors and a minute or so later fetched out a powerful torch. He walked towards her, snowflakes falling through the beam of light playing on the ground.

'You've had an accident?' he said. 'Are you hurt? I'm a doctor.'

'It's all right,' she said. 'I'm a nurse myself. I'm not hurt, just annoyed and feeling a bit stupid. Not only have I skidded into a ditch, I also dropped my mobile into the slush and it's stopped working.'

'Ah. Then you'd better be careful. Accidents always seem to happen in threes. Think carefully, what else could go wrong?'

He had a gorgeous voice, deep and comforting. And now he knew no one was hurt, it held a touch of humour too. She felt as if she could listen to it for ever. He was probably a consultant, Grace judged, by the expensive car and the fact that he must surely be on his way to join some country party at a big house or a hotel. 'Nothing more will go wrong,' she told him firmly, feeling more cheerful by the moment. 'It's nearly Christmas and I won't allow it. But if I could just borrow your mobile to ring the garage…?'

He chuckled. 'What's the number? Are you cold? Would you like to wait in my car while we contact them?'

'I'm fine, really. Oh, damn.'

'What?'

'The number of the garage is in my phone.'

'Ah, that would be the phone that doesn't work?'

'Yes.' She took a breath. This was perhaps a bit much to ask but he could always refuse. 'Could you give me a lift to the nearest farm? It's only three miles down the road.'

'Certainly I can, but won't they mind?' He sounded startled.

Grace stared at him in the dimness. This was definitely no local. 'No, of course not! They'll either ring Bert Machin for me or start up the tractor and haul me out of the ditch themselves.'

'Goodness. Well, hop in.'

But as she approached the large, powerful Range Rover,

an idea occurred to her. 'Or we could maybe get the tow-rope out of my boot and use *your* car to pull mine out. That would be even quicker.'

He seemed startled again. Grace was reminded once more that he wasn't from around there.

'Sorry,' she said. 'You're on your way somewhere. A lift to the farm would be lovely, if you really don't mind.'

'It's not that.' He looked towards his car as if unde-cided, then the dark head nodded. 'Yes. If yours isn't damaged, that sounds like a good idea. Just wait there a minute.' He strode along the edge of the ditch, shining the torch at the Land Rover's back wheels. 'Seems possible to pull it out,' he shouted. 'I'll have a quick look at the front.'

He rejoined her, having apparently been able to carry out his inspection without getting anything like as muddy as her. 'I think we should be able to manage it,' he said. 'Sorry I didn't suggest it straight away. I'm not used to owning something this practical yet—even though that was the reason I bought it.'

It seemed a bit extreme, buying a Range Rover just for a trip across the moors, but that was consultants for you. 'That's very kind,' said Grace. 'I'll get the rope. Hopefully this won't hold you up for too long.'

'Don't worry, I bought a rope along with the car. There's even a section in the manual about pulling vehicles out of ditches.' He was hurrying back, peering through the window and reaching around vast quantities of luggage to get shiny new tools out as he spoke. Grace couldn't escape the thought that he probably imagined her tow-rope was as elderly as the Land Rover. 'I'm Mike, by the way.'

'Nice to meet you. I'm Grace. If you give me the rope I'll fix it to my—'

'Certainly not. This is a new experience and I want to see the whole thing through myself.'

With a touch of laughter in her voice, Grace asked, 'Not because I'm a woman and you're a man?'

'Ah, very possibly. I can on occasion be a slightly un-reconstructed male.'

'I've met my share of unreconstructed males, Mike. I don't think you're one of them.'

Had just a touch of bitterness crept into her voice then? She hoped not. She had meant to copy his light-hearted tone. She felt, rather than saw, his sudden assessing glance.

'Perhaps I've been reconstructed just a bit,' he said. 'Tell you what. You can hold the torch and tell me if I'm doing it right.'

His hands, though they must be as cold as her own, were deft and sure. Grace was amused at the way he kept glancing up at his car, just to check it was still there. In a very few minutes they were both behind their respective steering-wheels. 'I'm starting to pull now,' he shouted through the window. 'Try your engine as well.'

She did. Slowly, her car moved forward a foot or so then stopped. She heard her wheels skidding but then her car seemed to jerk forward, throwing her against the seat, and then bounced back onto the road. They had done it! She braked, got out of the car, and in the darkness made out him getting out of his.

'Thank you,' she said with real gratitude. 'That was very kind of you.'

He undid the tow-rope and smiled. 'I'm sure you'd

have done the same for me.' Then he glanced at the nearest of her tyres and frowned. 'You do know these treads are very shallow?'

Of course she knew. But did he know how much four new tyres would cost? 'Yes, I'll be replacing them soon,' she said. She would have to. She didn't want any more shocks like today. She just wasn't sure where she was going to find the money.

'Wait a minute. You'd better not go until we've tested your steering and your brakes. You don't know what damage might have been done.'

'It's fine. The road from now on is straight and flat. I'll check both along there. Then I'll—'

'No arguments,' he said. 'I'm not that unreconstructed. Why don't I follow behind you just in case? Come on, would you leave me if the situation was reversed?'

Well, no, of course she wouldn't. And he had thought about it first, so he was a considerate man as well as a helpful one. 'Probably not,' she said, 'but I'm going all the way to Rivercut village. It'll take you miles out of your way.'

He laughed. 'It won't, you know. I'm headed there too.'

Grace stared. 'Then what are you doing on this road instead of the main route?'

'Funnily enough, I was asking myself that very question just before I came across you. My sat nav,' Mike added dryly, 'has a mind of its own.'

'Then I'm very grateful to it,' said Grace, recovering.

And, in fact, all did seem to be well. Her car steered without a problem, the brakes were good. She drove slowly, Mike following thirty or so yards behind. She suspected that if he thought she was going too fast, he wouldn't hesitate to let her know. He seemed to be a man who was perfectly polite, but who always made his point. Who on earth could he be visiting if he was heading for Rivercut?

The journey took perhaps half an hour and then they were in the outskirts of the village. Grace felt a rush of gladness, seeing the snow-capped roofs, the streetlights and the Christmas lights in the windows. As always, though, there was a pang as she passed the manor. She remembered previous Christmases with two great illuminated fir trees on either side of the front door and decorations in all the downstairs rooms. As a child she had found it wonderful. And she had thought it would last for ever.

Stop it, she told herself. You need to sell it, and you need to do it soon. You're living on fresh air once the mortgage has been paid every month as it is. Maybe a family would buy it, then it would have light filling it again. Light and love.

Fifty yards down from the manor entrance she drew up outside the small cottage that was now her home. Mike pulled in behind her. She stepped down from her car, grinning at the contrast between her old Land Rover and Mike's magnificent new machine. Ancient and modern!

Mike got out of his car too. With a smile she said to him, 'Thanks for the help. I hope I don't ever have to do the same for you. I'm not sure my vehicle would manage it.'

'Glad to be of service. There is one thing that occurred to me on the way. You had an accident as well as your car. You should really get yourself checked over. Now, I am a doctor…'

'Certainly not!' The very idea horrified her. 'I am a nurse,' she pointed out. 'I can tell whether I'm injured or not.'

'If you're sure. Sometimes injuries aren't obvious at first.'

She knew that, but… She looked distractedly past him. And gasped. 'Something moved,' she whispered. 'Inside your car.'

Instantly Mike whirled away from her. She hurried after him as he opened the rear door and caught her breath again. There, safely cocooned in the back seat, was a child of about five or six years of age, just stirring into wakefulness. It was the last thing Grace had expected.

'It's all right, sweetheart,' said Mike softly, tucking the child's arm back under a cosy scarlet blanket. 'We're nearly at Grandad's house.' He glanced at Grace. 'My daughter, Bethany. It's not far to James Curtis's place from here is it?'

Grace knew her mouth was hanging open. Mike. Of course. She'd completely forgotten. Dr Curtis had said his son Michael was moving up here to join the practice. 'No, no, it's just along the main street and left by the green. I'm so sorry— I didn't realise who you were. No wonder you've got so much luggage in the back.' She was babbling. Get a grip, Grace. And yet… She'd seen the front of his car quite clearly in her rear-view mirror. There hadn't been anyone in his passenger seat. She couldn't help looking again to make sure.

And his voice changed so suddenly that it shocked her. 'Correct. No wife, just my daughter.'

Had he read her mind? 'Well, you'd better get yourself and Bethany to Dr Curtis's house. He'll be waiting for you. I expect I'll see you at the surgery once you've settled in.'

'Not before you have your car checked over,' he said, unsmiling.

'Sure. Thanks again. Without you I'd have been properly stuck.'

As he got in his car, the light shone fully on his face. An unexpected thrill ran down Grace's spine. Dr Mike Curtis was a very handsome man. She didn't meet too many of them in the village.

CHAPTER TWO

THE cottage was cold. Grace hurried to turn on the gas fire before pulling the curtains. Then she went into the little adjoining kitchen and put on the kettle. She needed tea! She took off her coat, replaced her Wellingtons with furry slippers, and when the tea was made sank thankfully into her armchair in front of the fire. What she *should* be thinking about was how she was going to afford four new tyres. What she was actually thinking about was a deep, comforting voice and a thoughtful, considering presence. Mike.

How extraordinary that the man who had pulled her out of that wretched ditch had been the new doctor at Rivercut Practice! She tried to remember what she knew about him, but it was woefully little. James Curtis—her boss—was an open book himself, but reticent about his family. Mike had already been at medical school when James had moved to Rivercut. He'd visited his father a couple of times. Now Grace came to think of it, she even remembered a wife and a baby at one point. And then—a year ago, had it been?— James had suddenly dropped everything and gone to London for his daughter-in-law's funeral. Everyone at the surgery had been shocked. They'd expressed inadequate sympathy when James had come back and said they hoped his son and the little girl were okay. Grace remembered James had said Mike was taking it hard.

She groaned. No wonder he'd sounded so bitter when she'd glanced at the empty passenger seat. Grace sipped her tea. They hadn't spoken much, but Mike had otherwise been friendly and good-humoured. It was part of a doctor's stock-in-trade to be approachable, of course, but even so Grace thought they'd be able to work together as colleagues without any of the awkwardness that sometimes took a while to settle down. And what's more, he'd fit in just fine in Rivercut. That lovely voice would have all the female patients eating out of his hand in no time.

Grace's toes were starting to thaw. She wriggled them, thinking how she really ought to keep a pair of winter socks in the car now that the weather had set fast. Even without today's accident, she'd been cold. And if Mike hadn't happened along, she'd have been frozen for sure, walking to the farm for help.

She smiled, remembering Mike's little girl snuggled up cosily in the back of his car. No wonder he'd kept glancing at it—not anxiety about the vehicle, as she'd thought, but concern for his daughter. Lucky Bethany to have such a caring father.

Grace sighed. Peter had been just as protective of her when she'd fallen pregnant. God save her, she'd been as foolish as her mother to be flattered by pretty words, chocolates and flowers. But Peter Cox's professions of undying love hadn't lasted beyond the moment when he'd caught sight of the probate papers and realised there was no money to go with the heavily mortgaged manor, and then her world had fallen apart yet again…

Mostly Grace was all right. She had her job, she had her friends, she had Rivercut. It was just that now and again— like when she saw a man tucking his small daughter's arm inside a cosy blanket—she missed her lost baby more than she would have believed possible.

It had been a long journey from London but, absurdly, Mike found himself slowing as he drove along the main street of Rivercut village from the church of St Lawrence, with its illuminated crib, to the green. It seemed like a festival of light. Every shop was decorated. Every house and cottage boasted at least one Christmas tree. Everyone here was making an effort. There was obviously a lot of local pride.

He'd seen very little of the village, only making a few short visits in the twelve years his father had worked here. With his busy lifestyle it had been simpler for his father to come to London. So there was no sense of coming home. Rather, a feeling of curiosity. What would it be like, living in a moderate-sized village rather than in London? Peaceful, he hoped. Certainly different. Dad had said there was a good community spirit in Rivercut, and Mike's brief encounter with Grace had definitely been an eye-opener. She'd shown no qualms at all at the prospect of knocking up the nearest farmhouse and asking for help. He still wasn't sure why he hadn't let her do just that, except that his masculine pride would have been stung—and she'd been right about that too.

He grinned wryly. If the truth were told, he'd been glad

to follow her to Rivercut, not having quite the same faith in his sat nav as the salesman who'd sold it to him. He'd thought about Grace quite a bit as he had driven slowly behind her. He had only seen her in the half-light, but he'd had an impression of an above-average-height woman with what he suspected was a generous figure hidden by her fleece coat. He couldn't be sure about her hair—dark blonde, he thought, tied up in a pleat.

It wasn't her appearance that interested him most, though. It was her openness, her happiness with life despite having just skidded into a ditch, her apparent willingness to trust. Until right at the end, when she'd seen Bethany, and he could have sworn he'd seen a flash of something vulnerable under the cheerful, competent exterior. Had he imagined it?

Mike came to a halt outside his father's surgery and, as if on cue, from behind his seat there came the sound of his precious daughter waking up. Mike took a deep breath. It was time for them both to start their new life.

'Are we there yet, Daddy?' said Bethany sleepily.

'Just arrived, darling. Wait a minute, I'll come and unstrap you.' He undid the seat belt and lifted Bethany out of the car. She already had her coat on, but Mike pulled her woollen hat tight over her ears and wrapped the red blanket around her for good measure. They both regarded the surgery—a large Victorian house with an extension built out to one side. As well as the consulting rooms and pharmacy there was his father's flat where he and Bethany would stay until they found a place of their own. Bethany looked round, enchanted. 'It's been snowing,' she said.

The front door of the surgery flat was suddenly thrown

open and a beaming James Curtis came out. 'Who's got a kiss for her grandfather?' he called. Bethany wriggled out of Mike's arms and ran through the snow towards the lit doorway. 'Grandad! We've come to live with you!'

She was growing up, Mike thought, left holding the discarded blanket. This was why they were moving up here. He looked at the delight on their faces, one young, one old. It would be all right.

Bethany's sleep had revived her. As Mike brought in the luggage, she ran from room to room, her dark curls bouncing, learning the layout, deciding where her toys would go and chattering nineteen to the dozen. Then she watched intently as Mike put her duvet and pillow on her new bed. She wore the same expression on her elfin face that her mother had always had when she'd been concentrating on a medical journal and, as always, it tore at Mike's heart. *Oh, Sarah.*

'She's very like her, isn't she?' said James in a low voice as Bethany ran in front of them towards the kitchen, just to prove that she knew the way. 'Must be a comfort.'

'Yes,' said Mike. 'Yes, it is.'

They had planned a special tea for this first night, Bethany's name written in alphabet spaghetti on a piece of toast. Then, of course, they had to write 'Daddy' and 'Grandad' and anything else they could think of too. Mike told his father it was a bit of a messy way of learning to spell, but he thought that it worked. Then came an even messier bath, with both Mike and Grandad ending up soaked. And last of all, after the teeth cleaning, it was her grandfather who was chosen to read her a bedtime story.

Much later, as they each nursed a glass of single malt in front of the fire, James said, 'It's a big change, Mike. From the heart of London to an isolated village on the Yorkshire moors. Are you going to manage?'

Mike shrugged. 'I think I will. The practice in London was growing faster than I wanted it to. I was doing more administration than medicine. I was too dependent on our friends for child care and…and everywhere I go in London I see Sarah. I need to get away. And I can do without the relentless social life that seems to be a necessary part of living there.'

'You might be surprised at the social life there is here,' his father warned with a grin. 'We don't all spend the winter sitting by the fire and watching TV. But I suppose you're right. It will be quieter here. And I told you there'd be fewer private patients. One or two—but not many.'

'I'll be glad to give them up. I don't need the money. I was paid a stupidly large amount when I was in the Middle East and I saved most of it. I've done well out of finally selling the flat and my partnership. I want to get back to basics. I want a quiet decent life for Bethany and myself, with more medicine than paperwork.'

'Seems a fair ambition. You know you'll be taking over most of the outside calls? There are plenty of them and we cover a large area here. I used to do most of them, but since I had that fall my doctor says I mustn't go out as much as I did.'

'Your doctor is?'

'Me,' said his father smugly.

'What about your partner? Can't she do them?'

'Rosemary? She's heavily pregnant. I don't want her going out any more than she needs to.'

'Well, I'll be happy to do as much travelling round as necessary. Provided my sat nav cooperates. Get some clean air into my lungs for a change.'

There was silence for a moment as James filled both their glasses. Then he said, gently, 'it's been almost exactly a year since Sarah was killed. How are you coping with it?'

Mike gave a short laugh. 'Mum died over twelve years ago. You still have her picture in your bedroom and I'll bet you think about her every night. How do you cope?'

'By remembering her and telling myself that she'd want me to be happy. And I am happy, most of the time.'

'Lucky you. I miss Sarah so much I ache. My friends seem to think I should be better by now, they keep trying to fix me up with suitable women. I've had a year dealing with a heartbroken little girl who'd lost the mother she doted on. That's taken all the emotional energy I've had to spare.'

'Ah, well. Grief has always had its own timetable. You might find you have more energy after you've spent a few months in Rivercut. Things are calmer here. Now, I'll just nip along to the kitchen and see how the casserole is coming on.'

Mike took another sip of his whisky, leaned back in his seat and sighed. Perhaps his father was right. Perhaps here he would find peace and contentment. Perhaps even an end to the nightmare that still came far too often—with a vision of his wife in the burnt-out wreck of her car.

No! He was starting a new life. He reached resolutely for the leaflets and brochures his father had left on the coffee table, all with details of the property available locally. Staying with his father was all right for the moment, but he wanted a place of his own. He wanted a house with space and a garden. Somewhere Bethany could walk on her own down to school without him worrying about her as soon as she was out of sight. But as he turned page after page, his hopes fell. 'Nothing suitable for sale at all in the village?' he asked James when they were sitting down to lamb casserole and baked potatoes.

James shook his head. 'Not many people move out,' he said. 'And there's hardly any building allowed because we're in a national park. In fact, the only thing available here at the moment is Rivercut Manor. It belongs to my district nurse, Grace Fellowes.'

Mike looked at his father in amazement. 'Is she the only Grace in the area?'

'As far as I know,' said his father, mystified.

'Dad, I met a nurse called Grace on the way up. I pulled her car out of a ditch. A tatty Land Rover. But I left her at a cottage at the end of the village, not a manor house.'

His father sighed. 'It's a sad story. The wonder is that Grace keeps so cheerful all the time. Everyone feels sorry for her but she refuses to feel sorry for herself. Just keeps smiling and getting on with life.'

Mike was intrigued. 'So what happened?'

His father settled himself. 'The Fellowes family has been here for centuries. Once they owned most of Rivercut valley. Even seven years ago when Grace's father died, they were tolerably well off. They owned several local farms, they were good landlords. When Grace's father realised he was on his way out he sold the farms to the tenants. Grace was in the middle of her training and he knew his wife wouldn't be able to cope with rents and maintenance and all that. He put the money into two trust funds—one for his wife and one for Grace. Then a couple of years go by and Grace's mother takes up with a car dealer from Birmingham. Charming chap, squired her about, did the pretty. She fell for him in a big way, married him, signed every document he put in front of her, and then last year he did a runner to Spain, leaving the manor mortgaged to the hilt, the trust fund broken and Grace's ma without a penny to her name.'

'Oh, Lord. What happened?'

'Heart attack. Massive and merciful. But Grace still owes the bank a lot of money, she's barely clearing the mortgage payments and she has to sell the house to get straight.'

'And she's the Rivercut community practitioner?'

His father gave him an old-fashioned look. 'Up here she's the district nurse. She also does two or three clinics in the surgery for me. She's a brilliant nurse, knows everybody and everything. You'll enjoy working with her.'

'I think I will.' Mike was interested in this story. It suggested that Grace had a toughness that he had half suspected. He was looking forward to working with her.

As it happened, Grace was working in the surgery next morning. In theory she had appointments for wound management, injections and medical support for the first half of her clinic, then contraception, sexual advice and women's health. In practice, the receptionist fitted in people where she could. Grace enjoyed both sessions, even if the second one made her privy to rather more secrets than anyone else in the village suspected.

She had just finished giving a set of vaccinations to a couple who were going to Cuba for a long stay. Vaccinations against hepatitis A and B, typhoid, rabies, diphtheria and tuberculosis. She had given them the necessary brochures, but went through them herself so that they knew exactly what to expect. After the couple had left her consulting room, before the next patient was due, there was a tap on the door.

'Just grabbing a quick minute to introduce you to our new member of staff,' James said cheerfully. 'This is my son, Dr Michael Curtis, and his daughter, Bethany, who has a passion for knowing who works in which room and what goes on in all of them. I gather you've already met.'

'We have, and I've cause to be grateful.' Grace held out her hand. 'Good to meet you formally, Dr Curtis.'

He took her hand, shook it. 'Please, it's Mike. And it's good to meet you properly too. Dad tells me he's delegating all the home visits to me, so I expect I'll be working with you quite a lot. I'm looking forward to it.'

Last night had been an episode of torchlight and shadows; she'd hardly seen him clearly at all. But now was the bright light of day—and she had to admit that he was impressive. He was wearing a smart dark suit, a light blue shirt with some kind of college tie. He looked every inch the successful London doctor. Oh, dear, and yesterday she'd been covered all over in slush and mud.

To her embarrassment, he guessed what she was thinking. With a smile, he said, 'Bethany and I decided I should put on my interview suit because it's my first day, but in future I'll wear something more in line with the work I'll have to do.'

'In that case I advise clothes that are waterproof and easily cleaned,' she joked. Then she looked at the little girl holding her father's hand and smiled. 'Hello, Bethany, I'm Grace. You were asleep yesterday when your daddy's car pulled mine out of the ditch.'

Bethany's bright eyes darted about the room. They widened when they got to the photos on the shelf. 'That's a horse,' she said, and ran over to look closer.

Grace noticed the plastic pink horse clutched in Bethany's hand. She grinned. Was there a little girl alive without a pony fixation? 'She was called Sugar. She was my first pony. That's me riding her when I was a little girl.'

Bethany studied the photo. 'My teacher said I could ride a horse if I moved to the country.'

'I'm sure you will. There's a riding stable just outside the village where they have special classes for new riders.' Too late she saw Mike's muscles tense up. 'Once you've settled down, of course, and only if Daddy says you can.' And wouldn't the girls at the stable be all over him! Divested of last night's bulky coat, his body was trim— broad shouldered, narrow-waisted. Hair and eyes were both dark, his mouth well curved. Dr Mike Curtis was quite something.

'Yes, well, we've both got to find our feet first,' he said noncommittally.

Grace could read signals as well as the next woman and this one clearly said stay off the subject. James must have sensed it too. He suggested Bethany come and meet the re-ceptionist and her daughter Rachel, who was off school with a sprained ankle. She'd seen the play area earlier, hadn't she? The little girl danced off happily. Grace and Mike were left alone.

As he looked at her she wondered if she could detect

something in his eyes. Appreciation, perhaps, or even admiration? She had taken just a little extra care that morning. A little more attention to her hair, just a touch more make-up than usual. She didn't know why. Perhaps just to show a London sophisticate that not all country people were bumpkins with straw in their hair. Or to impress him? Whatever it was, it gave her a warm feeling when he looked at her with that searching expression.

'How's the car?' he asked.

Grace came back to earth with a bump. Fair enough. They *had* only just met after all. 'I took it into the garage first thing. Bert Machin said he'd have a look at it this afternoon.'

'You're not going to need it before tomorrow?'

'If necessary, I can borrow a car from Bert. I've done it before.'

He smiled. She liked his smile. It was starting to have the same effect on her that his voice did. 'The Rivercut spirit again, eh? I'd still be happier knowing that you—' But there was a knock on the door and a face appeared round it.

'Are you ready for me, Grace? You said… Ooh, sorry. Didn't know you had someone in here.'

'Wait outside a minute, Nina,' Grace said. 'I'll be right with you.'

Nina looked assessingly at Mike and then slowly disappeared.

'You've got work to do. I'd better go,' Mike said. 'I'll see you later, Grace.' And he too was gone.

The minute he was out of the door, Nina Carter rushed in. She was nineteen, a pretty girl who worked in a hairdressing salon in the next village and was the number one gossip in the area. A month ago, Grace had prescribed the contraceptive pill for her. Even after explaining patient confidentiality at some length, she'd still had to swear not to tell Nina's mother. And Nina had already said she wasn't going to use the practice pharmacy. She'd go into Whitby for it.

But now... 'Was that the new doctor, Grace?'

'Yes, young Dr Curtis.'

'He's fit, isn't he? Is he nice?'

'He's only just arrived. He seems to be a very practical doctor.'

'Is he married? Got a girlfriend?'

'Nina, I don't talk about doctors any more than I talk about patients. Now, you've been on the Pill for a month. Have you managed to take it regularly?'

'Yes. It's a bit of a job keeping it from Ma, but I've managed.'

'Have there been any unusual side effects? Headaches, mild depression?'

'No, nothing like that.'

'And you're still certain you want to go on with it?'

'Ooh, yes.' Nina grinned. 'Definitely.'

'Good.' Grace sighed. For a moment, she envied Nina her carefree attitude to relationships. It must save an awful lot of heartache. After ensuring that Nina was still practising safe sex, she dismissed her with a repeat prescription and welcomed in an older patient who was finding her unwelcome hot flushes rather hard to deal with.

It was a normal morning's work and she was enjoying it. But she couldn't get Mike out of her mind. What had James said last week? That his son could do with a whole new lifestyle? Mike was evidently going to be what she privately termed the 'outside man', doing all the driving to the

outlying farms, so they would be working together quite a
bit. She wondered if that would cause him any problems.
She guessed he was four or five years older than her. They
were both single. She could guess what conclusions the
local gossips would draw. Oh, well, they'd soon find out
they were wrong. Mike may be an attractive man, but the
baleful memory of Peter Cox was still very much with
Grace. She wasn't making new commitments any time soon.

Whilst talking to her patient, she rang through to James.
'I've just come across something, Dr Curtis, and if you've
got a moment I'd like your advice.'

But it was Mike who walked in through the door, not his
father. 'He says I'm to earn my keep,' he said with a smile.

That was fair enough, with the extra pressure they were
under due to Rosemary Watson's unfortunate pre-eclampsia.
Grace introduced Mike to Mrs Leaman, a fifty-five-year-old
lady who had just started on HRT drugs to deal with her
menopause. 'So far Mrs Leaman has benefited from the drug,'
Grace said, 'but it seems to cause her the occasional headache
in the morning. She'll put up with it because in general she's
feeling much better. But if it was possible to—'

Mike smiled at Mrs Leaman. 'I think HRT drugs are
wonderful,' he said. 'They make life so much more
pleasant. But let's see if we can get rid of the headaches
too.' He looked at Grace. 'What did you prescribe?'

She told him and he nodded. 'A good choice. But since
Mrs Leaman's having these headaches, how do you fancy
trying something with slightly different proportions of oes-
trogen and progestin?'

He wrote down the name of a drug on her notepad.
'Perhaps we could try this?'

Grace looked at the name. 'It's new to me.'

'Not been out long. I can tell you more about it, though.'

They discussed the new drug with Mrs Leaman and Mike answered all her questions.

'So what do you think?'

Grace liked the way he asked her opinion, too. 'I think it's a good idea. Mrs Leaman, would you like to try this?'

'I certainly would. And thank you both.' The woman took her prescription and left.

'Mrs Leaman now thinks you're a wonderful doctor,' Grace said. 'The news will be all over the village by the weekend.' Which had no doubt been James's intention. He could be a cunning soul at times.

'Does that mean that if I get something slightly wrong, it will be all over the village just as quickly?'

'You're catching on. This is an instant response environment. The Internet has nothing on Rivercut.'

'Going to have to keep on my toes,' he muttered. 'Actually, I'm quite looking forward to working with the same people over and over again. In London, a lot of my patients I only ever saw once or twice.'

'London has a larger floating population.'

'And some of them are sinking rapidly. I'm hoping that things will be a bit better up here.'

'Don't know about better,' Grace said, 'but probably different.'

'People seem more relaxed. In London everyone is in a hurry. There are things that they have to do.' He looked thoughtful for a moment and then added, 'Perhaps people aren't in a hurry here because there aren't so many things to do.'

'Ha! Just you wait. We don't want any of that fancy London talk in Rivercut. You'll be kept busy.'

It was fun talking to Mike. He had a sense of humour, wasn't going to take unimportant things seriously. Her phone rang. She picked it up. 'Yes, James, he's still here,' she said, and handed it to Mike.

Mike listened a minute, his face changing, then said, 'But what about Bethany…? Oh, okay, I'll be right there.'

He looked ruefully at Grace. 'Did you say I'd be kept busy? There's a small emergency and I'm to start work at once. I'll see you later.' And he was gone.

Grace had been right to think she would like working with Mike. She liked that his first thought had been for his daughter, not his own lost morning. As for anything else— and, yes, Grace admitted now that she was attracted to him—those sorts of thoughts were best banished. She'd made a huge fool of herself over Peter and she wasn't about to let herself in for any more hurt.

As Mike hurried to his father's room, stopping in Reception to tell Bethany he was going to be working for the rest of the morning and she was to be a good girl and play with Rachel where the other girl's mother could keep an eye on them, part of his mind was thinking about Grace. He was being perfectly detached about it. There was the same mild pleasure in thinking of her as he might feel watching a sunset or the snow on the hills. But, he had to admit, she was gorgeous. It wasn't just her height or figure, it wasn't even her dark blonde hair and clear complexion. It was her smile, her beautiful mouth, the way she was so happy with the world. And yet there was an alert look in

her grey eyes that told him this woman was nobody's fool.
He was going to enjoy working with her.

His first surgery. He hadn't expected to start work on
his first day. He and Bethany were supposed to be settling
in gently, meeting people gradually, looking for somewhere to live. But one of his father's long-term patients
in the village had been suddenly taken ill, and James had
offered to go round at once to see him. The other practice
doctor being off with enforced bed-rest due to a sudden
complication with her pregnancy, Mike had been volunteered to carry on with his father's morning list. This was
not the kind of flexible arrangement that Mike would have
expected in London, but he could see that it worked here.

So, his first Rivercut surgery and in his father's consulting room. A couple of suggestions that this was the room
of an old-fashioned doctor—the panelled walls, the old
roll-top bureau in the corner. It sat oddly with the computer
on the desk and the printer under the window. Adjusting
the swivel chair, Mike realised there were photographs on
the wall opposite. A photo of his mother. A photo of him
aged seventeen, covered in mud, racing down the pitch
clutching a rugby ball. He smiled, remembering that game.
And smiled more at the three photographs of Bethany. No
wonder the receptionist had recognised her on sight.

Mike felt at home. He pressed the intercom to summon
his first patient. Being new to the practice, he had to introduce himself to everyone, shake hands, explain that his
father had been called away. And then there had to be a few
words of general conversation.

He recognised what was happening after a while. He
was being welcomed to the area. Yes, there was more snow

here than in London. Yes, he had seen the poster inviting everyone to the Christmas carol service. Yes, his daughter would be going to the village school. No, he didn't think he would be lonely here.

His patients came in with the usual mixture of complaints, more minor than major. Gone suddenly deaf? A quick examination, then ear drops prescribed and come in to see the nurse in a week's time to have them syringed. A very bad cold? No, no point in antibiotics, they don't have any effect on a viral disease. Rest, plenty of fluids and paracetamol. A mole on the cheek that seemed to have grown over the past few weeks? Probably nothing, but we'll refer you to a consultant dermatologist at the local hospital—once he'd found out which one that was.

Then a case came in that was typical of the area. Dave Hart was clutching his back, obviously in pain. 'I was taking some feed out to the sheep, Doctor. I was loading up the trailer and I twisted a bit and suddenly there was this great pain in my back. Never felt anything like it.'

'OK, come and lie on this couch and I'll examine you.'

Sometimes Mike thought that the worst designed bit of the human body was the spine. He felt Dave's back, noticed where the pain was and observed what movement Dave had. 'Well, the good news is that I don't think that you've slipped any of the vertebrae. The bad news is you've strained the muscles quite badly. I'll prescribe painkillers, but the only real cure is rest.'

'Rest? Doctor, I'm a working farmer!'

'If you try to lift anything heavy, you'll only make things worse. Much worse. Isn't there anyone you can get in for a while?'

'I suppose so.'

Mike spent quite some time trying to make Dave see just how serious things could get if he did too much, but he had an uneasy feeling the man wouldn't know how to rest. And that would mean he'd be back.

His last case made him think too. Pip Lawrie, another young farmer, came in with a fungal infection of his feet, probably caused by getting them wet too often. 'The wife sent me,' he said sheepishly. 'Fed up with me itching all the time.'

Mike gave him advice and prescribed a spray that should clear up the condition. Then, just as he was leaving, Pip said, 'I don't suppose you can recommend something for a pain in the chest, can you? Just a mild pain.'

'You've got a pain in the chest?'

'Not me. Pa. He lives with us. He gets out of breath more than he used to and sometimes he complains about this pain. Says it's just down the front of his chest. It goes away when he sits down.'

Mike had a nasty feeling about these symptoms. 'I'd like to see him. Can he come down to the surgery?'

'Come all this way for a bit of a pain? No chance. No way will he leave the farm. He was born there and I don't think he's ever been more than fifty miles away from it in his life. He'll just carry on taking aspirin.'

'Not always the best thing,' Mike said cautiously.

'He's a tough old boy. You ask Nurse Fellowes. She used to come to the farm when he broke his arm.'

'Right,' said Mike.

* * *

It was lunchtime. Mike typed the last notes onto the computer, stretched, went into Reception to collect Bethany—and found the place empty! Where was she? Terror caught hold of him without warning. He flung open the front door but there was no one in sight. Really panicking now, he tore down the passage to Grace's room. 'Quickly,' he said. 'I need to—'

Grace looked up at him with a smile. Bethany also looked up from where she'd set up an improvised gymkhana on Grace's desk. 'Look at Twinkle, Daddy. He can jump right over the blood pressure machine.'

'Rachel had to go home,' said Grace, 'so Bethany's been keeping me company while you finished your list. My, but that Twinkle's an energetic little pony, isn't he?'

Mike just stood there, hanging on to the doorframe, feeling the adrenalin draining out of his limbs.

Grace's steady grey eyes rested on him for a moment. 'Tea, I think,' she murmured. 'Sit yourself down on my squashy chair with Bethany while I make it. Go and sit on your dad's knee, poppet.'

Bethany rushed across and threw herself into Mike's arms. 'Rachel goes riding,' she said. 'And Grace says she knows where. And—'

There was a knock at the door. James peered in. 'Where's the young lady who promised to have lunch with me?'

'Grandad!' Bethany leaped off Mike's knee, ran open-armed across the room. James winked at Grace and Mike. 'Just like her father used to be,' he said. 'Never walked when he could run.' Then the two of them were gone.

Grace put a cup of tea by Mike's elbow. 'I couldn't say

I didn't know about the stables when she asked. Sorry if I've put my foot in it. Have you ever ridden?'

He shook his head. 'Once, when I was working in the desert, I was persuaded to go for a camel ride. I decided then that I was happier walking on two legs than being shaken about on four. I'll stick to walking.'

'Camels?' Grace grinned. 'I don't see you as Lawrence of Arabia.'

'Neither did the camel. Take a word of advice, Grace, stick to horses. They don't spit.'

'I'll remember that. Horses—good, camels—bad.'

He'd been feeling better until that moment, until an echo from the past seared across his brain, so painful that he gasped.

'Mike! Mike, are you all right? Your face has gone white. Are you going to faint?'

There was Grace in front of him, reaching out to him, her hands on his shoulders. Her smiling face was now concerned and he felt terrible for worrying her.

'I'm all right,' he managed to mumble. 'A bit tired. Yesterday was a long journey and…'

'Hush. Drink this tea, and I'm putting two spoonfuls of sugar in it. No arguments.'

He was in no condition to argue. He drank the sweet tea—which was disgusting—then felt angry at himself. He was a doctor, for goodness' sake. What had got into him? It was over now, done, finished. It had finished at ten p.m. on a wet November night when he had known at once what the news was. The A and E consultant had come out of Theatre and his face had told it all.

He would have to say something to Grace. He owed her

that much for giving her such a fright. He'd make it short. 'My wife was killed in a car crash just over a year ago. I loved her very much but I've tried to put it behind me for Bethany's sake. Every now and again something brings the hurt back and it's...it's hard. You just said, "Horses good—camels bad." What could be more harmless? Except that I remember Sarah saying it to me, those exact words. And we laughed about it.'

'Oh, poor Mike—I'm so sorry. So, so sorry.' He saw tears in her eyes. And then she was beside him, her arms wrapped round him, rocking him as his mother had done so many years before. 'So sorry,' she whispered again. 'So sorry...'

It was comforting, being held like that. He felt the tearing emptiness in his chest ease. But he was a man, not a child. He was a professional, a doctor. He didn't make an exhibition of himself. Reluctantly, he pulled away.

'It's me who should be sorry,' he said. 'I don't usually make a fool of myself like that. I—'

'You're not a fool! You were in love with someone who loved you and that is to be celebrated! And if you feel pain there is no shame in showing it. Right?'

'Right,' he said after a moment.

'I think that anyone who can love like that is...is wonderful. Wonderful and very lucky to have had it in their life. Would you like more tea before you go back to James and Bethany?'

'Please. But this time without sugar.'

He sat quietly sipping it, watching as she typed up her morning's notes. He found it comforting, he was glad he was with her. 'Thank you,' he said at last.

'No problem. I'd hazard a professional guess that you've been working too hard to grieve and have just bottled it up. You men are all the same.'

'Oh, that reminds me. Do you remember treating a man called Lawrie for a broken arm? About two years ago?'

Grace grinned. 'Joshua Lawrie. Lives with his son on High Scar farm. He's a cantankerous old so-and-so. Broke his arm in a farm accident—compound fracture, left radius—and it took twice as long to heal as it should have. He wouldn't stop working. I caught him trying to fork up hay one-handed. Why are you interested?'

'I've just had his son in. Apparently Joshua is complaining of chest pains, but he won't come down to the surgery.'

'I'm not surprised.' Grace looked at Mike. 'Are you worried about him?'

'It doesn't sound right. But I'm new here and don't want to be seen to interfere.'

'Well, I got on quite well with him in the end, so I could call in on them this afternoon and see how he's doing. Oh. No, I can't. My car's in the garage.' She bit her lip, then looked at him speculatively. 'You could drive me up there *because* my car's being fixed—then you could see him for yourself.'

'It's a good plan, but I promised Bethany we'd unpack this afternoon,' said Mike. 'I've neglected her all morning as it is. I wonder, though… I don't suppose you ever do calls in the evenings, do you?'

Grace laughed. 'Sorry. That really would put the wind up them. You're truly worried about this, aren't you?'

Mike shrugged. 'Occupational hazard. How about if we just say you're showing me the area? Bethany will be all right with Dad for the evening. I really would appreciate your assistance on this, Grace.'

She was silent for a moment. 'All right. About half past six?'

'That would be perfect. I'll see you then.'

Walking down the road to her cottage after Mike had gone, Grace thought of what she had just learned. His wife had been killed just over a year ago in a car accident. She'd known that already. What she hadn't known was that he was still in love with her. Grace was a trained nurse, she could read people, she had recognised the anguish on his face as being entirely honest.

So what did that mean to her?

Grace sighed. It meant she'd have to be careful. It meant that—whatever vague thoughts she might have been having about how nice he was, how attractive—she'd just have to give them all up. They would work together. They could even be friends. But nothing more.

Mike was in love with a ghost.

CHAPTER THREE

Given that they were never going to be any more than friends, Grace was having a surprising amount of difficulty deciding what to wear. Not her uniform, that was certain. But did she dress as someone going out on a snowy winter's night—boots, trousers, thick sweater and anorak? Or did she dress more smartly? Like someone going out on a date?

Hmm. Mike's car was large, luxurious and capable of dealing with the worst conditions that there could be round here. So she would dress smartly. Not overdo it, but just make a bit of an effort. She started to run herself a bath. It would take time; the boiler was old and temperamental. Meanwhile, she went to her rather chilly bedroom and laid out three dresses on the bed. Which to wear? The dark blue lacy dress, the light blue wispy silky dress or the grey jersey dress with the swooping neckline?

Oh, for heaven's sake! She was going out to see a possible patient with a man she had only met yesterday. What was the point of dressing up? They were going to be *friends*. There was no need to impress Mike Curtis. She hung all the dresses back in the wardrobe and took out a pair of black trousers.

But she'd still look smart. She liked to look smart on occasion. In fact, when she had bathed and washed her hair, decided on a white silk shirt and a blue bolero jacket to go with the trousers and spent half an hour on her makeup, she decided she looked quite presentable.

To finish, a pair of black court shoes. Then she sighed and put her Wellingtons in a carrier bag. There would be the inevitable muddy walk between car and front door.

Mike was exactly on time and she felt a faint flutter in her stomach when she opened the front door to him. He was now in a black leather jacket and a dark sweater. There were snowflakes on his head and shoulders. He looked distinctly male, even more so than in his formal suit. In fact, he looked decidedly sexy.

'I'm ready,' she said, catching up her coat. 'Let's get straight off.' She didn't give him the option of coming into the cottage. For a start there was no need. And also this was in a sense her refuge, it was geared to *her*. If he came in he might feel to her like an intruder and she didn't want to think of him that way.

He didn't seem upset by any possible rebuff. 'Your carriage awaits you, madam,' he said.

She waved the carrier bag in front of him. '*Mesdames* in carriages don't carry Wellington boots with them to get through the mud.'

'If there was mud I would happily have carried you.'

Now, that was a thought that was rather exciting. But she said, 'We don't go in for a lot of carrying around here. Modern women make their own way, even if it's through mud. Come to that, they probably always did. Besides, your legs would buckle—I'm not exactly a stick-thin model.'

'I'm glad you're not,' he said, and she had to blush. But after she'd locked the door she didn't object when he took her arm to walk her through the snow.

Being driven in his Range Rover was infinitely preferable to driving her faithful old vehicle. It didn't rattle, it didn't smell of diesel, it didn't hesitate before climbing a hill. And the seats were so comfortable!

'I like your car,' she said.

'I think it's right for the job. The equivalent of my London Jaguar. I'm going to enjoy driving around here. I'm already getting used to the novelty of not stopping for traffic lights every hundred yards. Incidentally, what's the word on your car?'

'Very good. Nothing bent or broken. Bert's retuned the engine and done something incomprehensible with the carburetor. And he's getting me a set of re-moulds as soon as possible.'

'Re-moulds?' Mike's voice was sharp. 'Why not new tyres? You need them.'

'Bert says re-moulds will do the job.'

'They might do a job but not the best.'

Grace sighed. 'I can't afford new tyres. Re-moulds will be fine. It's hardly as if I'm going to do any racing. Getting from A to B is all I ask.'

'Point taken,' he said. He drove in silence for a moment. 'Just one thing—if this weather gets worse and you have to make a trip out to somewhere that's going to be really hard to get to, I'd like you to borrow this car.'

'What! Are you mad? This Range Rover costs something like double my annual salary!'

'It's insured. Tell me, Grace, if there was trouble and

if I needed to borrow your car, you'd lend it to me, wouldn't you?'

'It's not the same.'

'How is it different?'

'It just is. You need to take the left fork here and keep going up. The road's a bit precipitous.' She pointed to a rack of CDs just below the dashboard. 'Shall I pick some soothing music?'

'Soothe away,' he said.

She needed to stop talking for a while. Mike was unsettling her. His offer to lend her his car—she could imagine some men making it solely to impress her. But she didn't think Mike was like that. It was a genuine, helpful offer and it only added to his attractiveness. Which, given the way he still felt about his dead wife, could be a real problem. Putting some music on would mean they didn't have to talk. It would keep things impersonal.

What was the last thing he had been listening to? She ejected the CD, looked at the title in the dim light from the dashboard and laughed out loud. '*Nursery Rhymes To Sing Along To?*'

He slanted a look at her. 'When we're bored with driving, Bethany and I sing duets. We're very good. Would you like to join me in a rendition of "*Ba Ba Black Sheep*"?'

'I think I'll pass.'

'We sing Christmas songs too. There's a CD of them in the rack. With finishing for the holidays so early, Bethany's been practising non-stop for her school Nativity since half-term, so we're pretty hot on carols.'

'That's handy. You'll be a big asset at the carol service. Talking of school…'

'She's booked into Rivercut Primary for January. I want her to grow up in the village.'

'That's good, but it wasn't what I was going to say. It occurred to me that the school here has still got a couple of weeks until the end of term. The reception teacher is a pal of mine—I'm sure she'd let Bethany start now if you wanted.'

'Well…'

'You know, Christmas is a great time for a kiddie to settle into a new class. It's all glitter and paper chains and snowflakes. And with you taking over Rosemary's list, it would mean Bethany is safe and occupied and happy while you're working.'

There was a silence as Mike negotiated two hairpin bends in succession. Grace held her breath. Had she said too much? Would he accuse her of interfering? 'You're right,' he said at last. 'I'll take her down there tomorrow and introduce ourselves.'

Phew, he hadn't taken her suggestion the wrong way. Grace riffled through the CDs with a feeling of relief. A lot were Bethany's but those he had picked for himself were a wide-ranging selection.

'You've got an interesting taste in music,' she commented.

'I have to give the non-musical answer. I know what I like.'

Grace slipped in a disc, but turned it down low. 'I like this,' she said. 'It's cheerful.'

Ten minutes later they drove into the courtyard of High Scar Farm. 'We were just passing,' said Mike with little regard for the truth. 'Nurse Fellowes is showing me the area and I thought we'd drop in. Mr Lawrie, this morning your son said that you'd been having some pains in your chest?'

'Indigestion,' growled Joshua Lawrie.

'Right. We can fix that—if it is indigestion. How have you been getting about in general?'

'All right.'

'No you haven't, Pa,' said his daughter-in-law. 'You've slowed right down and you know it. You can't get to the top of the stairs without catching your breath. And then these pains have started. Why indigestion now? You're eating the same food as you have for the past fifty years.'

'It's the sort of thing you expect when you get older.'

Grace looked at Joshua thoughtfully. She'd not seen him for quite a while, and it struck her that he had aged. He didn't move as smartly as he had done, his back was more bowed.

'Are you still forking the hay into the top loft, Mr Lawrie?' she asked. 'I remember how strong you were. You did it with just one arm.'

'Takes him all his time with two now,' said Pip. He got a malevolent look.

'Why don't we go into your bedroom and let me have a quick look at you?' Mike suggested. 'It'll only take a couple of minutes.'

'I don't see any point—'

His son interrupted. 'Go on, Pa. Doctor's come all this way to see you. It's only polite.' Evidently Pip didn't believe the story about the two of them just passing.

'All right, then.' It took quite an effort for Joshua to get up from his seat.

Mike followed him as they went upstairs. When they came down again, Grace could see that something had changed. Mike's expression was stern. Joshua looked half upset, half obstinate.

Mike stood in front of the fire. 'I've examined Mr Lawrie. What he's suffering from is not indigestion but angina pectoris. I think his blood vessels have narrowed, meaning his heart isn't getting enough blood. And this cold weather is only making things worse. I'd like him to go to hospital—and I'd like him to go now.'

'I'm not going to hospital! Not at this hour of night!'

'Pa! You've got to do what the doctor tells you. He's the expert.'

'I would like you in hospital tonight, Mr Lawrie. If you stay here, I know you'll go out in that farmyard tomorrow morning and the cold could kill you.'

'I was born here. I can die here.'

'No, Mr Lawrie.' All of them were silent. Mike's words had been said quietly but with considerable force. After a while he went on. 'Tell you what, I'll meet you halfway. You go to bed now, you stay in your own bed tonight, you wait indoors in the warm tomorrow morning until the ambulance comes for you. Okay?'

'I think that's very fair of the doctor,' Pip put in.

Seeing that everyone was ganging up on the old man, Grace added that the sooner he was in hospital, the quicker he'd be out. 'You might have an angioplasty or perhaps even a bypass operation, but it can be done in a day and afterwards you'll be well on the way back to the man you used to be.'

'All right,' growled Joshua, after a silence just long enough to indicate that he wasn't going to be a pushover. 'I'll be ready tomorrow.'

'Good,' said Mike. 'This is your chance to be both fitter and happier.'

The old man looked at Mike, then nodded imperceptibly. 'I'll go to bed now, then.'

They watched as he left the room. 'Nobody in the past fifteen years has been able to change his mind, Doctor,' said Pip. 'You're a miracle worker.'

'They'll work miracles for him in hospital,' said Mike.

'You achieved a miracle there,' Grace said as they travelled back down the snowy lanes. 'You managed to change his mind.'

'I knew if I insisted that he go to hospital tonight, and he didn't go, then he'd feel that he'd won a bit of a victory. He was entitled to that.'

'That's sneaky. You can be as persuasive as your father sometimes, can't you?'

'Perhaps.'

There was silence for a while. 'I'm starving,' he said suddenly. 'Have you eaten yet?'

'Cup of tea and a biscuit when I got in from work.'

'That's not enough. Is there a pub nearby where I could buy you a meal? We're both looking smart this evening and I think we deserve a treat after our successful visit.'

She looked at him assessingly. 'Just as colleagues?'

'Just that.'

'Then I'd love to,' she said lightly. Even so, she wouldn't choose anywhere too expensive. That would send out exactly the signal she wanted to avoid. 'I know the perfect place—providing you're prepared to be a little more flexible with your arteries than you are with Mr Lawrie's?'

'You're the navigator—direct away.'

'Well,' she said with a grin, 'the place is called The Hilltop for a reason...'

It was an excellent meal. They had a table in the wooden-beamed parlour, by the window so they could see the snow swirling around the moors outside. They had a bottle of good white wine. Fish fresh that morning from Whitby and the hotel's famous—or infamous—speciality: chips guaranteed deep-fried in pure beef dripping.

'I see what you meant about arteries,' said Mike. 'I don't think I'll ever eat another chip cooked in oil again. These are just heaven.'

For dessert, equally wonderful, they had rhubarb crumble and thick, home-made custard.

And then a cafetière of coffee. As she smelled the rich Brazilian coffee beans, Grace closed her eyes and smiled. 'Thank you, Mike. That was the best meal I've had in ages.'

'Likewise. We must come again. Soon.'

She opened her eyes in surprise. What did he mean, soon? She'd only known him for...was it really only twenty-four hours? But she reflected that in London he probably ate out with colleagues a lot. Networking. His offer wouldn't mean anything.

'So tell me about you,' he continued diffidently. 'My father told me you were having to sell the family home. Does it hurt to talk about it?'

His voice was gentle. Grace felt he genuinely cared. 'It all hurts, but it's something that has to be done. The mortgage payments are crippling. Did James tell you why?'

'He said your stepfather cheated your mother.'

'Cheated, but did it quite legally. There's no hope ever of getting the money back. Most of it has been lost in poor investments, from what I gather. I can't blame Mum. She was horribly lonely—and the man was a real charmer. I was happy for her—can you believe that? I hate men like him.'

'Not all men are the same.'

'So I thought. Until I found the man of my own dreams and it turned out that I was as big a fool as my mother. He was even more worthless than my stepfather.' She sighed. 'But I don't want to talk about Peter right now. I enjoyed the meal—and the evening—too much to want to be made angry.'

He reached across the table for a moment and gripped her hand. The physical contact warmed her, showed he understood. Grace was a tactile person. She understood how important touch was when used for comfort or silent sympathy. Mike's brief grip was judged just right and she appreciated it. But when he'd let go and was signalling to the waitress for the bill, she wished it could have gone on a bit longer.

As they walked down the hallway he paused by the il-luminated Christmas tree. 'That's nice. I promised Bethany we could have a real tree this Christmas. Where do I buy a good one? The Forestry Commission?'

Grace shook her head. 'There's a plantation called Kilham's out on the Penthwaite road, it's not too far away. If you've got somewhere to plant it, get a tree in a special pot that you can put in the ground. Then you can keep it from year to year. But order one quickly, they soon disappear.'

'I'll do that.'

They walked out of the warmth of the pub into a moonlit wilderness. The snow had stopped, there was only the blanket of white over the peaks around them. Grace felt an uplifting excitement at the sheer beauty of it.

'Now, that's something you don't see in London,' said Mike softly. 'Truly magnificent.'

'I love it,' said Grace. 'It's so pure, so wonderful. It makes me think that everything just has to be all right really. Christmas will be white. Every child will get their favourite toy. People will laugh and be happy and…'

'You're an idealist, Grace.'

She grinned at him. 'Someone has to be.'

He cupped her elbow to steer her to the car. Did his hand take that bit longer to fall away?

As Mike started the Range Rover, feeling replete, he was shaken by a giant yawn.

Grace glanced across. 'Are you all right? Do you want to go back inside and have another coffee?'

He was touched at her quick concern. 'I'll be fine. It's been a long day, that's all.' It had too. He let out the clutch and started back down the swooping road, mulling over the events. Beginning work two weeks before he was expecting to. The sense that the patients were comparing him with his father. The successful visit tonight. The hearty meal. No wonder he was tired.

'Yes, of course,' murmured Grace. She bent her head to search through the CDs and with a jump Mike knew she was thinking of his fright over Bethany's apparent disappearance that morning and that horrible, searing moment when he'd been reminded so vividly of Sarah.

'Don't you ever get furious?' he suddenly burst out. 'You lost your mother to a heart attack that could have been avoided. You were let down badly by someone you trusted. How can you be so calm all the time? So certain that the world is a good place? It isn't!'

Grace's head came up. 'Pull over,' she said.

'Don't be ridiculous. I'm driving you home.'

'Pull over,' she repeated. 'I want to show you something.'

There was a stopping place just ahead. Mike did as she asked.

'Come on,' she said. 'You can't see it properly from here.'

See what? But Mike followed her out of the car and across the road to where a bare-leafed tree stood sentinel on the wide verge of the ridge. The snow squeaked under their feet. 'Careful,' he muttered, taking her arm. She didn't pull away.

'What do you see?' she asked, nodding across the valley.

Mike looked. The village lay below the ridge: a crescent of snow-covered roofs and stained-glass curtains, all lit by the moon. 'I see Rivercut,' he said.

'Exactly. I did my training in Leeds. I enjoyed it—it's a nice city. But it's a *city*, Mike. When you look out of a top-floor window at night there are lights all around you— as far as the eye can see.'

Her breath made clouds in the frosty air. 'Meaning?' he asked, his breath mingling with hers.

She gestured below them. 'Look—it's like an illustration from one of those annuals I used to get every Christmas. I can see every house, every window. I can see the decorations. I can guess what's on the children's lists for Santa. It's… It's enclosed—and it's mine. I know them, Mike. I know every family. I look after them. And they look after me. It's what makes a person whole. It's what makes life good.' She looked up at him, her grey eyes clear in the moonlight. 'You're not convinced, are you?'

He was still holding her arm. Through the sleeve of her coat he could feel her warm, vital strength. 'I'd like to be,' he said. He sighed and tipped his head backwards, gazing up through a tracery of bare, snow-lined branches at the great silver disc of the full moon. Was Sarah up there? Watching over him now? Telling him to make a go of this new life?

Grace was still looking at the village. 'The Carters have put up even more lights. I'd hate to have their electricity bill.' But her face was gentle, not condemning. 'I do love Christmas,' she murmured. 'I know it's over-commercialised, but underneath there's still that hope, isn't there?' She glanced up. 'Oh! I can see a star in the east!' Then laughed. 'Except it's moving too fast and it's flashing.'

Mike laughed too. 'These aeroplanes get everywhere.' He continued to track the plane as it passed behind the tree. He frowned. There was a strange collection of twigs attached to one of the branches. 'What kind of bird makes a nest like that?' he said.

Grace turned her head to see. 'It isn't a nest. It's mistletoe.'

Mistletoe. Instantly there was a silence between them. He was aware of her breath on the night air, of her arm under his hand. The tension in her muscles told him she was just as aware of him.

He hesitated just a moment too long before he said, 'Mistletoe? I've never seen it growing wild like that.'

And Grace hesitated just a moment too long before she said, 'Well, there you go. You're in the countryside now.'

And neither of them looked at the mistletoe again as they headed back for the car.

CHAPTER FOUR

IN THE morning Grace had a number of calls to make in the village. Where it hadn't been swept, last night's new snow crunched under her feet as she walked from one house to another. The sun was shining, the snow sparkled and Christmas was most definitely in the air.

She came level with the school playground just as a barrage of shrieks announced the arrival of playtime.

'Hello, Grace!' shouted several of the children, tearing across with their coats open and their scarves flying. 'Where are you going?'

'I'm off to see a patient.' She smiled.

'Hello, Grace,' called another voice. It was Bethany, pink-cheeked and bright-eyed, holding hands with a new friend on each side.

Grace was pleased. She'd rung her friend Liz, the reception class teacher, last night, but she hadn't been sure Mike would actually take the plunge and bring Bethany down. 'Hello, poppet. Are you having a nice time?'

The little girl nodded enthusiastically. 'We made snowflakes and glittered them all over. I made one for you.'

'Thank you. I'll hang it up with my other decorations

when I get them out. I hope you made some for Daddy and Grandad too.'

'I did. And Miss Lang says I can be in the Nativity!'

'That's lovely. Off you go and play now.'

Hmm. If Bethany was at school, Mike would be free after morning surgery. Thinking about a certain phone call she'd received earlier, Grace rang the practice.

'Grace? What's the matter? I can hear children screaming!'

'It's playtime, Mike.'

'Oh, sorry.'

Grace grinned. 'And before you ask, Bethany is building a snowman with a whole lot of new friends.'

'Has she got her coat on?'

'They've all got their coats on. She told me she's been decorating snowflakes and she's going to be in the Nativity play.'

'She's *been* in a Nativity play. She was a king's page. You've no idea how much spin I had to put on to convince her it was superior to being an angel.'

Grace chuckled. 'The reason I'm ringing is to ask if you could drive me up to see a patient called Edith Holroyd this afternoon. She's a farmer's wife and is suffering from rheumatoid arthritis. I thought she was more or less stable but she phoned this morning asking if she could have a stronger dosage of drugs because the pain was coming back. I'm just a bit concerned. I'd like another opinion before she gets a fresh prescription.'

'It's what I'm here for—as long as I'm outside those school gates at three to pick up Bethany. And talking of picking up, you might like to know Pip Lawrie phoned to say Joshua grumbled his way into the ambulance which is even now heading for the hospital.'

'I know,' said Grace. 'I saw it coming through the village with Joshua's daughter-in-law driving behind to stop him escaping through the rear doors and doing a runner. I'll see you at the surgery after lunch, okay?'

'I'll be here.'

Mike found he was looking forward to doing another visit with Grace. He got a small rush of pleasure when she tapped on his door to ask if he was ready. She looked a typical district nurse with her neat uniform, tidy hair and minimal make-up, but there was a joyous inner core to her that in Mike's view made her a very superior community practitioner indeed.

As she directed him out of the village and up into the hills, he said, 'I had a look at Mrs Holroyd's notes—has anyone ever told you you write a fine report, by the way?—and I've signed out what extra medication might be needed from the pharmacy. It might save her or her husband a trek to the nearest chemist.'

'That's thoughtful,' said Grace.

Mike felt an absurd warmth at her praise. 'It's not something I'd have been likely to do in London, but it seemed obvious here. There is still the possibility that surgery might be necessary. Tell me more about her. What is she like as a person?'

'Sixty-three, daughter of a farmer, married another farmer who lived ten miles away. One daughter living locally, one son who emigrated to Australia and is farming a station out there that seems to be the size of Yorkshire.

Never known any other life than farming and never wanted to. She can…she could…drive a tractor, shear a sheep, fork out feed. Only four years ago she could work in the fields for twelve hours and still turn out three hot meals a day for the family. Then she got rheumatoid arthritis and suddenly couldn't work at all. It's a tragedy! She hates just sitting around. Her husband loves her and wants her to be as comfortable as possible but he must miss the work she could do.'

Not a story you'd hear in London, Mike thought, but said nothing.

Grace continued. 'She knows that, barring some miracle cure, she's never going to get back to the person she was. She's never complained—but it grieves her. Life isn't fair sometimes.'

He was amused by her vehemence. 'Do you care for all your patients as much as this one?'

She shrugged. 'In this case, the family are friends. When I was a Guide my patrol used to go and sleep in their barn and Mrs Holroyd kept an eye on us. She used to accidentally cook too much dinner and need us to use it up for her.'

'She sounds like a good person.'

'She is. Her husband too.'

The farm was large and well kept. Mike didn't miss Grace's wistful expression as she glanced at one of the barns. Did she wish she was a young girl again?

Inside the farmhouse Fred Holroyd was on constant alert, fetching things for his wife, even though she scolded him and told him it wasn't necessary. Mike could feel the love between them. He liked Edith Holroyd too. He could tell the disease was sapping her strength, that she hated not being able to do the things that had once been so easy. He gave her a thorough examination—and sensed Grace's approval as she looked on—but he knew from the beginning that there was going to be no miracle cure.

He left Grace to help Edith get dressed and went back into the parlour. Fred was trying not to appear too hopeful. Mike examined the pictures on the wall while they waited. Most of them were photographs—some obviously of children or grandchildren but others were much older. Pictures of a kind of farming that had now disappeared.

When Grace and Edith came in, he said, 'Mrs Holroyd, I'm going to alter your medication. It should make your life a little easier, help you to sleep better. But you know this is in no way a cure.'

'I know. I've accepted that. There's worse off than me.' There was toughness in the voice but also just a thread of desperation.

'What do you do to occupy your time?'

'I cook still. I read. It's nice to have the time, now I'm not in the fields any more. I like it when my grandchildren come round. Helen brings them at least once a week. And I write to my son in Australia.'

Mike nodded, an idea forming. 'You must have seen a lot of changes. I've been looking at your photographs—some of the farming scenes date back to your childhood.'

A small smile creased Edith's face. 'I was helping in the yard when I was six,' she said. 'Not getting in the way, mind, but helping. My father paid me—he gave me a shilling and some sweets.'

'Ever thought of writing down your memories? To pass them on to your children and grandchildren?'

Mrs Holroyd looked shocked. 'Me! I couldn't write!'

'You write to your son. Just think of it as a series of letters. Start by listing all the jobs you did in the yard. It's a fast-disappearing way of life. People will be interested in the years to come.'

'I think that's a great idea,' said Fred. 'You always tell a good story, Edith.'

'Well, I've got some memories,' she admitted. 'I'll give it a go.'

'You're an odd sort of doctor,' said Grace as they crossed the farmyard to the car. 'I'm really impressed. That idea you gave Mrs Holroyd—that she write out her life story—that was inspired. It'll probably do her as much good as the medicine.'

'Just so long as she keeps taking the medicine! But thanks—one of the reasons I wanted to come up here to Yorkshire was that I thought there might be the chance to spend more time talking to patients. Not the ten minutes allocated to them in the surgery but an opportunity to get to know them.'

'In an ideal world,' Grace said. She opened the passenger door, then paused. 'Can you hang on a moment? There's something I need to collect. I won't be long.' And she walked quickly over to the barn she had looked at before.

Mike watched, surprised, as she pushed open the unlocked door. She obviously knew what she was doing, but even so…

It wasn't a barn for agricultural use. He'd been on City Farm excursions with Bethany and this building didn't have anything like the requisite dusty, cobwebby atmosphere. Or the smell, for that matter. As Mike stepped through the doorway his eyes took in a new concrete floor, a sound roof and solid walls. There were packing cases stacked along one wall and furniture, wrapped in thick insulating sheets, at the far end.

Grace was rummaging through a packing case, lifting out cardboard boxes.

'I assume the Holroyds don't mind you making off with the crown jewels, do they?'

She didn't look round. 'It's not the crown jewels and they know all about it. Please, Mike, just wait in the car. I really won't be a moment.'

He was startled. Her voice was ragged with tension. 'Can I help you carry anything?'

'It's fine. The boxes are very light. Please, Mike.'

He put his hand on her arm, just for a second. 'No hurry.' But it was a puzzle—the first time he'd heard her sounding less than in control. It made him feel... He didn't know how he felt. So once they were in the car heading for Rivercut again, boxes safely stowed in the back, he started talking about the government's latest plans for reorganisation of the health service. It wasn't exciting, but it was something that concerned them both, and on which they both had views. A sensible talk between two professionals. He was sure they both benefited from it.

When he drew up outside Grace's cottage, she unloaded her three cardboard boxes—they really were light, he noted with interest—looked at her watch and said, 'Ten minutes for you to get to school. Perfect timing.'

He glanced across at the side road leading down to the school. It wasn't exactly solid with cars, but enough to make parking interesting. 'I couldn't leave the car here while I collect Bethany, could I? Save doing a turn in the road in the snow with everyone watching.'

She raised her eyebrows. 'Says the man who used to drive a Jaguar in London. Yes, of course you can. Go on, you don't want to be late.'

'Thanks. Well, see you tomorrow, I expect.'

Grace shut the door behind Mike and let out a breath she hadn't realised she'd been holding. Her gaze fell on the boxes of Christmas decorations the Holroyds had been storing for her. Ridiculous to get so upset. She gave a mighty sniff and went to put the kettle on for a comforting mug of tea.

But the kettle had only just boiled when there was a knock on the door. On the doorstep stood Mike, a beaming Bethany—and a very, very glittery snowflake.

'She made it for you,' said Mike with a perfectly straight face. 'So I knew you'd want it right away.'

'Thank you, poppet. It's lovely,' said Grace. A small shower of silver transferred itself to her uniform cardigan as she took the star.

'Yes, it is,' agreed Bethany. She gave an excited skip. 'I'm going to be an angel!'

Some spin, thought Grace, looking at Mike.

He looked back. 'And, um, she has to have a costume as soon as possible. Tomorrow, for preference. I asked about hiring one. Everyone fell about laughing. The teacher thought you might be able to help.'

Oh, did she? Grace was going to have words with Liz next time she saw her. 'Well, all you need is a white pillowcase and a couple of lengths of tinsel, but... Wait a minute...' She'd remembered something. 'Actually,' she said slowly, 'I do have an angel costume ready made. It used to be mine. But it's at the manor. In the attics.' And that would mean going back there.

'That would be great. Can we take you? Bethany and I? In the car?' said Mike, and then he saw her expression. 'But, of course, I understand if…'

Grace shook herself. It was just a house and an attic and a box of dressing-up clothes. She smiled at Bethany. 'I'll fetch the keys.'

The manor stood on rising ground just outside the village. No one had been up the drive for quite a while, so the snow lay thick along it. The afternoon sun gilded the mellow Georgian facade and there were flashes of light reflected from the icicles hanging from the eves. Grace hadn't expected this to hurt quite so much.

Bethany was clamouring to get out as soon as Mike stopped the car.

'It's beautiful,' he said quietly. 'Like an illustration out of one of Bethany's fairy stories.'

But without the prince, thought Grace. She unlocked the double outer doors, then the inner doors. There was a film of dust everywhere—and it was cold. But that was why she'd moved out. It took too long and cost too much to heat. She simply hadn't been able to manage it by herself.

Mike followed her in. 'No furniture?' he queried.

'The agent advised it. He said the corporate bods prefer to see floor space if they're thinking of out-of-town head-quarters.' But it was horrible, hearing their echoing foot-steps where once the sound would have been absorbed by sofas and bookcases and low tables and colourful rugs. She tried to see the empty hall through Mike's eyes. An elegant oak-panelled room, built in the days when the hall had been the main room of the house. An ornate fireplace, now blocked up against the draughts from the chimney. A graceful staircase leading to an open landing.

Bethany gave a squeal of delight and ran past them to start climbing the stairs. Grace gave a shaky smile. 'We used to have parties in this room. You should have seen it—they were glorious. And beforehand I'd borrow one of my mother's long skirts and walk down the stairs, holding my dress just above my ankles and feeling beautiful. Exactly like the actresses in the films Mum loved watching.'

'I imagine you outshone them all. Bethany, sweetheart, be careful on the stairs.'

'They're shallow, Mike. It's quite difficult to hurt yourself falling down them.'

But he was hurrying up after his daughter, so Grace followed.

On the landing, Bethany demanded to know what was in all the rooms. 'Sorry,' said Mike. 'It's a passion of hers.'

Grace would have preferred to collect the dressing-up box and go, but she couldn't disappoint that bright, excited little face. 'This used to be my bedroom,' she said.

It wasn't too bad, coming in here. She saw Mike look around, noting the brighter patches of wallpaper where her wardrobe, bed, chest of drawers and dressing table had stood. Bethany ran to the window to look out.

'My desk was under that window. When I was tired of studying, I could stare at the moors. Probably why I love them so much.'

'I'm trying to imagine you as a schoolgirl. What were you like?'

'Gawky,' she said, and Mike smiled. 'With pigtails. That wall was covered with pictures of pop stars and horses. Dad always said the horses were better looking. You've got all that to come with Bethany.'

She led them down the passage towards the attic staircase. But Bethany reached up to open the next door along. 'Daddy!' she gasped, looking in. 'It's a princess bed!'

'Ah,' said Grace. 'That was my parents' room. The bed was built actually in there goodness knows how many generations ago. The only way to get it out would have been in pieces, so I left it for the time being.' Peter had talked grandly about knocking through the wall when they were married and turning her room into a palatial en suite. She wished she'd known before she'd got engaged how much of his love had had its roots in pure, unadulterated snobbery.

'It's a hit with one little girl, that's for sure,' said Mike. 'Sweetheart, don't bounce up and down on the mattress like that. It's ever so dusty.'

Grace was glad to be distracted from her memories. 'Bethany's not asthmatic, is she?'

'No, I just…' He broke off. 'It's a lovely light room too, with these windows on two sides. Views of the whole valley.'

'Yes.' Peter had loved that too. The fact that up here he had been lord of all he'd surveyed. Suddenly Grace wanted to retch. 'The attic is this way,' she said abruptly. 'You'll like this, Bethany. There's a cupboard door—and when you open it you find a staircase instead.'

Mike's daughter immediately bounced off the bed and raced past Grace round the corner to open the next door.

Except that wasn't the attic staircase. Grace stood rooted to the spot, the desire to be sick even stronger.

Mike brushed past. 'Bethany, wait for me before you start climbing…' He looked into the room, stood perfectly still for a second, then shut the door gently. 'Not that one, darling. Let's try the next. Wow! Stairs! Just as Grace said. Carefully now.'

Feeling came back to Grace's nerve-ends. She followed them up the enclosed staircase, smiled wanly as Bethany ran in and out of the little attic bedrooms, unlocked the end room she'd been using for storage. Then she retrieved the box with the angel costume in, and went downstairs.

'Sorry,' said Mike again. 'She's going to want to look everywhere on the ground floor too. I swear she's going to be an estate agent when she grows up. It's hurting you, isn't it, showing someone around your home?'

'I've had easier tasks,' said Grace.

'You don't do it when someone is interested in buying it, do you?'

'No, I leave it to the agent. I couldn't bear to see their faces as they look at the shabby wallpaper and the old Victorian toilet fittings. Any big company would gut the place and refit it anyway.'

'You love it very much.'

'Of course I do. It's my home. Mike, do you mind if I wait outside while Bethany looks at the downstairs rooms?'

'We'll be quick.' He put his hand on her shoulder, gently. She reached up, touched his hand and then moved to the door.

She had time to regain her equilibrium before they joined her. It was ridiculous to get so worked up. The manor had to be sold and that was an end to it. She locked the doors and turned to see that Bethany, like all children every-where, had been unable to resist the lure of the wide sweep of untouched snow in the orchard to one side of the drive.

'Not too far, sweetheart,' called Mike, an edge to his voice. 'It's getting dark and I don't know how deep it is.'

Grace looked at him curiously. Surely even in London there were places where a child could fall full length in the snow with perfect safety? How on earth did he think snow angels were made? 'Let's run and catch her,' she suggested. 'I used to love it when my parents did that.'

He cast her a swift, grateful glance and pelted one way. Grace ran the other way in a pincer movement. Bethany shrieked happily and did indeed fall full length in the snow, suffering no ill effects at all.

She let her father scoop her up. 'What's that?' she said, pointing up into the branches of the nearest apple tree.

'Mistletoe,' said Mike knowledgeably. 'People kiss under it.' And he kissed his daughter on the forehead.

Bethany was charmed. 'Grace kiss me now,' she de-manded.

So Mike put her down and Grace bent to give the little girl a hug and a kiss.

'Now Grace and Daddy.'

There was a tiny silence. Grace straightened up. Her eyes met Mike's.

'Absolutely,' said Mike. He put one hand on her upper arm and moved forward. Just the most delicate touch of lips on lips. They were cold, but a thrill passed through Grace that she had never quite felt before. She rested one hand on his body, felt the fast beating of his heart through his coat and leaned forward. He kissed her again, warmer, slightly longer, but just as soft. 'For luck,' he said. Then let out a breath, hoisted his daughter up to his shoulder and walked back to the car.

CHAPTER FIVE

TEA was over. Bethany was having a bedtime story read by Grandad. There was no evening surgery—and Mike was walking down Rivercut High Street to Grace's cottage. She'd noticed some places where the tinsel trim needed to be sewn back onto the angel dress. She'd take it straight over to the school tomorrow. No need, he'd said, I'll come down later to pick it up.

Which he was. Wondering at himself the whole way. That kiss. Just a friendly peck he'd meant it as. But the moment their lips had touched it had ceased to be a friendly gesture and had *meant* something. Trouble was, he didn't know what. And with Sarah an ever-present ache in his mind, if the kiss had meant something to Grace too, he'd have to break off whatever it was. It wasn't fair to her. But it had been lovely. And—yes, he admitted it—too short.

'Hi,' said Grace when he knocked at her door. She'd changed into jeans and a jumper and let her hair down. It was longer than he'd thought, and very attractive. 'Come in—and before you say anything, yes, it is a bit of a contrast to the manor.'

Mike smiled. 'On the contrary, you've made a tiny space look quite large.'

'Thank you. Mrs Johnson up the road remembers families of eight or nine children living in these cottages. Personally I think it does just nicely for one—like a comfortable set of clothes that I put on when I enter the front door.'

'I shouldn't gain any weight, then,' he said with a grin.

'I can't, I'm too busy. I've got the angel costume for you. Oh, and I found my photo albums for Bethany so she can see what the manor looked like with furniture in. You're welcome to borrow them.'

It was a clear hint but, 'I don't need to rush home straight away,' he said.

'That's a pity,' said Grace.

He laughed out loud at her honesty. 'And that's why. I think we might need a small talk, don't you?'

'I suppose so. I'll make some coffee. Sit on the couch—you won't loom as much.'

But he didn't sit. He wandered around the room. It wasn't very warm. Did she not notice? Or was she really too hard up to heat it properly? He turned to see her watching him from the door to the kitchen, an anxious look on her face. 'This is a handsome sideboard,' he said, stroking the polished walnut surface.

'It's Georgian. Practically the smallest piece of furniture from the manor.' Then she hesitated. 'You've probably guessed what was stored in Mr Holroyd's barn was the rest.'

'I wondered.'

'I know I need the cash, but I just couldn't bring myself to sell everything I'd grown up with. And if I get some-where larger to live then I'd like to keep a few more pieces.'

'Seems a good idea. What was in the boxes you brought back today?'

She grinned. 'Christmas decorations. I realised when Bethany told me about the snowflakes this morning that I hadn't put mine up yet.' She ducked back into the kitchen and reappeared with two mugs of coffee. She handed him one then sat cross-legged on a large cushion by the wall.

Mike felt the tiniest bit impatient. 'Oh, come on, Grace. This might be a small couch, but there's plenty of room for two.'

She waved him to sit down. 'I sit here a lot. Good for the posture.'

'Really? Your posture looks pretty good to me.'

'Shows it works.' She reached under the coffee table for a couple of albums. 'Here,' she said, passing them to him. 'The manor.'

'Grace, this is silly. Come over here and show me them properly. I don't bite.'

'It's not biting I'm worried about.'

Mike's gut clenched. 'And *that's* what we need to talk about. Grace…'

Her mobile rang, making him jump. 'Sorry,' she said. 'The trouble with having been born in Rivercut is that people don't always realise I have off-duty hours.'

But it wasn't someone needing medical attention. And the moment Grace said 'Hi, Bert. The car's ready? That's great! How much do I owe you?' Mike suspected he ought to be leaving.

He downed his coffee double quick, burning his throat, grabbed the bag with the angel costume in and had nearly made it to the door when Grace put out a hand, barring his way.

'I don't quite understand, Bert. Why is there no charge for the tyres?'

'I'd better go. Bethany will be—'

She toggled the mute button. 'You're in no hurry, remember? Yes, Bert, I understand they're fantastic tyres and will probably outlive the car, but how much did they cost?'

Mike winced.

'*How much?* Six hundred pounds? That's three times the... Pardon? Dr Curtis said the practice would pay? Yes, wasn't it nice of them? Yes, it was a surprise to me too. Refresh my memory, Bert. Would that be old Dr Curtis or the young one?'

She listened for a moment more and rang off.

Get in first, thought Mike. 'No arguments, Grace. You use your vehicle to work for the practice and it just wouldn't have been safe enough with remoulds. You are no good to us or to your patients if you break down.'

'You pay me for using my car! I claim every inch of mileage I'm entitled to.'

'Forty pence a mile doesn't come anywhere near covering your usage. The cost of those tyres is worth it to me because I now know that you're safer in bad weather than you were.'

'I thought you said the practice paid.'

'Me, the practice—what does it matter?'

'It matters because I have to know who to pay back!'

'Nobody!' He bit out his words in frustration. 'You weren't safe in that car and I'm not having anybody else I care about die in cars when I can do something about it!'

He didn't realise he had a look of anguish on his face until Grace put her hand up to his cheek. 'Mike?'

He stumbled back to the sofa and put his head in his hands. 'Leave me alone.'

He felt the sofa dip. 'Not a chance.'

'Okay, then. You've been warned. This isn't pretty.' He took an immense breath. 'Sarah—my wife—worked with me in the practice. She was a good GP—better than me. Neither of us were supposed to be on duty that night, but Sarah got an emergency call from one of her patients and felt she had to go. It was raining, the roads were slippery, she was in the little runabout, not the Jaguar.' He took another deep, shuddering breath, conscious of Grace's arm around his shoulders but seeing only the slick, wet tarmac and the blazing lights of the traffic. 'It wasn't her fault, the inquest decided that. A lorry coming the other way swerved to avoid a car pulling out of a side road and lost control. Sarah braked, she had lightning reflexes, but she skidded and the lorry smashed into her. It almost flattened the little car and it caught fire. She died in A and E.'

Now both her arms were around him. 'Oh, Mike. Oh, Mike.'

He turned instinctively, buried his head in her shoulder, curling into himself with the pain of the memories. 'I looked at the police report afterwards, got to talk to the mechanic who had examined the wreckage of the car. He told me the tyre treads were within the legal limits. But if there had been just a little more tread then she might have stopped just a few feet sooner, might not have skidded. I was the one who saw to the maintenance of the cars. I can't forgive myself for that.'

Grace was crying too. Mike felt her tears splash against his forehead. 'You weren't to blame for the accident!'

'But I'm to blame that Sarah died.' He pulled away. 'I'd better go.'

'Not like that, you won't. I'll make some more coffee.'

He leant back against the cushions, drained. But in a strange, horrible way he felt better. He'd never said it out loud to anyone before, that he knew he was to blame for Sarah's death. Grace returned, sat down next to him and put a warm mug between his hands.

'Drink,' she said. 'It'll do you good.'

More silence. He sipped the coffee, felt its warmth trickle into him. For want of anything better to do he opened one of the albums. 'The manor,' he said. 'All dressed up for Christmas.' To be accurate, it was the manor at night. All the windows were lit, swags of coloured lights had been fixed to the elegant facade and there were two large Christmas trees, one either side of the front door.

Grace smiled. 'Those trees are still at the back of the hall. They're quite a bit bigger than that now. We used to enlist the regulars at the pub each year to heft them into place. Lots of people have said it doesn't seem the same without them this year.'

Mike turned the pages. 'Oh, wow,' he said at a photograph of the entrance hall set out for a party. A party in the grand style too. 'I see what you mean about it looking splendid. You ate like this every night?'

'Idiot,' replied Grace.

The hall was decorated and there was a huge Christmas tree next to the fireplace with presents piled underneath. Tables had been arranged in the form of a big T and covered in white cloths. Arranged on them was a vast buffet. And frozen in time were the smiling guests. Mike could almost hear the chink of glasses and buzz of good-humoured conversation. It could have been an old-fashioned Christmas-card scene of the squire and his guests making merry—but brought up to date.

He realised that Grace was leaning against him. She seemed to be doing it quite unconsciously, a woman who was used to touching, who wasn't uncomfortable with herself. 'Now do you see why I like Christmas so much?' she said. 'Everyone looks so happy. As if they think this can go on for ever. I wish the manor looked like that now, instead of horrid and echoing. Look, there I am! Holding my mother's hand.'

Mike bent to look closer. Grace's hair brushed his cheek for a moment. Yes, he could see her now. A young Grace, about ten years old. Her hair had been a lighter blonde then, but she radiated the same inner joy. 'And with a smart long dress,' he said, trying to sound prosaic. 'Is that the skirt you borrowed?'

She chuckled. 'No, it's a real dress—sort of. I threw a tantrum because I didn't have anything long to wear. Everyone else was in a full-length dress, why not me? So my mother fashioned that dress out of a real Indian silk scarf. Took her half an hour. I thought I was the best-dressed woman in the place.'

At which point Grace did notice that she was leaning against him. She got up hurriedly. 'There are photos of the other rooms there too. The music room, the dining room, my father's den. Take them to show Bethany.'

Mike stood reluctantly. It had been nice, sitting there with Grace. 'I will. She'll be fascinated.'

Grace moistened her lips. 'Mike—I do need to repay you for the tyres somehow. If you've ever been…quite well-to-do and then find yourself quite definitely poor, then you get very edgy if you think you're being offered charity. And before you say anything, I know at times people offer things and you should accept them in the spirit they're meant, but it's not so easy when you've only met that person three days before.'

He sighed. 'Without boasting,' he said, 'a large sum of money to you is not so large to me. For various reasons I'm…well, comfortable. It pleases me that people should be able to share in my good fortune.'

'Maybe so. But I'm not very good at being indebted.'

'You could help us integrate with the village, if you like. You know everyone and we know no one.'

'Except your dad, who *does* know everyone,' she murmured.

'I want Bethany to be settled here. Part of the community.'

Grace laughed. 'She'll do that without any help from me. I've never met such a friendly child.'

'Tell me about it,' muttered Mike. 'Do you know how many sleepless nights that friendliness gives a father?'

'She'll be fine. Now she's at school she'll be invited to tea and to parties. She'll go swimming and riding with the other kids. She'll… Now what's the matter?'

'Nothing.' And it was nothing. He would have to get over this protectiveness. And he may as well start now. 'There is one thing,' he said slowly. 'She wants to ride. Will you take her for me?'

Grace looked puzzled. 'The beginners' class is in the afternoon straight after school. You could take her yourself.'

'No, I can't,' he ground out. 'Horses are large and dangerous. Bethany is small and infinitely precious. If I take her, I'll be up there on the horse's back with her. Probably not very clever in the street-cred stakes.'

'Mike, the instructors are trained. This is their livelihood. Why would they teach kids something dangerous?'

Suddenly he needed to be out of this small room. He needed air to breathe and space around him. 'I have as much right to be irrational about my only daughter as the next man,' he said. 'But, equally, I don't want to infect Bethany with my prejudices. Just make the arrangements and stay with her the whole time, will you? Please, Grace?'

She opened the door for him. 'I'll give the stable a ring. She will be safe, Mike.'

'Good,' he said. 'Good.' And strode up the high street through the cold, crunchy snow, feeling as if he was about to throw up.

Thursday morning. Grace did her early calls, then went to the surgery to write up her notes and get ready for her diabetes clinic. After last night's emotional exchanges she had thought long and hard about how to behave around Mike and had decided it would be best for both of them if she adopted the same cheerful camaraderie with him as she did with his father. As for that kiss yesterday afternoon (over which she had expended even more long, hard thought), that had been so fleeting, such a nearly precious moment, that she wasn't going to let any highly charged personal stuff get in the way. Truth to tell, she wasn't sure yet how she felt about Mike. The pull of attraction was there—on both sides, she thought—but she didn't think he was ready to love another woman yet, and she couldn't see herself trusting another man with her heart for a long time to come.

Accordingly, when Mike put his head round the door and asked if she minded him sitting in on her clinic, she said, 'Yes, I do mind. Go and play with your own patients.'

It was evidently the right tack. He moved a chair to the corner of the room, unperturbed. 'My list this morning seems to be composed entirely of young women who have come down with mysterious colds or unidentifiable aches. I've shifted them to Dad and the nurse.'

Grace grinned. 'Well, you can't blame them. You're novelty value.' *And great eye-candy.*

'That's what Dad said.'

'Okay, you may observe my clinic with pleasure—not that it would make any difference if I did object, I suspect—but first I've got bad news for you. Bethany can start her riding lessons today. For now she just needs a pair of jeans, a jumper and a loose coat. I can take them home with me, get her changed at my place, and then drive her to the stables. It's a couple of miles past the manor.'

Mike didn't look thrilled, but said he'd get the clothes out.

Grace's first patient was Angela Mather, a busy mum who nodded approvingly as Grace explained to Mike that Angela had had type 1 diabetes from an early age, managed it herself with insulin injections and was here for her annual check-up.

'I saw you yesterday at school,' she said while Grace was checking her blood pressure and taking a blood sample. 'My Joanne was telling me all about your Bethany. Played together all lunchtime, she said. Would she like to come to tea one day? Oh, and you must bring her to the Rivercut children's Christmas party next week. I'll put you down for sausage rolls, shall I?' She rolled down her sleeve, nodded when Grace said she'd be in touch about the results, and hurried off.

'Children's Christmas party?' said Mike faintly.

'In the village hall next to St Lawrence's. I'll do you a check-list.'

Her next patient, Mr Dobbs, told Mike at length that North Yorkshire had a 98.9 per cent record of good diabetes health care as opposed to the national average of 98 per cent. Grace didn't dare meet Mike's eyes as she relayed the information that Mr Dobbs was a newly diagnosed type 2 who needed regular monitoring and had never missed an appointment yet.

'Good grief, he knew more about diabetes than I do,' said Mike when the elderly man had left the room.

'That's the Internet for you—as soon as he got the diagnosis he read every leaflet I gave him and then monopolised the library PC to check that I knew what I was talking about.'

Mike stood up. 'Well, you've got my vote. Can I just cast an eye over the surgery's diabetes register?'

Grace waved him towards the PC. 'Help yourself. It's open on one of the windows.'

Evening surgery didn't start until six p.m. on a Thursday. The riding lesson was due to finish at five. After a short struggle with himself, Mike drove to Rivercut Stables despite the fact that Grace had said she'd bring Bethany back. Inside a large, brightly lit barn, a dozen or so little boys and girls were solemnly walking round in a giant circle. There were a sprinkling of parents, a handsome woman in riding breeches lounging to one side of the ring and a couple of others calling instructions. Bethany was perched on a chubby barrel of a pony, being led by Grace.

Mike's heart leapt into his mouth. Bethany looked half entranced, half terrified. When she saw him she let go with one hand and managed a quick wave before grabbing the reins again.

Grace turned, and smiled with delighted approbation. Mike smiled back, his nerves easing. Grace looked good in riding breeches, boots and sweater. In fact, she'd looked good every time he had seen her.

Then he shook himself. Hadn't he decided it would be better if he *didn't* react to Grace as a sexual being? She was a colleague, a friend. It was foolish to mix work and pleasure.

It was nearly the end of the riding lesson. The children were told to give their pony an encouraging pat on the neck. Then they had to dismount, take off the saddle and bridle, and carry them back to the tack room before leading the pony to its stall. The two riding-school ladies trotted up and down the line, keeping an eye on the older ones and showing the newbies what to do. Mike hurried over to carry the saddle, which was far too heavy for Bethany. But his daughter was emphatic that she would lead the pony herself.

Grace kept an unobtrusive hand on the pony's mane as the string ambled out of the barn. 'She did really well,' she said.

'Damn. You mean she wants to carry on?'

'Not a doubt, I'd say. You can buy her the most expensive riding hat in the catalogue if it makes you feel better.'

Mike sighed. 'Sadly, I can't imagine a Christmas present she'd like more.'

The older woman who had been watching from the side broke off her conversation with one of the parents. 'Grace Fellowes. What a surprise. What brings you here?'

Mike saw Grace stiffen. 'I've been leading Bethany Curtis around. She's a new pupil. Dr Curtis, Lorna Threlkeld is the owner of Rivercut Stables.'

Cool eyes assessed him. 'Welcome to Rivercut, Dr Curtis.'

'Thank you, I—'

But the woman behind them had hurried forward. 'Dr Curtis!'

Lorna strolled back into the barn. Mike turned. The voice belonged to Grace's diabetes patient. 'There, now, I thought I recognised you. Would Bethany like to come to tea tomorrow? I can pick her up from school and you can collect her after surgery.'

Instinctively, Mike looked at Grace. She gave the tiniest nod.

'Thank you, that would be lovely. Bethany, sweetheart, Joanne's mother has invited…'

But he heard Grace's intake of breath and saw her nudge the pony forward. Angela Mather was still talking, holding up the rest of the line, giving him yard-by-yard directions to her house. He nodded and smiled, but his eyes were on Grace. And on the man coming from the car park who had just altered course to cross her path.

The man had the smug air of a chap who was well aware of his own good looks. He was wearing a good suit, good shoes. Mike disliked him on sight. His eyes flicked from Grace to Bethany, to Grace's hand on the pony's mane. 'Supplementing your income playing nursemaid, Grace? Or is it wish fulfilment?' He laughed and went into the barn. A moment later Mike heard him laugh again—and a female laugh tinkle in reply.

Mike strode forward. 'I could thump his teeth down his throat for you, if you like?'

Grace's set face broke into a forced replica of her usual smile. 'Don't bother. He's not worth the grazed knuckles.'

'No, really, I'd like to.'

Her mouth wobbled into a shaky laugh.

He studied her face. 'Are you all right?'

'Me? Never better.'

CHAPTER SIX

GRACE was half expecting the knock on the door.

'Hi,' said Mike in an unconvincing I-was-just-passing tone. 'We didn't realise until bedtime that you still had Bethany's clothes for school.'

As excuses went, it was a pretty good one. 'Sorry,' said Grace, 'I forgot. Here you are.'

But he'd stepped into the cottage's small front room, ignoring the proffered carrier bag, and had shut the door. 'It's all right,' he said, sitting on the sofa. 'I'm not going to loom.'

Grace sighed, accepting the inevitable. 'Coffee? Tea?'

'Whichever will make you feel most comfortable.'

'That'll be tea, then,' she muttered.

'And no sitting on that cushion on the other side of the room either,' he said when she came back in.

Grace put two mugs on the coffee table. 'If that's your version of "Trust me, I'm a doctor", it needs work.'

Mike smiled. 'You don't need a doctor, you need a friend.' He patted the seat next to him.

Grace sat down. Truth to tell, she had—quite badly— needed an arm around her all evening. 'A friend?' she said.

'A friend. A listening ear. Tell you what, let's start with the woman who owns the stables and carry on from there.'

Grace sipped her tea. 'Lorna Threlkeld? Oh, she's just a minor irritant. Her father is a big landowner around here. He was most put out when Dad sold our farms to the tenants, not to him. He kept ringing up and offering more money, but Dad simply said he was quite well enough off already, thank you, and turned him down every time. So Lorna doesn't like me by way of perpetuating her father's ill-feeling. I can live with it.'

Mike's voice was gentle. 'And the idiot who arrived as we were leaving?'

Her heart gave a sharp twist. 'Yes, well, that was Peter.'

'I hoped it was.'

She looked up at him, startled. 'Hoped? Why?'

He wrapped his arm around her shoulders and gave her a comforting squeeze. 'Because I don't like to think of there being two men who could upset you like that.'

She laughed. 'Thank you. That's very sweet.' She put her mug down on the table and leant against him. It felt comforting and strangely natural. But he was waiting for the story with the air of a man who was prepared to sit there all night if necessary, and this time she was ready to tell him.

'Peter Cox is a local solicitor. He grew up near Nestoby and now he's got a thriving practice based mainly towards Whitby. I've sort of known him for years, but we didn't get together properly until I came back to take up the job here. We went out a few times, bumped into each other at parties, you know how it is.'

'All too well.'

'Anyway, when Mum had her heart attack, he was a real

tower of strength, comforting me, saying he'd take care of all the formalities, saying she wouldn't want me to be unhappy. I didn't let him deal with the legal stuff, of course—for one thing we had our own family solicitor and for another I knew it was a task I must do myself—but I did let him comfort me in other ways. And somehow there we were, engaged, and he said he'd been waiting all his life for a woman like me.' She put up a hand to dash away a tear. 'And I was so happy—in spite of all the awfulness of Mum's death and the mess her affairs were in. I thought… I thought…'

'Shh.' Mike pulled her close and kissed her softly on the forehead. 'What happened next?'

It was a strange way of being kissed. The kiss of a friend. Non-threatening and non-sexual. But she still didn't want to say the next bit. 'Mike, I can't.'

'How about if I help you? That room you didn't want us to see yesterday—it had been decorated a lot more recently than the rest of the house. There was nursery paper with cheerful, smiling animals on the walls. There was fresh paintwork. There were new light fittings, a dimmer switch on the wall, brightly coloured curtains. Grace, it's not difficult to work out.'

Grace felt the tears leaking out of her eyes again. Blast him. Why was he making her dredge this up? 'Yes. Yes, you're right. I was pregnant. It wasn't planned, but there had been times when we hadn't been very careful during sex, so at the backs of our minds it had always been a pos-sibility. I told Peter and he was thrilled and I was happy about it too. I wanted a family. I longed to bring laughter and love back to the manor. Peter was virtually living with me by then and really enjoyed planning how the manor could be updated, how it could be modernised. It would be luxurious, he said, welcoming and habitable and a lovely home for our children. It was far too early, but we got carried away, We even decided on the name for the first one—Jonathan or Eleanor. And he encouraged me to decorate the nursery. He said I should do it up exactly as I wanted it.'

'Oh, Grace.'

'I worked on the nursery while he drew up plans for the rest of the house and got estimates from builders. The estimates came in, they were expensive but reasonable. I was so happy that he was enjoying the thought of turning the manor into a home again.'

'Then?'

'Then the probate papers arrived. It was what I'd expected, but I must have made some sort of face when I opened the packet, because Peter asked me what the problem was.'

'He got a shock?'

'A shock! I wondered if I'd have to resuscitate him! His mouth opened and shut for a minute, but no sound came out. My family had been almost rich before my mother's second husband came along. Not any more. Poor Peter was horrified. He'd thought he was marrying money. And it transpired that when he'd said he'd see to all the renovations himself, he hadn't meant that he'd pay for them, he'd meant he'd supervise them. He yelled and shouted and said I'd led him on—letting him think I had money when all the time I wanted his.'

Mike's grip around her shoulders tightened. 'Bastard.'

'I said I couldn't believe he hadn't already known. The rest of the village had got wind of it. Why did he think Mum had had her seizure, for goodness' sake? And I knew I'd wept all over his silk shirts about the whole thing. He said I'd taken care to be incomprehensible while I was sobbing. What he meant was that he hadn't been listening.'

'A man who hears what he wants to hear, in other words.'

'You've got it.' Grace fumbled for a tissue and blew her nose. 'He stormed back to his own place, and for the first time ever I had to phone your father and tell him I couldn't work that day. I felt dreadful. I was shivering, nauseous, I couldn't stop crying, I had a blinding headache and appalling stomach cramps. I fell asleep out of sheer nervous exhaustion. And when I woke up, I realised I was having a miscarriage.'

'Oh, Grace.' He hugged her tight. 'You poor thing. You must have been devastated.'

'I was. And to make things worse, he went around telling people that I'd tried to trap him. That I wanted his money and had got pregnant to force him into marriage. But lucky for him...'

Mike swore, long and comprehensively. Listening to him, Grace felt surprisingly better.

'It's all right. Really. I won't say it hasn't left a scar, but I'm fine now. I'm just very glad I found out what Peter was like before I married him. In that way I was luckier than my mother.'

'Grace, only you could find a bright side in that experience.'

'Well, I don't think I'll ever be quite so trusting again.

But none of the folk in Rivercut believed him. The good things in life still outweigh the bad.'

'Humph,' said Mike. 'What was he doing at the stables? Are we going to meet him every time Bethany goes riding?'

'I doubt it. He's Lorna's father's solicitor. I expect he was there on a matter of business. Lorna isn't usually there herself. She lets her staff see to the running of the place.'

'Those two instructors we saw? They seemed nice.'

'They are.' Then his words filtered through. 'What do you mean, "Are *we* going to meet him?" I'm supposed to be paying off my tyres, taking Bethany riding. I thought you couldn't bear to watch?'

'I can't. Not for the whole time. I was being brave this afternoon.'

She smiled up at him. 'You did very well. I was proud of you.'

He looked down at her. 'You were?' he said, an odd note in his voice.

Their faces were very close. Grace felt a small tremor run through her. 'I was,' she said.

The next bit happened in slow motion. Very tentatively, Mike bent his head. Grace found herself stretching up to meet him. As she felt his lips on hers, felt the warmth of his body, the strength of his arms as they tightened around her, she knew that this was more than Mike trying to comfort her. It was the kiss of a lover for a lover, a kiss promising everything. She could stop him if she wanted to, but she didn't want to stop him at all.

He pulled her closer. She eased herself towards him and slid her arm around his waist. His hand cupped the back of her head as his kiss became deeper, more intense. She found herself exploring his mouth as eagerly as he was exploring hers, and she gave an inarticulate murmur at the unexpected excitement it generated in her. Her body moved against his; it was telling her that this was good, this was wonderful, that she needed more and…

She pulled back, breathing fast. What was she *doing*?

He understood the message at once. He slackened his hold. 'That… That was…so good,' he said, just as the silence got beyond bearable.

'Mike, I…' She broke off. 'Oh, Mike. I don't know.'

'Grace…'

She shook her head. 'Don't say anything.'

'I have to. Grace, I didn't intend that. I don't know why I did it.' He hesitated. 'But I'd like to do it again.'

Without another word they came together for a second kiss. This was less tentative. Their mouths had already accepted each other. Grace felt herself tingle all over as her tongue twined with his, as she learnt the shape of his lips— both strange and immediately familiar. It was just a kiss, just holding each other and kissing. It ended naturally, with a lingering reluctance. There could have been so much more— part of her wanted so much more—but it was too soon.

Grace knew she would have to explain something of what she felt. But how to find the words when she didn't understand herself? She put a hand to his cheek, meeting his eyes squarely and openly. 'Mike, that was lovely— more than lovely—but I don't think I'm ready for it and I'm fairly sure you aren't either. Can we leave it like this for now? Can we be just friends?'

He took a ragged breath. 'I'm not sure we can. Not

after that. Not after the way you made me feel then. But we can try.'

For a moment more she leant against him, secure in his hold, the memory of the kiss still with her. 'We've only just met,' she said, as much to herself as to him. 'We barely know each other. I'm scarred. You're still wounded. You are, aren't you?'

He passed a hand across his eyes. 'Grace, I can't not be honest with you,' he said slowly. 'Yes I miss Sarah. How can I not? I loved her very much. But while I was kissing you there was no one in my head but you and nowhere else in the world that I wanted to be but right here on your sofa. So I'm feeling guilty now because I didn't feel guilty then. And that's not fair on you.'

She nodded, still tucked into his side. 'Look at us,' she said softly, 'we're like two birds with broken wings. We can flap and make a lot of noise—but we can't fly.'

'Broken wings do mend,' he told her. 'Perhaps we'll learn to fly again.'

'I hope so. I really do.'

Mike strode out into the night, hoping the cold air would cool his brain. What had he been thinking of? How could he have lost his wits so thoroughly? A snowflake melted on his eyelid, several snowflakes. He groaned. He'd come out without a hat—a fine one he'd been this morning to lecture Bethany about wrapping up warmly. *Bethany. Sarah. Grace.* Oh, Lord, what a tangle.

He heard footsteps thudding in the snow behind him, and a voice calling his name. 'Mike—you forgot this.'

He turned to see Grace in flapping duffle coat with a

woolly hat jammed on her head, holding out the bag containing Bethany's clothes. He gave a shamed laugh. 'I must have had something on my mind.'

'Don't let it give you sleepless nights,' she said with a smile.

The falling snow made the village look like a scene from a Christmas card. Lights blazing out of the narrow windows of St Lawrence's church simply added to the illusion. As they stood there the choir began to rehearse another carol, 'Good King Wenceslas'.

'They must have timed that on purpose,' Grace said. 'Listen, "When the snow lay round about. Deep and crisp and even."'

Mike laughed. 'It's not like this in London, you know. In fact, much more of this weather and it'll be "In the Deep Midwinter". How d'you fancy driving when there's water like a stone?'

She grinned. 'I've got new tyres. I can drive anywhere.' Then reached up and kissed his cheek, before turning and hurrying back to her cottage.

Despite her admonition, he did wake up in the small hours thinking of her. He'd been dreaming of Sarah, dreaming of holding her asleep—she'd used to sleep in such a fierce, concentrated way—but when he woke it was Grace in his head and Grace's lips in his memory. He lay there, aching and not knowing why, for a long time before his eyes closed again and he drifted off.

He only saw Grace briefly on Friday. She'd popped in between visits to supplement her medical kit before heading back out again.

'Grace,' he said, hurrying outside after her. 'I was wondering what you were doing at the weekend. Bethany and I are going house hunting. The estate agent has sent us a list, but a couple of the locations look pretty inaccessible without local knowledge.'

She smiled at him as she stowed her kit in the back of the Land Rover. 'Sorry, I can't help. I'm off to a nursing reunion in Leeds. You'd better take your father with you instead.'

His face must have registered his surprise. She grinned. 'Don't look so injured. I do have a life, Mike.'

'I suppose you must have. Oh, well, enjoy yourself.'

'I'll do my best.'

He glanced at the rear of the car. 'Good grief, you're not camping, are you?'

'No, I'm staying with my old roommate. She married a local doctor and still lives in Leeds.' She followed his gaze and laughed. 'That's my out-in-the-snow survival kit. Sleeping bag, reflective blanket. Thermos. Chocolate, Kendal mint cake, thick socks… You ought to have something similar—especially driving Bethany around. Ask James what you need.'

It was a good thought. 'I will. Thanks for the tip. Wait a moment. You'd better give me your mobile number— just in case.'

She raised her eyebrows. 'In case of what? If my patients have an emergency, they need you, your father or the ambulance, not me.' But she gave it to him anyway, and then at his insistence added his mobile number to her phone's address book. 'See you Monday, Mike.'

They had now seen four properties and none of them had been right. Driving back through the falling dusk on

Saturday afternoon, Mike reflected gloomily that at this rate Bethany would have grown up and left home before they'd moved out of his father's surgery flat.

'I know it needed work, but it was a good size for its price, that last one,' said James.

Mike wasn't convinced. He drew to a stop outside the estate agent's office to drop the keys off. 'You two stay in the car. No point all of us getting cold.'

'Sorry,' he said to the agent's polite enquiry. 'Too far out, too cramped, too lonely and too dilapidated in that order.'

The agent accepted this philosophically. 'You're sure you can't go higher on price?' he asked. 'I do have something—perhaps bigger than you were envisaging—but it's slightly over your maximum.' He turned to rummage in a filing cabinet. 'It's a very superior property actually in Rivercut, which, if I remember, was one of your main requirements. It would benefit from a little modernisation, but I assure you it is perfectly habitable.' He found the details and drew them out, tapping the pages in an undecided manner. 'I don't know… My colleague has had one or two nibbles—a local landowner is most interested—but if you are in the position to make a cash purchase… The owner is desirous of selling as soon as possible.'

Mike shrugged and held out his hand. 'I may as well take a look. I can always say no, can't I?'

'Indeed, yes, sir. Good evening.'

Mike took the brochure and hurried back to the car. He wanted to get back home, he wanted warm food inside Bethany and a hot mug of coffee inside himself. He dropped the house details on his father's lap and started the car. And then stalled with a jerk as he caught sight of the photo of the property. 'That's the manor,' he said, flabbergasted.

James looked down. 'I did tell you Grace was having to sell.'

Yes, he had, and Mike knew it perfectly well, really. It was simply that he thought of the manor as Grace's house. She had fitted the place so well—worn it like a ballgown, to use her own analogy. The stark reality of her situation honestly hadn't struck him until he saw that colour photograph, flat and businesslike on the top sheet of the agent's property details.

It was Grace's house. Anyone buying it would be an interloper. Yes, she'd be solvent again, but how would she feel, seeing someone else parked in the driveway? How would she feel, seeing builders' trucks outside? Hearing the crash and rumble of internal walls being demolished and rebuilt into quite a different floor plan? Catching glimpses of skips on jolting lorries, brimming over with old, cracked Victorian bathroom fittings?

It wasn't to be borne.

And she didn't need to bear it.

If James noticed that his son was quiet for the rest of the evening, he didn't mention it. In truth, Mike had already made his decision. Buying the manor may not have occurred to him before, but as soon as it had all that remained was for him to work out how.

Grace arrived home just after lunch on Sunday. Or, rather, just after when her friend Natalie's lunch would have been. She'd been pressed to stay, but she'd said she wanted to get back in daylight. Nobody queried the fact that a good proportion of her working life was spent negotiating lonely moorland roads with the aid of her headlights. It had been a good weekend. She'd enjoyed staying with Natalie and spending time with Chloe, her god-daughter. She'd had fun meeting up with the old crowd, catching up with what they were all doing. But she'd stopped drinking as soon as she'd started seeing Mike's face everywhere, and now she was home with presents to put under her tree, looking forward to a bowl of home-made soup and a satisfying session of Christmas decorating. It did give her a nasty moment, driving past the manor and seeing car tracks and footprints in the snow, but she told herself she was being ridiculous. Just think how much better off she'd be without the mortgage payments emptying her account every month. She pulled up outside the cottage and took a deep breath. Right, first the soup, then she would get the tree in.

Mike walked down the drive of the manor, mulling things over in his mind. It was bigger than the sort of place he'd envisioned buying, but it had land for Bethany to run in and she would love it. He stopped and turned back to gaze at the facade. It was a jewel—perfectly in proportion—he'd be a fool not to buy it. But, and it was a big but, what about Grace?

He resumed his progress through the snow. It was getting cold again and the parts that had turned to slush were freezing. He hoped Grace would take care driving back from Leeds. And on that thought, he saw her Land Rover parked snugly outside her cottage! Mike was amazed at the rush of gladness that filled him. Pleasure that she was back in Rivercut where she belonged. Thankful that she'd made it across the country without mishap.

Then he got the shock of his life. The tall, bushy tree by the corner of her house moved across to the front door by itself! What the…?

'Come on,' said the tree, pushing into the aperture. 'Let's see if you fit *this* way.'

Mike let out a shout of laughter and hurried around the car to give Grace a hand. 'Do you know your Christmas tree sounds just like you?' he said.

Grace was wearing her duffle coat and had gloves on. Both arms were wrapped around the trunk. 'It should,' she said with a grunt. 'I've had it fifteen years now. Come on, tree, don't get stuck *there*.'

Mike hastily propped up the very hefty mid-section and got a shoulder full of pine needles as a thank you. 'Perhaps you could ask it to breathe in,' he suggested. 'Or buy it a diet book. Grace, this is too big for the doorway.'

'It isn't. It's just a case of getting the angle right.'

From what Mike could see she was braced on the other side of the door, pulling for all she was worth. He sighed and felt through the branches, trying to get a purchase. 'Ouch, this tree's dangerous!'

'That's why I've got gloves on.'

'Grace—have you thought that even if we get it into the room, you're not going to have anywhere to stand it?'

'I've moved the big cushion.' She heaved again and he heard a shower of earth tip out of the pot.

Mike stopped trying to feed the branches one by one through the doorway. 'This is silly. You're trying to fit a manor-sized tree into a cottage. You think *I* loom when I'm standing in your front room? This will fill it! You'll have to clamber across the furniture to get from the stairs to the

kitchen.' He shifted his grip and a branch took the opportunity to slap him across the face. 'And the scent will be
overpowering.'

'I like pine,' said Grace, sounding muffled.

'There's a difference between liking pine and living in
a tree house!'

Silence. Then a sniff. Mike cursed, let go of the tree and
pelted around the side of the cottage to the back door. He
threaded his way through a tiny kitchen and found Grace
with a green streak on her forehead, pine needles in her hair
and a tear rolling down her cheek.

'Oh, Grace,' he said, and wrapped his arms around
her, just as he might with Bethany when she'd been
trying so hard to tie her own shoelaces and hadn't
managed it.

'My father gave me this tree,' she said, a quiver in her
voice. 'To replace the one he gave me when I was little for
my very own because I loved Christmas so much. That one
died. But this one's good and strong and I brought it with
me so I'd have something of him. I've lost so much, Mike…'

He held her tighter. 'Shh. I've got an idea. Why don't
we stand this tree outside your front door, so you can put
lights on it the way the manor trees were always decorated
in that photo you showed me? Then the villagers will know
you're keeping the tradition alive. And we can go over to
the place you told me about and buy you a *small* tree for
inside the cottage.'

In the circle of his arms, he felt her let out a half-sigh. 'I
suppose you think I should have thought of that for myself.'

He hugged her quickly and released her. 'We aren't always
very sensible when grief is involved. How far is the Christmas

tree place? I'll come with you now if you like. Then I'll know the way for when I take Bethany to choose one.'

'You don't have to.'

'Oh, I think I do. You obviously have zero spatial aware-ness. I need to stand next to all the trees on offer so you can find one that won't loom at you.'

She turned out to be a good driver, considerate and careful even when she wasn't being followed in a Range Rover. It might not be the most comfortable of vehicles, but Mike felt himself relax, knowing she was safe to be out on the hills in all weathers. He was glad he hadn't given in to the urge to kiss her again. Or at least only one soft kiss on her hair that he didn't think she'd noticed. It was much better to keep things friendly between them.

On the way back she glanced towards the manor. Mike guessed she did it habitually. 'I'll have to go and collect the outside lights,' she murmured, 'and maybe other bits as well. The estate agent left a message on my mobile yes-terday to say someone had made an offer. It's a lot lower than I was asking, but it might be worth it, just to get rid of the mortgage.'

Yesterday? That had been before he'd viewed it offi-cially, before he'd even been given the details! 'No,' he said before he could stop himself. 'Don't accept. It's a bargain just as it is.'

She turned a laughing face to him. 'Mike, it isn't. The central heating costs an absolute fortune to run, the plumbing needs modernising, the electrics badly need rewiring and the kitchen is well overdue for the biggest makeover in the world. And the whole place should be redecorated.'

'But the roof is sound, it didn't feel damp the other day,

and it has mistletoe in the garden. The manor is a gem, Grace. When the right person comes along and falls in love with it, they'll pay the asking price.'

'Will that be before or after I go bankrupt?'

'Before,' Mike said firmly. 'Let's fetch your string of lights now before it gets dark and we electrocute ourselves on the dodgy wiring.'

As they entered the manor, Mike watched Grace's face. He felt her love for the place. Her smile was half sad, half happy memory.

'Oh, Grace,' he said. 'How are you going to feel with someone else living here? This was a good home for you.'

She walked resolutely up the stairs. When she spoke her voice was stronger. 'I loved it here. I hope whoever buys it will love it just as much.'

It was no good, he was going to have to say something soon. If only he knew how she would really feel!

CHAPTER SEVEN

AFTER the third patient in a row told Mike on Monday morning that they'd no doubt see him at the party, he thought it might be an idea to ring Grace.

'Which party?' he said, trying not to let a plaintive tone into his voice.

She chuckled down the phone. He could hear her walking briskly along. 'The children's one. In the village hall tomorrow afternoon after school. Angela Mather told you about it, remember?'

'Angela Mather. Type 1 diabetic. Joanne's mother. Talks.'

'That's her. Also party organiser.'

Mike remembered something else. 'Sausage rolls!' he said, aghast. 'Do they sell them at the village shop?'

'Mike, you can't send Bethany to her first Rivercut party with shop-bought sausage rolls! It's a matter of honour.'

'The children won't notice,' Mike protested.

'The mothers will. And you're an honorary mother.'

Mike leaned his head against the window pane. 'Dear Grace, if you are not doing anything when you finish work, you wouldn't like to come and construct sausage rolls with

Bethany in our kitchen, would you? I can offer you supper. Dad makes a mean casserole.'

'How can I resist? I'll buy the ingredients while I'm doing my rounds, shall I?'

Mike sighed. 'Yes, please.'

Grace arrived that evening, put down a promisingly bulging bag and started divesting herself of her outer garments. 'Oh, it's lovely to be warm,' she said, getting her hair caught as she unwound her scarf. 'One of the reasons I enjoy farm visits so much is that I mostly see patients in the farmhouse kitchen, with the Aga permanently on and wonderful smells seeping out of the oven. It's a shame modern houses don't have kitchens big enough to really live in.' She was wearing a big floppy sweater under her coat, but stripped it off in a double-overarm movement to reveal a figure-hugging dark blue angora jumper underneath. It had a V-neck and three-quarter sleeves and made Mike wonder very much what the layer below that was like.

He blinked as Grace produced a spray cleaner from her bag, squirted the table and wiped it with a kitchen towel. Then she gave the spray to Bethany, telling her to do her side as well, all the time explaining bacteria in terms a five-year-old could understand.

Mike was impressed. He poured out three glasses of Rioja, took one through to his father, who was shouting points of medical procedure at a TV hospital soap. When he came back Bethany was wrapped in a cook's apron, had just had her hands washed and was installed at the table to weigh out the flour and margarine. Mike leaned against the worktop, ready to be amused.

Grace narrowed her eyes. 'Now, then, is this fair?' she asked Bethany. 'Us doing all the work and Daddy just standing there, drinking a glass of wine?'

'You've got a glass of wine too,' he pointed out.

'Daddy, help,' decreed Bethany.

'I haven't got an apron,' he said cunningly.

Grace crossed to her bag, pulled out a blue-and-white-striped barbeque number and dropped the neck loop over his head. For a moment she was standing very close to him. 'You planned that,' he said, an unexpected tightness in his chest.

She grinned. 'Would I do such a thing? Okay, here we are. Sausage rolls.'

She had a children's recipe book with her, with big clear writing and step-by-step photos. 'You didn't buy it especially, did you?' said Mike, worried about her spending money she didn't have.

'No, I picked it up at the last church sale. I was going to give it to my god-daughter, but when I got there last weekend, I saw it on Natalie's kitchen shelf already. I'll leave it here for Bethany if you like.'

This was fun. Bethany's first two attempts at scooping flour out of the bag into the measuring bowl resulted in a small-scale snowdrift on the table.

'It'll be useful for rolling out the pastry,' said Grace, unperturbed. 'Shall we let Daddy have the next turn?' She reached for the scoop at the same time as Mike. She drew back at once, but he thought she'd probably felt the same frisson that had run through him during the brief moment when the backs of their hands touched.

By the time there was enough in the mixing bowl there was flour everywhere, but Bethany had learnt what the gradations on the scale meant in real terms—in a way Mike doubted she'd have managed at school. Grace was really good with children. And when he caught himself drawing a fancy pattern on the pastry with a zigzag roller, he suspected she might be good with him too. All the same, the sausage rolls were a lumpy, misshapen lot. 'Shall I buy some from the shop anyway?' he asked in a low tone as she put the tray in the oven.

'Certainly not. These have got character. Besides, kids aren't bothered what things look like at a party, just what they taste like.'

'If you say so. Oh, Lord, look at this place. Bethany, sweetheart, I think I'd better put you in the bath clothes and all tonight.'

His daughter giggled. The apron had kept most of her clean, but she had flour in her hair, flour and margarine and sausage meat on her hands and suspicious bits of pastry around her mouth.

'You can talk,' said Grace, carrying Bethany to the sink and rinsing her hands.

'What do you mean?'

'Well, let's just say you're going to look very distinguished when you're older.'

Mike hastened to the mirror in the hall. He appeared to have gone grey at the temples since they'd started baking. 'Could be worse. Go and sit with Grandad while we clean up, darling.'

Grace scrubbed efficiently at the table. Mike fetched a broom for the floor. 'Wait a minute,' he said. 'Take off your apron.'

Grace looked at him in surprise, but undid the ties. A

small shower of flour fell from behind the bib to the floor. She tutted and brushed at her jumper. The white streaks became more pronounced.

'No, don't. You've got damp hands. You're making it worse. Here, let me.'

He brushed the loose flour away from her midriff. Her angora jumper was soft to the touch, and warm where it lay against her body. Grace, however, had gone suddenly still. 'Lift your arm,' he said, and very, very carefully he brushed the flour away from her side, his fingers tantalisingly close to the swell of her breast. 'There's, um, more…'

'Go on, then,' she invited softly. Her breath was coming slightly faster and the pupils of her eyes had dilated. Then the oven timer broke into a flurry of beeping, sending them instantly to either side of the kitchen.

'There,' said Grace, clattering the tray down with a hand that wasn't quite so steady as normal. 'A beautiful batch of sausage rolls.'

Surprisingly, they did smell wonderful. As Bethany and James both bounded in to sample them, Mike hoped his father would put his heightened colour down to the heat from the stove.

It had been a lovely evening, thought Grace. The moments alone with Mike in the kitchen had been especially lovely. After the baking she'd helped bathe Bethany and agreed with her choice of a pretty pink full-skirted dress for tomorrow's party. She'd also been shown her 'Adventure Calendar'—'Every day I can open a window and there's a chocolate inside, but I mustn't open two windows at once and get two chocolates'—and read a bedtime story.

After that Grace had eaten James's casserole and drunk another glass of Mike's Rioja and now Mike was walking her home.

'There's no need,' she'd said, but he claimed he wanted a stroll to clear his head so he may as well stroll in the direction of her cottage. Grace wondered what was coming next. She wasn't at all sure that she wanted things to move too fast.

They walked side by side, not touching, talking of nothing in particular. Mike had his hands in his pockets. He seemed to have something on his mind that hadn't been there earlier in the evening. They reached her cottage and stopped. She hadn't quite decided whether to invite him in for a coffee when he spoke abruptly.

'I've got to ask you something, Grace. If I leave it any longer, it's going to get too difficult and I won't know how to say it at all.'

Grace was apprehensive now. What did he mean?

'You know Bethany and I were house hunting over the weekend?'

'Yes. Did you find anything?'

'Sort of. It hadn't occurred to me at first. But there's nothing else, and the more I thought about it, the more I realised it would be perfect.'

'Mike, what are you talking about?'

He slapped his forehead. 'I am making such a mess of this. Grace, how would you feel about me buying the manor?'

Grace's mouth fell open. It was the last thing she'd expected him to say.

He groaned. 'You hate the idea. I don't blame you. It's *your* house—it would be like evicting you.'

She found her voice. 'No,' she said slowly. 'No, I don't

hate the idea. I mean, it is for sale. I need the cash, it's owed to other people. Someone's got to buy it. And I evicted myself because I couldn't afford to run it. That central heating just *eats* money.'

'Yes, but we have to work together. You'll see me several times a week at close quarters, not just passing in the road. I think what I'm saying is would you mind if I was the new owner? Would you be upset when you saw me driving out of what used to be your drive? Or if I invited you for a cup of tea in what used to be your living room?'

'It would be odd, certainly. But it would be odd with anybody.' He looked so distressed that she put her hand on his arm to reassure him, still not sure of what she really felt herself. 'I think you would at least be sympathetic to the renovations it needs. But, Mike, they'll cost a fortune.'

He smiled briefly. 'I've got sufficient funds, Grace.'

'If you're serious… Oh, Mike, I don't know. I think I'd rather it went to a friend than a complete stranger. And I'd love to think of Bethany growing up there.'

'Then shall I do it? Contact the estate agent in the morning?'

'Yes. If you're sure.' And because she didn't know how to say the next bit, she let her hand slip down to squeeze his wrist. 'Mike, I won't invite you in. Not because of you buying the manor. Not because of anything that might have happened earlier, which felt…nice. Just because it's been a really lovely evening and I don't want it to get…messy.'

He smiled. 'It *has* been a nice evening, hasn't it? Thank you.' He hesitated, then kissed her cheek and left, striding back up the high street.

Grace went indoors, her thoughts all over the place.

Mike at the manor. It was an awfully large house just for him and Bethany. But she recalled he'd been in with a big crowd in London—his partners and their families, his wife's friends. They'd all pitched in when Sarah had died. Kept him going, looked after Bethany. No doubt they would be coming up to stay from time to time. Sleeping in the guest bedrooms, cooking in the kitchen, having drinks in the hall, their children playing in the gardens with Bethany.

It would be strange to have the manor full again and her not there. And she wondered if any of those friends were single, just waiting for Mike to stop grieving.

This was no good! What should have been uppermost in her mind was that soon she would be free of debt, free of responsibility. She could start to plan her life again. But mostly what she was thinking about was Mike's kiss on her cheek—and the thrilling touch of his hand on her body.

The waiting room was full when Mike arrived from taking Bethany to school. James always started his appointments at eight-thirty, but Mike had been amazed at how no one—surgery staff and patients alike—expected Mike himself to begin until after he'd got back from Rivercut Primary. Even so, he rang through to Grace's room before telling the receptionist he was ready.

'I know you're in the middle of a clinic, but I just wanted to know whether it was still all right for me to go ahead with the manor?'

'It's still all right.'

'Good. Don't run away at lunchtime. Have a sandwich with Dad and me. I need to know what else I'm supposed to do for the party.'

'Very well, Dr Curtis.'

Mike smiled as he buzzed for his first patient. He loved Grace's 'official' voice.

He was surprised later when she put a small present, wrapped in Christmas paper, on the kitchen table. 'Is that for thanking me for buying the manor? There ought to be a message for you from the estate agent, by the way.'

'There has been and I said yes. *This* is to go under the Christmas tree at the party. Each child puts one there and they take a different one home with them.'

'That's a nice idea. You must tell me how much I owe you.'

She grinned and pointed to the receipts tucked discreetly under the parcel.

James bustled in. 'Tut, tut, no one got the kettle on yet? I'm parched. I've had Mrs Carter in talking at me. Says she's worried about Nina. Seems she's started getting secretive and hiding things from her and sometimes she giggles for no reason at all and did I think she could be taking drugs?'

Grace laughed. 'Oh, dear, what did you say?'

'I said she was a healthy nineteen-year-old with a good job and a refreshingly honest take on life and I didn't think Mrs Carter needed to worry. I *didn't* say that if Mrs Carter herself had taken what I very much hope young Nina is on, there would be rather fewer Carter offspring mopping up the buffet at the Rivercut children's party this afternoon.'

It was nice, having Grace there. His dad was obviously fond of her and as she talked over a couple of cases with them, Mike could again see just how good a nurse she was. He wondered if he could make the sharing of lunch-time sandwiches a routine on her surgery days. Then he got a callout, and she looked at her watch in horror and bolted the last of her tea, saying she was late for Mr Blenkinsop's blood-pressure check and Mike remembered all over again why medical personnel bought more indigestion tablets than any other profession in the country.

'See you at the party,' she said as she hurried out. 'Don't be late.'

Far from being late, Bethany was so eager to be gone that they were early at the village hall. She was buzzing with excitement. There were fairy lights, a large Christmas tree and a decorated chair all ready for Father Christmas. There were even Christmas songs belting out of the loudspeakers.

A handful of mothers were busy putting the final touches to the decorations. Mike was surprised to see Grace amongst them, a mound of paper chains in her arms.

'Mike,' she said cheerfully, 'just the man we want.'

'You need a doctor?'

'No, we need someone tall. Could you get the stepladder from under the stage and loop these paper chains round the back of the light fittings and down each side of the hall, please? Then hang the big pictures of Father Christmas underneath the lights.'

'Can do,' said Mike. 'Can someone watch—?' But Bethany was confidently running over to join a couple of little girls from school. No problem there. Other assorted parents were going backwards and forwards, laying out food on the white-covered trestle tables, arranging jugs of squash and plastic cups, counting rows of tiny presents and frowning over lists. The mothers smiled at him briefly. The fathers rolled their eyes. This was obviously not a time for standing around chatting.

Mike got on with his paper chains. 'Brilliant,' said Grace, appearing by his side. 'Tea's up, everyone. Grab a cup while it's hot, the kids will all be arriving in a few minutes. And give yourselves a pat on the back too. The place looks wonderful.'

'Let's hope the little darlings appreciate it,' said a passing mother. She gave Mike a friendly smile. 'Come on, the tea urn is this way.'

Mike glanced around for Bethany. Grace had moved over to the children and was keeping an eye on them.

'Dr Curtis, isn't it?' continued the mother, leading him towards the kitchen behind the stage. 'I understand there is no Mrs Curtis?'

'No,' said Mike, 'not now.' He marvelled at the efficiency of village gossip.

'Ah, well, we're a friendly bunch here. Let me introduce you to a few people…'

He found that he was expected—and that he wanted— to stay. He watched one or two party games and saw that Bethany, as always, was enjoying herself. It struck him that the Rivercut mothers were in essence no different from the ones in his London crowd. They pulled together, looked after solitary males in their midst with kind efficiency, organised themselves to cover all bases. No one person was doing all the work.

'This village is better organised than the Mafia,' he said to Grace, finding himself standing next to her later.

'Except there's no vow of silence,' she said with a laugh.

She had taken off the apron that had covered her dress— and her dress was wonderful. Simple, in a blue silky material, it did nothing but show off her figure. And that figure was gorgeous. 'How do you come to be involved in all this?' he asked, trying to disguise the fact that he was appreciating her body rather more than was seemly.

'We always used to hold the children's Christmas party up at the manor. The last couple of years... Well, let's just say it's been more sensible to move it down here. But everybody has always taken turns to do the games and swap around doling out food and drink. It's my game next, and then tea.' She cocked her head at him. 'Are you enjoying yourself?'

'Very much. It's nice being a dad today, not a doctor. Everybody is making me feel welcome. What game are you doing?'

She laughed. 'An incredibly ancient Pin the Tail on the Donkey. We have to have it before tea, otherwise the kids throw up when we spin them round. Would you like to help me?'

'I'd love to,' he said. And meant it.

But suddenly there was a shout that was a little louder than the general noise in the hall. People began moving to the far end of the room and a woman's voice was raised in a terrified wail. 'Help him, someone, help him!' There were other confused shouts and even as Mike started running, Grace alongside him, he heard the words, 'Turn him upside down... No, thump him on the back...'

'Let me through,' shouted Mike, adding the time-honoured words, 'I'm a doctor.'

A hysterical woman was clutching a boy aged about four. She looked up at Mike and sobbed, 'It was that cake, the big one with the silver balls on top. I told him he wasn't to touch, but he got one and when I saw he had it he put it in his mouth and now he can't breathe and I've tried banging his back and...'

'Give him to me. What's his name?'

'Alex.'

Mike took Alex, turned him for a quick look at his face. It was turning blue, cyanosis already obvious so the blockage must be nearly complete. Alex was pawing weakly at his throat.

'Did anyone try smacking his back?'

'I did,' a woman volunteered, 'about ten times. But not too hard.'

'Good.' The first step when trying to deal with asphyxiation caused by a foreign body in the trachea was a set of blows to the back. An old remedy, sometimes it worked—but not this time.

Alex was only small, light-boned. Mike turned him around, wrapped his arms round the tiny waist, positioned his hands on the bottom of the diaphragm. The Heimlich manoeuvre. Jerk the hands into the abdomen so the blockage is forced out. But with the weak bones and muscles of a four-year-old child, it was essential not to pull too hard.

Mike ran his fingers up and down the ribcage, felt the softness of the abdomen, tried to assess just how hard he should pull. Now! No result, not hard enough.

He had to remain calm, to think the almost unthinkable. If this didn't work then he might have to perform an emergency tracheotomy. Use whatever knife was handy, cut a hole through the throat into the thorax and use some kind of tube—even a ball point barrel would do—to make an airway. But, please, not yet!

Try again, a little harder. Now! And this time it was

exactly right. A silver ball shot onto the floor, the first great shuddering breath was taken, the blue tinge started to fade at once.

There was a huge sigh of relief from the collected parents. The hall, which had been eerily silent, burst into life again.

'Result,' said Mike, feeling the adrenalin in his body die down. 'Now take him somewhere quiet, give him a drink and let him rest for a few minutes. I'll come and have another look at him.'

He turned to the circle of his audience. 'Everything's fine, folks. Alex will be as good as new in five minutes. Let's get on with the party.'

Alex was led away by his grateful mother, but there was another white-faced woman in the crowd. 'It was safe,' she said, her voice getting higher. 'The bag said they were safe to eat.' She was clutching Grace's arm, shaking. 'What if he'd died…?'

'Of course they're safe,' Grace reassured her. 'Pauline, you've been making beautiful village cakes for years and no one's ever had an accident before. Maybe the silver ball Alex grabbed was a bit bigger than the rest. Maybe it got stuck to a lump of icing. As long as we tell the children to crunch and chew properly when it comes to teatime, there won't be a problem. Now, I'm going to do Pin the Tail any minute, so can you put the urn on for the parents' cuppas? Then it will all be ready and people won't have to wait.'

As he crossed the room to help hang up the donkey and get the Victorian tails out of their tissue paper, Mike was struck dumb by Grace's humaneness. Yes, he had saved Alex's life—but Grace had known who'd made the cake.

She'd known how the woman would feel and had been there on the spot to administer sensible comfort and a distraction technique.

The party continued, but with a difference. During tea and the last few games, most of the parents found a moment to come up to Mike and say what a good job he'd done.

'You aren't an incomer any more,' said Grace as they got the children settled down and dimmed the lights to wait for Santa. 'You're accepted.'

Every child got a present from Father Christmas, chose another one from under the Christmas tree and started putting coats on to go home. Bethany wanted a goodbye cuddle from Grace.

'Off you go, poppet,' said Grace. 'I'll see you on Thursday for riding.' And to Mike, 'Thanks for your help, even if it was a baptism of fire.'

'I enjoyed it—well, apart from the emergency. Come back with us, if you like. There's still some of that Rioja left.'

'No, I'll just finish tidying up here, then go home. I'm a bit shattered.'

It was snowing again. Mike lifted Bethany up onto his shoulders for the walk back. She'd had a wonderful time. She had got a fairy wand from Santa—all pink ribbons and glitter—and insisted on waving it around her head, putting magic spells on all the houses they passed. As soon as they got back she had to tell Grandad all about the party.

James chuckled, but looked at Mike shrewdly. 'What's up?'

'I had to perform a Heimlich manoeuvre on a little boy.' He passed a hand over his face. Suddenly he too was shattered. 'Look, Dad, are you all right to do Bethany's bedtime? I left Grace tidying up and I just want to have a word with her.'

'She works too hard, that girl. Why don't you take her to the Coach and Horses for a meal? It does lovely food.'

'Good idea. Thanks, Dad.'

He found Grace alone when he got back to the village hall. She had moved the trestle tables, was sweeping where they had been. He didn't say anything, but found a black bag and started to collect the abandoned plastic plates, cutlery and cups that had been left around.

'There's no need,' said Grace. 'A couple of the others are coming back to help.'

'I need to wind down,' said Mike. 'Bethany's reliving the whole party for Dad.'

'That was a great job you did on Alex. You were so *fast*.'

'Thank God it worked. And you did a good job with the cake-maker too.'

'Poor Pauline. She was horrified.'

'You are one special nurse, you know that? Grace, things are happening fast and I need some time out. Will you come to the pub with me when we've finished this? Dad says the food is good there.'

For a moment he thought she was going to refuse. Then she smiled tiredly at him. 'Time out? That sounds very restful. Thank you. I'd love to.'

CHAPTER EIGHT

GRACE felt her tension drain away as soon as they walked through the door of the Coach and Horses. The pub was warm, full, bright with decorations and a welcoming fire and cosy with good cheer. The Christmas spirit was alive and well. As they threaded their way to a corner table, they got nods and greetings. 'Evening, Grace. Evening, Doctor.'

Mike grinned. 'I've a feeling I should have come in before. Now, then, first a drink, then a bit of business. Then we can relax. What would you like?'

'A red wine, please.' She watched him cross the room and discuss options with the bartender, scanning the shelves with a considering look. He came back with a bottle, two glasses and the menu.

'Cheers,' he said, pouring them each a ruby-red glassful.

It tasted wonderful, soft and rich. 'Cheers,' she replied. 'So, what's this matter of business?'

'The manor,' he said. 'It's going to take the solicitors a while to get their act together and produce contracts for us to sign. I've no idea why it should, but it always does. But I really want to make a start on things now. Overhauling the central heating, for instance. Refitting the kitchen. Getting quotes on a conservatory. What I'm saying is—can I go ahead? Do you trust me not to back out of buying the house?'

Did she? The last two men who'd had anything to do with the manor hadn't been trustworthy at all. But this was Mike. He was different. Besides, she knew where his father lived. 'Yes,' she said.

'You're sure? Because I don't want you to hear I've got a surveyor in and be worried that I might try and beat you down on the price whilst making your house temporarily unsaleable. I only want to find out early whether any treatment is needed so I can get it sorted as soon as possible.'

'It's fine, Mike. I trust you. You can have my spare set of keys. When do you want to begin?'

'I thought tomorrow, for preference.'

Tomorrow! That really was eager! This was a side of him she hadn't seen. Or had she? Wasn't this the same solid intractability that had got Joshua Lawrie into hospital for treatment? A pleasant, no-nonsense, velvet bulldozer?

He laughed at the look on her face. 'No point hanging around. Dad loves having us in the flat, but two men in one kitchen is a strain on any relationship. And now I need your help some more. I'd like to use local people if possible. Builders, plumbers, electricians, carpenters. You know everyone here. Can you make me a list? I realise they might not be available right now, but I would at least like to ask.'

'Of course I will. That's great, Mike, but why?'

He took a sip of his wine, his face thoughtful. 'I think it was what you said about incomers. Bethany and I are moving to Rivercut and we want to belong. And at the party

I overheard one of the chaps saying he'd been laid off by a building contractor because there wasn't the work around and the company was being forced to retrench. Now, I don't know what sort of workman he is, but that man's child will be going to school with Bethany. I'd rather put bread in my daughter's friends' mouths than fill up the coffers of some big firm from Salford or wherever.'

Grace's eyes stung with tears. It was the same attitude her father had always had, but from a Londoner, a stranger… 'That's… That's…' She broke off, searching in her bag for a tissue. 'You're too good to be true.'

He looked at her seriously. 'I just want to do it right, Grace.'

She blew her nose. 'There are some people in here at this very moment who would be interested. I think you're about to make Christmas a lot brighter for a number of families. I'll introduce you and you can have a chat while I get my emotions in order.'

In fact she'd refilled her glass and had perused the menu several times before Mike rejoined her.

'Thanks,' he said, looking cheerful. 'Sorry if I took a bit long. That was really useful. I don't feel nearly so daunted now.'

'Daunted? You?' How did one daunt a steamroller?

He sat down next to her and picked up the menu. 'I'll have you know I frequently tread a fine line between bluff and counter-bluff. Mmm, home-made game pie. Wonderful. What are you having?'

It was a good meal, and by the end of it Grace felt mellow and well fed. But the pub was getting noisy and she was struggling to hear what Mike was saying.

'This is hopeless,' he mouthed. 'Shall we go?'

Grace nodded and put on her coat. Outside the Coach and Horses it was spectacularly silent. Maybe it was the change in her routine, but she felt different tonight. The cold made her tingle, not shiver. 'I don't feel as if I've drunk half a bottle of wine,' she said. 'The food must have soaked it up.'

'Same with me,' said Mike.

He stood there, perfectly at ease, gazing down the snow-covered street. Grace began to suspect that he was in no hurry for the evening to end either. She took a quick breath. Say it now and say it quickly. 'I've got a bottle of claret that was given to me by a grateful farmer. I haven't liked to drink it alone, so if you fancy another glass...'

Now he turned and looked at her steadily. 'Are you sure?' he said.

Ah, so she hadn't imagined those moments during the meal when their arms had accidentally brushed. 'Of course I'm sure. It's just a bottle of wine after all. And you can collect the keys for the manor at the same time.' She kept the tremor out of her voice.

'So I can.' They started strolling towards her cottage. 'Why was the farmer grateful?'

Grace laughed. 'Oh, he liked the way I'd dressed the wound on his shin. He said it didn't hurt at all. All I'd done was shave the hairs on his leg before attaching the plaster.'

'Florence Nightingale would have been proud of you.'

Coloured lights shone merrily around the Christmas tree outside her door. Grace got a small pleasurable lift from the sight.

'Very handsome,' said Mike.

'Isn't it just. And there's more.' She opened her door and bent to flick the switch on at the socket. Dozens of fairy lights sprang into twinkling life on her inside tree.

'Now, that's pretty. Seems a shame to turn the main light on.'

Grace's heart beat faster. 'We don't have to. Wait a moment.'

She crossed the room to the mantelpiece, on which she had arranged two bright red candles amidst Christmas foliage. She lit them carefully and the room was changed. It became a place of shadows and magic.

Mike hung his coat on the back of the door and sat down on the settee. She could almost hear him saying, *See, I'm not looming.* Nevertheless she went rather quickly into the kitchen to fetch the wine.

The couch was big enough for two. Just. But she could feel their shoulders touching and his thigh pressed next to hers. Her hand shook just slightly as she poured the wine.

'Do you know,' he said. 'I feel really positive. I've been *doing* something this evening. Not simply my job—that's an everyday thing. Not selling my flat and selling my partnership. Those are looking-backwards things. Today I've been doing something forward-looking. Planning what needs doing to the manor. Accepting deep within myself that Bethany and I are going to live here and make a future. I've been moving on.'

Grace smiled. 'You're right. That is a good thing.' It was what she should be doing, she realised. Now the millstone of debt was gone, she should be thinking positively too. Put Peter behind her once and for all. Start to trust again. 'To the future,' she said, holding up her glass.

He clinked his against it. 'The future.' They drank in silence for a minute. 'There is one thing I'm worried about,' he continued. 'The driveway. It's so open. Anyone could walk in. Bethany could wander out. Has it always been that way?'

Oh, Mike! And there she had been thinking that with the candles and the wine, things might be approaching romantic. He was looking at her enquiringly. Grace dredged her memory. 'I'm pretty sure there used to be gates when I was small. I remember looking through openwork scrolls at the road and I can't think where else I'd have been looking if not through gates. I guess the posts rotted or something. They'll have been too big to store in the attics. You'll have to investigate the barns.'

He raised his eyebrows, amused. His blue eyes danced in the candlelight. 'They won't have been thrown away?'

'Good Lord, no. Nothing has ever been thrown away at the manor.'

He chuckled. 'If that's the case you could probably have paid several months' mortgage money out of the scrap value in the outbuildings.'

'I never thought of that.' She found herself breathing in his clean-sweater scent and a faint tang of citrus. 'You smell nice,' she murmured inconsequentially. The claret must have been more potent than the wine at the pub.

It seemed natural for him to put his arm round her shoulders. 'So do you. You feel nice too,' he replied.

An inner certainty stole over Grace, as warm and languorous as the wine. She put her glass on the table. She knew what would happen next. And she knew what might happen after that if they both let it.

She heard the 'ting' as he placed his glass on the coffee table too. And then he kissed her.

He kissed her as he'd kissed her before. Gently, tentatively almost, as if he wasn't sure what he was doing or whether he'd be welcome. But he was welcome. She trailed her fingertips down the side of his face. She could feel the slight roughness of his cheek—it had been morning when he'd shaved.

This was so easy. There was no need to hurry. She could feel his tongue exploring the insides of her lips, touching the sensitive corners of her mouth. She mirrored his actions, feeling him respond, marvelling at how right this felt. When he pulled away she felt bereft, but it was only because he'd moved on to kissing her cheeks, her forehead, even the tip of her nose. 'That's lovely,' she said.

She realised that she'd never felt quite like this before. Mike was more than just a man—he was *the* man.

Then she gasped and called out his name. Very, very gently he had nibbled the bottom of her ear. How did he know that that was one of the most sensitive parts of her body? How did he know that that combination of pleasure and the tiniest pain possible could bring her so much joy? But he did know. And he did it again. How could he know her so well?

They'd somehow moved around, turned in their embrace until they were half lying on the couch. Her head had fallen back, her body was melded tightly to his. And now he was kissing her mouth again, but this time with a growing need that was fully matched by her own. She opened up to him without restraint, giving as well as receiving, letting his tongue join hers in joyous delight.

They paused, not really wanting to stop but knowing the next step had to be taken slowly, if it was taken at all. Grace's eye fell on their two glasses. 'Do you want a drink?' she asked with a mischievous smile.

'Grace!' Then he propped himself up on one elbow. 'What have you got in mind?'

'You'll like it. Yes or no?'

'Yes. But I'd rather kiss you again.'

'Well, it involves kissing…'

She took a small sip from her glass, then raised her face to his. He kissed her. And she let the wine trickle from her mouth to his and it was more wonderful than she could have guessed.

'Oh, I like that. In fact, I think I'd like another drink— just like that one. Or would you like me to feed you some wine this time?'

The claret was warm when it arrived in her mouth, slipping over her tongue and tasting of him. Their kiss took on a momentum of its own as she ran her hands around his back, feeling his palms sweeping over the silk of her dress. She shifted, trying to indicate without words that if his hand wanted to roam lower she wouldn't object. But her leg hit the arm of the settee and her foot found the branches of the Christmas tree.

She lifted her head. 'There's not a lot of room here. Would you…? Would you like to move to somewhere more comfortable?'

For a moment the sound of his breathing was the only noise in the room. He knew as well as she did what she was asking him. What had happened so far could still be drawn back from. It could be passed off as momentary madness, perhaps to be smiled over and forgotten. But after they had gone upstairs there would be no turning back.

Huskily, he asked, 'Grace, is this really what you want?'

'Yes—if you want it too. If you don't we'll just have a lovely last kiss and then I'll put the light on and we'll finish our drinks and talk about the manor. I won't be hurt. I won't be offended.'

'I do want it,' he muttered. 'Part of my head is telling me to walk away, but most of me thinks you are gorgeous and generous and intelligent and I would like very much indeed to make love to you.'

He'd said it. It was out in the open. Grace's whole body quivered. 'Come on, then,' she whispered, and took his hand to lead him up the narrow stairs.

Upstairs she switched on her bedside reading lamp and pulled the curtains. Mike held her hand again as he sat on the edge of the double bed and looked around at the small items of furniture she'd brought from the manor, at the faded duvet and matching curtains that had been hers for years, at the pictures—as many as the room would hold.

'Thank you,' he said softly, squeezing her hand. 'Thank you for trusting me enough to bring me up here. This is a very special room for you, isn't it?'

Grace felt her eyes sting again. He was right. And because he had sensed what her bedroom meant to her, she knew everything from now on would be fine.

'Yes,' she said simply.

He smiled, his face gentle in the shadows. 'Come here and lie down next to me. Just for the moment I'd like to kiss you without getting a crick in my neck.'

So they slipped off their shoes and lay side by side on the duvet. Mike eased his arm under her head and she rolled gladly towards him, her knee bending naturally so that her leg was half on top of his. As they kissed, his hands unhurriedly roamed her body, feeling the pulse in her neck, stroking her back, cupping the edge of her breast.

This was good, simply relaxing and getting to know his body, enjoying the shivers of pleasure as he got to know hers. And all the time something was building inside both of them—the urge to move on, to take this new, tentative delight to greater heights.

His fingers ran down the indentation of her spine, curved over her hips, found the hem of her dress. And then up her nylon-clad leg until…

'Stockings,' he said, his voice breaking. 'Oh, Grace, do you know what you do to a man?'

'I can take them off if you like,' she said, a laugh in her voice.

'Don't you dare.' He brushed the bare skin and moved on up underneath the blue silk. He found the lacy cup of her bra, lingered for an exquisite moment then slid around the back to the fastening. A moment later it was undone. Grace felt her whole self trembling as his hand moved back to cover her breast.

'Oh, Mike,' she breathed, and rolled onto her back, lifting her arms in mute invitation for him to ease her dress up and off. She heard his intake of breath, his inarticulate gasp of pleasure.

The bra came off with the dress. He leaned over her upper body, slowly stroking from the shoulders down and around each curve. Grace felt the skin of her breasts tighten, her nipples harden in anticipation. He brushed them with his palms, rubbed with his fingers—but so slowly!

'Mike…please…' she murmured, aching for more.

At last his head bowed over her and his tongue touched first one then the second proud peak. She moaned—then cried out with delight as he took one into his mouth. That was so good!

She reached out, wanting to touch him too. Her fingers encountered fine Shetland wool. Her eyes flew open. 'Mike, you're still dressed!'

'Mmm? Oh, so I am.'

Grace snatched her dressing gown from the bedpost, pulling it around her. 'Just to make us even,' she said at his protest. 'Stand up—I want to do this properly.' She slid off the bed to face him. First his sweater joined her dress on the floor. Then she undid all his shirt buttons and slid it off. He had a magnificent torso. She spent a moment admiring it before running her hands lightly down his front to his belt. It was a matter of seconds before he was stepping out of his jeans, but when she gripped the waistband of his black silk boxers he put his hands over hers.

'Aren't we forgetting something?' he said. 'We're not even any more.'

Grace's insides turned to liquid. She raised one foot and rested it on the bed so he could peel off the stocking. Then did the same with the other. She loosened the belt of her dressing gown but just as the front was about to part she put a hand to her mouth. 'Oh,' she said, suddenly re-membering something. 'Mike, it is Christmas, you know.'

'I do know. Why do you mention it?'

'Because last weekend my six-year-old god-daughter

gave me a very silly present that she had picked out herself
and made me promise to wear to my first Christmas party
of the season.'

'Which was today.'

'Er, yes.'

'Okay, I'm warned.' He untied her belt and pushed the
dressing gown off her shoulders to fall in a soft heap on
the carpet. He looked down—and a smile crossed his face.

'I'll have you know they're very warm and comfortable,' she said.

'I still want to take them off you.' And then he laughed
joyously. 'I'll bet no one at that party today guessed that
underneath your gorgeous slinky dress you were wearing
a pair of white satin knickers with happy Father
Christmases all over them.'

Delicately he slid the white satin downwards, his hands
lingering on her skin. Delicately she did the same for him,
feeling the first thrilling touch of his warm maleness against
her abdomen. With one hand she pulled back the duvet.

He swore.

'Mike?' What had she done?

He growled in frustration. 'I…I didn't expect… It's
been such a long time since…'

She giggled. 'I've got a box of condoms in my bedside
drawer. I was going to throw them out when…' She broke
off. 'But I never got round to it.' She looked up at him shyly.
'I'm glad now.'

Mike took her in his arms and swept her off her feet and
into the bed. 'So am I.'

It was different now when she felt him beside her, both
of them lying down between her sheets. For a moment

there had been a respite, time for a joke even. She realised that she had been more nervous than she knew. But now they were in bed together, they were naked and the delight she had felt before returned, but heightened so much.

He pulled her close to him. Kissing him was even more wonderful now. Not only their lips but their entire bodies were touching. She could feel the warmth, the softness of his skin pressed against hers. Her breasts, the peaks stiff and unbearably sensitive, were crushed against the muscles of his chest. Her smooth legs rubbed against the faint roughness of his. And pressed hard against her thigh was the indisputable sign of his need for her.

Every kiss, every touch told her that she wanted him, needed him with an urgency she had never experienced before. She had met this man only a few days before but now it seemed she had known him for ever. It was as if their coming together had been ordained since that first encounter.

She could tell he shared her frantic need. This would not, could not last long. One more searing kiss and she rolled onto her back, pulling him until he was poised above her. 'Grace... Grace... I...'

'Don't talk. There's no need. Make me complete, Mike.' Her arms encircled his neck, she urged him down onto her. Into her. She cried out at the same time as he gasped.

'Oh, Mike.'

'Oh, Grace.'

It was good, more than good. She was taking him, but giving to him. He was taking her, and giving to her. They were in perfect unison.

No use now trying to wait, to tease, to pretend that they had all the time in the world. Together they moved towards a climax, an ending that had them both gripping each other and calling out in ecstasy.

He collapsed on her, holding her tight, and kissed her again and again. 'Oh, Grace.'

'Shh. That was lovely. Shh.'

They lay side by side, curled into one another, their arms across each other's bodies, drifting into sleep. But always there was that consciousness of his arms round her, his body next to hers. She was content. She was complete. She was happy.

It was dark, Mike was warm and in his half waking, half sleeping state he was aware of burgeoning love and great fulfilment. Something had been missing for such a long time—a part of him ripped away and only an aching gap left in its place. But here, now, he was whole again. There was regular breathing in the darkness, drifting hair tickling his cheek. He reached out and his hand slipped over warm, smooth skin. 'Oh, Sarah,' he murmured.

Sarah. Grace lay curled up on her side, tucked into Mike's warm body, his arm loosely around her. Her eyes were shut, her limbs relaxed. Only the tear trickling down her cheek as her lover spoke his dead wife's name showed that she was awake.

CHAPTER NINE

MIKE came awake properly. For a split second he was surprised beyond belief to find a woman in his arms. But memory flooded back—and what a memory! He kissed Grace's neck softly. 'Grace, I have to leave. I can't not be at home when Bethany wakes up in the morning.'

She stirred, twisted to face him, pushing her hair out of the way. Lord, she was gorgeous. Her breasts rubbed against his chest, bringing a resurgence of desire. 'Are you going?' she said sleepily.

'I must.' He kissed her eyelids, pausing at the taste of salt. 'Have you been crying?'

'Yes... No... That was lovely, Mike.'

'It was. Don't get up, it's too cold. I'll see you tomorrow—today—whenever it is. Come and have a picnic lunch with us again.'

She padded downstairs anyway, wrapped in her dressing gown, to bolt the door after him. That last view of her, tousled and beautiful, stayed with him as he strode up the high street through cold, crunching snow under a waning moon. Something to keep him warm.

But as he opened the door to the flat he heard Bethany's rising wail. 'Daddy! I want my daddy!'

He tore off his coat as he raced to her room. 'I'm here, sweetheart. What's the matter?' He scooped his daughter up, feeling his heart thud as he cradled her to his chest. She was limp. He peered anxiously at her face in the light from the hallway. Was she flushed? Sweating? How long had she been crying?

She gave a small murmur and turned to snuggle into his sweater. False alarm. She was still asleep. Thank God. He held her a moment longer—then very gently slid her back into bed, testing her forehead to be on the safe side, lifting her wrist to check her pulse.

'Everything all right?' asked his father from the doorway.

For a moment Mike felt a quite shattering anger. Bethany had cried out and James hadn't been instantly with her. He'd trusted him to look after her. But then he had a vision of himself in Grace's arms, oblivious to the rest of the world. He was the one to blame, not his father.

'Talking in her sleep,' he said in a low voice. 'Nothing to worry about.' He followed James out of the room and pulled the door to.

'Good evening?' said his father.

'The best.' But he felt a small core of misery settle in his chest. He couldn't do it again. Bethany had needed him tonight and he hadn't been there. He wouldn't risk that happening any more.

Sarah. No matter how many times Grace replayed the events of the evening, she couldn't get that one word out of her head. He had said it in that moment between sleeping and waking, said it when the rigid guard on his memories was lulled. She had to face it. Whatever she had been beginning to believe, whatever hopes she had allowed to come into existence, the fact was that Mike still mourned his wife. He was still in love with Sarah.

Which left her where? Friends with him? Just friends after what they had shared? The idea was laughable.

Grace was clear-sighted enough to recognise that she had been in need of their lovemaking tonight just as much as Mike. He hadn't had any intention of taking her for granted or making a fool of her. Maybe he had no idea himself how much of his heart was still Sarah's.

So…she would be there to talk to, there to listen to him. And, God help her, she would be there to satisfy that other need if loneliness overtook them again. But it was a hell of a way to live.

As it happened, she couldn't make it to the surgery for lunch the next day. One of her outlying patients needed stitches removed. Another had an appointment with a home care visitor and Grace had been asked if she could be present. She sent Mike a friendly text to explain. As she drove through the snowy hills, she reflected that it was probably just as well. The less she saw him physically, the easier it would be to keep a mental distance. Kinder for both of them. Less heart-breaking.

She was surprised by one thing: the estate agent phoned to tell her he'd had another offer for the manor *above* the original asking price.

'It's too late,' she said. 'I'm selling the house to Dr Curtis.'

The agent pointed out that the contract had yet to be

signed. Grace replied that the formal offer had been
accepted and that she didn't go back on her word. Odd, she
thought, but put it out of her mind.

It didn't take too much effort to be busy the following
day as well, but she was conscious that she had promised
to take Bethany to her riding lesson. Subtle questioning of
the surgery receptionist elicited the information that young
Dr Curtis would be out all afternoon. Grace asked her to
relay the message that she would pick up Bethany's riding
clothes from his room at two-thirty.

There were vans in the driveway of the manor as she
went past. She drove resolutely on, ignoring a sharp stab
of pain. Mike was buying the manor from her. He would
make it beautiful again, a proper home for himself and
Bethany. But seeing workmen there, she finally realised
that what once had been a much-loved haven was lost to
her for ever. She let herself into the surgery as near deso-
lation as she had been in a long time.

She paused on the threshold of Mike's room. He had put
his stamp on it already. He'd shifted the computer onto his
desk and moved the desk nearer to the window. There was
the same tang of citrus in the room that she'd smelled on
his skin on Tuesday night.

She mustn't think about that. Not go there. Where were
Bethany's clothes? Ah, in a bag on the desk. She reached
for them quickly—and was arrested by the sight of a
framed photo.

It was large, ten inches by eight, and it showed a
laughing family. There was Mike, his head thrown back and
a wide smile splitting his face. He looked younger, carefree,
happy. And there was Bethany balanced on her father's hip,

dark curls dancing, giggling as if she would never stop. And there…there was Sarah. Also laughing, her head tipped towards Mike so that they framed their daughter.

Grace sat down numbly, unable to take her eyes off the photo. No wonder Mike was still in love with Sarah. She was an adult version of Bethany. Every time Mike looked at his daughter he must see his wife's face. How could any woman compete with that?

There was a note on the desk. *'Grace—busy this afternoon. Can you bring Bethany back, please? Thanks. Mike X'*

X. A kiss. Grace remembered his real kisses, pressed into her skin, taking her to such places of delight. She looked at the photo again. Even if they made a go of this, even if she let herself trust again, she would always be second best.

Lorna Threlkeld was just getting into her car as Grace and Bethany arrived at Rivercut Stables. She stopped, waiting for them, her face set in sour lines. 'Bethany Curtis, isn't it?'

'That's right,' said Grace. 'She enjoyed last week's lesson.'

'The little girl whose father is buying the manor. How very convenient, Grace.'

Grace's chin came up. 'It's convenient for Bethany because she won't have so far to walk to school.'

'And convenient for you too,' said Lorna with a malevolent look.

Grace knew perfectly well what the other woman was insinuating, but she kept her voice pleasant. 'It's certainly nice to have found a buyer at the right price,' she said, holding Bethany's hand somewhat tighter. 'We mustn't miss Bethany's lesson. Goodbye.'

A nasty little interlude, but as they walked on, a sudden amusing thought struck Grace. Could it have been Lorna's father who had put in that cut-price offer for the manor some time ago? Yes, she could just see him wanting to add it to his other properties in the area and turning it into holiday apartments or a country house hotel. He'd probably been holding back until she was desperate to sell at any price. But Lorna must have driven through the village and noticed the comings and goings so he had hurriedly contacted the estate agent and raised his bid. Ha! Too late, Mr Threlkeld. That will teach you to be greedy.

Her phone bleeped part way through the lesson. At the next pause, Grace looked at the text. 'It's from Daddy,' she said to Bethany. 'He wants us to call at the manor on the way back. He says he's found something exciting.'

'Treasure!' said Bethany straight away.

'I wish,' replied Grace. Sadly, knowing Mike, it was probably the old driveway gates so he could keep Bethany safe and sound and fenced off from the world.

They parked next to Mike's Range Rover. There were another couple of cars there too. Bethany danced in through the front door. It was a good thing it was open, thought Grace, it would have felt really weird using the knocker to her own home.

And there was Mike in conversation with a builder from the village, glancing towards the door and breaking into a smile. Grace stopped with an almost physical blow. So much for increasing mental distance. Just seeing him brought it all back. How could she have forgotten how wonderful he looked?

'Did you have a good lesson, sweetheart?' he said,

lifting Bethany in his arms. He kissed her, but his eyes were on Grace. 'Hi, Grace. How have you been?'

She had to keep up the pretence. Everything between them must appear unchanged. 'Oh, busy as usual. I might need your advice on one of today's calls.'

He was instantly alert. 'Serious?'

She shook her head. 'No. But a visit sooner rather than later would be good.'

Bethany was wriggling. 'Where's the treasure, Daddy?'

He laughed. 'It's not treasure, darling. It's a thing. What do you know about this, Grace?'

Such a strange exchange. The last time they had seen each other had been in her bedroom. They had just… It had been one of the most marvellous experiences of her life. And now they were casually chatting about patients and houses. Grace knew it was how she'd wanted it, but even so it took some getting used to.

Mike put Bethany down and led the way over to the fireplace. Grace saw with a jolt that it had been unblocked. She hoped he could afford the fuel bills that would be needed to combat the draughts.

Then she looked at the hall properly and was amazed. Mike had had the oak panelling cleaned. What a strange place to start! Surely there were more pressing aspects to be sorted out? But he was looking at her expectantly, his hand on an area of panel to the left of the fireplace.

'Ta-da!' he said, and pressed on the panelling. A black oblong appeared behind it.

'The secret passage!' exclaimed Grace, utterly delighted. Memories crowded back. She rushed to put them into words. 'To be exact, the secret entrance. When I was a little girl I thought it very Enid Blyton. Secrets in a house! There was a doorway here that led into a kind of long alcove at one end of the kitchen. It meant servants in the old days could serve drinks and food in the hall without having to walk all the way around through the corridors. But when the door was shut it just looked like the rest of the panelling. We didn't have servants so my father had the doorway bricked up and a big fridge-freezer installed in the alcove instead.'

'That explains it. We found it when we were cleaning the panelling. I couldn't resist trying to discover where it went so we knocked the bricks out and then pushed the fridge-freezer out of the way at the other end.' He grinned. 'Must say, I felt a bit Enid Blyton myself. Do you want to walk through? Revisit your childhood?'

'I do,' said Bethany, tugging his hand. 'Open the secret door, Daddy.'

'Careful of the brick rubble,' he said. 'Grace?'

There was an infectious excitement in his face. Grace felt herself melt. 'I'd love to.'

He eased the panelling door open. Bethany was instantly through it. Grace followed Mike more slowly. The arched passage was shorter than she remembered, the air hazy with brick dust and the tiled floor gritty underfoot. But it was magic. Mike was right—it was childhood revisited.

In front of them Bethany was already squealing with delight at having come out in a whole different room. Mike looked over his shoulder at Grace, his eyes brimming with amusement as he reached to clasp her hand. 'Fun?' he said.

His hand was strong and vital and alive. His joy in this simple thing was overwhelming. For a moment she was too full of emotion to speak. This was the man he was supposed to be. She settled for nodding. 'Fun.'

And she knew, here and now, permanently and for ever, that she loved him.

'Again,' shouted Bethany, running from the kitchen past Grace back to the hall. Mike jogged after her.

Grace remained in the kitchen, where they both joined her a few moments later.

'I'll have the alcove swept and cleaned and painted,' said Mike, panting slightly as he caught his over-excited daughter. 'And I'll have the secret door oiled. The passage is going to be so useful to get to and from the kitchen. Oh— and I got hold of a firm that refurbishes old ranges. And then later on I'd like a conservatory built onto the end wall there. It'll be a real living kitchen.'

'It sounds—it sounds lovely, Mike. I think you're going to be really happy here.'

He caught his breath. 'I hope so.'

'So who's this patient you were worried about?'

Grace looked up in surprise. She'd been immersed in writing up the morning's notes and hadn't heard Mike come into her room. She was even more surprised when he put a mug of tea on the desk in front of her.

'Peace offering in advance,' he said. 'I need to drag you down to the solicitor so we can sign a notice of intent of buy and I can pay you a deposit. Someone's been leaning on the estate agent—this should settle their hash.'

'Lorna Threlkeld's father!' exclaimed Grace wrathfully.

'I'll be glad to sign anything you like. But there's no need to pay me yet.'

'You don't have Christmas presents to buy? Besides, the money's better in your account than theirs.'

'If you insist, then.' She got the feeling that refusal would be futile at any time, but especially today. There was something different about Mike. He was edgy, his voice held an underlying tension. Had the surveyor uncovered something wrong with the manor? She kept her voice cheerful. 'And, yes, I always need to get more presents. I'm having a day's shopping in Manchester with Natalie tomorrow. It'll be nice to know there are funds to cover the credit-card bill.'

His face lightened. 'Natalie? The girl you trained with? The one whose daughter has such exceptional taste in underwear?'

Grace's heart skipped a beat at this reminder of the other night. 'That's her. But you'll be glad to hear Chloe is having a daddy day, so we'll be alone this time.' What was she saying? She'd intimated there might be another bedroom occasion! 'Always assuming we get out of the café, that is,' she said hurriedly. 'Put two friends together with unlimited coffee and we might just talk all day instead.'

'But that's good too. It's always good to have a friend.'

Oh, dear, was he reflecting that he'd left all his friends in London? She couldn't seem to say anything right. Then she remembered why he'd come into her room in the first place. Talking about work was safe. 'That patient I mentioned. Mrs King.' She brought up the file on the computer, shifting so Mike could read it.

He pulled across a chair and studied the screen.

Suddenly he was a doctor, a professional, not just Mike. 'Ivy King,' he murmured. 'Seventy-five years old with high blood pressure. What's the problem?'

'I called in to do her regular check-up. All seemed normal, the diastolic pressure was slightly up, but nothing to worry about. Then her daughter mentioned that Ivy had had several falls recently. It's not like her.'

'Did she appear weaker? Slurred speech?'

Grace made a helpless gesture. 'A bit more frail. I just…'

'You're wondering whether they were transient ischaemic attacks? Grace, it's not the end of the world if they were.'

Grace nodded, but still felt worried. A TIA happened when a small piece of fatty material came away from the wall of an artery, was transported to the brain and caused a temporary blockage. They were often the result of high blood pressure and they tended to grow more frequent with age. Recovery was usually quite quick. The danger was that in time the underlying cause might lead to a stroke.

'I'd still appreciate you doing a proper examination.'

'Then I will. Do you want to call in after we've seen the solicitor?'

Grace glanced at the clock on the wall. 'Will you have time before collecting Bethany from school?'

'She's going to a friend's house for tea. I've been instructed to pick her up at six o'clock.'

'Then, yes, please. Can you give me twenty minutes to get these notes finished?'

'Sure. I'll go and read up properly on Mrs King.'

It was all quite straightforward at the solicitor's office. Grace signed and was witnessed, signed again and was witnessed again. In a tone decrying his bad taste for mentioning it, the solicitor murmured that Mike's deposit would go straight into Grace's bank account. Grace said cheerfully that her bank manager would probably go out and get quietly drunk.

That almost brought a smile to Mike's lips, and when he was examining Mrs King he seemed normal too, if slightly withdrawn. But after he had suggested gently to Ivy that he arrange a trip to hospital for her for further tests, and they consulted a calendar to fix on the best time, Grace saw a shutter come over his face. Instinctively she took over the conversation, chatting in a friendly way as they moved to the door.

'So,' she finished, 'you're not to worry, Ivy. We just want to be on the safe side.'

'All right, young Grace,' said Ivy King. 'As long as the tests don't interfere with my Christmas, I'll go quietly. Run along now. Dr Curtis will be wanting to pick up his little girl. Bonny little thing she is, by what people say. Oh, and we're all pleased as punch that you're taking over the manor, Doctor. And there's not one of us believe the gossip neither.'

'Gossip?' said Mike when they were eventually in his car again. 'Which gossip would that be?'

Grace felt her cheeks heat. 'Nothing that matters.'

He looked at her as if he didn't believe her.

'Drive,' she said. 'You can tell me something soothing about how much you're having to pay to refurbish the central heating as we go. I saw the plumber's van turn up this morning as I was leaving for work. I can't believe you've found a system that will actually keep the main hall warm in winter.'

He gave her another of those piercing looks, but talked amiably enough until they came to a halt behind a line of traffic.

Grace peered ahead. It was obvious what had happened. A wedge of snow had slid suddenly down onto the road, causing a car to veer off. It didn't look as if anyone was hurt, but the road was blocked by the recovery lorry. Grace was used to this sort of scenario. She got Mrs King's case notes out of her case to annotate them. Mike, however, sat tensely, his eyes on the lorry, tapping the steering-wheel and casting harried glances at the dashboard clock.

'Why did this have to happen today?' he muttered. 'If I knew the roads around here I could take a back route home.'

Grace looked up. 'Mike, I know the roads and there aren't any back routes. Who is Bethany having tea with? Give her mother a ring. She'll understand. Or ask James to collect her if you're really worried about her outstaying her welcome.'

'I can't. He's going out for the whole evening.'

'Then ring,' she advised placidly. 'It'll be fine. We're used to unexpected snow-dumps in this part of the country during the winter.'

Bethany, predictably, was not in the least alarmed at Mike turning up late. She'd had a lovely time and was delighted to see Grace in the car too. But back at the surgery she set up a wail when she realised Grace was unlocking her Land Rover instead of coming indoors.

'I want Grace to stay!'

'Grace has things to do. It's nearly Christmas and she has to—'

'But I want to show her the bath toys Grandad gave me!' Tears started to roll down Bethany's cheeks.

Mike glanced at Grace, who nodded her head. 'All right, Bethany, just this once because it's nearly Christmas. But then you go straight to bed and be good!'

'All right,' said Bethany, demure now she had got her own way.

In fact, she was very tired after the excitement of playing with her friend. Bathtime was soon over and teeth cleaned. Grace offered to read a story, but the little girl was asleep before she reached the end of the first page. Grace looked down at her, wondering if this was how Sarah had looked in sleep. She withdrew quietly to the living room.

Mike was sitting staring into the fire, legs stretched out in front of him, his head resting on his hand. Grace saw his expression before he realised she was there. He looked sad, something she hadn't seen before. She wondered what he was thinking.

'Bethany's worn out,' she reported. 'It must be terribly tiring being a sociable five-year-old.'

He stirred. 'Thanks for putting her to bed. I don't usually pander to her but...' He broke off. 'Are you hungry at all? I was thinking of warming up some soup. And maybe a glass of wine?'

Grace remembered the last glass of wine they'd drunk together. She smiled—about to make an allusive remark—but realised with a slight shock and just a tiny touch of pique that sex wasn't on Mike's mind at all. But something was. Something that had brought a grey look to his face and defeat to his voice. 'That would be nice,' she said neutrally. 'Shall I help? Where is it all?'

He started to get up—almost had to drag himself. 'Sorry, I'm not being much of a host.'

Then Grace remembered something he had said earlier. *It's always good to have a friend.* 'Mike, tell me if I'm wrong, but is now one of those times when you'd like a friend?' she asked.

'Sorry?'

'There's something troubling you, it's obvious. And earlier you said that it was always good to have a friend. Well, I'm here and I'm a friend. What's the problem?'

He laughed shortly. 'Ten out of ten for observation skills. Yes, there is something bothering me, but it's not a problem. It's an anniversary.'

'Anniversary? Of what?'

Another silence, and then he said, 'I've been trying to forget it all day. Today my wife would have been thirty. But there'll be no party.'

'And it hurts.'

'It hurts. Last year her birthday was sheer agony, coming so soon after…after the accident. I thought this year it might be easier. And I suppose it is. A bit.' He frowned. 'Grace, this isn't the kind of thing I should be talking to you about. We've got very close and—'

'Mike, I want you to talk! You loved her, and I…I think that's great. So tell me about her, tell me about her birthdays.'

He laughed, and this time Grace thought there might be some genuine humour. 'I can take them or leave them but Sarah was like Bethany. She was so serious and intent for most of the time, but she loved birthdays and birthday parties. We always went to a bit of trouble for her. Two years ago I took her and Bethany on the London Eye at night. As it went round we had a picnic out of the rucksack

I'd packed. Then I told her to close her eyes, and Bethany and I gave her her birthday cake.'

'A birthday cake? In a rucksack?'

Mike almost smiled. 'Two birthday cakes. Two little iced cakes, one with two candles on, one with eight. Because she was twenty-eight.'

'That sounds magic.' Grace couldn't help herself. She took his hand. 'Tell me what Sarah was like,' she said. 'It might be painful but it might help. I think it's wrong to try to forget, it's better to remember—to remember the good times, remember how much they outweighed the bad. Describe her to me.'

For a moment she thought he was going to refuse, but then he took a deep breath. 'She was a very slim woman, athletic but not as tall as you. She had a young face, sort of pointed—elfin some people called it. Dark hair, wavy like Bethany's. She had big dark eyes, dark green, and a piercing look. Sometimes she'd stay silent and just look at you so you wanted desperately to say something to her.'

'And she was a doctor, like you.'

'Yes. She never believed that some problems are insoluble, are beyond a doctor's abilities. She got involved when she shouldn't and when she failed it hurt her.'

'That's a good fault, don't you think? Better than the opposite.'

'True. You remind me of her that way sometimes.'

Grace felt like crying. 'Thank you, that's a lovely thing to say. I can see why you miss her.'

'I do. Sometimes I think I always will.' He buried his face in his hands. 'And sometimes I resent that. How can that be? How can I resent Sarah? I loved her. I loved her so much.'

Grace watched, alarmed now, as he crouched forward, his hands gripped together. 'Grief doesn't follow normal rules, Mike. Love alters us. Maybe…maybe our bodies can't cope immediately. Maybe when the one we love has gone, our bodies try to snap back to how they were before. But they can't. I think…I think the thing to do is to move on, but remember the past.'

'Easier said than done. Do you still want some soup?'

She followed him into the kitchen where he took a large bowl of home-made chowder out of the fridge and ladled it into a saucepan. There were crusty rolls to go with it, and half a bottle of red wine. He brushed against her as he reached for his glass. His wedding ring knocked her knuckle. Mike studied his hand for a long moment before carrying the food through to the other room.

This time the conversation was easier. They talked about some tiny changes Mike wanted to make to the practice, but wasn't sure whether his father would agree with. By the end of the simple meal, Grace thought Mike was probably all right again. She was glad she'd been here— as a friend—when he'd hit that low point.

'I'd better go,' she said. 'I'll leave the car here and walk. Don't want to risk running over any stray carol singers when I've had a drink.'

'Wait a minute.' Mike sat upright, his voice strained. Grace realised she had been premature in thinking him over his earlier emotion.

He spread his hands out, looked at the left one. 'I remember the time in church, getting married, when we exchanged rings. For me it was the happiest moment of the ceremony. They didn't match, our rings. I gave Sarah one

I'd had specially made—in white gold. She didn't have much money of her own, so she gave me her grandmother's ring, enlarged to fit my finger. That's why it's so narrow. She joked that when she was a world-famous consultant she'd have a broader one made for me. I said I didn't want one. I just wanted this one, given to me with love.'

'That's lovely,' whispered Grace, tears in her eyes.

'Sarah's ring was ruined in the fire in the crash. This one…' He pulled at the narrow band on the third finger of his left hand.

Grace couldn't help herself. 'No, don't! It's a symbol, it reminds you that—'

'I need to look forward,' he said fiercely. He tugged the ring off his finger at last, kissed it then put it on the table. 'I shan't wear it again.'

This was wrong. This was so wrong. There were tears in his eyes and Grace couldn't bear it. She gave it a moment then asked, 'So do you feel different now? More comfortable? A new person?'

'No.' There was a world of pain in his answer.

Grace picked up the ring from the table, lifted Mike's hand from where it lay desolately in his lap and slipped Sarah's wedding band back onto his finger. 'You loved her, she loved you and she'll always be part of you. Don't fight it, Mike. Accept it. Go forward with her behind you, urging you on.'

She stood up. He stood too, slightly dazed, at a loss. Grace put her arms round him and hugged him tightly. 'You'll be all right,' she said, and kissed his cheek. 'But if you need a friend, phone me.'

It took a great, great effort of will to shrug into her coat and leave the house. But she had to. Because otherwise she might have said those fatal words, words Mike wasn't anywhere near ready to hear. She said them outside, though. Closed the door firmly behind her and then looked back at the solid wood panel.

'Sleep well, Mike,' she whispered. 'I love you.'

CHAPTER TEN

THERE was another snowfall that night but in the morning the sun was out and the light on the white moors was beautiful. No one could be unhappy on a day like this, thought Grace as she drove out of Rivercut and the full beauty of the landscape hit her. She had a brief moment of regret for her old bedroom at the manor—she'd have seen this view as soon as she pulled her curtains.

No. She set her thoughts resolutely towards lively, bustling Manchester and the day of Christmas shopping awaiting her. The manor belonged to Mike now. The view would most likely be Bethany's. She must be content with her small cottage and rejoice in the simple fact that she could now afford to pay the rent *and* have money left over for more than just the basics of life.

Mike. All the curtains had been drawn still when she'd picked up her car. She hoped he'd got some sleep last night, not stayed up wrestling with his memories. She hadn't had a phone call. That was a good sign, wasn't it?

In Manchester she met up with Natalie, who needed a posh outfit for a charity do on New Year's Eve. With a pleasurable thrill, Grace realised that she would not be restricted to merely admiring her friend—she could dress up too!

An entire morning later, Natalie was the possessor of a strapless number in dark red satin—and Grace had blown an awful lot of salary on a full-length gold taffeta gown with diamanté spaghetti straps and a seductive slit from thigh to ankle. She didn't give a thought to when she would actually wear such a dress. Whenever the occasion arose, she'd be ready! On the way out of the store they stopped in the children's clothes department. Grace was charmed to see full-length party dresses for little girls. 'I'll get one for Bethany,' she said aloud.

'Pardon?' asked her friend.

'Bethany Curtis. Mike's daughter. I told them how I used to walk down the staircase at home holding a long skirt above my ankles just like a film star. Bethany would love to do that. And I know she doesn't have any long dresses. This can be her Christmas present.'

'Good idea,' said Natalie. 'I'll buy one for Chloe too. How old did you say Bethany was?' And she continued to ask casual questions about Bethany and Mike as they looked through the racks.

It was when they were having lunch at a chic city restaurant that Grace felt a tap on her shoulder. 'Grace Fellowes! Haven't seen you for ages! And Natalie Wright too. What a sight for sore eyes.'

Grace swung round. It was Dr Robert Ross, a friend that she and Natalie had worked with some years before. He now held a senior position in a hospital in Manchester. And it seemed he was looking for staff. He joined them for coffee and told them about it.

'Half the time teaching—sharing your practical knowledge—the rest of the time proper hands-on nursing. Think about it, Grace. You've been a rural nurse for quite long enough. It's time your talents were recognised. There's more money in it.'

More money. Three weeks ago, those two words would have made Grace seriously consider the proposition. Now she laughed. 'Thanks, Robert, but inner-city nursing—even hospital nursing with all the up-to-date equipment—it's just not for me.'

'But you're wasting away out there in the sticks! Look around you—don't you deserve this?'

'Right here, right now, it's tempting. As soon as I get home I'll wonder what you spiked my coffee with.'

The afternoon was spent in more shopping. There were several people in the village Grace needed to get small presents for, but all the time she was conscious she hadn't bought anything for Mike. But what? What did you get for the man who was buying your house—a house that needed a considerable amount of work doing to it—at a far too reasonable price? What did you get for the man who had been your lover for a few glorious hours one magical evening?

'Penny for them?' said Natalie. She had the air of having said it before.

'Oh, sorry. I was trying to remember what else I wanted.'

Natalie looked smug. 'I just need the antiquarian bookshop. Perhaps you'll be struck by inspiration there.'

And perhaps not. She didn't even know what Mike liked to read.

At the shop, Natalie plunged into discussion with the bookseller to whom she had already emailed her husband's wish list. Grace riffled idly through a stack of framed maps and prints—and stopped, amazed. There was an old hand-coloured map of Rivercut Village and the farms around it! She knew instantly that it would be the perfect present for Mike. It was the whole area the practice covered. It even had the manor inscribed in the centre! She blinked a bit at the price but the shopkeeper, in a fit of generosity brought on by Natalie's lavish squandering of her husband's money, reduced the amount by a third.

'That's lovely,' said Natalie. 'Where are you going to hang it?'

'I'm not,' said Grace absently. 'It's for Mike.'

Natalie pounced. 'Aha! I knew it! When do we get to meet him? Remember, you always promised I could be your matron of honour!'

'It's not like that.'

But the trouble with friends who knew you rather well was that they didn't believe the 'just good friends' line for a minute. 'Grace, you've been talking about him all day.'

'I have not!'

'Well, he's made a lot more appearances in your conversation than anyone else has.' Natalie's voice warmed; she clasped her friend's hand. 'He sounds nice.'

'He is.'

'So what's the problem? Not still that jerk Peter, is it?'

Grace sighed. 'In a way. Partly. It's quite difficult to trust after something like that. But it's also Mike. I told you his wife died in a car crash last year. Well…he's still in love with her.'

Natalie looked at her solemnly. 'But you have slept with him, right?'

'Natalie!'

'Grace, you're acting sad, but your eyes light up when you mention him.'

'That doesn't come into it. I don't…' She paused, realising it was true. 'I don't want to be second best.'

It seemed a very long journey back. Leaving the bright lights of Manchester, leaving the shops and restaurants and wide streets and bold sculptures and bustling activity. But the moors soothed Grace as always, even ghostly white and deserted in the darkness. And coming into Rivercut's narrow main road with the Carters' over-the-top Christmas display visible from the edge of the village, she smiled, wondering how she could have been so daft to consider Robert's offer even for a moment.

The Carters had competition—the manor was ablaze with lights, several vans parked in the drive. Grace was impressed. Mike had meant it when he'd said he wanted to get started on necessary work as soon as possible. Part of her wanted to pull into the drive, to see what it was he was doing. But part of her preferred to leave well alone, to remember the manor as it had always been, decaying grandeur and all. All the same, curiosity might have won if her car headlights hadn't suddenly caught the glint of wrought-iron gates. A pattern of graceful loops and whorls she hadn't seen since childhood.

Grace rolled numbly to a halt, unable to look away. Mike must have found the gates in one of the barns. Not only found them—he'd had gateposts installed and fixed them back in place. She wound down her window to the acrid smell of new paint.

Gates across the drive again. No matter that they were

standing open now, the very fact of them being there at all proclaimed the change in ownership. The manor was no longer her home.

Mike was woken up by a heavy weight clambering on top of him. For a split second his sleepy body hoped it might be Grace, but the words 'Daddy! Daddy!' made him realise his mistake.

'Go away,' he grumbled. 'It's Sunday.'

His daughter giggled. 'I know.'

He growled and caught her in a tickling cuddle. It was only later, washed, dressed and breakfasted, holding Bethany's hand as she skipped beside him on their way to the manor, that Mike realised his first thought that morning had been for Grace, not Sarah. The revelation came as such a shock that he missed his footing and thumped down hard in a sitting position, half in snow, half in slush. Bethany found it highly amusing.

'If you're tired you should have knocked,' called a voice. 'You could have rested for a moment before going on to the manor.'

Grace! She was just putting her bag into the Land Rover. Mike scrambled to his feet, brushing snow off his anorak. She looked gorgeous. Wait a moment, though… 'Why are you in uniform?' he said with a frown. 'It's Sunday.'

'One of my patients had a fall overnight and the dressing is oozing.'

'But you're off duty. Can't they ring the out-of-hours service?'

'Mike, it'll take me forty minutes maximum. Don't fuss.'

Don't fuss? He was a doctor! It was his job to fuss.

'Grace, I've seen too many medical professionals have breakdowns because they do too much. You have to look after yourself. Time off—time spent doing things for yourself—is important.'

She smiled and opened the driver's door. 'All I had planned for this morning was wrapping presents. How can that be more important than a patient in pain?'

There was no answer to that. Mike felt all the frustration of arguing with a woman who knew she was in the right. 'Just you make sure it is only forty minutes, then,' he said grumpily.

'It will be.'

'We've got presents,' said Bethany, fixing on the important bit of the conversation. 'Under Grandad's tree.' She sighed. 'But I'm not allowed to open them until Christmas.'

'Fair's fair,' said Grace. 'Baby Jesus had to wait for his presents, didn't he?'

'Our baby Jesus is a doll. Will you come and see me be an angel? Daddy's made me a halo to wear.'

Mike caught his breath, waiting for Grace's answer. He thought she looked touched and very pleased to be asked.

'I'd love to,' she said. 'When is it?'

He cleared his throat. 'Tuesday afternoon in the church, with a repeat performance on Sunday. You have no idea what strict instructions we've been given about when to get there and which carols to practise and to make sure they all know their lines and don't wear coloured knickers under the angel dresses. This isn't a nativity—it's show business!'

Grace laughed. When had that rich tone started making him tingle? 'It will be lovely,' she said, getting into the car. 'My friend Liz is a bit of a perfectionist, that's all, and the

Reverend Christine wants her first Christmas here to really stand out.'

'Believe me, it will! I'm willing to sing "Once in Royal David's City" just one more time but then that's it till next Christmas.'

'I'd better go, Mike. Try not to fall down any more on your way to the manor.'

'I'll do my best.' He shut the door for her, waited for her to wind down the window to say goodbye. 'Oh, did you see I found the gates? Eventually I'll have an electric system fitted so you can open them without getting out of the car.'

'That would have shocked the people who originally built the house.'

'Cheaper than employing a full-time gatekeeper.' He studied her face. 'What's the matter?'

She shook her head as if impatient with herself and started the car. 'Nothing. The gates are great. I suppose I'm just taking longer than I expected to get used to the change.'

'But you liked the thought of the secret passage being unblocked. You liked the idea of the kitchen being thrown open and a conservatory added.'

She raised her voice to carry over the sound of the engine. 'Yes, I did. Don't worry about it, Mike. I'm being irrational. Bye, Bethany.'

He and Bethany watched her drive off up the village street, then they resumed their walk to the manor. What was wrong with the gates? They were safe, practical, original... She *was* being irrational. All the same, her words about it taking time to get used to change started an interesting train of thought in his mind.

* * *

The cold weather was starting to take its toll. Grace had a lot more calls than normal from patients who wondered whether she could just call in on her way past rather than them travel into Rivercut. She was finishing typing up her notes for the day when there was a tap on her door. Mike on his way to start his evening surgery.

'Grace, I was wondering about instigating a weekly review of the patients that don't pass through my or Dad's hands. Just to keep us aware of any problems that might be brewing.'

Grace looked at him levelly. There was a touch too much innocent helpfulness in his tone. 'This wouldn't be about you deciding whether I should or shouldn't go out on my own time to patients, would it? Because a district nurse is generally held to be autonomous and capable of making up her own mind as to whether she's needed or not.'

'Nurse Fellowes, I wouldn't dream of calling your professional judgement into question!'

Grace raised her eyebrows. 'But?'

Mike sighed. 'But I've seen your workload. I'm not sure your heart knows the difference between genuinely needy and taking advantage.'

She was torn between irritation at the interference and warmth that he cared about her doing too much. 'Away to your patients, Dr Curtis. You're just going to have to trust me until we're less busy.'

All the same, because of the extra calls she was late finishing and late leaving, and more tired than normal when she got home. Maybe Mike had a point, she thought as she climbed the stairs wearily and fell into bed.

Next morning she realised with horror that she'd either slept through the alarm or had forgotten to set it. She washed hastily, dressed, grabbed the local paper out of the letterbox and hurried up to the surgery for her regular Tuesday clinic without stopping for breakfast. She got a couple of odd looks from people on the way, but it wasn't until she slipped into the surgery kitchen for a coffee in a short lull between patients and opened *The Moors News* that she found out why. There on the third page was the announcement of an engagement and an article—with photographs—about the engagement party at a posh country house hotel.

MATCH OF THE YEAR, it was headed. Prominent landowner Raymond Threlkeld had apparently had great pleasure in announcing the betrothal of his only daughter, Lorna, to local solicitor Peter Cox. He had welcomed many eminent county residents to an opulent dinner-dance in order to celebrate alongside the happy couple.

There followed a list of said guests, a description of the menu and a report on the male half of the happy couple's speech. 'I have spent my whole life looking for a woman like Lorna,' he said, looking deeply into his fiancée's eyes. 'And now I have found her.'

Grace felt sick. *I have spent my whole life looking for a woman like Lorna.* Those were words Peter had used to her as well. Just at this moment she didn't think she would ever trust a man again.

The door opened and Mike dashed in. 'Excellent, you've got the kettle on. I could kill for a mug of… Grace? What's up?'

'Nothing.' She fumbled a second mug out of the cupboard and put a spoonful of coffee into it. She heard the rustle of newspaper, an intake of breath.

'Oh, Grace.' Mike's arms came around her in a comforting hug. Just for a moment it was so nice to be held like that. He moved his lips to her ear. 'You really should have let me punch him, you know.'

Grace gave a shaky laugh. 'He'd sue you. Thanks, Mike. I'm all right.' She splashed milk quickly into her mug and headed back to her room. Any more of that and she'd melt. She *wanted* to melt. But that would be a disaster. She needed to be Nurse Fellowes again, professional and in control.

'I still say he was mad,' Mike called after her.

Several patients' heads swivelled interestedly. *Oh, thank you, Mike,* thought Grace.

'Getting on well with young Dr Curtis, are you?' wheezed her next patient.

'He's a very good doctor,' said Grace repressively. She slipped the blood-pressure cuff on and set the timer. 'Relax, please.'

But gossip was life blood to Mrs Smithson. 'We've all been saying how suitable it would be, what with his poor little girl motherless and you not getting any younger. And when we heard how your car was outside the surgery all night last week, well, we were pleased as punch. Nobody's worried about that sort of thing these days, are they?'

'I had a meal with both the doctors Curtis and there was wine, which is why I walked home. Your blood pressure's fine, Mrs Smithson. Now, can you breathe deeply and then blow as hard as possible into this tube for me? See how efficiently your lungs are working.'

Not as efficiently as the local grapevine, that was for sure. Grace went through the rest of the checks resolving to be discreet with a capital D in her future dealings with the Curtis household.

* * *

The Nativity play was to be at two o'clock in the church. Grace had a couple of visits to make in the village, but got a phone call while she was at Mrs Johnson's house to ask if she could pop in to see Mr Harris, whose daughter was concerned that he'd had a dizzy spell. Unfortunately, Mr Harris lived at the other end of Rivercut, which meant by the time Grace had got there, diagnosed the problem and hurried to St Lawrence's she was late. Not to worry, she'd slip into the back and would still be able to tell Bethany truthfully that she'd watched the whole thing.

First problem—there was standing room only. Evidently the school parents wanted to make a good impression on the new vicar. Also, a good half of them had camcorders. She'd be continually in the way. Second problem—Mike was twisting round from his position in the front pew, looking for her. When he saw her he beckoned that he'd saved her a place. Oh, great. Grace walked the entire length of the aisle feeling as if her face was blazing as brightly as Rudolph's nose.

'All okay?' he asked in a low voice. 'Do I need to see Mr Harris?'

'Not unless you take a glass with you,' Grace murmured back. 'He'd smuggled himself in a bottle of whisky and had started on the Christmas cheer early. I'm not surprised he'd had a dizzy spell.'

Mike chuckled. 'I'm glad you're here,' he said simply.

How could he make her heart ache with just one sentence? 'Is everything all right backstage?' she asked. 'Not too much stage fright?'

'Couple of nasty moments when the halos slipped on

the walk up here from school, but otherwise they seem to be all right.'

The organ started playing. Good, she didn't have to talk any more.

Christine—Rivercut's new vicar—welcomed the audience and said how happy she was that the youngest children at the school had chosen a traditional Nativity to perform on this, her first Christmas here. Then there was a scuffle in the screened-off side chapel and Liz was heard exhorting the shepherds to get out into the nave and start watching their flocks. The play had begun.

The moment the angels filed in, Mike grasped Grace's hand. She couldn't blame him. Bethany looked enchanting. Perhaps she spoiled it a bit by looking into the audience and smiling widely at Grace and Mike, but most of the children did that. It added to the charm.

Strangely, though, it was when Mary and Joseph came on stage, looking for an inn to stay the night, that Grace broke down. Tears ran down her face. Over twenty years ago she had played the pregnant Mary and she had loved it. And now a child that she…that she loved was taking part in the same play.

Mike saw her tears and squeezed her fingers before passing her a tissue. After she'd dried her eyes he didn't take her hand again. She told herself this was sensible. There was enough talk as it was.

It was a magical afternoon. Everyone remembered their lines or were gently prompted by Liz. Bethany was a wonderful angel and spoke clearly. The familiar carols sung in children's voices brought a lump to her throat. The Christmas story ended, the cast lined up, smiling and waving in relief; the applause was tumultuous.

'I need to collect Bethany,' said Mike over the noise.

Grace nodded. She'd wait for them outside. It was too busy in here and she wanted to be alone to collect her thoughts for a moment. She threaded her way through the press of parents to the church door, twisted the iron ring and stepped out into a world where the sun was just disappearing behind a bank of lowering snow-laden clouds.

Straight into the path of Peter Cox and Lorna Threlkeld.

'Well, well,' said Peter. 'Fancy seeing you here.'

Grace stiffened. 'If you wanted the Nativity, you've just missed it.'

'Why would we?' drawled Lorna. 'I get enough of kids at the stables. We're here to see the vicar about arranging our wedding.'

'Come to that, why are you here, Grace? You don't have any—' Peter broke off, looking into the church. 'Oh, I see. Congratulations. You really have found someone to keep you and the manor in the style to which you'd like to be accustomed, haven't you? Quick work.'

Grace turned to see Mike hoisting Bethany in his arms, about to set off up the aisle.

Peter was still talking, softly poisonous. 'And a surrogate child too to slake those maternal longings. Clever Grace. You get his gratitude and an instant family in one fell swoop.'

Mike had been detained, talking to the mother of one of Bethany's friends. Thank goodness for small mercies. 'You're wrong,' said Grace between set teeth. 'There is nothing between Dr Curtis and myself except work.'

'Don't give me that. A widower with the inconvenience of a small child? You're a gift from the gods,

Grace. Over-sexed, pathetically grateful and poor. And right on his doorstep.'

Lorna laughed and linked her arm in Peter's. 'A match made in Heaven, in fact. Come on, darling. The vicar must be finished with this lot by now, surely?'

They strolled inside. The parents and children streaming out blocked Grace's view of the nave. She felt ill. Sick and shaken. Was it true? What Peter had said? Was she all those horrible things? And was Mike taking advantage of her?

Her phone went. One of her more cantankerous patients wanted to know how much longer she was going to be. Grace had never been more pleased in her life to hurry off.

Away from the church.

Away from people.

Away from Mike.

CHAPTER ELEVEN

MIKE zipped Bethany into her coat, picked up the bag with her school clothes in and hoisted her into his arms. It was going to be easier getting out of the church if he was carrying her rather than worrying about her tripping everyone up. Bethany was pouring an excited monologue into his ear, but for once he wasn't giving her his full attention. Where was Grace? He'd assumed she'd be waiting for them. He couldn't believe she wasn't by the door. He'd felt so close to her, watching the Nativity. It had almost been like… Almost been as if they were a family. He looked down the street through the thinning crowd of parents—and saw her Land Rover pull away from the side of the road. Of course. He'd forgotten she'd be still working this afternoon. She must be on her way to her next appointment. He set Bethany on her feet—an angel in anorak and Wellington boots—and trudged back home with her, feeling flat with disappointment.

There was no message from Grace on the surgery phone or his mobile. Once evening surgery was over and Bethany in James's care, Mike walked down to the cottage.

'Hi,' he said, when she opened the door. 'I wondered if you fancied a drink at the pub?'

'Last time we had a drink at the pub we ended up in bed.' She looked normal, she sounded normal, but she wasn't quite. If she'd been a patient, Mike would have said she was hiding something. 'And that was bad?' he asked, probing lightly.

'No, it was very good indeed, as well you know. But I don't want to be a habit, Mike. I don't want to be a convenience.'

'You weren't!' he said, stung by the injustice. 'Can I come inside? I think we need to talk about this.'

Grace moved to let him in. 'You haven't mentioned that evening,' she muttered.

'Neither have you.' He sat down on the sofa. 'If you must know, when I got back Bethany was—'

Grace's phone shrilled, interrupting him. She answered it. 'Hi, Robert! No, I haven't forgotten your offer… Yes, well, you know Natalie. I just hope her credit card's made of stern stuff.' She listened a moment more. 'I'll let you know. Have a good Christmas. Thanks for ringing.'

'An offer?' said Mike, before he could stop himself. What was the matter with him? Why did he feel so aggressive all of a sudden?

After a moment's hesitation she perched next to him. 'Robert Ross is an old friend from my training days. He's setting up a back-to-basics teaching department for hands-on nurses. He was trying to convince me I should move to Manchester.'

Alarm, rage, *something* swept over Mike. 'You can't. You're needed here. You belong here!'

She blinked. 'I'm only the district nurse. I'm easily replaceable.'

'Any other district nurse might be—not you. You're

special. Who else is going to turn out to patients at unsocial hours because they can't work the childproof cap on their tablets?' He was trying desperately to hold on to his sense of humour, but he was filled with such horror at the thought of her leaving Rivercut that he was having difficulty stringing a sentence together.

She was looking at him oddly again. 'Relax, I'm not going. Or I don't think I am.'

Oh, thank goodness. He reached for her in relief, drew her towards him. Their lips met in a clash of urgency and need.

A brief, sweet moment and then she drew back. 'Mike, I can't do this tonight. I don't know what I want, and I don't think you know what you want, either.'

He wanted *her*, that's what he wanted. But dimly, through his frustration, he recognised that telling her so would probably be counter-productive.

She was talking again. 'Can you give me a few days? I'm sorry, Mike, but I really need to think something through.'

What could he say? No matter that all he felt like doing right now was dragging her to the nearest cave and barricading the pair of them inside.

'Sure,' he said, getting up. 'I'll go and have that pint.' At least the temperature outside was as good as a cold shower.

By Thursday afternoon, Grace was feeling thoroughly frustrated. Mike had taken her at her word and not raised the subject of their relationship again. He appeared to be settling into the district well and was finding his way about. A bit too well, actually. Grace dropped in at Holroyd Farm to see Edith and was surprised to see his Range Rover coming the other way out of the farmyard. Just checking on those new tablets, she was told when she asked. Grace was niggled—Mrs Holroyd was supposed to be *her* patient.

Still, it was now Bethany's last riding lesson before Christmas and Grace had picked her up from school and was helping her change. She happened to know that Mike had bought his daughter a complete riding outfit for Christmas—Grace wished she could see the little girl's face when she opened the present on Christmas Day. In fact, she wished…

No. She must stop thinking that way. Mike was still in love with his dead wife. She and Mike might be attracted to each other, but a relationship based on physical needs and her own neediness would be doomed to disaster.

At the previous lesson, Bethany had graduated to going around the ring without needing to be led, so Grace leant on the rail and watched her. It was so sweet, all the ponies had tinsel twined into their tack and the children had been promised the treat of feeding their mounts a Christmas carrot each at the end of the lesson. It reminded her of years ago when she too had started learning to ride.

A low, furious voice broke in on Grace's thoughts. 'Why the hell aren't you in the ring with her?'

Grace jumped, startled. 'Mike, she told you last week when we got home that she could ride by herself.'

'I didn't realise she meant all the time! She's far too small and inexperienced. What if the horse bolts?'

'She's coming on really well and these ponies are so old and staid they wouldn't know how to bolt. Calm down.'

'Easy for you to say, she's not your… Oh, no, that's too fast…'

The circle of children had increased to a trot. Grace

smiled at the look of delight on Bethany's face. The little girl saw Mike and beamed, then blinked and slid off the pony's side. Mike instantly made to vault over the rail, but Grace hung on to him. The circle had slowed and one of the riding instructors was already there, picking Bethany up.

'Oh, well done! You fell beautifully. Just as we told you, no feet tangled in stirrups, no hanging on to the reins, nothing. What a clever girl you are. Up we get again.'

Mike was incandescent, trying to pull away from Grace's restraining grip. 'That does it, she's never riding again ever.'

'She's already back on the pony. Does she seem worried?'

'She's too young to know the danger!'

'Mike, you can't keep her wrapped in cotton wool for ever.'

'I lost her mother. I'm not going to lose her as well. Let me go!'

'No. You're going to stay here and watch and smile and be proud. If you leave, she's going to think you were disappointed when she fell off. If you take her away, she's going to think she's done something bad and be upset.'

He looked at her, his eyes blazing. 'You don't know what you're asking me.'

Inside, Grace cried. Outside, she remained calm. 'I do! This is important, Mike. Your dad is always saying how like you Bethany is in temperament. "Never walked when he could run," remember? You *have* to let Bethany push her own boundaries. How else is she going to grow? Did James ever stop you climbing trees, even though you might fall out of them? Did he forbid you to jump in the deep end of the swimming pool? Riding is only dangerous if you haven't been taught properly. Bethany is being taught properly.'

Mike didn't say a word, just shook her off and stared ahead at the ring in silence, his whole body rigid. After five minutes, he rasped, 'Have I watched for long enough now? May I go?' He waved to his daughter, turned and left.

After the lesson was over, the carrots duly given to the ponies and Christmas wishes exchanged all round, Grace strapped Bethany into her car. No Lorna this week—that was good. She was still shaking with reaction after the exchange with Mike; any more unkind words would probably finish her off. She *hated* telling people home truths, but at least doing it in the line of work meant she had proven medical research to back it up. Why should Mike believe her about Bethany? Especially after the trauma he'd been through. He had every right to hate her for telling him to loosen up with his daughter.

Drearily, Grace drove back. She automatically glanced up the drive of the manor as they passed. Mike's car was there. Her heart twisted.

'There's Daddy!' squealed Bethany.

Grace took a deep breath and turned in between the new-old gates. Her headlights illuminated a solitary figure swinging an axe at a log pile.

'Daddy,' said Bethany excitedly as soon as he opened her door. 'I gave Foxtrot a carrot!'

'That's lovely, darling.'

He looked so, so tired. Grace ached for him. She cleared her throat. 'Is the kitchen still working?' she asked. 'I could kill for a cup of tea.'

Her voice sounded strange. Hopefully Mike would accept the olive branch.

It was touch and go for a moment, then, 'I think we

could run to that.' He unfastened Bethany and lifted her out. 'Foxtrot's the horse that's ten feet tall with a mouth full of teeth, I take it?'

Grace's heart banged painfully. 'Oh, more like twenty feet tall. With a dreadful temper and a trigger-happy kick.'

Mike gave a lopsided smile. 'Grace, I'm sorry. I over-reacted.'

She laid a hand on his arm. 'You had reason. Goodness, haven't you made the hall look bright?'

'Scrubs up nicely, doesn't it?'

It did. The panelling had been cleaned, the floor polished and the ceiling whitewashed. She only now appreciated how careworn it had got.

'Come and see my bedroom,' shouted Bethany, tugging her towards the stairs.

Oh, no. No, Grace wasn't at all ready for that. Another little girl in her room. Someone else's decor in the sanctuary she had known all her life. Different curtains framing 'her' view of the moors.

'Go on,' murmured Mike. 'Be brave.'

She supposed she deserved that. She girded up her courage and followed Bethany. And was astonished beyond measure when the little girl danced along the passageway to what had been Grace's parents' room.

'It had the princess bed in,' explained Mike. 'Would your mother have approved?'

Grace looked dazedly around the freshly decorated corner room. The bed canopy was now pale pink. The wallpaper had unicorns, fairies, rainbows, hearts and butterflies on a pink background. 'Definitely,' she said. 'A fairy bower. Mum didn't live in the real world either.'

She was shown the rest of the rooms on the way back down to the kitchen. The nursery she had designed with so much love was untouched. She didn't know whether to be pleased or unsettled. The other rooms looked much as she remembered them, though there was something different, something she couldn't quite put her finger on. It wasn't until she had finished her mug of tea and was preparing to leave that she realised what it was.

'Mike! The upstairs rooms! The paintwork…the papering… They look exactly the same as when I left, only brand-new! Why would you re-create the house as it was?'

He looked just a tiny bit disconcerted. 'I suppose I liked the way it was,' he said evasively. 'It was easier to restore it rather than dream up something new. The architect I asked to check the building out was enthralled. He said he'd never seen a small manor house like this one with so much apparently original work. He's got some excellent suggestions for how to modernise the plumbing and heating without it being intrusive.'

'I see. It's going to be lovely.'

'I hope so.' He glanced at her. 'So do you think you can bear to come to the party?'

Grace frowned. What party?

'Bethany! Didn't you give Grace the invitation?'

'Oops.' Bethany giggled. 'I forgot. Sorry.' She raced down the remaining stairs, peered into her school backpack and pulled out a rather crumpled envelope. 'Here you are! I helped Daddy write it and I signed it and he says it's my party as well as his and I can have a new dress that's long just like you.' She thrust the envelope into Grace's hand and added, 'I drawed the holly. It's good, isn't it?'

'Very good.' Grace opened the letter—an invitation from Miss Bethany Curtis and Dr Michael Curtis to a celebratory party at the manor on Christmas Eve. She swallowed. There had always been a Christmas Eve party at the manor. But her family had organised it. It would be different going as a guest.

'You can come?' Bethany pleaded.

'Of course I can come. Nothing would keep me away. I shall write you a proper reply this evening.'

'You've got to. That's what RSVP means. It's so Daddy doesn't buy too many packets of crisps.'

'And you're going to have a long dress. That's exciting.'

'She's been looking at your old photographs,' said Mike. 'I'll ask one of Sarah's friends to send something up. They've been bombarding me with emails for a fortnight, wanting to know what to send us from civilisation.'

Grace lowered her voice and leant towards his ear. 'If it's any help, I bought one for her in Manchester as a Christmas present.'

It was lovely, being this close to him. But all he said was, 'Grace, that's fantastic. Do you want to give it her before Christmas Day? She'll be over the moon.'

After Bethany was in bed, Mike sat with his father, watching television.

'You all right, lad?' asked James.

Mike sighed. 'Just thinking.'

James cleared his throat. 'I know we haven't been close these past few years, and neither of us are good at saying what we feel—but I do want you to be happy. I got the feeling that you and Grace might…'

'Dad, it's complicated.'

There was a small silence. James sipped his whisky. 'Sarah wouldn't have wanted you to mourn for ever.'

But when was the right time to stop? Grace was lovely—her dark blonde hair, her wide smile, the way she wanted to eradicate all suffering everywhere. The truth was that Mike wanted to be with her all the time. He'd refreshed the manor because of her distress at the changes. He couldn't care less what it looked like as long as she was happy. Her honesty this afternoon at the stables had been devastating—but she'd been right, reluctant though he was to admit it.

But how could he betray Sarah's memory by even contemplating sharing his and Bethany's lives with another woman? Was he quite sure it wasn't just his bodily needs that were driving him? At the thought of Grace's body an exquisite cramp gripped him. He wondered what his father would say if he went down there now, tonight. Come to that, he wondered what Grace would say. He needed to know her better. He would ask her to have lunch with them again tomorrow. He would talk to her—really talk. Show her he'd heeded her advice. Find out about *her*, her hopes and dreams and aspirations. And, meanwhile, he would carry on with his plans for the party.

The next day, however, fate seemed determined to thwart him. It had snowed again overnight and when Mike put his head around Grace's door he found no one there. So many patients had cancelled that Grace was doing house visits instead, the receptionist told him cheerfully. He rang her mobile at once.

'Hi, Mike.'

'Grace, what do you think you are doing?'

She chuckled. 'My rounds.'

It was unfair of him to feel cross at a perfectly good answer, but he'd wanted to see her—how much he hadn't realised until this minute—and a crackly phone call was no substitute. 'Did it not occur to you that if the weather conditions are too bad for your patients to come to you, they are also too bad for you to go to them?'

'My patients are old and frail, so it's not the same thing at all. And the roads aren't too bad—don't forget that we are used to the snow up here, not like you Londoners.'

That hurt. 'So used to it that you needed me to pull you out of that ditch the first time we met!'

'Now you're being petty. And I need to concentrate and my battery's low. Bye, Mike.'

He exhaled irritably and called for his first patient. An hour later he decided maybe he *had* been petty. He tried to ring Grace again but got voicemail. *Please leave your message after the tone.* Mike was flummoxed. What did he want to say? 'I, er… Just drive carefully. No heroics. Don't go and see anyone who doesn't need it. Call me when you get back.'

He returned to his own list, even more disgruntled. There was nothing from her by the time he had to collect Bethany. Everyone at Rivercut Primary was hugely excited by it being the end of term. They raced around the playground, scraping together snowballs and skidding in the slush. Their parents stamped feet to keep warm, balancing bags of this term's artwork and exchanging last-minute Christmas cards. Mike smiled and wished people all the joy of the season, but his mind was on an elderly Land Rover somewhere up in the tops of the hills. He held Bethany's hand tightly.

The sky was leaden and grey now. Thick flakes of snow fell on them on the way home, that morning's footprints filling fast. Grace's cottage was lifeless, her car nowhere to be seen.

Mike knew it was probably just because he wasn't used to conditions on the North Yorkshire moors, but he was really uneasy. He checked his phone—nothing. He called Grace and got voicemail again. James hadn't heard anything either but, then—as he pointed out—he wouldn't have expected to. 'District nurses are autonomous. They don't have to account to us for all their comings and goings.'

'Well, that's going to change for a start,' said Mike grumpily. He left James and Bethany making pancakes—an exercise they both enjoyed—and opened the connecting door to the surgery for a last prowl around.

There was a note on his desk. Grace must have rung while he'd been at school. She was all right. Thank goodness. Then he frowned. The receptionist had written that the road from Kender Downfall was blocked so Grace would put up at the pub on the main road for the night.

Mike stared at it. Where on earth was Kender Downfall? Which pub would it be? So many things he didn't know! His eyes fell on his computer. Grimly he switched it on and pulled up Grace's diary, laboriously tracking her route around the high moors. A couple of questions to James and he had the name of the pub. He phoned it—ready to blast her for her stupidity in going out to such inhospitable places in appalling weather.

A few moments later he was back in the kitchen doorway.

'Found her?' said James, pouring batter into the frying pan. Then he turned and looked at Mike's face. 'What's up?'

'The pub is full of people but she's not one of them.' His heart was thudding against his chest. 'Can you look after Bethany? All night if need be?'

'Of course, but shouldn't you leave it to the rescue people? Dusk's falling. You don't know your way about these hills yet.'

Mike gave a strained smile. 'No, but my sat nav thinks it does. Time to see if it can put its money where its mouth is.'

'Be careful, lad.'

'I will.' He dropped a kiss on Bethany's head. 'I've got too much to live for.'

Where the hell was she?

CHAPTER TWELVE

IT WAS going to be a whiter-than-white Christmas, thought Grace as she drove carefully along the snow-packed roads, blessing her new tyres. It was nice that Mike had phoned that morning, nice that he was concerned enough to forgive her interference yesterday, but right now the deserted landscape, the relentless wind and the whirling snow suited her mood. In her trusty vehicle she was the sheriff of the moors, with a hypodermic on each hip instead of a six-shooter. She brought comfort and reassurance. She kept the dreaded spectre of hospital in-patient wards at bay. She made it possible for her people to live the independent lives they wanted. And if the thought strayed across her mind that it would be nice to come home from all this to a warm house with a loving partner and a scamp of a little girl to cuddle, Grace ignored it. Mike needed to sort out his own life—she wasn't going to get in the way of that again.

She glanced at her watch—it was touch and go, but she thought she had time to squeeze in one last call. Nellie Farthing had mentioned that her foot was a bit sore, if Grace happened to be passing this way. Grace had decided to be 'passing' as soon as possible. Nellie was eighty-three and too tough for her own good. She lived with family who would soon ring if there was an urgent problem, but Grace wasn't convinced Nellie always told them the 'silly little things' that bothered her.

Because of the driving conditions it took longer than usual to get to Longsky farm. The place was well named. It stood on a hilltop, the highest point for miles. The views on a good day were entrancing. Today—with a sinking heart—all Grace could see were advancing stormclouds.

Still, she was welcomed, told she was mad to come out in weather like this, given a mug of tea. Then she took the ever-cheerful Nellie into her bedroom for a quick examination. She was glad she had done so. Some time ago Nellie had had herpes zoster—shingles—and it had been painful. The pain had not quite disappeared. This was a condition known as post-herpetic neuralgia. Grace decided to give her more analgesics.

There was another problem with the sole of Nellie's left foot. She had developed an ulcer that would not heal—largely because she kept walking on it. Grace scolded, cleaned and dressed it, and obtained a promise that Nellie would spend less time standing and more time with her feet up. 'I'll be back in a week or so, but if your foot gets bad again, phone at once. I'm going to tell your son and daughter-in-law.'

'I feel much better already,' said Nellie. Grace thought that if this was true it would be a medical miracle—but she didn't say anything.

Nellie's son was waiting for her at the front door. 'Weather's taken a turn for the worse,' he said. 'Look at that snow fly. And it's falling dark too. I reckon you ought to stay the night.'

She shook her head. 'No need. Once I'm behind Kender Downfall I'll be in a bit of a shadow. The wind and snow will be less there.'

'Well, come back if there's any trouble. Or phone me and I'll come and fetch you on the tractor.'

'I will, that's a promise. Merry Christmas!' She ran to her Land Rover.

The weather was bad. Her windscreen wipers could only just keep the screen clear. The wind buffeted the car so it rocked, shaking her. The tyres had to fight for grip. A small voice in her head whispered that Mike might well have been right about her not going out on rounds today. Or at least cutting them short early. But she cheered herself by reflecting that Nellie at least had needed her. That ulcer on her foot could have got really nasty if left any longer. She drove on carefully, slowly, knowing that she would get home eventually.

Coming down the steep slope into Kender Downfall was more like sledging than driving. But she made it, and progressed along the narrow road around the hill on the far side. And there with a jerk, she stopped—an inch from deep, piled snow. No way was she getting any further. There had been a mini-avalanche, the road was covered with loose snow to a depth of several feet. She sighed. This was what came of being awkward.

She considered her options. She shared the general country view of people who got into trouble through their own stupidity, blithely expecting others to sort them out. The first thing she must do was reassure anyone who might worry about her, but she certainly wasn't going to ring Mike and tell him he'd been right! With the last of her phone battery she called surgery Reception instead, saying she wouldn't be back that night because of the bad weather. She would stay at the pub on the main road. Would the receptionist tell anyone who asked?

It was a likely enough story—the Drovers' Rest a few miles away was constantly putting up marooned travellers—but Grace had no intention of going there. She had a full 'stranded' kit in her car—a sleeping bag, blankets, a complete set of winter clothing and Kendal mint cake. From time to time she could start the engine to warm the inside of the car. The thing to do was not to panic. In a way she was half enjoying herself.

She kept the car engine running while she swiftly stripped off her nurse's uniform and pulled on heavy walking gear. Most important, a woolly hat pulled right down over her ears. A quarter of the body's heat could be lost through the head and neck. Then she reclined the passenger seat, wriggled into the sleeping bag (not as easy as survival handbooks made it look), wrapped blankets round herself for good measure, and lay down to sleep. She was just a bit disturbed by the snow piling up on the windscreen and tried the radio to see if there were any weather alerts. Sadly, the signal was so badly distorted as to be unrecognisable. And it was a nuisance getting her arm in and out of the sleeping bag.

Grace dozed, and woke again with Mike's image in her mind. Now, what was the point of that? But her subconscious didn't know any better. To make sure it got the message, she said 'I love Mike Curtis' out loud. Then added the killer sentence. 'But he doesn't love me.' The words formed a tiny cloud of condensation over her lips.

Does it matter?

Now, that was a revolutionary thought. Mike was attracted to her physically. He cared for her in a friendly way, felt responsible for her. Did it matter that he didn't love her to the exclusion of all else?

She dozed again, worrying away at the problem she'd set herself. Then she woke and frowned. The windscreen was solid with snow, but there was a small light bobbing up and down on the road outside. She struggled to get her arm free and wound down her side window, shivering at the blast of cold air and snow.

A light was coming towards her. A small light and a darker shadow behind it. A light carried by a man. The light flashed onto her face. A moment later the shadow stopped beside the car. 'What the hell do you think you're doing?' it said forcefully.

Mike Curtis's voice. Grace blinked, unable to take it in. Was she having hallucinations? Could one hallucinate a voice? 'Um, sleeping,' she said.

'Is the driver's door unlocked?'

'Yes. I didn't expect many thieves down here tonight. And I took the ignition key out.'

'Do you know there are times when you have too much to say?'

He disappeared round to the other side of the car. She shut her window, adjusted the seat so that it was upright again. From outside she heard the sounds of a man brushing the snow from his clothes. Then the door was opened, a rucksack bundled in—landing heavily on her lap—and Mike followed.

He sat in the driver's seat, grunting as he adjusted it to

make space for his legs. From out of the rucksack he took a Thermos, poured a drink and handed it to her. 'Here. Drink this before we start arguing.'

The smell of coffee filled the car. She thought just that would be enough to revive her, but the coffee itself was even more blissful. She had to say something. 'Do you know, I could kiss you for this?'

'I don't make a practice of kissing people I'm about to have a flaming row with.'

'It's all right, it was just a figure of speech. Mike, why have you come out here when I sent a message saying that I was all right?'

'Because I want to shout at you very loudly and you aren't answering your damn phone! How stupid can you get, Grace? I found your message on my desk! I might not have known at all. You hadn't even had the courage to ring me yourself. "The pub on the main road" indeed—anything less helpful would be hard to imagine. I worked out where you'd been and phoned everywhere along the route. Longsky farm said you'd left in dreadful weather, even though you'd been offered a bed for the night! Dad told me about the Drovers' Rest, so I phoned them, intending to give you hell—and you weren't there! So I guessed you were stuck. I put my faith in the sat nav and arrived on the other side of this snow-dump.'

Grace finished her coffee, feeling better by the minute. 'Only to find that I was well wrapped up and sleeping peacefully.'

'You were shivering.'

'Because you opened the door! I would have been warm enough all night long otherwise.'

'I doubt that.'

She decided not to argue. 'Anyway, I do appreciate the coffee. And now I suppose you're going to frogmarch me back to your car and take me home. Shall I bring the Kendal mint cake?'

'You've got to be joking. Have you seen the weather out there? It's evil! I've used up all my luck getting here—I'm not driving anywhere else tonight.'

Grace looked at him blankly. 'Then what was the point coming to find me?'

'So I'd know you were safe! Look, I passed a barn a hundred yards or so back—that'll be safer and warmer than sleeping in the car, won't it?'

'I suppose so.' She paused a moment and reluctantly added, 'Thank you for coming to find me. It was good of you.'

'I suspect you'd have done the same for me—if only to prove what an idiot I was. Come on, let's go. What do you need to take from here?'

'Everything. Have you got a sleeping bag?'

'I've got the full kit. Following your example, remember?'

'Right,' she said gloomily. 'I'll put on my boots.' She wasn't exactly comfortable—but she was settled. Still, what he said made sense.

It was freezing outside the car, the wind cut through all her layers of clothes. Mike hoisted his rucksack onto his back, helped her into hers, took her arm and led her through the snow. His torch flickered. Without a word she got hers out of her pocket and flashed it on.

It seemed very hard work, pushing through the blizzard to the barn, but once inside the relief from the wind was immense. 'Sit there,' he said, and started hauling bales of hay to make a draught-proof wall.

'Not a chance,' she replied. She hung the torch on a convenient nail and did her share of dragging bales of hay together until they had constructed a small nest.

'Cosy for the night,' he said. 'By the way, I never asked, you're not wet, are you? No falling into streams or anything?'

'I'm perfectly dry. Not even the snow has wetted me.'

'Good. I wouldn't want you to have to take your clothes off so I could warm you with the heat of my body.'

'I'd rather freeze, thank you.'

'Even if I bribed you with a sandwich and the rest of the coffee? Body heat is still something we have to conserve. I was going to suggest we zip our sleeping bags together and cuddle up to keep warm.'

Grace scrutinised his face. Was he joking? Half joking? 'Mike, we'll be wearing all our clothes.'

He looked unperturbed. 'Of course. It would be stupid to do otherwise. It means we won't notice the crumbs.'

She laughed. 'You're impossible. Let's do it. Boots off, though.'

There was a surprising amount of room in the zipped-together sleeping bags. They sat in them first of all, drinking the coffee and eating the sandwiches he had brought. Grace told him about Nellie Farthing, pointing out with only minor triumph that the old lady had indeed needed to see a nurse. It was odd—intimate in a strangely non-invasive way.

Mike got out to turn off the torch, and she held her breath as he slid back in beside her. 'Go to sleep,' he said, his voice deep and comforting. 'I'm not about to make advances.'

Pity, she thought, and matched his chaste kiss on the cheek with one of her own. But it was no good, she couldn't sleep. She loved him, and here he was lying next to her. And even if it had been unnecessary, he had come out in evil conditions to rescue her. It was bound to have an effect.

She was surprisingly warm, much warmer than she had been in the car. Various layers of clothes, sleeping bag and then hay, they all warmed her. And Mike's body heat, though he had rolled to the other edge of the sleeping bag.

'You know, it'll get colder,' she murmured. 'And to maximise our body heat we should be closer together.'

'You mean it might be sensible to hug each other to keep warm?'

'I think it could.'

Well, of course, it made sense. They wriggled together. Grace found herself with one of Mike's arms under her neck, the other round her waist. Their bodies were pressed together, one of his thighs was over hers. She buried her face naturally into his neck and felt his lips against her hair.

'I've missed you so much, Grace,' he breathed.

He'd missed her? Grace pulled back in shock, straining to see his face in the irregular bars of moonlight. He'd missed *her*? Not Sarah? She made some sort of disbelieving, inarticulate sound.

And then he kissed her.

There was a world of longing in that kiss. And it felt so right, so very right. Had he come all this way, in this weather, to kiss her? And to do other things, judging by the way his hand had bypassed several layers of clothes in order to tug her vest out from the waistband of her trousers? There had been no need to bother, he could have...

This was a pain! If she hadn't known before why people got undressed before they went to bed, she certainly knew now. But with an excess of fumbling it was possible to loosen this and that, to unzip, to ease these down a bit…

To feel suddenly flooded with heat. To cry out with desire. To experience his banked-up passion.

Mike gave a low laugh. 'I never thought I'd ever make love to a woman with woollen socks on up to my knees, whilst wearing a bobble hat.'

'And I never thought I'd have a vest, T-shirt, shirt and sweater tucked under my chin and the bobble of his woolly hat tickling my nose.'

'Sexy, isn't it? We ought to write an extra chapter for one of those sex manuals. How to make love in a sleeping bag in freezing conditions whilst fully dressed.'

Grace chuckled. 'I'd love to see the diagrams. Oh, Mike… Oh, yes… No… Oh!'

Outside there was the howling of the wind, the banging of a loose plank, the weight of the ever-falling snow. But inside they had made their own little world and they were happy in it.

Afterwards they tenderly pulled together various bits of loosened clothing and hugged each other warm again. Grace snuggled into Mike's side. 'I feel warm and happy and content. But shouldn't we talk?'

'No,' he said drowsily. 'Not now. For now let's just be.'

So she slept. Tomorrow would come soon enough.

In the morning, bright sunshine shone through various cracks in the barn walls and there was the clanking of a tractor outside. Grace blinked her eyes open. Heavens above! What time was it? She kissed the forehead of a still-sleeping Mike, wriggled out of bed, pulled on boots, zipped her anorak hastily over the haphazardness of her loosened clothes and went to look at the day.

The storm had blown itself out. It was noticeably warmer. Mike's car was parked outside the barn and Tom Farthing had just broken through the snowfall on his tractor.

'Want to move your car down next to the doctor's, Grace?' he called. 'Then I can clear the road properly.'

'Um, yes. Yes, of course.' She hurried to the Land Rover, fumbling for her keys. Was she blushing?

'That's grand,' shouted Tom over the noise of his engine, and chugged on his way.

Grace returned to the barn. Mike was sitting up in the sleeping bag, rooting around in his rucksack. 'Aha!' he said, and drew out a second flask. He waved it at her. 'Breakfast,' he said.

'Is that more coffee? Mike, you're a marvel!'

'Now and again. Was that the rescue brigade outside?'

'Only Tom Farthing, clearing the road. But I think our cover is blown.'

'Ah, well.'

He didn't say any more and Grace didn't push it, just drank her coffee, more lukewarm than hot. He'd talk when he was ready.

He slid out of the sleeping bag and they tidied up in a nearly companionable silence. 'It's very Swallows and Amazons, all this,' he remarked. 'I used to love the books when I was a boy. Sailing and camping and surviving in tough conditions.'

She laughed. 'And everyone living happily ever after.'

'Yes,' he said, his face sobering. 'That's the rub, isn't it? Children's stories always have happy endings. The burglars get caught, the horses escape the fire, the kids survive. Life isn't always like that.'

'No, it isn't,' she said. 'But sometimes enough good things happen that you can pretend it is.'

Had she said enough? She desperately hoped that he was going to open up to her. Surely after last night he'd have to admit they had the ability to make each other happy? It would do as a beginning.

But instead he hoisted his rucksack and took it out to his car. 'Grace, isn't it lovely here?'

The two of them looked around in silence. It was truly beautiful, the curves of the hills outlined by the sparkling white of the snow.

'Yes, it is lovely,' she agreed. 'I don't think I'll ever forget it.'

Another pause, the chance for him to say something more. 'Do you want to follow me back?' he said.

'Mike!'

He sighed. 'I know, Grace, I know. Listen—yesterday, for the first time in over a year, I didn't think about Sarah all day. I was too wound up thinking about you instead.'

And now she wished she hadn't provoked him. 'I'm sorry,' she said. Her stomach was solid with misery. 'I didn't mean to make you feel guilty.'

'You ridiculous woman! I'm not feeling guilty towards Sarah! I'm feeling guilty towards you for not being able to sort my emotions out!'

Was that good? She thought it might be. The misery melted a little. Now, should she tell him she loved him? Would that make his dilemma better? Or worse? 'Mike, I—'

He put his finger on her lips. 'Dear Grace, give me a day

or two to wrestle. Right now I want to get home and have a hot shower.'

Ruefully, Grace had to admit that was what she wanted too. 'Snap. Would you and Bethany and James like to come to lunch tomorrow? Then Bethany can have her Christmas present in time for your party.'

'That would be lovely.'

With a sigh of relief, Grace stripped off the clothes she had worn all night and ran a bath. As she luxuriated in her favourite bath foam she thought about her lovemaking with Mike. It *had* been lovemaking. It had been fumbling, uncomfortable, awkward, at times almost impossible. But they had enjoyed it, the joy largely coming from the pleasure each was giving the other. There had been no mistaking that. At that moment Mike had really loved her. She just had to wait for him to realise it.

She hadn't intended inviting them for lunch, but it was a perfect way to establish friendly—maybe more than friendly—relations. Except… Oh, Lord, did they do traditional Sunday lunch? And she only had a tiny freezer compartment, there certainly wasn't a joint for four in it. She hastily finished her bath and dashed up to the butcher to see what he had left.

They were prompt the next day—which was good, because Grace had started far too early. Her kitchen wasn't big enough to spread the preparations around. It had to be done task by task. The living room wasn't big enough either, even without the tree taking up so much room. Grace banished the large cushion and unfolded one wing of the table so they could all sit together. Bethany thought it highly amusing that she had to scramble over the arm of the couch to get to her chair.

'We brought wine,' announced James, kissing her on the cheek. 'Point me at the glasses and I'll pour.'

Grace thought Mike was going to peck her on the cheek as well, but at the last moment his lips met hers, light but definite. Did that mean he'd come to a decision? Or was it simply an acknowledgement of something between them?

'If you don't like roast beef,' she said, bringing the joint to the table, 'I'd rather no one tells me. I would have done chicken, but with Christmas next week…'

'Quite right,' said Mike. 'This looks lovely. And all of us eat any amount of Yorkshire pudding. I'm afraid we even have it with turkey.'

So that was all right. And with a glass of wine inside her and everyone making trencherman-like inroads on the food, Grace felt herself relax.

'Where are you spending Christmas Day?' asked Mike at one point.

The question was casual, but Grace didn't miss his swift exchange of looks with his father. 'At Natalie's,' she said.

'That's nice. And I suppose you'll be working flat out until then, will you?' Mike sounded resigned rather than reproachful.

'People don't stop being ill just because it's the holiday season. You're not telling me the pair of you won't be on call?'

'Guilty,' said James cheerfully. 'And in that case, you'd better have my present to you early. It's an in-car charger for your phone. Can't have my district nurse going awol again.'

It seemed to be the cue for them to pile the washing up into the kitchen and move across to the tree. Bethany was ecstatic about her party dress, insisting on putting it on there and then.

'Beautiful,' said Mike. His eyes met Grace's. 'Thank you.' James was just as pleased with his bottle of whisky, but it was Mike's reaction that Grace really wanted to see. She handed over the carefully wrapped package, praying that he'd like it.

He did. He looked at the old map of Rivercut in its frame and his face lit up with joy. 'Grace, this is wonderful, it couldn't be more... You must have known...' He kissed her impetuously, unguardedly. 'It's just perfect.' And then he hesitated. 'My present to you isn't wrapped yet. I thought I'd give it to you when you come to the manor for the party on Christmas Eve.'

Grace felt just a tiny bit let down. It was a tactful way of saying he hadn't got her anything yet. 'That's fine,' she said. 'Who's for coffee?'

She kept herself busy over the next couple of days. Mike was looking after Bethany as there was no school, so he wasn't in the surgery. He wasn't idle, though. She seemed to be forever passing his Range Rover on the road. It was almost as if he'd committed her schedule to memory and was avoiding her. She couldn't work him out. Since that night in the barn she thought they'd come to some kind of understanding...but what? Ah, well, there was just his party to get through, then she'd be off to Natalie's where they could discuss the strangeness of men to their heart's content.

On Christmas Eve itself, she'd arranged to finish work at midday. Half her patients had been invited to the party at the manor anyway. During the morning she got a phone call from Mike. 'I have a favour to ask. Could you come over to the manor early this evening? Say about seven? You've done parties there before—I'd like your advice on a couple of things. Come in your party dress in case there isn't time to change. Can you do that for me?'

'Of course,' she said. 'Seven it will be.'

In truth, she was not sure how she felt. A party at the manor but not her party. It seemed really to be the end of an era. She had a bath and dressed slowly in her new gold taffeta gown. Was this too much? No. She lifted her head proudly. She owed it to the manor itself to pass her much-loved home on graciously.

It was a gorgeous night. The stars shone in a black velvet sky, she could hear the choir practising in the church (she'd been told that they had all been invited up after choir practice), and the air had that sharpness that came with a frost. The snow crunched softly under her feet. She looked down and grinned. Here she was, walking to a party in a gold taffeta gown slit to the thigh—and Wellington boots.

The gates were open. She turned the corner into the drive—and gasped. Tears came to her eyes. At the front of the house on each side of the door a tall Christmas tree stood. Just as they always had at this time of year. And on them were coloured lights—mirrored by the coloured lights in the downstairs windows! Just as they always had been. Even the fairy on top of each tree—this was a re-creation of her childhood!

She felt like a child again, moving up the drive in a dream to stand and gaze up at the trees. It was like a miracle.

Mike must have been looking out for her. He appeared in the doorway. She had just time to notice that his dinner jacket looked the last word in elegance and that he himself looked more than a little apprehensive. But she had to ask.

'Mike, the Christmas trees, they're wonderful! They're exactly like they used to be. How did you manage it?'

'You're sure you don't mind?'

'Of course I don't mind! How could I mind?'

'You lent Bethany the photograph albums, remember? And I asked Dad what the trees used to look like. And I copied them. Come inside, you must be cold.' He took her arm to draw her into the hall, then angled her towards the cloakroom to one side of the door. 'Can I take your coat? And your...' He looked down, past the seductive slit in the skirt to her Wellingtons.

'Don't you dare laugh. Stand right there without a word while I put my party shoes on.'

'I wouldn't dream of it.' But there was a suspicious wobble in his voice.

'Fibber.' Grace leant on him to change first one foot and then the other. 'There,' she said. 'You can look now.'

The admiration in his eyes was all she'd hoped for. 'May I say you look wonderful?'

'You may.'

'And may I welcome you properly?'

She felt suddenly breathless. 'Properly?'

'Like this.' He took her by the shoulders, his hands warm over the diamanté spaghetti straps, and kissed her. He might have intended to stop before it became a proper, full-on kiss, but the moment their lips met it was heaven.

'You... You said you wanted my advice,' she said faintly.

'Did I?' He seemed as shaken as she was. 'Oh, yes.' He

took a deep breath and rotated her gently. 'How does this look to you?'

Grace stood transfixed at the sight of the hall. The old electric fire was long gone, of course, but in its place was a roaring wood fire. To the side of the fireplace was a Christmas tree—with all the big decorations that hadn't fitted on her tree at the cottage! In the centre of the room were two great tables arranged in a T just as they had once been for parties. And around the room were pieces of her own furniture, last seen stored at the Holroyds' farm.

She looked at Mike in bewilderment, feeling tears fill her eyes. 'I don't… How have you…?'

'You told me how lovely it would be to see the hall all grand and festive again. So this is my attempt at showing you. I borrowed your furniture from the farm. I hope you don't mind.'

'Mike, I don't mind! This is so wonderful. I can remember it being just like this and… Thank you, Mike.' Her turn this time to kiss him. But not for long. She wanted to look around, drink it in with her eyes. She only had one tiny, sad thought. This was wonderful—but it wasn't hers any more.

Mike looked a bit more relieved, but there was something else he was nervous about. What else had he done? She was almost afraid to ask.

'You said you used to play party games,' he said. 'I want to try one with you now, a guessing game.' He walked to the big fireplace, its mantelshelf now covered with cards. Above was the mirror that had always been there. Mike really had studied those photos well. But above the mirror was something new—a rolled-up screen, perhaps eight feet long. Mike pulled at a cord, the screen unrolled.

It had a border of Christmas scenes—pictures of holly, mistletoe, church bells, candles. In the middle there was a message—*Merry Christmas. Welcome home, Grace.*

'Guess what this means?' he said.

She shook her head. 'It's lovely, Mike. But this isn't my home any more. It's yours.'

'It could be your home. If you wanted it.'

'But you're going to live here. You and Bethany.'

He felt in his pocket. 'I said I hadn't wrapped your Christmas present. I lied. The manor is half your present— and this is the other half. If you don't like it we can change it for something else, but I did take a long time picking it.'

Her gave her a small parcel, wrapped in Christmas paper, with a card attached. The card read: *For Grace, with all my love. Mike.*

Grace's heart was beating much too fast. '"With all my love"?'

He put his hand to her face. 'I had to write it before I could say it. It's taken me a while, but I'm there now. With all my love, Grace.'

She tore away the paper with shaking hands, opened the little leather box inside. There was a heart-shaped ruby surrounded by tiny diamonds. She stared at it, speechless, entranced. Then she took it out of the box, held it up so the jewels sparkled and flashed.

He took the ring from her, folded her hand in his. Dimly, dazedly, Grace was aware of Bethany and James at the top of the staircase.

'I love you, Grace. Will you marry me? Marry me and make the manor your home again?'

'I love you too, Mike. Of course I'll marry you.'

She held out her hand, he slid the ring on her finger. The kiss this time was all she had ever wanted, all she had ever hoped for. And was cut short by a delighted little girl in her first long party frock, pelting down the stairs towards them.

'Congratulations, son,' said James, beaming all over his face. 'Grace, I couldn't be more pleased. This is more than a Christmas party now, it's an engagement party! I'll go and break out the champagne!'

Mike nudged them all towards the old kitchen passage-way. 'Look up,' he said softly.

Grace smiled. He'd fixed a sprig of mistletoe in the archway. 'Just in case,' he said, and kissed her again.

EPILOGUE

A NEW season. It was the first day of spring, and as beautiful in its way as the winter had been. There was blossom in the fields, the trees were showing new green leaves.

Gardeners had been working hard at Rivercut Manor. By summer the rose garden, herb garden and the shrubbery should be as wonderful as they had been in the manor's heyday.

But they hadn't started to re-lay the new lawn. The old lawn had been left for now—it was just the right size for the marquee that had been erected on it.

This was a village wedding. It seemed as if most of the village were guests, and they all agreed how stunningly beautiful the bride looked in her simple cream silk dress with a full train. Her bouquet was a pretty posy of white and yellow roses. Mike looked handsome in his dark grey morning suit, while Bethany and Chloe made enchanting bridesmaids in long dresses of yellow tulle with circlets of flowers on their heads. The matron of honour was, of course, Natalie, in an amber gown, while James wore his old regimental uniform.

After the service in St Lawrence's, the reception was

held in the gardens of Rivercut Manor, the home of the newly married couple. And after a delicious meal, everyone danced long into the night.

'Do you think anyone noticed?' Grace whispered in a rare moment they had alone.

Mike slid his hands over his wife's slender waist. 'There's no sign of Bethany's new brother or sister yet.' Grace's hand moved to cover his, brushing over his third finger where her narrow ring to him nestled snugly alongside Sarah's, both of them making a whole band, and he kissed her tenderly and deeply. 'But do you know how happy it makes me to know he—or she—is there?'

She smiled radiantly up at him. 'As happy as me.'

MEDICAL™ 2-in-1

Coming next month

POSH DOC, SOCIETY WEDDING
by Joanna Neil

Dr Izzy McKinnon knows she must keep things strictly
business with Glenmuir's handsome Laird, Dr Ross Buchanan.
But Izzy has won Ross's heart – he's determined to give
Glenmuir a celebration to remember and make her his bride!

NEW BOSS, NEW-YEAR BRIDE
by Lucy Clark

When obstetrician Melissa Clarkson goes to the Outback to
find the family she's never known, she finds herself sharing a
sizzling New Year's Eve kiss with her dreamy new boss! Can
Joss convince Melissa to unpack her suitcases for good?

THEIR BABY SURPRISE
by Jennifer Taylor

Turning to each other for support after the disastrous *non-*
wedding of their children, single mother Rachel Mackenzie and
widower Dr Matthew Thompson find that old friends can make
a new beginning! Then Rachel discovers she's pregnant...

GREEK DOCTOR CLAIMS HIS BRIDE
by Margaret Barker

Tanya left Greek doctor Manolis after she lost their baby,
so seeing him again throws her into emotional freefall. Manolis
must persuade Tanya to risk her fragile heart again for their
happy-ever-after to finally happen!

On sale 1st January 2010

MEDICAL™

Single titles coming next month

A MOTHER FOR THE ITALIAN'S TWINS
by Margaret McDonagh

Single father Dr Luca d'Azzaro moves to Penhally Bay
to bring up his precious twin girls. His unassuming
colleague, Dr Polly Carrick, enchants Luca with her quiet
beauty, but there is such pain in her eyes... Luca is
determined to heal her heart – he'll make Polly see that
she is the missing part of his family.

THE DOCTOR'S REBEL KNIGHT
by Melanie Milburne

Dr Frances Nin has come to Pelican Bay in search of
tranquillity...but motorbike-riding local rebel Sergeant Jacob
Hawke gets her pulse-rate spiking! This gorgeous cop must
convince Fran to stay and not just because the community
desperately needs a doctor – Jacob wants Fran by his side, to
love, cherish and protect...for ever!

On sale 1st January 2010

1209/03b

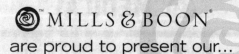

millsandboon.co.uk Community

Join Us!

The Community is the perfect place to meet and chat to kindred spirits who love books and reading as much as you do, but it's also the place to:

- **Get the inside scoop from authors about their latest books**
- **Learn how to write a romance book with advice from our editors**
- **Help us to continue publishing the best in women's fiction**
- **Share your thoughts on the books we publish**
- **Befriend other users**

Forums: Interact with each other as well as authors, editors and a whole host of other users worldwide.

Blogs: Every registered community member has their own blog to tell the world what they're up to and what's on their mind.

Book Challenge: We're aiming to read 5,000 books and have joined forces with The Reading Agency in our inaugural Book Challenge.

Profile Page: Showcase yourself and keep a record of your recent community activity.

Social Networking: We've added buttons at the end of every post to share via digg, Facebook, Google, Yahoo, technorati and de.licio.us.

www.millsandboon.co.uk

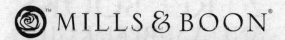

2 FREE BOOKS
AND A SURPRISE GIFT

We would like to take this opportunity to thank you for reading this Mills & Boon® book by offering you the chance to take TWO more specially selected books from the Medical™ series absolutely FREE! We're also making this offer to introduce you to the benefits of the Mills & Boon® Book Club™—

- **FREE home delivery**
- **FREE gifts and competitions**
- **FREE monthly Newsletter**
- **Exclusive Mills & Boon Book Club offers**
- **Books available before they're in the shops**

Accepting these FREE books and gift places you under no obligation to buy, you may cancel at any time, even after receiving your free books. Simply complete your details below and return the entire page to the address below. You don't even need a stamp!

YES Please send me 2 free Medical books and a surprise gift. I understand that unless you hear from me, I will receive 5 superb new stories every month including two 2-in-1 books priced at £4.99 each and a single book priced at £3.19, postage and packing free. I am under no obligation to purchase any books and may cancel my subscription at any time. The free books and gift will be mine to keep in any case.

Ms/Mrs/Miss/Mr _____ Initials _____

Surname _____

Address _____

_____

_____ Postcode _____

Send this whole page to: Mills & Boon Book Club, Free Book Offer, FREEPOST NAT 10298, Richmond, TW9 1BR